I0653791

FIRES OF THE NEW ALLIANCE

NEW ALLIANCE SERIES
BOOK 1

ALEX GREEN

CHAPTER 1

DRACONIS SYSTEM | PRESENT DAY

Whipping his head out of the path of the shattered breeze block that accelerated towards him demonstrated impressively sharp reactions for someone of Nigel's imposing bulk. The uncharacteristic agility he displayed leaping across the room would also have surprised anyone watching. With video surveillance temporarily disrupted, the central monitoring suite were unaware of Nigel's abnormal activity.

Before the dust cloud could settle, more blocks blasted into the room, increasing the size of the opening and with it, Nigel's anxiety. Running with sweat, his horrified face grew increasingly pale as he observed the disintegration of the cell wall, and in his view, possibly his life. Squeezing his gargantuan frame as far back into the opposite corner from the architectural carnage as he could, he developed a severe case of uncontrollable shakes. The visual effect was somewhat like a blancmange on a skateboard crossing a cattle-grid.

In a final crescendo of grit and debris, two figures burst through the wall. Nigel threw both hands up in front of his face as completely ineffective protection.

"Grab him Remi," shouted the bigger of the two colossi that had charged into the room. "Ash will be neutralising the remaining guards on the exit ramp, we need to be quick."

"Come on Tariq," barked the moving stack of muscles that Nigel now knew was called Remi, grabbing him by the scruff of the neck. "You're going to 'ave to move fast big boy, we're on le clock 'ere. Putain[i]... 'ow the... What the..."

"Merde[ii] Sam, did they build this maudit[iii] cell around ami obése 'ere?"

"Uh... excuse me, I'm right here!" protested Nigel, "And my name's not—"

"Shut up and get your sorry butt into that corridor Michelin Man before it kicks off like an action holo out there." The figure Nigel had now identified as Sam snarled at him from the door she had wrenched open.

Not wanting to cause a scene, Nigel opted for discretion and figured they could iron out this misunderstanding later. He kept his mouth shut as advised and with a significant amount of effort and 'mechanical encouragement' from Sam, squeezed himself through the cell door. As he stood, sweating and swaying from the effort, Nigel realised he hadn't exerted himself that much in years. He was also forced to admit that he had really let himself go and was rather out of shape.

"No time to rest now big T," growled Sam, "shift yourself down

---

[i] Over the years, three languages became dominant across the galaxy - English, French & Mandarin. English eventually prevailed for common conversation while Mandarin was often used for cursing and derogatory speech. Some people preferred the eloquence of French for vulgar insults. Translation for the more complex ones will be provided. Putain: Common Fr. 'Whore' / 'F**k'

[ii] Fr. 'S**t'

[iii] Fr. 'wretched' / 'bloody'

that corridor and take the third left, in fact, follow Remi. I'll cover the rear and pick off any unwelcome followers."

Desperately trying to keep up with the considerably fitter and faster Remi who had sprinted off ahead, Nigel set off with an ungainly shuffle at tortiosian pace.

Within the first ten metres, the effort required to keep himself moving was taxing Nigel to the point of delirium. His brain put him into a kind of trance just to escape the burning pain that screamed through his whole body.

In his altered cognitive state, Nigel's mind wandered, recalling the first time he had traversed the corridor he was now being kidnapped, rescued, or escaping through. He wasn't yet sure which verb it was.

———

Eleven and a half years ago, Nigel had been marched down the stark, grey halls of Incarceration Zone Five and ignominiously dumped in a 'single occupancy detention unit'. The cell was designated as a "sleep cube with open toilet & wash area", as if that was something to be promoted. That was not a big problem for Nigel. There were no windows to look through. Anywhere!

Also, nobody needed to peer in at the door as all cells had a permanent video feed to the central monitoring suite.

His shock at being detained for twelve years for a crime he hadn't even committed caused a rapid descent into depression. This was followed by burgeoning weight gain due to levels of inactivity that would shame even the most lethargic teenager.

Incarceration Zone Five or IZV as it was commonly known was a medium-secure detention centre for a combination of petty thieves and white-collar criminals. In itself it was unremarkable and its detainees were generally civil and well-behaved. The worst that could happen was losing a shoelace or entry access pass to one of the pickpockets and then subsequently a toothbrush or your last set of clean underwear. IZV was also, however, a temporary holding location for level-one dangerous and violent criminals in the last six months of their sentence. It was designed to rehabilitate and re-integrate the unhinged and misguided thugs back into civilisation. They were to be readied for their release and transfer to Omega-4 where they would be given a clean record, a new identity, and 1000 galactic credits to launch them on their way to a new life.

More often than not, instead of providing the desired reformation, it served as a redirection gateway. Heavy-handed hoodlums transitioned into more delicate and less detectable felony.

There was very little entertainment for the inmates so they grouped together in their "exercise and social time" to hone their deception and sneak thieving. They would share ideas on how to slip corporate fraud past the authorities and conjure up new ways to swindle emerging digital markets from their galactic credits.

Nigel wanted nothing to do with a potentially lucrative and almost completely undetectable life of crime. He was intent only on serving out his time without any fuss, keeping his head down, and putting the whole episode behind him. As such, he avoided social contact and therefore took almost zero exercise. Entering IZV, he was a measly 23-years old, 10 stone weakling with failing eyesight. Today, he was a lumbering 52 stone amorphous mass of wobble who could barely see beyond the end of his outstretched arm. In all honesty, due to the lack of physical training and significant muscle wasting, he was barely even able to lift an arm *to* outstretch.

––––––

The commotion of a fierce firefight jolted him from his reverie, throwing him back into the pain of his present existence: Agonisingly plodding one foot in front of the other in repetitively painful monotony.

Just as he was about to round the corner, Sam grabbed his shoulder and slammed him to the floor, creating the sound and visual effect of a dropped bowl of jelly at a children's birthday party.

Before he could complain, the fizz of energy weapon discharge whipped past his left ear and the smell of ionised air filled his nostrils. Chest heaving, Nigel clumsily rolled past the whiff of scorched plas-steel to look at the black pock-mark on the mains electricity conduit running along at floor level. He was relieved that it hadn't been pierced to let out the jumble of high voltage cabling beneath.

"Stars! Keep still you dumb-ass mutie[iv], have you got a kriffing death wish?" Sam's voice, that close to his ear, was gruff and menacing.

"No, just a—" began Nigel before he was cut off again.

"Shut your foutu[v] mouth and save your energy for moving or you'll get us all killed." Remi glanced behind her as she let off another barrage of plasma.

Rolling out into the centre of the corridor, Sam pulled two hand-weapons from her shoulder holsters.

"We can get to the dock on the next level down if we punch through those blast doors and hang a right." She let fly with

---

iv Mutie - Derogatory term originating from the radiation-damaged mutant creatures that evolved in the wastelands outside developed cities on Earth during the nuclear winter. May be human or animal forms in origin, but exhibited the horrific deformities and mutations of your worst nightmares. Always hostile to humans, would feast on any creature unfortunate enough to cross their path. Subsequently it developed into the name given to any creature that you wouldn't want to meet alone in a dark alley without your plasma pistol and then became a general insult.
v Fr. 'freaking'

deadly accuracy. "Cover me while I clear out the last of those jagweeds."

As she finished her sentence, four more guards crumpled into immobile heaps, leaving the way clear for the exiting party to access the aforementioned blast doors.

At the end of an insufferably long and strenuous mental queue, Nigel's brain clocked out again. In contrast to his normal idle drifting through space in the bowels of IZV, he was barely able to compute his current frenetic experience.

————

The reformatory institution orbited the yellow dwarf sun just between Omega-4 and Omega-3: the second of the three terraformed planets in the Sigma Draconis System. Nobody was entirely sure why the first planet had been called Omega-2 rather than Omega-1.

Nigel didn't care. He didn't care about anything to be honest. He cared less and less each rotation because all he had to look at was the blank mid-grey of the plas-steel floors and rendered concrete walls. There weren't even any rivets to count or seams to pick at with his nails.

IZV was, in its time, the pinnacle of engineering. Huge smooth sheets of plas-steel, welded together into a vast, sleek, hulking penitentiary, the insides partitioned into basic living units by concrete blocks rendered featureless with fibre-carbon resin. Everything was electro-coated with the classic prison-cell grey, save for the rows of recessed inmate navigation lights that lined the corridors.

The construction phase was quick and very expensive, the specification being predictably impressive, but the maintenance budget was woeful. 250 cleaning bots weren't enough for the 4500 cells to be kept spotless, and the maintenance droids now spent almost as much time cannibalising each other as they did repairing the everyday wear and tear of the station.

Despite the ruggedness of the build, cosmetically, it was beginning to show its age. The list of areas that escaped regular cleaning was expanding and new species of mould were evolving to cover the already discoloured surfaces. Nothing was seriously toxic yet, but there was a growing incidence of respiratory illness aboard. Fortunately, Nigel was housed in one of the more frequently-scrubbed core-ward cells and so had escaped the fungal spore-induced asthma that afflicted so many of the rimward prisoners.

Nigel didn't have anyone that missed him, the only thing he left behind was a stuffed gerbil. He had grown very attached to his first pet, 'Frisky', so when the creature no-longer lived up to its name, Nigel contacted the local taxidermist and, for a small fee, had it preserved. He had forked out a little extra to inject some drama into the frieze. Frisky was captured in an action pose with a bandanna tied round his head and a mini plasma-cannon slung over his shoulder. A classic Space-Marine stance was beautifully reproduced, standing on some baize grass next to a fake tree. Proudly displaying Frisky on his work desk probably marked the limit of Nigel's adventurousness, but demonstrated a nostalgic sentimentality uncharacteristic of the age of New Alliance (NA).

———

Surfacing momentarily, Nigel watched Remi hold one of the limp guards up to the retinal camera whilst grabbing the lifeless arm to position it over a hand scanner. Sam was lacing the corridors with indiscriminate weapon-fire, in full battle-frenzy so Remi turned to Nigel.

"Putain, make yourself useful mutie. Poke your foutu finger in this lid to get 'is eye uncovered."

The stomach-churning sensation equivalent to fingering a peeled grape almost lost Nigel his last meal. It was immediately made worse when he caught a slightly torn fingernail in the side of the eyeball and in a moment of panic, pressed too hard.

Warm, thick liquid spurted out over his hand and he desperately held back another retch.

"Merde. What on Omega are you doing Tariq? That is unnecessary, we 'aven't got time for this you foutu sick bâtard.... Try the other one."

Remi trapped the guards hand against the scanner with her knee, raised her plasma cannon again and let off a volley of shots over Nigel's cowering hulk, sending several guards tumbling and others running for cover.

Managing better with the guard's other eyelid triggered a whirring, grinding sound from below their feet and the blast doors began to inch upwards.

From his disadvantage point, head once again slumped back against the cold floor, even with his atrocious eyesight, Nigel could see that the space behind the vast metal barrier was clear. In a vain attempt to avoid the ire of his new companions, he hastily gathered his folds together and made a valiant attempt to pick himself up off the floor.

Not used to the extreme effort, his brain disconnected once more, depositing his limp body on his gelatinous belly. He lay, panting, weakly vacillating, somewhat reminiscent of a beached walrus. The memories came flooding back again.

———

Without a family who would customarily have accompanied him to the spaceport and wave him off in a dejected and ashamed way, Nigel's hapless lawyer had performed the relevant duties with one raised middle finger, as a "gesture of goodwill".

Nigel would have much preferred for the legal incompetent to have put some effort into defending the shoplifting charge. There was no evidence that Nigel had stolen anything. In fact, the CCTV had clear images of three young children collecting numerous items of low value from Reggie's shelves and making off down the precinct at top speed.

When presented with all the facts, the prosecuting attorney all but admitted that it was easier to attempt to incarcerate Nigel and face the miscarriage of justice appeals (that would never arise owing to the cost) than trace the juvenile criminals. Even if caught, they would be almost impossible to identify and hard to charge. All in all, it was more convenient for someone traceable to take the rap and justice be damned.

The judge's final statement was a flaccid admission of the waning powers of the entire legal framework.

"Whilst there may be scant and flimsy evidence to link Mr Colemin to the robbery, it could be ascertained that he was in the vicinity at the time and therefore his detention will, in these circumstances, suffice."

On Omega-4, the judicial system was swift. Tidy but inaccurate, precise yet fundamentally flawed. This meant Nigel's entire case was seen and ruled on within a week.

No sooner than he discovered his standard twelve-year fate, he was bundled into a Megacity Guard (MG) hover-transport with his entire wardrobe. Six identical plain body-suits with integral underwear, had been retrieved from his apartment without the landlord being notified of the termination of his rental. His employment was paused with immediate effect, without any given reason and Nigel was on his way to IZV. Without Frisky!

Any intelligent employer would, inevitably, correctly discern the cause of Nigel's twelve year 'sabbatical' and normally a quiet contract termination would ensue. As luck would have it, Nigel's employer was the Megacity Administration Department, (the name was clearly dreamed up by some bright spark purely for the appropriateness of the acronym) and therefore was, by very nature, not intelligent.

For normally luckless Nigel, this meant he would be able to resume employment without questions at any point, just by plugging his data interface into any MAD terminal. An unexpected down-side was that although his pay was not frozen, any surplus, after his tax, rent and bills were deducted at source, was accidentally diverted to the android donkey sanctuary by an overly complex, and clearly pointless algorithm. Nobody would miss him, but then again, nobody would notice him return. The landlord continued to be paid and his apartment cleaned. A situation of almost complete anonymity developed, which played both into and out of Nigel's hands in roughly equal measure.

As the transfer module floated gently away from Omega-4 towards IZV, Nigel questioned whether his intimate knowledge of the orbiting prison, its schematics, data points, and maintenance specifications would be any use to him.

He had been the 'Lead Conduit Tracer' on the project. Every bit of pipe and channel that went anywhere on the spinning penitentiary (and indeed any other New Alliance construction) was etched into Nigel's memory, mostly because nothing else of interest ever passed his eyes. The 'Lead' in his job title was purely a fluffed up administrative ploy to bolster the morale of low ranking MAD employees. It didn't work. Nigel neither deserved a position of rank nor aspired to one, he was by all accounts, 'bang average' and until his arrest, he had rather liked it that way.

Trunking, it transpired was a very good way of passing messages and contraband around the prison. His extensive knowledge of its layout bagged him an almost endless supply of energy-dense nutri-bars. He had underground minor-celebrity status and was able to trade New Alliance construction secrets for junk food, yet Nigel eschewed the attention, isolated himself, and allowed the 'black dog' to overcome him. After all, if you couldn't even get a cup of tea in prison, what was the point in anything?

———

The sensation of a heavy combat boot stomping on his neck snapped him out of the stupor again.

Leaping down the corridor like an oversized panther, Sam was over him and laying down cover fire with something that looked like it would normally be mounted on a star-fighter.

Desperately trying to preserve what hearing remained, Nigel tried to lift his hands to cover his ears.

Half way through the excruciating procedure, a gorilla-esque paw clamped onto the back of his sweat soaked shirt and, somehow, hoisted him up. While Nigel dangled 20cm from the floor like an obese squid, Sam, temporarily pausing her demolition of the facility, half dragged, half slid him towards the next corridor junction faster than he was able to move himself. With a final heave, he was lumped onto the steep ramp that led to the cargo bay and he tumbled his way down it like a jumbo slinky.

"What the drokk have you done to yourself Tariq?" Ash suspiciously eyed Nigel as she retrieved the weapons that a mound of inert security guards was gifting her. Nigel slithered to a stop at the bottom of the ramp and somehow managed to kneel up. Proffering a hand to the woman in full combat armour, laden with multiple weapons, Nigel began:

"I'm actually not—"

"Get him on le putain de transport fast, 'e'll only try to slow us down waffling," cut across Remi, cleaning off a wicked-looking knife as she pounded down the ramp. "Merde! Bandits on our six."

"Better find some haulage restraints too," said Ash. "Ain't none of our seats that will carry that gorram beast."

Scooped up by the armpits, Nigel felt himself swiftly propelled into the back of a small transport shuttle by Remi and Sam and roughly secured under a cargo net with wide webbing restraints. The ramp was still closing as Ash leaped in behind the pilot's console, plugged her data interface into the ship in one smooth movement and fired up the thrusters to lift the vessel off the cargo deck. It was only moments before the little ship was barrelling toward the atmo-shield and bursting out into the inky void of space like a speck of glass from a shattering window.

CHAPTER 2

AURIGA SECTOR | YEARS EARLIER

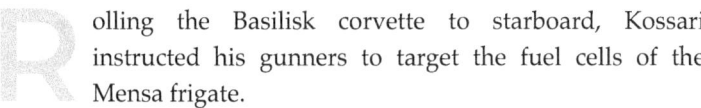 olling the Basilisk corvette to starboard, Kossari instructed his gunners to target the fuel cells of the Mensa frigate.

The return fire on the Phoenix was sporadic and though her shields were depleted, they had more than adequate power to absorb the energy.

"Cease-Fire" came the command as one set of fuel cells ignited into vapour. "Let's wait for a moment. We can salvage the ship to replenish our own supplies so I want minimal damaged. I think we've managed to disable her now. Anvi, pilot us in close, I want teams G and N EVA'd and ready for boarding in ten minutes."

Anvi swung the ship round to line up the access hatches and slowly nudged the Phoenix in towards the frigate, perfectly matching her listless rotation.

Proximity alarms sounded as the ships almost touched and the pilot extended the docking tunnel towards the frigate's airlock. As the locks engaged and pressurisation began, only the noise of nervous breathing could be heard in the boarding teams' helmet-comms.

Standing by the inner airlock in the throb of the red-flashing warning lights, Kossari addressed the heavily armed group.

"This is not a rescue mission, it's salvage and safety. Neutralise any hostiles with extreme prejudice. Any unarmed or surrendering crew are to be escorted to the brig for processing. Saleera from comms is now broadcasting to the interior of the ship for unconditional surrender. I'm sure if anyone is still alive, they can be persuaded to lead a team to any onboard resources. Hopefully they will concede defeat and assist us, most folks know when they are beaten and these guys folded like a cheap deckchair."

Without even a faint hiss, the airlock opened to allow the boarders to enter, closing softly behind them. Moments later, the pressure seal indicator illuminated with a soft chime and Huron pressed the sequence to open the outer airlock.

Tapping the side of his helmet in the traditional manner, he spoke across the team's comm-channel to test everyone could hear.

"Comm check." Every gloved hand immediately lifted in acknowledgement. "Good, let's move out into defensive as soon as the doors open and be ready to proceed when we get an all clear.

"Stay focussed, use hand signals to keep chatter to a minimum but make sure everyone stays informed. We must think individually and intuitively but work as a team, we can't waste time constantly waiting for instructions."

Knock knock knock

The whole team turned towards the frigate airlock and brought their weapons up. Several of the team took one knee and put an eye to their rifle scopes.

Knock knock knock

"What on Omega is that boss?"

"No idea. Hold positions."

Knock knock knock

As the outer airlock door slid open, all the air swept out instantly, slapping the odd loose webbing strap across static arms or legs. The inside of the frigate was dark and eerily silent except for the gentle echoing voice of Saleera requesting peaceful surrender.

Breathing apparatus clicked on and head-torches automatically brightened to illuminate the depressurised, creaking vessel.

Waving a hand, Huron indicated for the teams to diverge and quietly spoke his orders.

"Move out, Team G to supplies, Team N split and sweep each deck, keep moving, cover each other."

Forty helmets nodded silently and the teams crabbed out in noise-less manoeuvres, flowing around corridors and rooms like well-trained oil.

Turning back to the airlock, all boarding units despatched, Huron was surprised to see it had closed. Speaking full-net, his voice came over confused.

"Boarding teams active, sweep in operation… Who closed the airlock doors?"

"It was initiated from the Mensa side. We figured you were doubling up on safety, what with the hull breaches and the frigate being fully depressurised." came the response from Saleera.

Huron thought for a moment.

"G, N. Did anyone close the airlock?"

"No boss," chorussed multiple voices.

A few minutes later, over the comm, there was a sharp intake of breath, followed by a piercing scream which choked off almost immediately. Then static.

"Saleera... Saleera!

"Saleera?

"Kossari what the kark is happening?"

"I'm on my way to find out."

"Everyone, we need radio silence until the Phoenix can give us a status update. Continue to recon, mission objectives haven't changed." Huron turned away from the airlock and focussed his attention on his HUD. Zooming in and out, he checked the locations of his teams against the 3D projection of the Mensa frigate. All vitals still registered green and mobile.

Anvi's voice broke the silence.

"Captain, I'm picking up tr— aaaaagghhhhhhh."

"Anvi, Anvi, what is it? Anvi! Report in. Anvi???

"Kark!

"Huron. Recall teams, something serious is happening, we need backup."

"Sir!"

Huron quickly switched back to combat network only comms.

"All fire-teams return to boarding airlock immediately. Abort mission."

Within ninety seconds, the clatter of heavy boots on the steel deck came to an end leaving a ghostly silence in the vacuum of the ship.

"We're going back to the Phoenix. Something crazy is happening. Be on full alert, I have no idea what we're going to face. Standard manoeuvres, cover each other, watch corners and doorways.

"Move out."

Clustered together once again as the airlock re-pressurised, the stoic faces on his teams gave Huron a feeling of pride.

On the signal, they formed an attack V with all weapons pointing out of the opening airlock door. Six soldiers on one knee, rifles at their shoulders, the remainder covering the whole antechamber outside the airlock.

Silence met the squad and it took until the airlock door warning system started beeping before they moved again.

"New objective: return to the bridge and find out what the kark has gone on here. I'm getting nothing from the rest of the crew."

Slower than normal, the two teams edged their way out of the airlock and crept towards the front of the corvette.

Turning the corner into the main concourse, bodies were strewn in increasing regularity. Dark stains grew over the floor and patches of maroon spatter decorated the walls.

"Watch out private!"

The foremost soldier slipped on the slick surface and face-planted, letting off a couple of rounds that ricocheted down the corridor, eventually bouncing to a halt at one of the blast doors.

"Sorry Sarge."

"You trying to get us all kriffing killed?"

Huron waved them forward and activated the doors.

Behind them was a scene of devastation of holocaustic proportion. Every other fire-team lay piled over one another, arms and legs at awkward angles. At regular intervals, admin staff were spreadeagled, hewn down mid-flight. A river of coagulating brown liquid slowly seeped across the plas-steel, the rest of the concourse resembling an explosion at a morgue.

The stunned silence in teams G and N left the whisper of a crackle in their helmet comms accompanied by shallow, rapid breathing.

Approaching the triple-thickness door to the bridge, they stopped again as it slowly slid open.

15 silent muzzle-flashes dropped almost half off the two fire-teams positioned behind Huron, leaving 15 small smoking holes in their armour and 15 rapidly growing pools of blood.

The remaining soldiers froze instantly.

"You have ten seconds to provide the codes for full access to this ship's command centre before the rest of your crew is dispatched." The voice came from a completely black torso, seemingly floating in mid-air by the central control console. One arm wrapped across the chest of Anvi. Against her dark throat, the other hand held the sharpest, blackest blade Huron had ever encountered.

"If that doesn't convince you, next step is your girlfriend here losing her head! This is where you Basilisks lose."

Taking a deep breath, Huron lifted his hands in front of him and slowly walked towards the figure.

"It's vocally imprinted with..." looking at Anvi's pleading eyes the whole time, Huron's voice cracked "with palm-scan verification. Please don't hurt her. Nobody else needs to die today."

"Suddenly grown a conscience officer?" The torso continued to taunt the stunned mercenary.

"Huron, no!" Fire-team leader Dybalo half-stepped forwards.

Raising his fist at lightening speed in a 'halt' gesture, Huron instantly stopped Dybalo in his tracks and regained full composure.

"Nothing can go wrong now that can't get 1000 times worse by you being a heroic idiot," he growled through his stiffened jaw.

"Spoken like a true leader." The suspended torso sounded almost amused. "A wise choice."

Stepping over the inert figure of Kossari, Huron placed his hand on the palm-scanner and spoke the command into the console to activate manual control of the Phoenix.

"Another insightful decision Commodore Huron."

Despite the impromptu promotion, Huron didn't feel celebratory. However, his pulse relaxed a little as he watched the hijacker loosen her grip on Anvi.

"Now, just to make sure we're all on the same page here, you will be unharmed as long as you remain non-hostile."

Releasing her hold of Anvi, who immediately ran to Huron's side and buried her head into his shoulder, the floating torso clicked her fingers.

The sound of Anvi's sobs, mostly absorbed by Huron's chest, still muffled the gasp that came from his remaining soldiers as 25 bodies seemed to appear out of thin air in front of them.

"You will be continuously monitored. Please lay your weapons down on the deck and proceed in an orderly fashion to the brig. Do not pass 'Go', do not collect 200 Galactic Credits!"

Huron thought he detected a smirk in the comment, but he motioned his team to comply and carefully placed his own blaster, grip-first, on the floor.

"I am Scarlett, and this is now my ship," spoke the now fully-visible figure. "Retract the docking tunnel, slave The Bufalus to The Phoenix, let's get going." With a further click of her fingers, her fighters re-cloaked and vanished.

"Set course for Mensa-Prime. Hard burn."

"Anvi, are you ok?"

Huron gently cupped the side of her face in his hand, lifting her head up to see into her eyes.

"Damn stealth armour! That's a trademark of the kind of advanced technology the Mensa system has. We were duped into that phoney battle. No wonder they capitulated so easily."

———

Sitting with their backs to the cell wall in the ship's brig, Huron let his head thud back against the steel plates.

"You'll relieve yourself of your last remaining brain cell Huron!" Dybalo's sneering face across the room radiated contempt.

"If you thought it was a trap, you should have said earlier," Huron replied. "Nobody saw this coming, it's a shrewd move by whoever we've come up against and I doubt you'd have done any better dealing with the situation. In fact, you almost got us all killed back there so why don't you wind your neck in."

"You never should have been Captain on this mission or this ship Huron, you don't have the brains to understand tactics or the guts to take the necessary risks."

"If you don't shut your kriffing cake-hole, I'll take my boot and shove it so far—"

"That's right guys, fight amongst yourselves, it's just what they want, keep that up and we've lost already." The voice had a cold edge and commanded respect.

"We need a plan to escape, re-take our ship and get back to the Chimera. First, we have to make sure there aren't any of those muties earwigging."

Huron looked across the brig to where the voice was coming from, knowing it to be speaking truth.

"How on Omega are we going to manage that Ash?"

With a sparkle in her eyes, she beckoned to them.

"Come in close guys, I've got a great idea, you'll love this."

Dybalo and Huron caught each other's gaze with a growing feeling of foreboding. Rarely were Ash's 'great ideas' comfortable or anything other than humiliating for the male members of the team.

CHAPTER 3

DRACONIS SYSTEM | PRESENT DAY

Another huge shockwave rattled everything on the small cargo shuttle, rocking the occupants and sending various ropes and other unsecured hardware flying across the hold.

"Stars Ash, what are you doing in there? Anyone would think this was a bag of gorram 'salt 'n' shake' crisps for kriff's sake."

"That wasn't me, we've been hit," came back the reply from the scruffy pilot's console. "My data interface has come loose, hold on while I reconnect and assess the damage."

Immediately, Nigel noticed his shapeless aggregation of organic material pulling against the cargo net and offered his viewpoint:

"It feels like the engines have failed!"

"Which degree course did they implant you with professor graisse d'oie[i]? You've pushed le tug out to come up with that enlightened nugget," sneered Remi. "Don't get ideas above your station Tariq,

---

[i] Fr. 'goose fat'

you always were and always will be the túnbù liè kǒu[ii] of the team."

"There seems to be a—" began Nigel, before he was interrupted again.

"What's the news Ash?" Sam's gruff voice was clear in the eery silence.

"Port engine is damaged, sucked some debris through an intake and we seem to be venting pressure somewhere on that side of the ship. Everything else is re-booting, the main multithread went into panic.

It was a good thing the impact threw out my connection or I might be re-booting too right now."

"How long til we know anything useful boss? We're sitting tribbles here."

"Stop panicking Sam. As we have just found out, this asteroid field is as inhospitable as Tariq's scrotum and the ship is practically invisible even without a cloak."

————

A grappling hook dinked against the bulkhead and graciously floated past Nigel's nose, lazily turning over and over as it migrated across the zero-G landscape. Several other unpleasantly sharp chunks of serious-looking tackle drifted over him as his chest pulled against the restraints. Nervously, Nigel started to draw attention to this impending situation.

"Excuse me, but… well I don't want to cause a fuss… It's just… my arms are sort of stuck and when we start burning and gravity

---

[ii] Ch. 'a** crack'

kicks in again... I don't want all that effort that you put in to my kidnapping to have been a waste!"

It was the first sentence he had been able to complete in several hours.

Three heads turned slowly in his direction as the words sank in for his fellow occupants.

"Kidnapping?" They chorused.

"Is 'abduction' a better word?" Nigel offered.

"Have you lost what tiny kriffing mind you once had Tariq?" began Sam in a less than comforting tone. "We rescued you from IZV for a category five job, dragged your sorry ass through a firefight with, I might add, very little initiative or effort shown on your part, and you start talking about kidnapping?"

"Ah, well..." said Nigel. "Here's the kicker. My name isn't—" But he was interrupted by that familiar light-stomached feeling as his intestines suddenly seemed several feet higher. The inevitable sinking sensation as gravity exerted her firm hold once again followed promptly, pinning his body down to the deck and raining heavy military equipment on his unprotected anatomy.

Fortunately for Nigel, most of his wounds were only superficial.

The whining of an unhappy sounding ion thruster snapped him out of his daze, but the spiralling rotation of the shuttle immediately started to make him nauseous.

"Hold tight everyone. We've got our drives back," called Ash. "This is going to get worse before it gets better. I'm going to try to bump start the port engine in reverse, using the ion trace from the starboard one. You may experience uncomfortable levels of G as we get close to the optimal rotation velocity."

———

Nigel wasn't sure if he had vomited before or after he blacked out. He was also not sure if it was the continual battering of his head by random weapons or the rapid spinning in one direction that triggered it. Now he had a different problem:

Cleaning vomit in an enclosed space whilst boosting through an uncharted and rapidly changing asteroid field under the disapproving gaze of three psychotic mercenaries.

However, it wasn't a lot of vomit; he had barely eaten and that had been hours ago, plus it had happened after gravity had returned, with the ship now under thrust.

Nigel felt his luck was beginning to change.

CHAPTER 4

AURIGA SECTOR | YEARS EARLIER

Beating their hands repeatedly on the glass of the cell door, Huron and Dybalo shouted as loudly as they could to get the attention of any guards.

Several minutes of hollering and a pair of hoarse, rasping throats later, a head appeared behind the window.

"Kark! I wish you wouldn't do that," rasped Dybalo. "It's freaky and unnerving. Grow a kriffing body will you!"

His request was met by one hand, middle finger raised, materialising in salute, before both body-parts vanished again.

"No, no. It's ok, don't go away, come back, come back. Ignore him, he's an idiot," yelled Huron.

The hand re-emerged, maintaining the same pose.

"Oh we've got a right comedian here haven't we," muttered Dybalo under his breath. "Look... guard?... uhh, several of us are desperately in need of relieving ourselves here, any chance you could escort us to the head?"

After a short pause, the hand disappeared.

"Yeah, belter of an idea Ash, they don't care if we piss ourselves—"

"Shut up Dybalo, stop being a moron." Ash stepped closer to the pair and kept her voice low. "Just stick with the plan. You couldn't organise yourselves out of a paper bag, let alone come up with a scheme to outwit a team of heavily armoured guards covered in stealth-tech. Just be patient, no man I've ever met has ever been as crafty as a pissed-off woman."

A couple of minutes later, the door clicked and swung open.

A disembodied voice spoke up with a warning.

"Try anything kriffwit Basilisk scum, and it'll be the last thing you ever do. Who needs to use the head?"

Five hands went up immediately.

"Bunch of mouse-bladders," grumbled the voice. "You're being watched and you are outnumbered. Follow me, single file, not too close."

Huron stepped out of the cell, followed by Dybalo and three other Basilisks.

They stomped off towards the corridor, but as the door slid shut, Ash jumped up and called out.

"Wait. Please can I go too?"

Signal sent, Huron stopped abruptly and the ensign at the back of the line fell forward, arms outstretched.

The mayhem that happened next was short-lived, but gave them all the information they needed. Windmilling whilst falling, the five latrine-bound men tumbled, rotating to the floor in a clumsy slap-stick manoeuvre that would have fooled nobody as to its intent.

Splayed out on the plas-steel floor, each member of Huron's squad gradually heaved themselves up, pressing as many fingers against the floor as stealth soldiers they believed they had touched.

As luck would have it, it seemed there was only one cloaked warrior between each crew and, disgruntled as they were, they refrained from further violence.

"Has nobody taught you kriffwits how to walk?" screamed their captor. "Get up and stop karking around. You, lady, out of the cell, come with me."

Just as the door started to close again, another cry came out from the cell.

"Sorry, I've just realised I need to go too."

"Oh for kark's sake. Come on, then."

Giggling like a group of teenage schoolchildren, Huron's team walked out of the anteroom and into the corridor. Following up the rear, Ash could sense a body in front of her and the one that seemed to be the leader behind her.

"The ladies is this way," Ash cooed.

Splitting off from the group, Ash and Sam turned left and saw the door to the female head slide open. Stepping inside, she paused in front of a stall.

"Any chance of a bit of privacy?"

"No." came the stiff reply, an entirely predictable response that sparked the two ladies into action.

Ash swung her elbow backwards at lightening speed towards where she estimated the noise had come from and was rewarded with the satisfying crunch of a helmet-comm meeting its demise. Spinning on her heel at the same time, she dropped low and swept the legs from under the stealth soldier before leaping on top of her.

As she saw her partner make her move, sensing the slight distraction of the other invisible guard, Sam also sprang into action. Throwing her torso forward, she let the momentum carry her rapidly extending foot backwards with a powerful kick, slamming the Mensa fighter back against the wall. Rolling over through a break-fall, Sam pushed off the opposite wall and launched herself at the space she desperately hoped her victim would be occupying.

She was met with the reassuring resistance of a partially stunned body so brought her knee up rapidly. The soft thud of patellar crushing groin was accompanied by the splatter of someone being sick inside their helmet.

"Oh kark, I'll have to clean that up," she muttered. "Why do these guys have such weak stomachs?"

"I wish we had Tariq with us," panted Ash. "We'd never have got ourselves into this predicament."

Sensing the fight-back coming, she grabbed for the shin of the soldier and recovered the blade she was expecting to find strapped to the inside of his leg.

"This stealth armour is pretty impressive, only works within a certain proximity." One hand placed on the chest of her victim, restraining any movement, foot trapping one leg and her knee on what must have been an arm, Ash momentarily steadied herself.

"I can't see anything I'm touching. This is going to be interesting."

Speculating that any body armour would have joints with a seam, she aimed just below where she guessed ribs might be and brought the knife up in a well-practiced manoeuvre.

The blade clipped the edge of an armour plate and deflected upwards, burying itself almost to the hilt where Ash figured a neck probably was.

"Oh drokk, I've nicked myself there." Ash pulled her hand away from the limp body and sucked at the blood welling up on her finger. "Not quite what I was aiming for but it's done the trick."

"Shut up moaning and help me subdue this mutie."

Ash turned to to see Sam wrestling with the invisible figure in a set of bizarre and amusing contortions.

"You look like you're managing ok." She smiled in response, trying not to laugh as Sam seemed to sink her teeth into thin air.

A round from the cloaked fighter's weapon flashed across the cramped room, catching a pipe and letting out a spray of pressurised hot water.

"Drokk it, this isn't going as smoothly as I'd hoped."

"Well if you would give me a hand instead of gawping across the kriffing room..." Sam grunted as she caught a blow to her stomach.

Swivelling round, hands clamped over what could have been an arm or a lower leg, she planted her feet against something invisible yet solid and yanked backwards.

A muffled yell came from half-way up the wall where Ash immediately aimed a thunderous kick.

Feeling a gratifying crunch and seeing Sam relax, she felt around for her own challenger.

"Let's get these helmets off, and see what we can do about the stealth-tech." The muffled sounds of fighting drifted through the half-open head door. "Those boys are going to need some help pretty soon Sam, I'm not expecting them to cope without us."

Pulling the helmets and gloves off the limp bodies, after a quick rinse-out they placed them on themselves. Ash and Sam soon worked out the gestures and commands that controlled the stealth armour.

"It's all run from that unit in the chest-plate, let's gear ourselves up in their armour and get over to the lads. I think they're still having trouble.

Grab the Captain, she's still breathing, we'll need a bargaining chip."

As per the plan, as soon as the men entered their head, all hell broke loose.

Estimating the position of their captor's weapons, Huron, Dybalo and the other Basilisks lashed out, ducked and dodged around. Frantically trying to get out of any possible firing line but also land enough blows to disarm, they fought blind but hard.

Huron managed to grapple a weapon from one of the Mensans and started returning fire from one corner of the room.

"Stars, I've been hit Huron." Blood flowed steadily from a sizeable hole in Dybalo's leg.

Holding on to whatever appendage he had caught, Dybalo fell to the side and heaved. Huron fired into the space that had just been created and struck home. More blood mixed with Dybalo's on the floor.

Behind him, one of the corporals collapsed to his knees, half his chest missing.

"Come on guys, we can't afford to lose anyone else." Dybalo started to droop, eyes dulling. Using his last ounce of energy, he propelled himself at an area occupied by the invisible half of a mortal struggle.

His arms connected with a pair of legs and then they were rolling on the floor. A heavy boot connected with his chin throwing his head back, but somehow catching the heel, he allowed his backwards momentum to unbalance the stealth fighter. He brought him down on top of himself, the other Basilisk landing on them both.

Huron fired several times at the gap between them until the thrashing stopped.

At that moment, the struggling form of the Mensa leader appeared, suspended in the air at the doorway.

"Stop or your Captain is finished," came Ash's breathless voice.

"We do not negotiate with terrorists, pirates, or mercenaries," slurred the Captain. "Fight to the death!"

"Your wish is my command." Blood spurted from the gaping wound as Ash dragged the knife across her neck and let her crumple to the floor. "At 'em boys."

The fighting intensified again after the slight lull and the cramped head began to resemble the inside of an abattoir. Blood spattered the walls, there was a severed hand and multiple sinks were damaged, water flowing out of bent and twisted pipes, mingling with the crimson flood covering the floor.

Huron was firing indiscriminately at anything that wasn't obviously one of his own crew.

"Alright, that's enough," Ash yelled above the melee. "Stand aside team." Picking out figures in her HUD, she waded through the bodies, stabbing and firing at any Mensa fighter that still moved. "Yes, the pirate did just say she wouldn't negotiate with pirates... You couldn't make it up! Now get yourselves together and retrieve any body parts that you might have been separated from."

Huron, Ash, and Sam stood amongst the carnage. Dybalo's arms were draped round Ash and Sam's shoulders for support. They were down another fighter and Dybalo was still losing a fair amount of blood. On the plus side, they now had enough stealth armour for everyone.

"Sirius, take Dybalo back to the brig. There's a med kit there. Release the others and wait for the signal, we'll tackle the bridge. Strip these of their armour and put it on. We have the element of surprise on our side and by my calculations, they are down to 17, all of which appear on our HUDs. Just remember not to fire at each other, stay in physical contact with someone on each side of you. We are Basilisks. We don't do defeat. We're taking the Phoenix back."

CHAPTER 5

PROCYON SYSTEM | MONTHS EARLIER

Fiercely sucking her teeth, Ash sat bent low over the ship's display holo, frowning. The schematics of IZV were zoomed in to a section surrounding one of the core-ward cells.

After what seemed like aeons, she waved her finger lightly over the projection and addressed the assembled crew of M94 Chimera.

"I think we can breach the hull here next to this service shaft with a self-sealing blister pack." A small section lit up with a pulsing red highlight. "This will get two of us into this empty cell. That one backs on to Tariq's and we can exit through his door."

She paused for a moment. "Meanwhile, I'll take the shuttle down to the service bay and land at the bottom of the ramp. I can come in hot and toast a few of the guards. They'll be in total confusion and won't know how to react if we hit them in two places almost simultaneously."

Looking up, Ash registered the agreement of her team and continued. "Remi and Sam, you get him out and swing left, left, get through the blast doors and then turn right down the ramp to where I'll be finishing off any stragglers. This will be the most straightforward hit we've done for a while, nobody busts people from IZV, they are light on security and have no auto-turrets. It's practically an invitation."

"No complaints 'ere," Remi drawled.

"Three of us will be enough," added Sam. "We'll meet what? Maximum 24 or 25 guards? You could probably do it on your own Ash."

"Yes but we want it to be quick, in and out before they can open any backup channels to call for help. By the time New Alliance System Security arrive, we need to be jetting rim-wards, at least 3000 clicks away."

"Copy that skipper." Sam adjusted her ammunition belt, "We can rendezvous with the Chimera on the outer rim. S3 has a 50AU range so we should be good if we hop out as the Chimera flies-by. It's only likely to be a three to four month mission. We can reduce our overall flight plan by six months and make the Magellanian job that we need big T for."

"I know you're capable boss, but is it sensible to risk yourself on this?" Vanja - the Super-cruiser's chief pilot interjected. "I'm happy to fly the Chimera, but it strikes me I'm more expendable than you. Maybe I should take S3 and you have a tactical over-view from here?"

"You're good Vanja, but you weren't a Galactic Marine! This will definitely be faster if I do it. And seriously, you'll hardly know we've been away. I predict station contact a few days after drop-off, seven minutes tops from first entry to clearing station atmo and then the return flight will be a couple of months."

"Well if you think it's going to be that easy…" Vanja left it hanging.

The ship's holo flashed red and chimed with a news notification. Ash accepted the message with a casual flick of one finger.

Everyone waited for her to assimilate the information and share the broadcast.

"It's from our source on the inside. If we can make our play at 12:00 Universal Standard Time, the guard will be changing shift. On top of that, they are running half security at the moment as, ironically, they are taking groups to Omega-4 for station defence training. Full contingent isn't due back on IZV for four days and we'll be at the furthest orbit point from either planet."

"Meaning we have the easiest job in the foutu galaxy," chuckled Remi.

"You remember what happened last time you said that?"

The velvety voice stroked every eardrum on the holo deck like liquid silk, causing some to shift nervously and others to snap to attention. "You lost Dybalo, 90 Basilisk fighters, 14 admin and flight crew and almost the Phoenix itself!"

"Yes Commodore," replied Ash. "That time we were young and foolish and underprepared."

"And this time…" Commodore Andrade strolled around the console, looking at the different parts of the projection, leaving her sentence ominously unfinished.

Andrade's svelte form glided with an elegance normally only seen on the dance floors of high society, silently taking in, calculating and evaluating everything.

"Yes, I can see how this *should* work… …barring any unexpected… let us say, hiccups… …I think your turn-around time should leave us with plenty of margin."

She turned and exited the deck, the air thick with trepidation as the weight of her slow and measured sentences left no doubt at her approval of the plan, with significant and foreboding caveats.

"We need a kriffing Commodore proximity alert," muttered Sam under her breath, "I hate it when she surprises us like that."

"Imagine how I feel," Ash replied, downloading the remainder of the mission data and resetting the holo display. "I'm supposed to have operational autonomy all the way up to category seven missions. She makes me feel like a drokking child sometimes.

"Right everyone, back to your stations. We'll muster at 22:00 Universal. Be ready to fly."

CHAPTER 6

OMEGA 4 | MONTHS EARLIER

C oming to a stop in front of a reasonably tidy, but clearly used desk, the MAD induction official half-turned, gesturing vaguely.

"This is your cubicle Mr... uh... Colemin. Oh, that's funny! Um... You will be expected at work by 08:30 sharp and you can clock off any time after 16:30. You can take up to two breaks of up to 30 minutes each, overtime is voluntary, you may use the shared sanitary rooms no more than five times a day, anything taken from nutri-areas is charged to your personal account and all VCs (that's what we call the vending centres) are monitored, recorded and cross-checked against your nutritional status to prevent over-nourishment..."

The official's high-speed staccato was delivered as one run-on, monotone sentence, without any pause for breath until he saw his audience begin to glaze over.

"You don't really need me to tell you any of this, it's all there in the Workers' Manual and Omniweb can answer any questions that the handbook doesn't cover, which, if the rest of MAD is anything to go by, is probably a lot."

The induction guide hushed his tone and partly covered his face with one hand, speaking out of the corner of his mouth.

"To be completely honest, nobody around here gives a drokk what you get up to as long as you keep your head down, and don't break any rules. It's anyone's guess why you can only piss five times a day, but if you need any useful tips on settling in, Doris on row seven has all the tricks covered and you can always find me on Node-233."

Finally able to get a word in edgeways, the new employee spoke up: "What's funny?"

"Funny? Nothing! ...Sorry, no idea what you're talking about, nothing here is ever funny... ever. Goodbye Mr Colemin!" The neat man left brusquely, without waiting for any further acknowledgment and quickly scuttled off around a corner, eager to move on to his next inductee.

Mr Colemin?

Nobody has called me that for years.

Slightly bemused, the burly rookie looked around the 10 cubic metres of his new 'home'. Rather than the common sinking reaction of most new employees, he stood a little straighter, adjusted his ear-comm and sucked in a deep breath.

A fresh start. This time it will be ok. This is a stable job, I will succeed and the make MAD proud of me. You don't get early release for good behaviour, then stuff it all up again... What the kark...? Mustn't swear, gives a bad impression.

His eyes, fully accustom to the gloomy interior, fell upon a small plinth in the corner of the desk, balanced on the Omniweb terminal.

Standing menacingly, brandishing a Sol Militaris Hellion Fire, a small, bandanna-clad rodent waved his invisible troops forwards. The detailing was fantastic. The burn-marks on the barrel of the weapon, the weary streaked face of the commander, ragged head-gear rippling in the imaginary breeze, energy cell belt slung across one shoulder. Waves of nostalgia welled up and the smell of sweat, scorched earth and blood swam into his memory. It faded away rapidly as he noticed the engraved title of the rather excellent taxidermy piece.

Frisky! There's an oxymoron.

After a good rummage through the desk cabinet, Frisky was unceremoniously stuffed under a pile of yellowing paper that must have been left several occupants previously.

He lifted a mug with a large N on the side and sniffed at the dried dregs of tea that covered the bottom. Pushing it to one side, his desk suitably cleared, a meaty finger punched the button on the front of the Omni.

Several minutes of listening to whirring noises, frowning at a blinking interface and idly flicking dust-balls from the desk passed until the sounds ground to a halt and the screen reverted to hollow blackness.

He repeated the process with no better result another couple of times before resorting to the time-honoured tradition of 'Percussive Maintenance'.

When that failed, he departed from male tradition and turned to the last resort of 'asking for help'.

After checking the directory on the mini omni-interface built into the side of each cubicle and tapping the right node-code on his ear-comm, he was instantly rewarded with a relaxed, but clearly slightly strained voice, laden with overtones of old-Earth Ireland.

"Hello IT."

"Hi, my Omni seems to be faulty."

"Have you tried turning it off and on again?"

"Well it was off when I got here and I just turned it on for the first time and—"

"I'm sorry I don't recognise your node, Have you paired your comm with your Omni?"

"No, it isn't working, I just—"

"Have you tried turning it off and on again?"

Keep Calm, explain slowly and clearly. "No, I literally turned it on for the first time just now and as—"

"I'm sorry, please can you state your name, job title, Node and Comm-code?"

"Mr Colemin, Junior Conduit Research Admin Partner, Node-877, Comm-code T7108."

"Thank you Mr Colemin, please hold while I try to remotely connect."

"You won't be able to, the Omni isn't on!"

"Please can you turn on your machine Mr Colemin. Ideally, you would be ready with your machine on so we can help you without any delay. The MAD Security Hub IT department is very busy and we can't really be wasting time hanging about if you aren't ready."

He felt the dents in the cheap desktop before he saw them and slowly unclenched his locked knuckles.

Stay calm, don't blow it before you've even got your feet under the table. This is your first day.

Taking a deep, shuddering breath, he composed himself again. And spoke slowly through gritted teeth.

"I commed to try to get my Omni fixed. It's my first day at the office, I have a temporary comm-code and I think, though I may be mistaken, that Node-877 is going to be my permanent residence."

"Mr Colemin, we don't have a lot of time, there are over 400,000 Omniweb terminals looked after by the Security Hub IT department and we aim to maintain a functioning cluster of 63 percent of those"

"63 percent?" *Small wonder Omega-4 Military has such a soft underbelly.* "Stars, that's 252,000 unusable Omni terminals just taking up space on people's desks! Paperweights for the paperless office. How does the MAD get anything done?"

"Drokk me you're quick at math. Now you've put it like that Mr Colemin, it does explain a few things."

"It's maths."

"Sorry?"

"Its maths, not math."

"I'm sorry, I don't get your drift. Anyway, as I was saying, I'm afraid our most recent shipment of the latest, high-specification Omnis has been delayed and we currently have no ETA on them so I'll put you on the list for a refurbished model."

"How long can I expect to wait?"

"Your guess is as good as mine sir, there are about 137,412 people in the queue ahead of you"

"For the love of Sol, wait what... how... "about 137,412"? Or 137,412? Because that's a very precise number for 'about'."

"Please stay calm Mr Colemin, we're working as fast as we can, we are a large department and the usual waiting time from request to delivery is about two months."

"Two months?" He felt his collar getting tight again and the desk top was definitely not going to withstand much more punishment from his vice-like grip.

Breathe, relax, count to ten, emotion is data not direction.

"What in Sol's name am I going to do for two whole months?"

"Read your Worker's Manual and—"

"It's digital... ...My Omni isn't working."

"Have you tried turn—"

"Are you seriously—"

"Sorry sir, just kriffing with you. I suggest you either do what everyone else does round here, which is drokk-all, or ask your supervisor for guidance Mr Colemin. Is there anything else I can help you with tod—"

With a slightly more aggressive swipe of his finger than was absolutely necessary, he ended the call and slumped back into his chair.

Is this as good as it gets? It was easier before, things always used to work before, we never had second rate equipment or non-functioning interfaces. Maybe a life of admin isn't for me, maybe I'm not cut out for this!

He paused in thought, frozen and pensive, contemplating the lifeless black screen in front of him. Shafts of afternoon sunlight picked out a scattering of dust particles suspended in the listless office air. A quiet background hum of Omni terminals crunching calculations was accompanied by the occasional soft tapping of fingers on desks and interface displays.

Given much longer, he felt that the backdrop of a room full of ageing Omnis, thrumming away in harmony was likely to put him into a coma.

All of a sudden, as if something has sparked him into action, he reached for his ear-comm and tapped in a code.

"That didn't take long Mr Colemin!"

"Yes, I know, look, sorry I didn't get your name before, um, well, the thing is, uh, can you find me a paper copy of a basic Omni manual and point me in the direction of the maintenance tool cupboard?"

"Excuse me? Can I... paper?"

"Ask me no questions and I'll tell you no lies, and you won't have to know anything that might jeopardise your job.... ...The tools."

"Certainly Mr Colemin, right away, in fact, why don't I just nip back past your node and you can follow me on a little walk about. No questions asked, no disintegrations."

"That's my boy!"

Within the hour, the insides of several abandoned Omniweb terminals were strewn across the desk, the smell of melted solder hung in the air and a satisfied grin cracked his face.

CHAPTER 7

DRACONIS SYSTEM | PRESENT DAY

Ash was clearly an extremely talented pilot. The smoothness of the flight belied the way she jinked and dodged through the asteroid field with supersonic-sharp reflexes and a good helping of finesse.

Nigel barely felt the direction changes as it seemed Ash was presciently responding to each oncoming threat. Before he even saw the onrushing chunks of rock, she had delicately adjusted course to slide round them.

The skill was even more remarkable owing to the port ion engine only functioning at 44% and all the compensations that came from flying a damaged ship.

Now was not the time to revisit the name confusion. Nigel, as usual, decided to lie-low and wait it out. He was sure something would turn up out of the blue to make everything right and normal again. Not that his optimism had a history of being rewarded, he generally found the worst-case scenario was his daily reality.

Having completed the vomit-clean, Nigel was re-tethered under the cargo net for his own safety. Remi and Sam had either clipped up, strapped down, or stowed the ironmongery away to prevent further injury and were making the most of their time by sleeping in their flight harnesses.

Nigel's stomach began to rumble. It started slowly and quietly, but very quickly, a noise like an approaching avalanche was broadcasting his hunger.

"Shut the drokk up snoring Tariq." Without a glance backwards, Ash threw a spare bolt at Nigel with pinpoint accuracy.

"Ouch!" squeaked Nigel, "I'm not snoring, I'm hungry."

"Uh uh, no nosh for you fatty, it's diet time."

Ash continued to boost through the last remnants of the asteroid field, clicked on the navigation lock and span round in her pilot seat to face the shuttle's interior.

"Not that it makes a weight difference at this point, but we are not dragging your scraggy, bantha-sized ass around on this job. You've got a crash diet ahead and some serious exercise to do over the next three months."

"Three months?" blurted Nigel. "Where are we going that will take three months?"

"None of your drokking business mutie, all you need to worry about is putting in the reps and cutting out the carbs." Ash smiled maliciously as she tidied up the flight consoles. She double-checked her coordinates, pushed the ion drives as close to their limits as she dared, and ignited the small antimatter engine.

Glancing at Nigel, she smirked again.

"You have your work cut out I grant you that, so we'll be starting in the next ten minutes. Grab a drink from that supply crate and let's work out where to begin. I'm surprised you've managed to slip this far to be honest Tariq. I know there's no gym on IZV but, drokk me, that didn't stop you staying in trim during your previous stay. What happened?"

Sensing his moment, as any good vampire might, Nigel went straight for the metaphorical jugular.

"I'm not this Tariq fellow you're talking about, my name is Nigel and I work in the conduit department at Omega-3 MAD."

Desperate to finally be heard, the words fire-hosed out of Nigel's mouth, pinning his captive audience to her chair.

"…the… drokk!" Was all that whispered from Ash's lips.

"Now that is *not* something I expected to wake up hearing," piped up the mellow voice of Sam. "Easiest kriffing job in the galaxy eh Remi?"

After a reflex 'putain', Remi sat red-faced for several minutes, opening and closing her mouth as if she was going to speak, but with nothing coming out. Ash's eyes bored into her and Sam just sat grinning inanely.

"Merde. I guess that pétasse[i] source inside wasn't so reliable after all," Remi eventually mumbled.

"No kark!" snorted Sam. "I can't believe we've got 5AU off-station before we found out."

Remi eyeballed Nigel with a look charged with sharpened steel blades. "Were you 'iding that little gem from us for any particular reason captain secret? Did you fancy a nice little vacance to le outer planets? Putain. Is this all just a petit joke for you? A jolie? A big, fat, once-in-a-bordel[ii]-lifetime adventure?" Remi menacingly advanced towards Nigel, drawing a cruel-looking, black blade from a sheath on the inside of her calf. "Shall we see 'ow funny it is with a couple of fingers missing?"

---

[i] Fr. 'bitch' / something even more vulgar.
[ii] Fr. 'fu**ing'

Confidence surging, following his ability to finally out the prover-bial Bantha in the room, Nigel faced up to Remi, in as much as a large blob of vaguely human, kneeling in vomit soaked overalls can 'face up' to anything.

"How is this suddenly my fault?"

"Yeah, stand down Remi," snapped Ash. "Looking back, he hasn't really had a lot of say in getting this far. Nobody needs to lose any body parts this time. However…" a smirk formed at the corners of her mouth again. "You can be in charge of the training regime to get our friend here into some kind of shape."

———

As the cargo doors gradually swam back into focus, Nigel's heart slowed and strength began returning to his legs. He rested his forehead against the cold metal and tried to get his lungs back inside his chest.

"Jus' one more set grande garçon and we're done for today."

Remi had been pushing him harder and harder each session. He could now walk the entire length of the shuttle's five metre freight hold twenty times without passing out or being physically sick. Tomorrow, she was threatening to make him do it without the support of the onboard hoist.

He felt like she was punishing him for her own mistake and at times, he considered giving up. The last couple of months had, essentially, been torture for him. The scant supplies of water and high-density protein bars were all he was given. Every step was tiring, his muscles screamed at him, he badly needed a shower and was only just beginning to fit inside and fully close the door on the inexpertly modified sanitary unit on the cramped light-haulage vessel.

The grind of Remi's voice slashed through his near delirium, calling him to get back moving again. Because he valued all his digits and didn't want to risk vexing that troll, he straightened and started marching again.

Only another couple of weeks Universal Time and he would be off this garbage can and thrust into a new environment to face whatever music was coming his way.

Nigel fought forwards, both to carry on walking, and to suppress the foreboding sense of nervousness at the onrushing change. A new and previously unexperienced feeling started to surface. Something he would later discover was called 'resolve'.

CHAPTER 8

OMEGA 4 | WEEKS EARLIER

"We weren't expecting you back quite so soon Ni... oh... uhhhh... Hi, my name's Doris, and I'm just over on row seven. I heard you were back... errr at this desk and wanted to introd— ...Hey where did you get all that stuff from?"

"Hi Doris, I... well... the tools are from maintenance and there were a few spare Omnis in a dusty store cupboard at the end of row three along with these."

He held up several wooden sticks with a graphite-coloured core sticking out of the end.

"I can't quite work out what they are for, but the cupboard was empty otherwise."

"Oh, the 'stationery cupboard,'" Doris adjusted her tight top, giving the effect of someone unsuccessfully taming a squid inside a party balloon. "We figured someone couldn't spell when they labelled it, that cupboard never goes anywhere. It hasn't been used by anyone except Nigel as long as I've been here... ...What are you doing?"

"I'd rather not say to be completely honest Doris. I'm not a hundred percent sure it'll work anyway... Hey..." He tried to bat her hand away as she reached out for the Omni button. "Don't touch..."

The Omni's light came on and the interface flickered. An altogether smoother whirring sound was coming from the device and moments later, the screen lit up with the ubiquitous 'O'.

As he touched the O, a keyboard projected onto the desktop as the Omni introduced itself in the usual way.

"Well that works alright," said Doris, half turning to go back to her cubicle, "lit up a darn sight quicker than mine too, what have you been playing at?"

"Questions, questions Doris, you know what they say!?"

"About what? *'They'* talk too much anyway!"

"Curiosity killed the cat Doris, curiosity killed the cat."

"Whose cat?"

"It's just a saying Doris, it means......oh never mind."

She was already half way down the aisle muttering to herself about 'cat murderers' and how 'it shouldn't be allowed' and 'who on Omega *"They"* think *"They"* are anyway, making up stuff about animal cruelty for fun' and other inaudible grumblings.

———

{Node:_ _ _ _}

877

{Com-Code:_ _ _ _ _}

T7108

{Processing...}

{No Match Found please call MAD Security Hub IT}

Not kriffing likely! Mustn't swear, mustn't swear. Breathe, relax, count to ten, emotion is data not direction.

{Omni MAD Security Bypass Hardware Detected}

Really? It worked!

{Security Level Request:_ _}

Ooh, why not!?

9

{Request Approved}

What?

{Linking…}

{Set Password:_ _ _ _ _ _ _}

*Ok? Um… *******

{Repeat Password:_ _ _ _ _ _ _}

****

{Authorising…}

{Node: 877}

{Com-Code: T7108}

{Security Level clearance:09}

{Remain still for facial recognition scan}

This is never going to work.

{Checking…}

{Checking…}

{Checking…}

{Clear}

{Welcome to MAD T7108}

{You can now use Secure Method Internal Login Everywhere on any MAD Omni Device or interactive console}

{Have a nice day}

I did not expect that.

The plain aluminium background with the blue O faded into a basic Omni interface screen and the Omni-Adventurer window expanded to fill the centre of the space.

Today's Tasks appeared in bold lettering, below which, a bullet list started to populate.

———

"Hey Doris, we never finished our introduction."

He stood behind her chair at a respectful distance, leaning casually on the cubicle partition. As the flimsy screen started to buckle under his weight, he quickly straightened up hoping no-one had noticed.

"I was wondering if you had a break coming up and wanted to walk to the VC with me?"

Without turning from her interface, Doris held up a hand, one finger pointing to the ceiling to acknowledge she had heard him.

"Yes sir... Absolutely sir... No problem, at all sir... You're welcome sir... Have a nice day."

She tapped her ear comm, swiped her hand across the keyboard projection to sleep her Omni and turned to him.

"Insufferable bore, he can stick his—" composing herself with a deep breath, Doris smiled that winning smile at Tariq.

"You know, kind sir, that would be delightful, I'm actually finished for today so—"

"Ah, I'm not going to rock the boat on my first day," he shot back, "I still have until 16:30 and I've got one more day-task. But this is my last break."

"Well, I'll happily teach you something about the VC before I go home." Her smile widened, revealing two perfect rows of sparkling teeth. "You'll need to have all the knowledge if you're going to survive around here."

A while later, he wandered back down the aisle, laden with Nutri-bars, energy drinks, some kind of compressed cereal cake and what purported to be a freeze-dried protein block but looked more like a line of vacuum packed-quail's eggs.

What a first day! I suppose I'd better go looking for furniture for my apartment. It's a bit bare at the moment, no way I could invite Doris back in its current state.

CHAPTER 9

Crackling came from the ship's internal PA and Ash's voice squirmed into the deep recesses of Nigel's ears like a burrowing weevil.

"Final approach ladies. We dock in five minutes, expect the deceleration burn in 5… 4… 3…"

"Why are you using the kriffing intercom?" Sam's head jerked up as she started adjusting her flight harness. "We're sat right behind you and the kriffing cockpit door hasn't closed properly since we got rammed by that frigate near Caroli."

"Well it certainly sprang you into action my dear! But now you've interrupted my ignition sequence, we'll have to start again! 2… 1…"

The force of the ship's engines running in full reverse slammed what was left of Nigel's dignity against the cockpit bulkhead. Loose folds of skin flattened out across the plas-steel panel; his clothes barely able to contain them. One of his chin-flaps pressed suffocatingly over his mouth and nose. With both arms being pinned back to the seat he had graduated to, all he could do was grind his head left and right to free his air-intakes.

"Merde, you're such a mutie Ash," the slurred insult forced its way out from the stretched face of Remi. "Why no warning?"

"I gave you plenty of time to adjust," came the rather lip-heavy reply from the figure at the pilot's console, accompanied by a mildly maniacal giggle. "Besides, this way is quicker."

"Yeah, by less than minutes"

"And much more fun," rounded off the ship's Captain.

Over the previous three months, Nigel had been worked relent-lessly. A diet consisting of only mineral infused water and protein bars had pushed his body into a severe ketosis, overloading the air scrubbers, leaving the ship with an atmosphere resembling the funk of a 2-week-old fruit-bowl.

Whilst his weight had plummeted, the elasticity in his skin was taking its time to catch up and his body resembled a Viennetta ice cream dessert crammed into a lycra sock. Uncomfortable though the experience had been, he was developing a spring in his step and his tormentor, Remi, had run out of portable equipment to force him to carry. Strength and fitness training was going very well from Nigel's perspective, his mood was improving and he didn't even mind Ash including him as one of the 'ladies' in her Captain's announcements.

The negative-G of the decelerating ship eased off and they swooped round in a graceful parabola, entering the hangar of the Super-cruiser M94 Chimera sideways.

Ash touched the shuttle down with a deftness borne of much practice, the passengers completely unaware of the contact with the hangar floor until the docking clamps clunked into place.

At the front of the welcoming party stood the tall, elegant figure of Commodore Andrade. Imposing in her tactical armour with only her white eyes standing out in the ebony skin of her face. Had she had her back to the atmo-shield, it would have been difficult to pick her out her against the space-scape.

"The next time you swing that shuttle in here like a teenage speeder-bike racer trying to impress his girlfriend with an air-brake turn, you'll regret it." Andrade's words were delivered like a titanium fist inside a silk glove. "And you're late. We'll have to increase our antimatter burn to catch up the time. You're fortunate I'm in a good mood or it might have come out of your wages."

"Good to see you too Commodore. Your enthusiasm for us all returning healthy and in one piece is heartwarming." Ash's thinly veiled causticity was not lost on the Commodore.

"Sarcasm is the lowest form of wit Captain." Andrade began to turn, the shuttle crew being expected to follow. "Banter may be contextually appropriate, but when it crosses the line into insubor-dination…" Momentarily, her words died away as her bright eyes widened at the sight of Nigel. "What in drokk's name is that?"

Standing in a sweat-stained body-suit, his spare flesh-rolls tightly gathered under the restrictive elastic material, Nigel was unsure whether he was supposed to offer his hand or introduce himself.

Despite the increased speed of his brain synapses since his improvement in physical health, the sharp-minded Commodore made his decision for him.

"At what point were you actually going to tell me that you were not bringing Tariq?"

In a move that some would later call cowardice but others applauded for letting responsibility rest on the appropriate shoul-ders, Ash stood to one side and let the penetrating gaze of the Commodore bore into Remi. Who, after a short pause, took her cue.

"We thought, as we were short on time, that it was better to make our rendezvous and come to a solution with your input

Commodore." Remi hitched her utility belt and shuffled uncom-fortably in the cavernous silence.

"Well, Corporal Remi, my time of not taking you seriously is coming to a middle." Andrade spun on her heel and swept grace-fully away, "we've wasted enough time and resources as it is, this excuse for a human is useless to us." Without pause for further consideration, she delivered her verdict. "Space it. Then meet me on the holo-deck in twenty minutes. That should give you enough time to freshen up and me enough time to calm down."

Three sets of eyes flashed at Nigel, then questioningly at each-other.

Remi was the first to speak.

"Putain! If she thinks I'm going to space this guy 'aving spent three months of my life burning the fat off 'im... ...Merde."

"I know, I know, we'll have to think of something quickly though, the Commodore doesn't suffer fools gladly and we don't carry dead-wood." Ash thought for a moment. "He must have some transferrable skills, anything at all, we can't go back to drokking IZV and we need the extra team member. Maybe we can trade with a different unit? Are any of the admin staff military trained?"

Pulling himself together from his temporarily slack-jawed state, Nigel felt a new stirring in his chest. Bravery was not something he had previously possessed. But even in the short time he had been with this female team of three, he had been confronted with more than life had ever pitched at him before. He didn't feel the fear anywhere near as much and, whether through boldness or indeed, stupidity, he spoke up again.

"I'm right here, right next to you!!" Their faces turned to him again. "You could always ask me!"

"Ok then smartarse," came the response from Sam, "what transferrable skills do you have that could save your soon-to-be-frozen kriffing spuds?"

Desperately trying to think on his feet had normally been beyond Nigel at the best of times. With a sleep-depleted mind, clouds of space-lag clinging to his ideas and slowing down his thoughts, he was at a distinct disadvantage. Ash unknowingly threw him a lifeline by stalling his reply, "Before you blurt out something drokking ridiculous and trivial, remember, Commodore Andrade is not to be trifled with and she may even have to pass it by the Fleet Admiral."

It came to Nigel in a flash of blinding inspiration, brilliant and clear. Never before had he thanked his incredibly dull former occupation quite as much as he presently did.

"Not only have you all seen just how hard I can work and how adaptable I am in a short space of time." A collective nodding ensued but he could see by their faces that they would need more convincing. "But…" And here was Nigel's trump-card. "I have a photographic memory."

"Well then. That settles it." Ash's grave face had a resigned expression. "Which of you is going to help me woman-handle this mutie to the nearest airlock?"

"What??? No, no, no, no, no, wait!" Nigel's blinding inspiration was rapidly replaced by blind panic. "You don't understand! I see things and they stick permanently. I never forget anything I've looked at." Struggling against the iron grip of Sam on one side and Ash on the other, Nigel squirmed and babbled, wondering, not for the first time, how he had become such a smeck-magnet.

"Still, you're going to 'ave to to better than that!" Despite the ruthless glee she had radiated as his principal torturer en-route, Nigel thought he detected some sympathy in Remi's voice. Almost encouragement. "I 'ate to see my time and effort go to waste

Colemin, but... merde, nothing you've said yet 'as come close to redeeming anything."

Still in a desperate panic, Nigel tried to calm his heart-rate, taking a few deep breaths, he closed his eyes and pictured himself at his old desk, Omni in front of him, Frisky sat on the top of the box-like unit.

Serenity descended on his troubled brain and the pieces of his hastily assembled jigsaw suddenly started to fit.

"I know the plans and specifications of every single, battleship, Megacity structure and trade vessel that has been manufactured by the New Alliance in the last twenty years. And most of the major civil and military projects since the foundation."

The sharp pain that accompanied his coccyx hitting the hangar floor convinced Nigel that his revelation had struck the right chord.

He had surprised himself to be honest. Maybe, he thought, to function at his true best, he really needed extreme levels of adrenaline.

"Why didn't you say that in the first place?" Ash's face was almost smiling down at him. "I think we can probably work with that. You need to get yourself cleaned up and into something a little more respectable. There's dribble on your top! Remi, drop your new boyfriend at the med bay for ship's Doc to check him over, then swing by with a new uniform for him. I'll find the Commodore and see if I can talk us all out of the court-martial we are due for disobeying orders."

"'E's not my putain boyfriend enculée[i]."

---

[i]   Fr. 'bugger'

CHAPTER 10

OMEGA 4 | DAYS EARLIER

lat-pack furniture littered the space around him, the discarded wrapping taking up a sizeable portion of the room. Despite his excellent manual skills, his spatial awareness left a little to be desired. He had definitely either underestimated the size of the units or overestimated the space in his apartment.

Busily, he manoeuvred the new storage units around to find their perfect fengshui positions. Shoving his freshly-constructed bed into one corner, he noticed a hair lodged in the side of the ventilation grille.

Don't think much to the cleaning bots here.

As he worked the hair loose, it gave some resistance until, glued to the end of it, a thin thread pulled through. Rubbing it between his fingers, he mused for a moment, then carried on pulling.

This feels like graphene-coated Spidroin silk. Easy enough to get hold of but not a normal thing to find in an average apartment.

As the thread continued, it widened into a flat-ish ribbon of a memory-foam which wound twice round the air vent and then pulled out completely, causing the grille to clatter onto the floor.

Behind the cover was a flat panel with a little depression on one side. It yielded to slight pressure and then popped open to reveal a numbered key in the middle of a small boxed-out area.

Well that's an anti-climax.

Pocketing the key and making a mental note of the hidden compartment, he replaced the grille and wound the padded ribbon back into its space, breaking off and keeping the useful spidrion silk.

Wrapping all the packaging material into one tight ball, he stuffed it into one of the empty boxes, folded all the rest into a neat pile and dragged it out to the recycling chutes in the shared hallway.

"New neighbours I see!"

A bespectacled lady in her early fifties with front teeth that could bite an apple through a letterbox grinned down the hallway at him.

"Neighbour," he swiftly corrected, adding "Hi, pleased to meet you." So as not to be rude.

"Ooh, *pedantic* new *neighbour* I see," she shot back. A fleck of spittle launched off at the 'P', caught the light breeze in the hallway and was whisked away towards the stairwell. "I'm Maeve, long-term resident; 28 years, one hundred and eighty days, seven hours and..." she looked down at the mini wrist-omni she was wearing. "...nineteen minutes, seven seconds."

"Great, um... very... err accurate," he grimaced, the smile rather narrowing his eyes as opposed to lighting them up. "Thanks Maeve, just settling in, I'm sure we'll have plenty of time to chat."

He beat a hasty retreat through his door and locked it behind him.

"Yes, let's definitely get to know each other better," came the muffled voice from the other side. "I've got a very interesting crystal collection, and I've been told I work wonders clearing people's bad energy. Have you got any bad energy? I'll happily cleanse your aura for you, shall we make a date?"

Slowly shuffling away from the door, he called back over his shoulder.

"Thanks Maeve, I'm good at the moment, any bad energy comes my way, I'll be right round. Got to crack on though, lots to do."

Already half way across his lounge and turning the volume of his music up, he didn't hear her muted reply.

"Welcome to the Motel California... Such A Lovely Space... Such A Pretty Face... " crooned Ron Shenley over the top of Maeve's continuing verbal diarrhoea.

Classic tune.

She seems lonely.

The agent didn't say how long this place had been empty.

I wonder when she last saw a real person?

Finishing plumping up his new bolsters and straightening the throw, he moved on to centring the vase of fresh flowers on the coffee table and treading out the creases in his new rug.

He stood up and surveyed the full effect of his home-makeover.

"If I lived there tomorrow, would you still dismember me?" Blasted out of the apartment sound system. Turning the volume down with a wave of his hand, he moved into the bedroom to check it still looked as good as he thought it did.

Running his fingers along the soft throw at the foot of his bed, he felt the warm glow of the micro-fusion heater on his back. He had opted for sleek and stylish but warm and cosy. Muted, neutral colours and minimal decoration pleased him, but he still wondered why the interior decorating guide recommended quite so many cushions.

"Omni, play something romantic from the 2000s but no James Blunt OK?"

"With all due respect sir, I wouldn't call James Blunt romantic! Wouldn't you be better off with some Barry White?"

Just what I need; a house managed by a sentient AI with opinions.

"I'm not generally keen on you answering back Omni but this time it's a good call."

Nervously, he waited for the door-comm to chime, checking and re-checking the room for anything out of place. He had chilled the drinks, provided tasty but not strongly-flavoured snacks and managed to get a local aspirational chef to cook up something exotic but not too adventurous. After all, he hadn't asked Doris what food she liked.

Why am I so much more nervous meeting this lady than any previous job I've had in my life?

The soft sound of someone knocking at his door made him jump, but he took a deep breath, walked over and opened it.

Doris looked stunning in a sparkly dress that hugged her figure tightly at the hips, then gradually floated out into multiple glittering ribbons of material, just long enough to reveal petite ankles in shimmering shoes. They were obviously made from the latest intelligent materials, with patterns swirling and pulsing, over her feet.

"I prefer the old-school ways," said Doris, noticing his eyes flick to the door entry panel. "A knock is more... exciting, more... unexpected!"

Seeing that his jaw was still gaping in awe at her appearance, Doris smiled demurely at him.

"Well are we going to stand here all night or are you going to invite me in? Something smells divine."

"Oh, sorry, yes, please… come in madam." He stood back out of her way and inhaled her seductive aroma as she glided past him. "I'll be honest, I'm not much of a chef, I had someone prepare something for us. I hope you don't mind, cooking was never really a priority in my previous employment."

"Oh, not at all, not at all," she cooed, putting her tiny clutch on the arm of the sofa. "As long as I'm not having to cook, I'm as happy as a tribble in a bag of popcorn."

"Well make yourself at home." He motioned towards the snacks. "Can I get you a cold glass of something?"

"Oh, whatever you are having."

As he carried two glasses of fizzing rainbow liquid through, pale-blue flames dancing around the rims, he reflected on just how fortunate he seemed to be.

"I'm so glad you could come Doris, it's a real pleasure to have you as the first guest in my new place."

"I'm honoured to be invited… I still never caught your first name and I'm sure as anything going to feel awkward calling you Mr Colemin all evening!"

"Oh, yeah, sorry, we got interrupted in the office didn't we," he joined in as she chuckled. "Tariq. Tariq Colemin."

CHAPTER 11

DRACONIS SYSTEM | PRESENT DAY

"Not a good look sir, not a good look!" The ship's doctor slowly shook her heads and scratched one of her chins with a spare arm.

Hello Mr Kettle, I'm Mrs Pot! Thought Nigel.

"Go through there and grab yourself a shower and we'll have a think about what we can do for you."

"I haven't asked you to do anything for me," came Nigel's confused reply. "Aren't you going to check my health over or something?"

"That has already been done. Your heart is surprisingly robust despite you previously resembling a rhino, your lungs clearly function fine and the analysis of your DNA shows no concerning predispositions. I assume the sweet aroma on your breath is down to the three months of zero-carbs and all scans and other breath-analysis has revealed nothing of concern.

"Now bugger off and get in that gorram shower before I throw up."

The doctor turned towards her consoles as if she was done with him.

"But how?"

"GO!" A spare arm pointed to a blank door whilst the other three flashed across the various displays, her heads staying concentrating on what she was working on. "I will come up with something, but GO, that smell is bad enough to gag a maggot!"

Nigel scurried through the door into the shower cubicle, peeled off his bodysuit and bundled it into a chute marked "Laundry"

Seconds later, the chute ejected his offering.

He tried again, twice, wondering how long he was going to stand naked, trying to get a warship's automated service-wash system to accept his garment.

At the fourth attempt, he found the chute wouldn't open but flashed a single word - Irredeemable - across the centre in bold, red lettering.

Immediately next to the laundry chute, the panel labelled "Garbage" glowed green around the edges and the door slowly gaped open.

————

Cold water pummelled his back, taking his breath away and ripping his brain out from the cobwebs of self-pity. Unable to fathom the ships plumbing, Nigel had settled for getting clean. The icy water hit him at such high pressure that heat was unnecessary. Precariously on the verge of brain-freeze, he battled with the soap and his excess skin-folds, desperately trying to get the grime from three months of sweaty workouts and several million kilometres of travel out of all the crevices.

Stepping out of the shower he noticed a pair of paper pants and a gown obviously placed specifically for him. He looked for a towel but then felt a warm breeze and radiant heat emanating from all around him. With some not-so subtle skin-flap juggling, he was dry rapidly and stepped into his pants, cringing at the thought of someone else entering the room while he was showering.

As he exited the shower area, the whole room seemed different. The bank of displays was gone, leaving a surgical table and his new four-armed, two-headed doctor friend standing, waiting for him.

He looked around in bewilderment, the doctor smiled and waved an arm at the bed, wandering off to a set of drawers that were built into the wall.

"Mmmm, lavender. Good choice Nigel. Just lie yourself down on there and I'll go through the process."

Perching on the edge of the bed, Nigel warily eyed the ferocious looking instruments the doctor was pulling out of her drawers. "Please can I ask what's going on?

"I've been accidentally rescued, dragged light-years through space, forced to exercise on almost no nourishment and blasted with liquid ice, all without any consent from me. It would be nice to have a choice in something for once."

One of the doctor's heads smiled kindly and her tone was definitely reassuring.

"It must be difficult for you with all these new experiences and constant surprises. You're in good hands now though so just relax, you can trust us, we only want the best for you."

At almost that exact moment, the doctor plunged a syringe device into Nigel's belly and depressed the plunger.

Feeling the tendrils of something creeping under his skin like a network of ant tunnels, Nigel frowned. "Now I'm finding it really difficult to take your last sentence seriously," he exclaimed, furiously rubbing his punctured paunch. "When am I going to have any say in what happens to me?"

"Listen Nigel. We were briefed on you and—"

"Well we know about the time you've spent inside and—"

"To put it bluntly, things have changed in the last twelve years."

"We have learned new things from other parts of the galaxy, new technologies are available too, and with the greatest of respect—"

"You don't really know what's good for you—"

"What's best for you—"

"Do you!?" The doctor's last words were couched half as a question, half as a statement.

Looking from one head to the other, doing his best to keep up with the two-part monologue, Nigel felt his focus beginning to swim.

"So, let's get these unnecessary bits taken care of shall we?" A hand idly wafted at his multiple muffin-tops.

"You won't feel anything at all—"

"Nothing at all—"

"Though… you might want—"

"To close your eyes."

Wondering whether it might be best to follow the advice or give in to his curiosity, Nigel's vision pulsed gently in and out of focus. Numbed to the peculiarities of his new world and all that he had faced over the last few months, his view of the doctor's two heads wavered in clarity like the snapshots of an amateur photographer. It was all he could do to follow orders and lie down without missing the operating table more than once. As he settled, took a deep breath to calm his nerves and closed his eyes, he heard the muttering of one of the doctor's heads.

"Lets get this hot-dog bunnery back under control shall we."

Several minutes of gentle tugging at his neck, thorax, abdomen, arms and legs caused Nigel's overwhelming inquisitiveness to crack open one eye.

"STARS! WHAT ARE YOU PLAYING AT? TAKE THAT SMECKING DEVICE AWAY FROM ME. BY DROKK, HOW DID I END UP AGREEING TO THIS?"

Momentarily, the doctor put two hands on Nigel's chest while she lay another length of skin, formerly known as Nigel, into a sizeable metal tray.

"We did say to keep your eyes closed—"

"Sir."

Realising he was not in pain or indeed any imminent danger, a not-particularly squeamish Nigel tentatively opened his eyes. Resisting the immediate urge to regurgitate his last meal or leap up and run screaming from the room, he slowly looked again.

Several neat lines crossed his chest and stomach where once lay redundant tissue. He blinked and looked again.

Noticing him looking, the doctor turned one of her heads to speak while the rest of her attention stayed on the task.

"We did say it was in your best interests and completely painless didn't we?"

"Does he look impressed yet?"

"Shocked presently, but I give it 5-4-3-2 there we go!"

"Those lines will fade in a few days, nobody will ever know."

"Oh, and we fixed your eyes too!"

"What happens to the left-over bits?" Nigel, again, cursed his questioning mind.

"Oh, we recycle it—"

"Yes, broken down into its constituent chemicals and mostly used as fertiliser for the onboard hydroponic farms."

"This lot could create a whole crop of carrots for the canteen."

Nigel was off the plinth and retching into the garbage chute faster than a knife fight in a phone box.

The doctor began to tidy away her instruments.

"I guess everyone has their limits."

"Yes, he did better than most though."

"Yes. He'll be one to watch."

"I'm not sure I want to watch that."

"I don't mean right now."

CHAPTER 12

OMEGA 4 | DAYS EARLIER

Rolling onto his side, Tariq propped himself up on one elbow and looked at the slow rise and fall of Doris' ample chest.

The fastidious neatness of his apartment and his new furniture had obviously impressed her.

What an evening. I could get used to this.

Silently slipping out of the bed, he crept into the lounge, softly closing the door behind him. He gestured for the solar blinds to let more light into the room, then wandered into the kitchen.

Finding something he could absent-mindedly chew on for breakfast, Tariq poured himself a glass of purified water and flipped on his interface.

Now that he had full security access and a remote connection, he could carry on his research from home and minimise the chances of arousing suspicion in the MAD office.

Checking his activities weren't being traced, he doubled down on staying undetected by initiating an IP cloaker and a trail-sweeper.

Contrasting with the monotonous rhythm of his chewing, his fingers tapped and swiped at a blistering pace, digging deeper and deeper into the bowels of the MAD classified files.

He wasn't completely sure what he was looking for, but he knew he would recognise it when he saw it.

"So who *are* you really Tariq?"

Time had passed without him realising it and regardless of the shock it gave him, there was no 'tell' in his body. Continuing to explore the innards of the MAD Omniweb, he turned to look at Doris.

"Who do you want me to be?" A most charming and genuine grin lit up his whole face.

"Well… I'm not sure I've worked that out yet. But I do want to know who you *were* and therefore who you *are* now." Trailing her fingers across his bare shoulders as she made her way to the drinks unit, her eyes sparkled with genuine intrigue and not a little mischief. "Where did you come from? Are you going to stay around? I'm not about to emotionally invest in someone that isn't going to share, or somebody that might make off at a moment's notice."

His eyes gorged themselves on her exquisite beauty, drinking in the irresistibility in the same manner that a desperate old soak at last orders sinks his penultimate pint.

Flipping the interface off, he pushed it into its storage drawer and turned to face her fully.

"Why don't you come over here and I'll tell you?"

As soon she was within reach, he enveloped her in his muscular arms and pulled her onto his knees, facing him.

"Once we've finished breakfast," he said, gently pulling her face towards his and planting a kiss on her expectant lips.

She melted into him, seemingly quite happy to invest physically at that moment, and kissed him deeply, running her soft hands over his back and chest.

———

"This shower is amazing," called Doris above the sound of the running water. "Do you have a towel handy? I forgot to pick one up."

"Just step out when you're done. The room is 'smart' and will work things out for you."

Emerging from the bathroom, glowing from her shower and recent exertion, Doris looked the picture of health and beauty. Tariq could feel his arousal growing again and looked away quickly.

He stood up and politely walked towards the door, "I'll be in the lounge area when you're dressed again."

A few minutes later, she joined him at the window, looking out over the city skyline and snuggled up under his chin.

"I..." He hesitated, one word in.

Lifting her almost flawless features up to him, she smiled encouragingly. "Don't be shy."

"Yeah... I... Promise you won't judge me if I'm completely honest."

"You know I can't possibly promise that Tariq. Nobody could. But I promise I'll be as generous as I can in my judgement."

"I suppose that's fair. Well... MAD has just assigned me to the Conduit Research Admin Partners team as the final phase of my rehabilitation."

Expecting her to pull away and rush to the opposite side of the room, he was pleasantly surprised to only feel her shudder slightly.

"I've just served my time in IZV for murder, extortion, theft, wanton destruction and probably a few other crimes I've forgotten about."

Reflexively she stiffened considerably and he relaxed his arm in case she wanted to move. At this, she hugged in tighter and delicately placed her hand on the front of his t-shirt. Raising her face again, she looked at him, expectantly.

"Well, aren't you going to comment?"

"I don't think that anyone that has been as gentle as you have towards me could still be a threat to anybody." She smiled and waited.

"Well… ok… I was never a threat to civilians anyway, not ones that didn't deserve it! I was part of a larger organisation that ran dark, taking military contracts from various large institutions and big galactic players. You may have heard of the Basilisks. Nobody got harmed by me if they weren't either holding a weapon or pulling the strings behind nefarious activities."

"But you're finished with all that now." Doris' eyes posed the question that her vocal inflection had not.

"NA has a good reintegration programme in many ways, but the things I have learned whilst 'inside' have made it harder to fully adapt. I really want to make a go of my new life here and I'm determined to make *this* work." Tariq's hand waved a vague circle, indicating the pair of them, and knocked over a chair.

"You were saying…"

"Yes, I want to make us work, and I want this new life to be a real new beginning but there's something that is bugging me at the back of my mind. Something I can't quite put my finger on. Something I think I know but won't really understand fully until I discover it. Unless I put this to rest I think I'll always struggle to settle down.

"But that doesn't change us! I won't drop you in it but you might be best not asking any questions. I don't want you caught up in anything."

Doris disengaged and slowly walked away, looking back coyly over her shoulder.

"Of course Tariq. I completely understand. Unless... I can help find that thing you're looking for."

CHAPTER 13

DRACONIS SYSTEM | PRESENT DAY

Standing in nothing but paper underwear, Nigel contemplated his new form. Spider-silk thin red lines threaded across his whole body where folds of skin once lay. He could see abs that he thought had wandered off years ago. Staggered at how his caravan-park-flood of a body had been transformed in the space of minutes, he started to smile.

"As I said, those lines will fade in a couple of days—"

"If you put this cream on—"

"Thank you… and you'll not notice them at all by next month."

"Wow, thanks very much." His grin had turned into something that radiated as much joy as a young boy in a sweetshop. "Maybe I can trust you after all."

Just at that moment, the door access panel chimed, and before anyone answered it, Sam muscled in.

"Get your kriffing clothes on already, gǒushǐ yùn[1] the Commodore wants to see you. Stars Nige, you look better. Wow you have abs! Who Knew? Some serious high-tech you got in here Docs. You sure you're allowed to do this magic onboard?"

"Thank you Lieutenant, it's called science—"
"Science, magic, whatever." Sam grinned widely.

"Please, come in, don't bother waiting next time—"

"Everything has been cleared with Fleet Command—"

"You know this is a privacy breach Lieutenant, you could be disciplined for this."

"Yeah but it's only Nige." Sam looked confused.

"We'll forgive you this time but it won't happen again Lieutenant. Move along now, we've got work to do."

Still frowning, the doctor, disinterestedly turned back to her consoles while Nigel hurriedly pulled on his new fatigues.

Moments later he was marching down the corridors in the wake of Sam, light on his feet and feeling more energetic than he had in years. The throngs of other shipmates, clearly making their way to the mess hall or training decks either parted as they saw Sam coming or found their noses bounced off the fabric-covered foam on the plas-steel walls as she made her own passage.

Nobody complained. Occasionally someone turned back with a look of anger, only to immediately get back to their business when they saw who had unceremoniously launched them across the walkway.

Nigel was beginning to think he quite enjoyed holding this kind of company when Sam turned her head to speak.

"Don't get any ideas mutie. This kind of respect takes years to earn and seconds to vaporise… Very much like your previously mammoth figure really."

"I wasn't—" stammered Nigel before he was cut off.

"I know exactly what you were thinking and to be perfectly honest, when we found out who you *weren't*, I wondered what kind of a garbage-ship fire we had walked into. You have a chance to come good but it is a slim chance and you have an even slimmer time window to convince the Commodore not to cut her losses and space you. So start working on your opening line. You'll get one shot. If you kriff that up, you'll be an icy husk within minutes and my team will be in for a world of pain."

"No pressure then eh?" Nigel attempted a grin.

"Exactly Nige. No Pressure. Just remember, one way or another, you're destined to be a diamond... In about 20 seconds."

———

"Ah, our honoured guest." Despite her saccharine tone, the Commodore oozed menace from every invisible pore. "I understand you may be of some value after all."

"Uh, yes, I guess so." Nigel half turned as he heard Sam muttering behind him.

"Stars! Way to go Nige, how to make an impact first impression."

"Thank you Lieutenant, that will be all." The glacial tone of the Commodore was clear and final. "Mr Colemin and I can take things from here."

"How did you—?"

"DNA Mr Colemin, DNA. Drokk knows how much of it you turned up with and left around the docking bay, you must be relieved to have been unburdened of some of it."

"But I—"

"Let us not get distracted. I am here for information, you are here to trade for your continued existence." She sat down in a comfortable seat by a large viewing window.

The panoramic glass allowed a magnificent star-scape to spill into the room leaving Nigel feeling overwhelmed. The sheer vastness of this arm of the galaxy reminded him of his smallness. In an attempt to preserve his sanity, his brain switched into survival mode and conjured endless images of food.

Sitting down in the chair that the Commodore had gestured towards, Nigel looked back at her, smiled weakly and wished he had a slice of cake... and a cup of tea.

"It's beautiful," he began, glancing at the light show.

"Cut to the detail Colemin. Start at the beginning. Give me a reason not to put you outside."

Nigel took a deep breath and promptly fell off his seat, banging his head against the window and landing on his back.

Getting to his feet in surprise, the incredulous look on his face multiplied at the second huge jolt from the ship that sent him tumbling into a glass-fronted drinks cabinet.

"Smeck!" Blurted out Nigel.

Alarms started blaring from every corner. Brushing the fragments of toughened glass from his bruised arm, he turned again to face the Commodore.

"STARS Man! What the drokk is happening?" Barked the ship's senior officer, getting up off her knees.

"I'm not sure Commodore, it wasn't me."

"Shut up Colemin. Not you, I was talking to my Commander." Commodore Andrade pointed viciously at her ear-comm.

"Oh, Sorry," mouthed Nigel as yet another massive impact sent him reeling again.

"I'm coming right over. Patch me through to weapons and shields, I need immediate damage reports and response statuses. Colemin,

I'll speak with you later, find somewhere to shelter and don't get lost or injured. And definitely don't drokking die. If you are to meet an untimely demise on my star-cruiser, it is going to be by *my* hand! Henshaw, where are those reports?"

The Commodore half ran, half staggered out of the room, struggling to maintain her balance as a succession of teeth-splintering blows rippled through the ship.

Nigel desperately looked round to find some kind of shelter. Stumbling around the huge room, he frantically pressed wall panels, pulled at anything that looked like a handle, randomly pushed buttons on consoles. Nigel's heart was pounding at the inside of his ribs like a hoard of angry zombies thirsty for a feast of brains.

A clichéd whooshing noise broke through the general cacophony as a circular glass doorway slid to one side. Without a moment's thought, Nigel rushed through and hit the big green button displayed on the control interface on the other side, assuming it would close the door.

Nigel's assumption was accurate and the big door rumbled back into its resting position.

Depressurising in 30 seconds

"Stars!!!! Why do I have to pick the only smecking airlock on this deck to shelter in?" He glanced at his dishevilled appearance in the air lock glass. "How has my life become such a rolling clustersmeck?And who puts an airlock on a viewing deck?"

Depressurising in 20 seconds

Nigel hysterically prodded at every light source and shape on the interface of the airlock, then took a deep breath and closed his eyes.

Deciding he wasn't going to get anywhere by mindless panic,

except rapidly turning in to a block of human ice, he opened his eyes and read the information on the screen in front of him.

Nothing seemed to offer any assistance and the large numbers in the middle of the screen counted down with depressing monotony. In the top right corner, there was a tiny cross inside a circle which Nigel only noticed when his face was so close that the control panel fogged up.

Depressurising in 10

Nigel touched the cross and the main menu opened. Sat in the middle, was the command he was looking for.

He tapped "Cancel Opening Sequence" and the first screen reopened, displaying a second timer next to the first one.

Airlock opening cancelled.

Nigel wiped the perspiration off his forehead with the back of his sweaty hand.

Depressurising in 5... 4... 3... 2... 1...

"What in smeck's—"

Zero

CHAPTER 14

OMEGA 4 | PRESENT DAY

Reaching into the safety deposit box, Doris glanced behind her to where Tariq was standing. His almost imperceptible nod showed that he was convinced they weren't being watched, so she pulled out the contents, jammed it into a soft hold-all and slung it across her back.

Walking across the concourse, she surreptitiously checked over her shoulders for any signs of being followed. Making their way to the underground, Doris subtly passed the bag over to Tariq as they crossed in front of the automatic barriers, shouldering the almost identical bag he had been carrying. Satisfied they were in the clear, they followed their overly-cautious plan. Doris took the Northbound Intra-City-Hyper-loop to MegaCity 2 (MC2), while Tariq went East for a couple of stops before shifting lines and transitioning cross-city until he picked up the high-speed line North to reconnect with Doris.

Stepping out into the fetid air of MC2 (MegaCity 2), Tariq set his jaw and scanned the immediate surroundings to find a vantage-point that was not overlooked or otherwise vulnerable.

Street-hawkers milled around selling their stimulants, suppressants and almost any other non-medical pharmaceutical concoction that anyone could imagine. Jostling past a sunken-eyed punter, Tariq spied a dark corner where he stashed his hold-all before swinging himself up to a grimy ledge. Squatting in the shadows, the aroma of xāhār rim thāng floated up his nose and reminded his stomach that his last meal was too long ago.

Focus Tariq, don't let your guard drop. Not long and you can go home again and relax.

Gently humming to himself, he crouched, lamppost-still, scanning the Hyper-loop exit as well as all the roads, paths and alleys that led into the grimier areas of downtown MC2.

"One of these days you'll feel the smell of speed and come crashin' in your house and say 'Hey, it's so late.'" Tariq nodded his head as her quietly sang along to that day's ear-worm.

"All your friends go driving around. Coming back to see the starship going up in smoke."

At that moment, he spied Doris exiting the Hyper-loop terminal. Two steps out onto the street, a previously unnoticed willowy vagrant leaped to his feet and rammed some kind of hood over her head. Immediately, another assailant had lifted the bag she carried, pinned her arms to her sides, and was rapidly but still fairly unobtrusively marching her off round a corner.

Leaping off the ledge with agility belying his muscular frame, Tariq was immediately in pursuit.

Who are they? How did they know?

Unhindered by a struggling kidnapee, Tariq rounded the corner and caught up with the attackers in seconds.

His elite training meant that his own movements were noiseless. Not that it made any difference, the fuss Doris was making could have woken the dead, probably even the undead.

Allowing his momentum to carry through, Tariq shoulder-barged the beanpole, sending him spiralling into a commercial waste unit. Not giving the other kidnapper any time to react, Tariq jammed his outstretched fingers into the man's Adam's-apple making him let go of Doris. Retrieving the hood from Doris' head, Tariq simultaneously swung his heel round, taking out the man's legs. He crumpled, coughing and holding his throat, leaving Tariq a moment to focus on the thin, tall opponent. Still reeling from the initial impact, his dazed expression turned surprised as Tariq caught him up by an arm and twisted him down next to his colleague. Covering them both with the same hood, Tariq pulled out the spidrion silk that was still in his pocket and took it twice round the neck of the hood, then tightly bound the hands of Doris' would-be kidnappers.

Yanking them both back up to a standing position, Tariq looked for somewhere he could interrogate the pair without being interrupted.

Seizing her moment, Doris aimed swift kicks to the crotches of both low-lives, causing them to buckle forward again in an awkward shuddering bow.

"I know that was a bit cowardly, but they started it." Replacing her stiletto heels that had fallen off in the struggle, Doris raised a questioning eyebrow to Tariq. "What are you looking for?"

"We need information from these goons and quickly. I want somewhere undisturbed."

Spying a rusty, battered-looking door at one side of the waste trolley, Tariq dragged his new quarry over and gave it a heavy kick with his heel. The lock pinged open immediately, allowing the door to swing a few inches back on its stiff hinges.

Leaning her shoulder against it, Doris pushed the door open enough for them all to come through, then carefully dragged the rubbish collection bin across the opening before closing it again.

Shafts of afternoon sunlight pierced through broken windows and ill-fitting fan-housings, lighting up the dust that slowly drifted around in the abandoned warehouse. The floor was thick with a layer of orange powder and the smell of ancient lubrication oil hung like fog in the air. Various machines in progressive states of dilapidation adorned the expanse of floor, but all materials and anything of value had clearly been stripped years ago. The place had an aura of decay and an eerie emptiness about it, the dirt covering the floor muting any sound.

Spotting a solid steel beam part way in to the room, Tariq pulled his new acquaintances to it and flung the other end of the spidrion silk over the top, securing his captives like hanging rabbits.

Before Tariq could make any further move, Doris produced a short lock-knife seemingly from thin air, pulled the top of the hood backwards and pressed the sharp tip to the throat of her original mugger.

Eyebrows raised higher than his hairline in surprise, Tariq spoke quietly. "Easy, easy Doris. Lets just take it slowly shall we. These chaps are clearly amateurs. Give me a minute, I have to retrieve the other bag."

Doris stepped into the shadows while Tariq slipped back out of the door, doing his best not to let it creak too loudly.

Almost as soon as he had left, Tariq returned with the holdall slung over his shoulder. He hung it next to the identical grip, over a rusty nail protruding from the wall and, still with a look of wonder on his face, nodded to Doris.

Stepping back to the suspended unfortunates, Doris applied the knife-tip again.

Coming up behind the taller of the two men, the one with Doris' blade at his jugular, Tariq growled into his ear.

"Who sent you?"

"What do you mean?" The man quivered. "Nobody sent me."

"I'm going to give you one more chance to tell the truth. Who... Sent... You?"

"I have no idea what you're—" His sentence was prematurely curtailed as the air was expelled rapidly from his lungs. Tariq's kidney jab leaving the man breathless, he switched his attention to the other aggressor-turned victim.

"Your friend can't breathe for a bit and unfortunately he is bleeding a little. Just a small nick, nothing terminal. Now, it's your turn to come clean. Who sent you?"

It was clear neither of the men were comfortable. The height differential between them required the tall one to stoop and the short one to continuously teeter on his tiptoes. A snivelling sound came from inside the hood, drowning out the heavy breathing of the other occupant.

"I promise, nobody sent no-one. No, no, no, no, don't hurt me!" He felt the tip of Doris' knife pricking him just under his sternum. "We have no idea what you are talking about, we just saw this pretty lady walking with a bag and thought it might have something valuable in it."

Swifter than a mousetrap, Doris made an incision in the material of the hood, pulled the shorter man's ear through the opening and rested the razor-sharp knife against it.

"I swear to you, you snivelling wretch, if you don't cough right now, you're going to start losing body parts. Beginning with this gorram ear."

At this, Tariq's jaw dropped, the space between his chin and his eyebrows resembling a gaping cave in a craggy - but clean-shaven - mountainside.

Trembling on the tips of his toes, sweat darkening the shirt under his arms, the man wailed for mercy.

"Please... I promise... I swear we were just looking for easy targets with expensive things so we can get our Tranquility fix. We've got nothing... Look." the man showed his wrists to Tariq and Doris, revealing characteristic 'convict in rehab' tattoo markings and pale, collapsed veins. "We've just been let out, no job, no prospects. We've done nothing wrong... Well, nothing more than a simple mugging or two. We're sorry, we'll do anything to make things right."

"Stop it," grunted Tariq, "have some dignity man, squealing like a stuck pig, for Sol's sake!"

Momentarily wandering off to one side, Tariq lost himself in thought.

"Doris, a moment..."

Moving away from the gibbering thieves, Doris ambled over the red dust to where Tariq was staring out of a dirty, part-shattered window.

They conversed in hushed tones so they wouldn't be overheard.

"That got dark very quickly Doris. Do we need to have a talk? That's the kind of life I came from, not the one I'm heading towards. I just didn't want to see you harmed, you're the best thing that has ever happened to me. And I'm paranoid that someone knows something about what was in that safety deposit box."

"I was just playing bad cop, violent cop for you, I've seen them do that on the holos. I quite enjoyed it."

"That's the problem Doris. The adrenaline is intoxicating. It makes you do things you wouldn't ever consider in your right mind. And you get addicted. The thrill of the chase, the capture, getting the information, eventually just causing the pain is a buzz you can't get enough of. You don't want to go down that alley. If you're not careful you lose yourself. I feel like I've found myself meeting you, I don't want to spiral back into the chasm again."

"Wow Tariq, that is deeper than I was expecting. You're very perceptive. You've been wasted as whatever you once were and I think you're wasted in your current MAD position.

"What do we do with these guys then?"

"I don't know. I have this distinct feeling that they might actually be telling the truth! I think they probably are just incompetent tranq-heads looking for their next fix. I was trying to think if I could find a way to help them. A life addicted to Tranquility or Stim or Esoteria or any of the other chems they peddle in the downtowns of the megacities is a horrifying existence and generally a one way highway."

The conversation was truncated by the sound of squealing breaks and screeching tires outside. Tariq ran to a window on the adjacent wall and cleaned a small patch of glass to look through.

Three large jeeps with blacked out windows had pulled up, engines throbbing. 12 burly men in dark clothing piled out of the vehicles. They looked well prepared with sleek, modern blasters holstered on their hips, but no sign of an insignia anywhere on their clothes.

"Quick, we've got to go." Tariq leaped back from the window. "We can't leave these guys here either. Oh man what have they dragged us into? There must be a way out on the other side of the room, you go and look for an exit, I'll get these two."

Tariq rushed back to untie their unfortunate nitties.

Quickly yanking off the hood at the same time as releasing their wrists, Tariq looked apologetically into their bemused faces.

"Time we were on the move fellas! I'm going to trust you not to try and escape because if you do, there is a world of pain waiting for you."

"Found it," Doris called from across the empty workshop. "The door is a bit stiff like the other one, but with a bit of teamwork, we can push it open."

Tariq half shepherded, half dragged their companions towards the far exit and leant his shoulder to the resistant door which gave way suddenly and vomited them out into another dingy alley.

They could hear the beginnings of a commotion behind them so they slammed the door shut and set off at a sprint that Doris' high heels were no match for.

Twisting and turning through rubbish-strewn ginnels, one of Doris' stilettos snapped, so she removed them both and held them, one in each hand.

"This is going to put dreadful ladders in my tights," she exclaimed.

"Right now I think that's the last thing you need to worry about miss," panted the tall scrawny druggie. "Stinks here is falling behind and I'm sure those banditos are hot on our tails."

"Stinks? Really? Stinks?" Called back Tariq who was charging ahead, trying to find somewhere to hide and stop for a breather. "I mean it's accurate, but hardly imaginative. What do they call you? 'Lanky' or 'Streaks'?"

"I'm Streaks, how did you guess?"

"Holy kark!" Blurted Doris "You couldn't make this drokk up.

"Also, did he actually call them banditos?"

"I think so" called Tariq, spying a door slightly ajar. He yanked it open and waved them through.

"This way, quick, stop wasting energy yammering."

Grabbing Stinks by the back of his shirt, Tariq propelled him through the door without looking, then dragged it shut behind him, to the sound of a satisfying click.

Pressing his ear to the door again, he motioned at the others behind him for silence. After a short while, dull sounds of heavily-booted running passed the door and faded down another passage. His breathing rapidly returning to normal, Tariq turned and rested his back against the door, unprepared for the scene that met him.

Several rails of clothing and accessories lay scattered across the floor, whilst Doris was already making attempts to dress Stinks & Streaks in new outfits.

"What in drokk's name are you doing Doris?" Not usually phased in many situations, Tariq was completely stymied this time.

"Disguises, we've got to have disguises!"

"Oh stars Doris. This isn't the holos, they didn't even see us, you're going overboar—" his last word was muffled as Doris planted a large, floral dress over his shoulders and pulled down hard, then crammed a blonde wig and wide-brimmed hat on his head.

"Oh, that's nice," Streaks started. "It really suit—"

Tariq's death-stare caused Streaks to choke off the words, leaving an awkward, hanging silence.

Wriggling his arms up through the dress sleeves, Tariq's exasperation broke through again.

"Doris what am I even doing letting you—" in a conversation of curtailed sentences, Doris' soft finger pressed over the front of his lips to silence him.

"I don't know who or what we're dealing with. You don't know who or what we're dealing with. We think Stinks and Streaks are probably genuine guys who have lost their way in life and nothing more. But… we can't afford to be complacent. We don't even know what's in that bag yet."

Eager nodding came from the pair of addicts, who now looked utterly ridiculous, Streaks in flared jeans, wide lapelled shirt and a kipper tie and Stinks head to toe in black biker leather.

"Now, help me find a helmet for Stinks and something discrete for me before we get moving again."

————

"Sorry, sorry, I'm ever so sorry madam." Doris, attired like a member of the aristocracy and sporting the accent to match swanned out of the store-room and into the shop-front, wafting her arms around like she owned the street. "I'll take all of these, just charge it to my sister."

The imposing frame of Tariq, barely contained by his lace-strewn dress, face partially covered by curly blonde hair ambled out behind her and offered up his wrist for the credit skimmer.

Doris ushered Stinks and Streaks towards the exit, quietly telling them to leave one-at-a-time and follow inconspicuously after her and Tariq.

"Thank you so much darling, you've been wonderful." Doris flashed her winning smile at the incredulous old lady behind the till.

"I thought you were trying to be discrete," muttered Tariq as they casually wandered out into the flow of shoppers in downtown MC2.

A mixture of old industrial installations & warehousing interspersed with commercial buildings in various stages of decrepitude rose up either side of the narrow street. Some of the ruins were squats, some better maintained properties were converted into apartments, albeit run by landlords of questionable moral character. The vertical sprawl of MC2 towered above them, the more prestigious dwellings being increasingly expensive and desirable, higher up the cityscape. Salubrious, luxury housing overshadowed the downtown district and limited the ability of daylight to reach ground level. Elderly sodium lighting only marginally increased visibility, creating a low-level murky orange glow to the whole district.

Beguiling smells infused their nostrils, punctuated by the occasional assault of raw sewage, vomit, and other unidentifiable, even less pleasant aromas.

"I want to feel sunlight on my skin, I see the scum cloud disappear under my chin. I want to shelter from the city rain. Where the tramps have no name." Tariq sang quietly in a comical falsetto as they picked their way between the food stalls and shops whose wares were tumbling out over the street, or attempting to escape.

"On that note Mr Colemin... Along with your lovely singing voice, I hope *your* sense of direction is going to return us to the Hyper-loop. We've got to get away from here and mine deserted me in our panic to escape. Who were those guys?"

"I can only assume we tripped a sensor and it was a private security firm sent to secure the premises. Maybe there's something important there or maybe the owner is sitting on property hoping for the market to pick up and doesn't want vagrants defecating in the corners. We'll probably never know. Either way." he tapped his ear. "My comm is cloaked and linked in to the Omniweb so we can easily find our way back. The bag is safe with us, I'm more concerned about what we're going to do with Streaks and Stinks!"

CHAPTER 15

DRACONIS SYSTEM | PRESENT DAY

E very swipe and tap that Nigel mashed into the airlock console just made things worse. He batted away pop-up dialogues and searched for hidden 'close' zones like he was fighting off the adverts to access an illegal sports stream.

Finally he took a lung-busting deep breath and held it. Willing his heart rate lower, he turned to the MAD mindfulness training that he had paid scant attention to during his previous employment.

A faint hissing sound started quietly and gradually grew to the point where he felt his new jacket whipping around his waist as the air gushed out of the airlock.

Opening his eyes again, he focussed all his new calm on the interface in front of him.

The lower part of the screen showed the current status, it read: "Depressurising | Outer Door To Remain Closed". The rest was a mess of circles, crosses, squares and jumbled information in a variety of typefaces.

Who the smeck wrote the code for this heap of junk? My 8-year old nephew could have done a better job. And I don't even have a nephew.

As his lungs started to burn, he methodically cleared all the myriad of clutter from the screen and paused again. Having a rare moment of oxygen-deprived clarity, he tried touching the status readout at the bottom of the screen.

Up jumped the magic words he was hoping to see. "Tap to cancel stop the depressurisation of sequence and the initiate re-pressurising airs command."

They couldn't even have it in standard Earth! Was this ship fitted out by disgruntled, underpaid workers in the Betelgeuse docks or something? How does anyone navigate this thing at all?

Firmly touching the relevant command, Nigel felt, rather than heard the re-sealing of the airlock and the warmth of ship air coming back in. Trying not to pant like an overheated dog, he relaxed further and studied the interface again.

Nigel was particularly careful in his painstaking analysis of the menu system until he found the commands for releasing himself from the airlock.

The shuddering of the ship had dropped to intermittent impacts that were a lot less fierce. Able to remain on his feet without much trouble, Nigel attempted to release the airlock to return to the viewing deck.

"Input Security Code: _ _ _ _ _ _ _ _"

"Oh for smeck's sake!" He expleted. Slumping down to the floor again, Nigel rested his head back underneath the command console and closed his eyes.

"Typical! It's always me isn't it." Expostulating at the empty space, Nigel ranted for a good quarter of an hour before he ran out of steam. "And to cap it all, now I need the toilet."

A mild crackling sound came over the ship's PA, followed by a polite voice.

"Attention all personnel. We apologise for the recent disturbance and any discomfort you may have experienced. Obviously, most of you are used to the rough and tumble of galactic warfare, but for those on-board that are not, please check your nearest interface."

Lost for other things to do with his time, Nigel dragged himself to his feet and steeled for another battle with the opaque software.

At the bottom of the screen, a ticker-tape newsreel pulsed in red, inviting him to tap on it.

The Chimera has been ambushed by a contingent of seven, cloaked Mensa cruisers.

Hull damage was only cosmetic as our reactive shields grow stronger with each energy pulse they absorb. We are in no immediate danger.

Internal damage from the initial shockwaves is still being assessed, a number of crew are attending the med bay due to minor injuries and damage to fixtures and fittings is now being catalogued.

If you find anything broken in your vicinity, please scan it and upload a picture to a ship interface. A printer will replace the item as soon as possible.

Please do not deliberately break anything just to get a new one.

Within the next hour or so, we will either outgun our attackers or transition through the outer-system jump-gate, leaving them behind.

The admin team apologise for any discomfort or inconvenience caused.

Drumming his fingers on the smooth wall, Nigel took stock of his situation. He was bed-wettingly-tired and it felt like decades since he had eaten a proper meal.

He started to wonder what the ship's chefs on a vessel this size could rustle up. Then, stomach grumbling, he wondered where the mess hall was and was just about to see if he could access a map or directions from the interface in front of him when he remembered his last demented experience and thought better of it.

The regular juddering of the ship under attack was almost soothing and despite the occasional flare of laser-cannons and plasma blasts flickering through the airlock window, Nigel felt his eyelids grow heavier. Taking off the soft shoes he had been given, he rolled them up and fashioned them into a rudimentary pillow.

Moments later, the tendrils of tiredness wove into his mind, blanked out the surprises of the last couple of days and dragged him into an uncomfortable but settled sleep.

CHAPTER 16

OMEGA 4 | PRESENT DAY

Playfully hopping down from a high step outside the Hyper-loop terminal, Tariq landed silently beside his unusually clothed companions, his dress floating gracefully out like that of a dancing fairy.

"You'll get arrested if a Megacity Guard sees you showing that much leg in public," sniggered Stinks, nudging Streaks into a fit of giggling.

"You're getting ideas above your station Stinks. Don't forget, you could be bleeding out in a dusty workshop right now."

"Yeah Stinks, wind your neck in," piped up Streaks unhelpfully.

The look that Doris cast him would have withered a healthy yucca plant and made greater men quail, but Streaks' obliviousness made him practically impervious to the stare.

Fortunately for him, he was about as intelligent as a ketamine-fuelled swamp-rat and had nothing else to add to the conversation.

"I have a friend who lives near here." Doris vaguely waved an arm, "I'm sure she'd be happy to meet you Tariq, and I doubt if she'd be bothered if we explored our mystery item in her apartment."

"Ok, let's go there and make a plan. Do you need to call ahead first?"

Doris shook her head, "No, we go back a long way. As long as we take some Bún Bò Nam Bộ with us, she'll be fine."

"Lead on." Tariq, like the elegant lady he had become, gestured for Doris to show him the way.

Despite their eccentric attire, very few people gave them a second glance. They weren't the strangest looking people around and most of the locals were either interested in hawking their wares or so high that they could have been seeing anything.

A few hundred metres down the street, a heavily bearded vagrant shuffled forwards, making straight for Streaks.

"Ere… don't I know you? I'm sure I do… Yeah, yeah, it's ole Streaks innit?!!?" Attempting to sidestep the weaving inebriate, Streaks stumbled into Stinks and sent him flying. Slowed by the collision, he was unable to get out of the way. Grabbing Streaks' kipper-tie, the beard continued to berate. "Yeah… and I'll never forget that stench any time soon, even though I want to! 'Ey lads it's Stinks and Streaks dressed all posh like, all lah-de-dah!"

"Get away, I don't know you," protested the wriggling Streaks.

Stinks picked himself out of the gutter and tried to look inconspicuous, brushing down his leathers and attempting to put his helmet on.

"Outa jail and too good for us now are we Streaks? Looks like someone's got a bit of an altitude problem."

The hirsute old soak was beginning to draw an unwanted crowd. Previously inert vagabonds were rousing at the disturbance, the atmosphere was becoming charged with electric anticipation as the throng grew around the developing scuffle.

"Get lost Beardy you deadbeat. You're nothing but mutie-feed. Go back under your rock." Finally having secured the crash-helmet, Stinks spoke through the open visor. "Beat it or you'll regret messing with us."

Adrenaline giving him more bravado than he would have mustered on his own, Stinks rolled his shoulders and planted his feed wide in a stance he thought he'd seen in the martial arts holos. It created the effect of having just soiled himself and left him vulnerable to the cowardly attack that Beardy followed up with.

Doubled over in exquisite agony, eyes watering, desperately trying to catch his breath, Stinks found it impossible to fight back as several of the local indigents set about him.

Never one to shy away from a fray, Streaks laid into Beardy, throwing punches in as ham-fisted a way as a blindfolded child attacking a piñata.

Insults flew together with the random blows, and before long, the melee had caused enough disturbance to allow Tariq and Doris to quietly slip away. In no time at all, the scene descended into a full-on tramp-fight slug-fest.

After five minutes of pandemonium, Stinks stumbled to rest against a wall, chuntering about rips in his new leathers and Streaks had resorted to the gouging and biting tactics of a classic street-brawl.

Doris and Tariq were long gone by the time the unmistakable sound of an approaching squad of Megacity Guard was close enough to stop the vagrant carnage in its uncoordinated tracks.

"MG, MG!" Came the collective cry, causing the mephitic sores of MC2's underbelly to suddenly disperse, shuffling back to their usual haunts, leaving the perplexed Stinks and Streaks looking round for any trace of Tariq or Doris.

The lucky shots that landed true were few and far between, several split lips and the odd black-eye were the only visible results of what had at times seemed like total annihilation. The presence of the MG (Megacity Guard) had rapidly served to calm the scene.

Unable to loosen the tie that he once proudly wore, Streaks started to search for a way to release himself from the choke-hold it had on his throat. Stinks wrestled with the motorcycle helmet that had, in the course of the scrimmage, been jammed so tightly onto his head that he could barely see out of his eyes.

Despite their enlightening recent adventure, the lure of total escape into pharmaceutical oblivion, all-be it temporary, was too great for Stinks and Streaks who re-grouped to spy out another victim to fund their next fix.

CHAPTER 17

DRACONIS SYSTEM | PRESENT DAY

"What in drokk's name are you doing Colemin? Why are you in 'ere, crouched up like an old wet poule[i]?" The thinly veiled contempt in Remi's voice startled Nigel from his torpidity. "Sam sent me. Goushi yun I found you. *I* didn't want to."

"Charming." Nigel dragged his weary body to his feet. "If it's any consolation, I'd rather have been found by someone else."

"Putain, it's not!"

"Right... good... So what's next?"

"Foutu[ii] if I know mutie. You'd better follow me. I expect someone will 'ave assigned you a cabin or something. We can go via the ship's bursar, they deal with accommodation too. Then we should probably visit the cleaning stores, it's unlikely the cabin will 'ave been atom-scraped, you're not exactly a special guest or VIP."

"You really have a way with people don't you Remi?"

---

[i]   Fr. 'hen'
[ii] Fr. 'fu**ed'

"You don't get to call me Remi, you call me Corporal because you're a foutu civvy. Not even a very good one of those if I'm being 'onest."

"Well Corporal, if we are being honest…"

Slamming her arm across Nigel's throat, Remi pinned him against the wall.

"*You* aren't." her eyes bored into his skull, daring him to resist. "You're just quietly following me around like the petite sheep that you are."

Gasping for air as she released the pressure on his trachea, Nigel felt a new, unfamiliar sensation stirring that he had previously only heard about. Bravery pushed the words out of his mouth before his fogged brain could evaluate the consequences.

"You can't 'out-rank' a civilian, and anyway, you're mercenaries; you just make up your own titles, you're not proper military. I'm not impressed and at this precise moment, you need *me* more than I need *you* Remi! If your adrenaline-shrivelled brain can recall, my continued presence here almost certainly saves you from the repercussions of bringing me to this smeck-hole in the first place, paradoxical though that might sound… And if you no-longer have the mental power to understand the word paradoxical, I suggest you get a smecking dictionary or query your closest Omni!"

Advancing towards Nigel's newly emboldened and significantly leaner frame, Remi closed the distance between their noses, homicide in her gaze.

"You'll pay for this Colemin. Jus' you wait!"

"And you should brush your teeth more often." Nigel wrinkled his nose up as he spoke but didn't give any ground.

"Lover's tiff?" Sam's rich baritone broke the tension, causing Remi to turn on her heel and storm off towards the elevator shafts.

"And after you'd both been getting along so well. I think you'd better go with her Nige. Maybe keep a lid on your newfound bravado, you don't want to loose any teeth now do you?"

———

Nigel's room-comm chimed and without thinking, he called out for the door to open.

Five hours of scrubbing at the walls and washing down the floor, scouring the sanitary area and generally cleaning all traces of mildew and grime from his new cabin had left his knees sore and his shoulders screaming for a rest. His prune-like wrinkled hands pushed the cloth and bucket to one side as he turned.

"My prison cell was cleaner than this dump," he said standing up, "and I think I need to visit the laundry to get some sheets or something."

Years of technological advancement still hadn't quelled the basic human desire to curl up under soft white bed-linen at the end of a hard shift and Nigel wanted to maximise any comfort he could while he still had the opportunity.

"Oh, it's you."

"Putain de merde Colemin, had you forgotten I'm still your physical training instructor?" Remi's eyed sparkled with renewed malevolence. "If you're going to be of any use to this mission, you'll 'ave to develop some muscles in place of those pendulous bingo-wings. 'ere, drink this, we're going to the training deck."

"Mission? What mission? I can't train now, I'm tired, I've only just finished cleaning my cell, err... cabin."

"Merde, why don't you ever stop asking dumb questions mutie?"

"Stars what the smeck is this? Brainworm mucus?" Having taken a deep draft of the beige liquid in the feed cup he had been handed, Nigel was retching, looking for a waste disposal chute. "Are you trying to poison me? It's revolting."

"More inane questions Colemin. It's protein mix. 'Oo cares where it comes from. You'll get used to it. Don't waste it you weak-ass, lily-livered, flocculent mutie."

"I said get a dictionary, not swallow one. Oh smeck this is rank!"

"Drink up, you're going to need it."

———

"And another one Colemin, you'll enjoy these before the week is out." The maleficent look in Remi's bright green eyes hinted otherwise. "If the Commodore thinks you've got it in you, I'll make a Basilisk out of your mutie-ass if it's the last thing I do connard office boy."

Nigel had no breath to answer, his face was puce and running with a small waterfall of sweat. Focussing on not bringing back the vile protein concoction that Remi was forcing him to drink took almost as much energy as pulling on the resistance elastic she was loading him up with.

Unsurprisingly, the ship's gym was a lot better equipped than the cargo bay of the shuttle that brought him there.

Predictably, Remi was relishing the tasks of making Nigel's muscles burn, his joints ache and emptying all the fluid out of Nigel's body via his pores.

"Remarkable Colemin! I didn't think you 'ad it in you to complete that set. Now it's time to work on those bamboo canes that you call legs."

Catching his breath momentarily, just enough to talk, Nigel spat out the question that had been burning almost as much as his biceps.

"Why aren't you screaming and shouting at me? Why aren't you bawling in my face and demanding I go faster and do thirty press-ups every time I get something wrong?"

"Merde Colemin, you are a product of the past aren't you!"

"Wha—?"

"Nobody does that kark any more Colemin. Screaming in the face of a recruit to 'break them' just isn't effective. We've moved on. For one, you'd never manage thirty push-ups and for two, psychology is way more advanced these days. Instead of punishing you for screwing things up, we reward you for your wins. Whatever is rewarded is repeated, so give me another ten squats."

"I'm not sure I've seen the reward yet Remi!"

"Putain! The reward for training your body is a strong, 'ealthy body and a more alert mind."

"You're smecking me. That still doesn't explain why you're being such a mutie."

"Colemin, it's not your place to question the methods or insult your mentor. It's your place to pump the iron. Another ten."

————

An hour later, knuckles dragging along the deck, drooling like a demented camel, Nigel's torture for the day came to an end.

Despite the chasm of exhaustion that he was tumbling into, he still managed to throw one last question at his tormentor.

"If physical training is so important to you Basilisks, why has nobody else come down to the gym deck since we've been here?"

"Oh Colemin, you poor lad. Nobody does that kark any more. We 'aven't got the time. We've moved on. Technology is way more advanced these days. We just plug ourselves in to our wellness pods for 30 minutes before we go to sleep and all our strength and 'ealthcare needs are fixed."

With that final barb, Remi turned and ghosted off to another deck. Nigel's stunned brain took a while to recover from Remi's malice, by which time he was showered and collapsing into his bunk, oblivious to the lack of sheets.

The fatigue built up over the previous few weeks dragged at Nigel's consciousness like a concrete bathing suit. He embraced the heaviness and allowed himself to finally, fully relax for the first time in what felt like years but was probably just months. Briefly considering how he could happily sleep, undisturbed, for a decade, Nigel let go of all conscious control and started to float off into a dreamless world.

At that precise moment, his stomach decided it was time to remind him that his last *proper* meal had been nearly twelve years ago!

"Why did you choose this smecking moment to interfere?" Nigel scolded his delinquent anatomy. "Can't I just get some sleep?"

Only moments later, Nigel was furtively checking the different interfaces along the corridors and cross-checking the way-finding signage on his way to the mess hall.

The rhythmic rumblings of the previously raging battle outside were almost completely absent now. The ships of the Mensa ambush, mostly out-run were only scoring glancing blows or using long-range missiles, all of which were ineffective against the Chimera's reactive shielding and Point Defence Cannons (PDCs).

Still getting the hang of his new mag-boots, often engaging them accidentally and unable to switch them off again, Nigel's zombie-like stagger speeded up as he caught the smell of food in the air. Growing impatient, he broke into a lop-sided shuffling jog that would have put only the most decrepit of the undead to shame, and, after a fashion, 'burst' into the ship's mess.

It was a vast hall taking up a full quarter of a deck, rows of moulded stools sprung up from the floor around large round tables. The whole effect was visually seamless, yet the stool's occupants seemed to be able to move the seats around to suit their needs.

The walls were adorned with friezes of space battles, some were artistic impressions, some were clearly real images and at strategic points around the room, excerpts from what must have been famous Basilisk victories played on loop. The effect was some-what spoiled by the footage being scraped from slightly grainy static ship's cameras rather than high-quality cinema-style holo devices.

At one end of the room, multiple portraits of Basilisk hierarchy lit up the wall, in front of which a bigger, half-moon table stood. In small clusters along this crescent, the ship's top-brass either laughed, schemed, ate, drank or in some cases, all four.

Hoping to retain his anonymity, Nigel sloped along one wall towards the service hatches in search of the source of the entrancing aromas.

Being used to blending in as a stone-wall average in his super-sized shape, Nigel found it even easier with his new svelte figure.

Possibly too easily, as he was barged out of the way and had his toes trodden on multiple times with no apology, before he made it to the food counter.

Scanning his eyes across the serving zone, his heart sank. No humans manned the area, all he saw was a massive bank of food printers and robotic hot-vending machines. The disappointment was crushing and led to Nigel pausing for a second too long.

"Move along yī zhī yùn qiú qīng wā hóu zi suǒ shēng de kuí chún[iii]!" The insult came from the lips of a fresh-faced teen, barely half Nigel's age. A disrespectful leer creased his face, three of his companions with similarly unpleasant expressions at his back, the teenager cussed Nigel again. "Come on gǒu tā mā de[iv] grandad, some of us want to eat today."

"I'm sorry, my Mandarin is quite rusty, we didn't use it much on Omega-4." Nigel reverted to his normal tactic of talking his way out of a conflict. "By all accounts, you go ahead of me, I'm still choosing what I want to eat—"

A tray slammed into the back of Nigel's head, rocking him forward into the fist of the first teenager which landed squarely on his chin. Reeling from the surprise, rather than any particular damage the feeble canteen tray or the admittedly well-placed punch had created, Nigel stumbled to one side. A perfectly timed wham from another mess-tray caught him flat across the side of his head, spinning him the other way, where a calculated kick in the back of one knee sent him to the floor. One ear ringing, head throbbing, Nigel curled into the foetal position while more blows rained in on him for what seemed like hours but was almost definitely less than thirty seconds.

"Gorramit stupid inbred schoolboys," the penetrating voice of Ash sliced through the maelstrom.

Wading in, she grabbed two of the youths by their shirt-collars, elbowed one in the throat and scored a severe shin-kick on another. "Enough of this nonsense little boys. Wǒ men qīng chu ma[v]?"

"Goushi yun you turning up Captain," one of the attackers muttered sarcastically under their breath.

[iii]   Ch. 'baboon born from a dribbling frog monkey'
[iv]   Ch. 'dog humping'
[v]   Ch. 'Are we clear?'

"Yeah, well you'll get more of that 'yun' if you don't keep your filthy little mitts off Colemin here. What in the name of all things sacred were you thinking? Fong luh[vi]. Idiots. All of you."

"Sorry Captain. It won't happen again."

Ash pulled her long dreadlocks back behind her head and turned towards Nigel again, offering him a rough, scarred hand to hoik him to his feet.

"I'm sorry about these boys Nige, straight out of the young offender's institute on Omega-3. They have far too much testosterone and no drokking brains. They need to experience real action to calm them down a bit. I'm not sure why the Commodore continues to believe she can do her bit for the galactic community by rehabilitating them. It's more trouble than it's worth." Ash finished shooing off the teenagers and wandered away again, firing a final verbal volley over her shoulder. "Just get some food already Nige. And keep out of trouble. I can't be saving your crazy ass every five minutes."

"Yeah, sure… to be honest, what I could really do with right now is a nice cup of tea," called Nigel as she wandered off.

[vi] Ch. 'Crazy'

CHAPTER 18

OMEGA 4 | PRESENT DAY

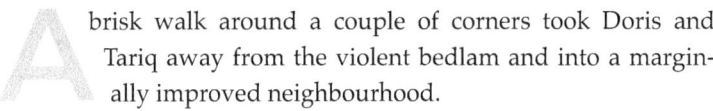brisk walk around a couple of corners took Doris and
Tariq away from the violent bedlam and into a margin-
ally improved neighbourhood.

Vast video-display boards that continually assaulted their eyes
still festooned the sides of the tenement blocks, blinking with
dead patches where the electronics had finally given up. They
stopped underneath the fizzing edge of one of the screens to pick
up some delicious-smelling street scran. Tiny sparks shot from the
exposed wires, intermittently showering the vendor below who
seemed completely oblivious.

Checking an old, scratched, public Omni-interface, they dialled up
the address of Doris' local friend.

The public elevator took them to the middle-caste level of the
high-rise, where they switched to the restricted access lift to bring
them to floor 832.

Battered and tired advertising monitors gave way to sleek, seamless, high-definition walls of individually-tailored marketing in
endlessly moving cinematic loops. Gone were the adverts for

rough approximations of nutritional substances that were constantly pushed at the lower echelons of society. Instead, luxury clothing, expensive gadgets and enticing holiday destinations were matched to the watching victim.

Doing her best to ignore the visual onslaught, Doris scanned her wrist at the control interface and opened the internal doors. She led Tariq down the corridor to a smart front entrance with a vintage bell-pull at the side.

Moments after her knock, the door flew open.

"Doris! You should have called ahead. Oh it's so wonderful to see you. Oooooh wow, you brought Bún Bò Nam Bộ, my favourite!!! My, my you look absolutely mesmerising in that ballgown. Are you on your way out? I mean it's hardly practical this time of day. Ah I love the handbag, it's so well matched to the shoes. Now who's your beautif...errr hands... ummm—" having turned towards Tariq she was fumbling for words.

"Tariq Colemin!" He introduced himself gruffly, dropping the clearly ornamental bell rope and offering his hand to shake.

Doris batted his hand down in rebuke. "We don't shake hands any more Tariq, not since the illness."

"The illness?"

"Sorry, I keep forgetting how long you've been... yes, anyway, long story Amelia." She turned back to her friend. "I'm just glad you're in. You wouldn't believe the little adventure we just had."

"Please, do tell, everything is so beige here these days. Since Martin got his new job, I don't have to work any more. Of course, I'm not complaining, it's such a relief not to have to worry about money. But every day just blends into the next. With him working from home seven days a week, we can't really go anywhere, the cleaning bots and the meal printer mean there's nothing to do in the house. I don't dare go street-side at the moment, what with the illness, the terrible crime waves that keep hitting MC2, not to mention the mutie sightings."

A beeping sound behind her made her whirl on the spot.

"Oh please, do sanitise before you touch anything madam errrr sir? Uhhh…" she ground to a halt again as she struggled to maintain eye contact with the peculiar vision of Tariq.

Taking things into his own hands, while the verbal diarrhoea from the lonely Amelia seemed unstoppable, Tariq had sauntered over to the meal printer and started dialling in the beginnings of a banquet.

"I'm sorry Amelia," he said, rapidly rubbing his hands with a squirt of alcohol gel. "It must be a shock to see me like this, just wandering into your lovely condo. Call me Tariq, here, let me make it easier for you."

In one swift action, he tore the dress off and removed the wig, depositing them into the atomiser disposal unit.

"I'll keep the hat, I think it kind of suited me."

The printer beeped again and the smell of freshly cooked thai-green curry exploded out of the unit. "Wow, this is a high-end model isn't it. I thought the military-grade ones we had on the Chimera were good but this is something else," Tariq eulogised through a mouthful of rich flavours. "Sorry again Amelia." He wiped sauce from the sides of his mouth and some 'rice' from where it had splattered on the worktop. "It's been ages since I've eaten, I'm not normally this much of an animal."

"At least not when you're eating." Doris quietly commented with a seductively raised eyebrow.

"Not at all, not at all Tariq." Amelia, clearly more comfortable with Tariq's plain dark fatigues, started eyeing him up and down, hungrily, "You clearly work out. What line of business are you in?"

"Oh, I just work with Doris here in the MAD. Really dull stuff. Tedious to the point of distraction."

"Amelia." Doris jumped in to rescue them both, "You don't mind if we might have inadvertently brought something um... potentially... illicit into your home do you?"

Amelia's face travelled through a range of expressions before it settled on a mixture somewhere between excited and concerned.

"No... that's... fine..." she said with an apprehensive, yet eager to relieve her tedium with something that might be a bit 'naughty' tone. She left a pregnant pause which Tariq took as clear indication to deposit the mystery hold-all on the worktop and commence opening it.

———

The contents of the package that had been stowed in the safety deposit box sat neatly arranged on the table top. Nineteen numbered notebooks, filled with meticulously neat handwriting. All the books were carefully numbered and titled "Nigel's Notebooks".

"All that effort and danger for those?" Doris allowed a look of partial disgust to wrinkle her cute, button-nose, "I was hoping for something a bit more glamorous, a bit more... I don't know... valuable?"

At the same time, the anxiety in Amelia's face vanished, relieved that there was nothing obviously illegal or dangerous in the bag.

"Let's see what Nigel's been writing about shall we?" Tariq picked up the first book and started to thumb through it.

Pages and pages of neat lines, columns and rows filled every book. Some names, some measurements, some calculations.

"Stars Doris, it's like a construction-geek's wet-dream. They're no different from the obsessive records of a maglev monorail-spotter... Only without the carriage numbers or departure times," Tariq murmured while he looked closer at the perfect jottings. "If we hadn't found these in a locked, anonymous deposit box, from a key hidden behind an air-ventilation grille, I'd discard them as pointless. But something tells me there's more to them than meets the eye. More than we're able to decipher just by looking at them."

"Sorry if the anticipation has led to disappointment Amelia," Doris apologised to her friend, "I hope you weren't hoping for anything more exotic or adventurous."

Before she could answer, Tariq spoke up again.

"It's been enchanting Amelia, thank you so much for the delicious food, I think we'd better be going. Doris and I need to examine these notebooks a bit more closely and I'm sure you could do with us getting out of your hair. What's the best way back to the Hyper-loop?"

Stunned into replying to the question, rather than begging them to stay longer, Amelia suggested they use the Skyway and transferred a couple of spare unlimited travel tokens to their wrist-chips.

The high-level enclosed walkway connected tower blocks on the expensive level of Megacity2 with variable-speed liquid-metal. At the edge it flowed slowly but towards the centre, it moved at a phenomenal speed. You could walk at normal pace but be travelling close to sixty or seventy miles per hour. The internal climate system compensated for wind resistance so every speed felt effortless. It allowed leisurely but rapid passage for the rich, from their homes to the commercial district, all the way to the exclusive, hanging botanic gardens, sports courts and entertainment zone.

Making a polite farewell, Doris and Tariq took an elevator up a few levels and exited onto the spotless moving thoroughfare.

"You take the skyway, right above the grimy scum-filled walkway. In my woolly socks and gloves, at night I lie alone, wonderin' if I'll sleep, wonderin' if we'd meet while on our feet," Tariq crooned again.

"Yeah, but this place doesn't get cold or have bums," said Doris.

Tariq turned to her with the biggest grin she'd seen yet.

"Really?" he beamed, "you know the song?"

"I'm a big fan of old-earth music. I love The Replacements. I don't expect Paul was quite imagining this though when he wrote it."

"No, I suppose not. So rare to find someone that appreciates a proper tune. Today's AI generated noise can barely be called 'music'."

"Why the big rush anyway? You couldn't get out of Amelia's Appartment fast enough!"

"Ah, yes," he stroked his chin, "did you see the way she was looking at me? And, there's something funny about these notebooks. Can't quite put my finger on them but I think we might have something big here. Some of the codes are ringing faint bells, we can't let any old person see them."

"What did you say Amelia's husband does?"

"I didn't. But he's some sort of executive accountant. High net worth clients, that sort of thing."

———

Once they stepped onto the Skyway, they were back to the Hyper-loop terminal in minutes. At the executive level, the Hyper-loop interchange had a more exclusive, more comfortable travel pod that dropped into sequence, but had priority status, so just for a laugh, Tariq tried his wrist chip.

First-class travel unlocked. Boarding initiated.

The doors slid open, much to their surprise, revealing a plush, four-seater cabin that smelled of a fresh summer meadow. An eye-watering credit number showed on the screen with a line struck through it and the words "Unlimited Travel Pass" flashing underneath.

"How the other half live eh! These tokens must be worth a small fortune."

Ever the gentleman, Tariq gestured Doris inside and followed, closing the doors behind them.

A soft voice asked them where they wanted to go and Doris replied instinctively with the name of Tariq's neighbourhood in MC1.

No sooner had she spoken, the car was dropping towards the Hyper-loop tunnel and a panel slid back to offer a range of drinks and snacks.

"I could definitely get used to travelling like this. You have some solid friends Doris, how do you know Amelia?"

"Well, that's a long story in itself. Perhaps not one for today, I think we might have to have an information trade sir. You divulge what you were snooping around for in the depths of the MAD databases and I'll tell you all about how I know Amelia."

"You drive a hard bargain Doris but I'll take you up on that." Tariq sipped his expensive-looking drink and pursed his lips. "I think it's probably best if we see what these books contain that is useful and then we can discuss the murky recesses of MAD Security Hub Information Technology."

"You're a dark horse Mr Colemin. A man of mysteries."

"I'd hardly call you an open book Doris. I sense you have secrets of your own that might surprise me."

"Yes." A smirk creased one side of Doris' face, "I think they might."

CHAPTER 19

DRACONIS SYSTEM | PRESENT DAY

R ob looked up from his book at the amber warning light. It blinked at him persistently until he silenced it with the tap of a button. He wasn't due a delivery today and wondered what unexpected nuisance was coming his way. He'd had enough trouble with his constant pain recently and it was all he could do to keep going.

Flicking a couple of switches, the command console hummed back to life, giving him immediate access to billions of data-points from hundreds of thousands of cameras and sensors.

He pulled up feeds from the proximity scanners and external security cameras and sent out a passel of inspection drones, just to be on the safe side.

Inhaling a long drag from the glowing reefer dangling precariously from the corner of his mouth, he brushed the hair out of his eyes and blinked hard at what had appeared on the screens.

The beginnings of panic crept across his pellucid face as he pulled several more live video streams up onto his main display.

"Well I'll be…"

Two New Alliance patrol ships were signalling their intention to dock. Rob's sensor array detected no presence of weapons being charged or shields up, so he presumed this was an inspection crew. As their comm came through, he saw something else on his deep-scan. It was fuzzy and indistinct but it was big and seemed to be moving in formation with the visitors.

Nervously, he accepted the hail request, pressing his receive button.

"This is New Alliance Patrol Vessels Hyuga and Yamato requiring clearance for a boarding party.

"You will comply immediately."

A thin film of sweat collected on Rob's forehead as he sent the relevant security data packets for the ships to dock. They came in smoothly, either side of the airlock gantry. The NA had appeared seemingly out of nowhere. Even his long-range sensors had been quiet. They had approached so quickly, he hadn't had time to tidy the place and disguise the evidence of some of his non-licensed activities.

Pinching off the end of his joint and tucking it into a discrete compartment, he quickly made his way out to greet his guests.

Slowing to a relaxed swagger as the inner airlock doors slid open, Rob's face broke into a disarming smile, showing all of his yellow teeth.

"Welcome to Galactic Waste HQ ma'am. I'm Rob, Galactic Obliteration Director. Pronouns he, him." He winced as the pain came again. "How can we help you t'day?" His lazy ancient-midwestern drawl, combined with an easygoing manner was all carefully curated to pacify the officials. Rob leaned on the deactivated shotgun that deputised as a walking-stick and adjusted the lapel of his long black leather coat.

A typically austere inspector, neat flat-cap over a pair of pene-trating eyes and a crisp jawline ending in a chin that jutted over a prominent data pad, looked down her nose at him.

"Mr…" she paused, scanning her interface for details, a frown growing under the rim of her cap.

"Rob." The 'o' drawn out into a long 'a' sound made it sound more like Raaab as he spoke. "Jus' call me Rob. Unless you're more happier with titles, in which case, call me GOD [gaaad]." He chuckled at his own joke, grimaced in pain again and then rolled casually on through his promotional patter.

"Waste obliterated to order, one-off loads, permanent contracts, you leave it, we heave it! All types of garbage catered for, scrap, chemical, vegetable, medical, hazardous, shint it off on us, take the weight off-of your ship, your planet, and your mind. No-one else does it quite like us, cos no-one else in the galaxy does it! Don't leave it in orbit, let us take your shi—"

"Thank you Mr Rob, I think we get the idea. We don't need your whole sales spiel."

"You're welcome ma'am. Now we've got a shipment comin' in about three hours so we'd appreciate it if we can git down to busi-ness soon as possible. It looks to us like you've got an inspection crew ready to audit this here station. We don't rememb'r havin' any warnin' about this. See, we norm'lly get us a message few weeks before, lettin' us know, so as we can arrange our schedule and not be botherin' you hard-workin' stylus-pushers." Again, he let out a short laugh, eyes narrowing briefly as his pain surfaced.

"Very efficient Mr… Rob. We approve. Let's get straight to it. We're not here to audit. We don't need to. Your record keeping is exemplary and every consignment you send to be incinerated in the sun is tagged and cross-referenced against it's incendiary signature. We very much value what you and your robot team do for the galaxy across the multitude of stations you operate."

"Why thank you ma'am, that's swell. It means a lot to us havin' your appreciation. Most folks don't know what happens to all their sh—"

"Yes, yes, and we're more than happy to turn a blind eye to the local agricultural project you have going on."

"I'm not entir'ly sure what you're drivin' at ma'am." Glacial in its expressionlessness, Rob's face had an inscrutable quality to it.

"The marijuana Mr Rob. The cannabis plants."

Still, he maintained his enigmatic look.

"The pot, weed, dope… grass, herb… Kush! Haze? Ganja! Drokk, the place smells of it strongly enough and I'm running out of terms here Mr Rob, but I think you get my meaning. Either way, we aren't interested. We have a business proposal for you."

"Well, now you're makin' sense ma'am. Are we talkin' jus' a one-off or somethin' reg'lar-like."

"Oh, just a single cargo, but if all goes well, there may be others intermittently."

"Alright ma'am. I'll put it into the queue. How big we talkin'?" Rob flicked his hair away from his eyes again and scratched his two-day stubble.

"About 43 Million Metric Tonnes."

"In one mass? We be needin' a bigger sling-arm and some kind a planetary stabilisation-beam to hoof that sorta haul. Not sure we can modify this station that much." To his credit, Rob didn't quail at the enormous job, immediately responding with a query on the practicals of the offer.

"Oh, no, it's all in standard container sizes."

"Ok ma'am, New Alliance getting rid of the paper archives?"

Once again, a sharp intake of breath indicated his regret at amusing himself with a wisecrack.

"The contents are not of your concern and we have some other conditions of passage. Firstly, we need to know that you will keep the whole operation confidential and stick rigidly to the terms of our agreement."

"I'm fine with that ma'am, but we be looking at somethin' three months down the line afore we can fit that kind of activity in."

"No, that won't do. The first batch needs to go by the end of the week."

"Well then, we're real sorry but we jus' have to decline your kind proposition. Jus' don't have the capacity right now."

"You will be well rewarded and… How can I put this… Refusal is not really an option. Presuming you still want to be in charge of your outfit and not spinning aimlessly around Omega-4 in IZV."

A brief quickening of Rob's pulse was demonstration enough that he was slightly rattled.

"How much we talkin' ma'am?"

The officer turned her data-pad in his direction for him to see a figure on the screen.

"Half now and half on completion."

Retrieving his eyebrows from the back of his scalp, Rob grinned again, revealing his nicotine-coated teeth.

"Stick *and* carrot eh? Well, now I come to think of it, we do have some space right about now. When will them containers arrive so we can git goin'?"

"They're already here Mr Rob!" Said the administrator, making a couple of entries on her data-pad.

In the viewing window at the end of the docking gantry, a vast flotilla of containers in formation, cordoned in the traction-net of a powerful space-tug, faded into view.

"I knew I'd seen somethin' on my scanners. I thought it was jus' the weed." A wide-eyed Rob took a deep breath. "Cloakin'. Damn, that's some good stealth you got ma'am, no wonder we din't notice you creepin' up on us."

"One last thing. Mr Rob... This is not going into the sun. This is only going close enough to use the gravitational slingshot to propel the cargo to *this* destination" She pointed at a map reference on her interface - "Without going close enough to damage what's inside. They are triple lead-lined containers so we have plenty of tolerance. I presume your computer systems are advanced enough to calculate that!"

Rob looked at the lady coldly before replying.

"I ain't a complete rookie! My data processors are the most pow'rful in the known universe. They can compensate for ev'rythin' round that ol' sun of ours an' avoid all shippin' lanes, not to mention every bit o' space debris ever logged. Don't you worry ma'am. We'll git started straight away."

Flanked by her security detail, the plainly-dressed messenger headed back to the airlock, turning only to send a final warning to Rob.

"Mr Rob. You may be GOD of waste, but if this job doesn't go well, or any word gets out, you'll discover who holds the real power in this sector.

"I hope you get my drift."

"Un'erstood ma'am. Have a nice day." Rob wheeled round and whistled his way back to the command room to retrieve his calming smoke and tend to his marijuana plantation.

CHAPTER 20

DRACONIS SYSTEM | PRESENT DAY

Squinting at his reflection, no-longer seeing a basset-hound face staring back, Nigel tried to take in everything that had happened over the last months.

Was he really on a Basilisk battle Super-cruiser barrelling through the outer reaches of the Draconis system towards a lesser-used jump-gate?

Had he really swapped the confines of an orbiting prison cell for a cabin that he could leave at any time?

Had he exchanged the multiple excess kilograms of surplus blubber for a lean, rapidly-becoming-toned, muscular frame?

Was he now headed for excitement in the outer rim of the galaxy rather than returning to the drudgery of life in the MAD?

Was it really happening to him?

Nigel was conflicted. He had both a low level of anxiety at all the unfamiliar territory he was exploring and also that light-stomached, anticipatory feeling for the new possibilities coming his way.

He wondered how he was going to adjust, *if* he was going to adjust and he wondered, most of all, where he was going to get a decent cup of tea.

––––––

"COLEMIN."

He hadn't heard the door-comm chime or the door open. Judging by the tone of Remi's voice, in his daydreaming, he hadn't heard her call him the first few times.

Sitting in a trance-like state on the edge of his bed, the interruption jerked him back into the present and he turned his head just as Remi opened her mouth to shriek at him again.

"The Commodore want's you Colemin. Crisis is under control, she wants to pick up where she left off."

"Oh, thanks… I guess."

"You're welcome Colemin." Remi's sarcasm-laced reply elicited no response so she carried on, "To be 'onest, I'm 'oping she actually discovers you are useless after all so I get the pleasure of putting you outside."

"Yeah, sweet," came Nigel's distracted voice. "I guess I'm to follow you?"

"Merde! If you can't find your way back to the viewing deck, there's no 'ope. The only reason I came was because nobody believes you're important enough to be issued a maudit ear-comm and you weren't answering the interface in your room."

Nigel looked across to the room control screen and saw 45 missed calls.

"You need to up your putain de jeu Colemin, this outfit doesn't carry dead-wood and you're barely 'anging on to your basic 'uman privileges as it is."

"You make it sound almost like you care."

"Well I don't."

Remi stormed off again, leaving Nigel wondering if he should try to find some new clothes or make his way over to the Commodore first.

He quickly brought up the ship's layout on his room interface and managed to find a route to the viewing deck that would take him past the laundry and stores without adding an appreciable amount of time to his trip. Easily committing it to memory, he closed his door and walked briskly towards one of the elevators.

————

Pulling at the new fatigues to adjust their position around his waist, Nigel marvelled at being able to see his toes again and knocked at the blast door that isolated the viewing deck.

What am I thinking? Nobody is going to hear that knock. How do I get in?

Spying the access panel, he touched a green button and the door slid open for him with a satisfying rumble.

Captivated by the view of the stars again, Nigel wandered to the huge window and lost himself in the light-show of the many galaxies and nebulae that, from this angle, he was completely unfamiliar with.

He was so utterly absorbed that he failed to notice Commodore Andrade entering the room behind him, until she cleared her throat, startling him.

"Yes Commodore." Nigel span round to face her, almost losing his balance.

"Colemin." She nodded curtly, "We were in the middle of a conversation I believe."

"Yes Commodore."

"Well…"

"Well, what Commodore?"

"Firstly, just call me Ma'am and secondly, please carry on from where you were about to begin before we were so rudely interrupted."

"Ah, yes, of course Ma'am. Um…" A long, uncomfortable pause followed. "I know I have a photographic memory, but I'm not quite sure where I was now I come to think of it Ma'am. A lot has happened since then and my memory is visual, not audiological."

"Look Colemin. We have protocols and policies that you are probably unaware of. Despite me not being particularly one for enforcing protocol, it helps for everyone on this ship to be on the same page. You call me Ma'am and any male officer ranked above you 'Sir'." Seeing Nigel was opening his mouth to speak, she quickly countered. "Yes, yes, I know you aren't ranked because you are a civilian… for the moment, just follow the structure!

She continued by laying it out simply for him. "For female officers ranked above you, address them by rank. Before you ask, there are combinations of little stars and stripes on collars or lapels that denote rank. Look up the org chart on the ships modified Omnis, you'll learn it soon enough."

"Thanks Ma'am."

"Oh, and only use the honorific once at the beginning or end of the first sentence you speak to an officer, unless receiving instruction or discipline. I don't want to hear you scattering Ma'ams in like you've got a case of over-polite Tourette's."

"Smeck Ma'am, that's a lot to remember. Oops, sorry Ma'am."

"And don't swear at senior officers Colemin. Insubordination is a court-martial offence."

"Uh—"

"I know, I know, you're a civilian, you can't be court-martialled! Please, try to make this easy for me, I've got a lot on my plate."

"Yes... Ma'am?"

"Correct Colemin. You're learning fast. Now, to bring us back on track from that long, tedious tangent, you were about to tell me what you know, starting at the beginning."

"Ah, yes. Well... ...I was minding my own business, sitting in my cell on—"

"Not that beginning Colemin. Don't think I don't know the complete drokkstorm that got you here. I'm interested in what you think you know that will prevent you having another encounter with that all-too familiar air-lock over there."

"Ah, yes, I see. I worked for the conduit tracing department of MAD up until—"

"Colemin! For drokk's sake. I know all this kark. Tell me something I don't know before I space you myself. You're starting to wind me up."

"I thought swearing was... oh yes, I understand... you're an officer and I'm—"

The death-stare that the Commodore gave him brought him to an abrupt halt. It would have withered stronger warriors, but Nigel only saw it as a warning not to digress again.

"Ok, well when I worked for the MAD, I saw almost—"

"What now?"

"Sorry? What do you mean what now? I've barely started."

"Shut up Colemin.

"No, I'm busy."

"But I thought you wanted to know—"

"Oh for the love of drokk. Colemin shut up!" She gestured to her ear-comm and made a lip-zipping gesture to Nigel who, slow to the party, realised she was having a conversation over the ship's communication network."

"What does he want now? Actually, don't tell me, I'm strategically not available, please take a message.

"Colemin, please continue."

"Ok, so I had to examine every ship schematic and construction that the New Alliance ever manufactured. On and off-world. Military, mostly, but also a lot of the commercial, and some residential. I traced conduit for IZV, for the New Alliance super-freighters, corvettes, battlecruisers and the rest of the star-fleet. I traced for most of the commercial district in MC2, for the luxury interstellar yachts of the rich and famous and even for the super-secret racing pinnace built for Minister Komarov and his villa on the outskirts of the Magellanic System."

"Stop."

"Excuse me Ma'am?"

"What did you just say?"

"I was going through all the things I've conduit traced—"

"COLEMIN!" Cutting him off again, the Commodore's voice hit an unexpectedly feverish pitch that worried Nigel. "Why are you so literal? And yet completely not literal at the same time? Repeat what you said about a secret racing pinnace."

"Oh, sure. I traced and logged all the power and cooling conduits on the super-secret racing pinnace built for Minister Komarov and also when his lavish villa was built on the outskirts of the Magellanic System, I had to check there was no conflict of air/water/chemicals/power etc. in the pipes and ducts."

"Drokk Colemin, you might be of use to us after all, what can you recall of that?"

"Everything!"

"Everything?"

"Everything!"

"Everything?"

"Every… thing!"

"Everything?"

"How long are we going to go on like this Ma'am?"

"…………Everything?"

"Yes Ma'am, I have a photographic memory."

"Yes…" It was ambiguous by the tone of her voice whether she was going to speak any more or not and the silence dragged on and on.

Nigel was desperate to say something to break it but was wary of facing the potential wrath of the ruthless Commodore.

He could almost see the cogs turning in her brain.

"What do you know about the clouds of the Magellanic System?"

"What?"

Mildly perturbed by Nigel's completely confused expression, Andrade carried on.

"The Magellanic Clouds of the Magellanic System - you know, them?"

"I can't say I do, I'm more of an indoors guy. To be honest, this is the first time I've ever been further away from Omega-4 than IZV orbits. I don't travel well and I always used to get really space-sick, even on short leisure trips, so I generally avoided them. It's—"

"Really not interesting Colemin." The Commodore finished his sentence for him, then continued herself, "You said Minister Komarov had a dwelling built on the edge of the Magellanic Clouds."

"I did!"

"Well…"

"I'm sorry Ma'am, I am so lost. I have no idea what you're driving at. I've barely slept for months and I really just want a nice cup of tea."

"You must know something about the Magellanic System if you worked on Minister Komarov's mansion."

"No Ma'am, I'm sorry, as I said, I'm an indoors kind of guy. I could draw the plans out and tell you where services come in and out but anything further than that, I'm not your man."

"You can what?"

"I can draw the plans from memory, label all the pipes and cables. It's my—"

"Photographic memory, of course. Look Colemin, I'm going to go out on a limb here and tell you something very few people know. We're supposed to be hitting a target on the edge of the Magellanic Clouds. It's a top secret location and we believe there's a huge silo of stockpiled energy cells, new weapons and some other valuable supplies. The sort of volume that could keep the Basilisk fleet running for centuries. According to our calculations, it would be enough to arm and power the New Alliance Armada for at least a decade."

"Why are you telling me this Ma'am?"

"Because, Colemin, *Drokk you are slow*, we need that stockpile. It would mean the Basilisk fleet could press on with activities without worrying about where our next supply is coming from. It means we can focus on proper missions rather than pirating and salvage. It gives us a stable umbilical cord rather than forcing us to take our eyes off the important jobs to scrabble around for scraps. Half the time we waste is on looking for part-used energy cells that might be polluted or damaged or paying over the odds for second-rate reconditioned power cores. Having this cache would mean we could shorten our space-miles, reduce wasted journeys, we can bid for the better jobs and be able to respond quicker. It means increased efficiency, superior technology, improved firepower."

"Lovely, that's really lovely Ma'am. I hope this works out for you. Are you finished with me?"

Andrade, having become uncharacteristically animated in her tirade practically screamed at him.

"COLEMIN, you just don't get it, do you? You don't."

"I… uhhh."

She strode up to Nigel in a more purposeful than menacing way and spoke quietly into his ear.

"Don't you move an inch." With those words, the Commodore completely disappeared; blinked out of existence from right in front of him.

He slowly turned on the spot, trying to work out what had just happened.

"Is anyone there?" Nigel called out into the room. Several security cameras swivelled towards him and stopped. He waved nervously at them and straightened his clothes again.

A monumental clattering came from behind him, causing him to jump and spin to face the noise.

Commodore Andrade had burst through a concealed doorway in the wall, knocked over an elegant, magnetic-based vase which smashed, spilling its contents over the deck and was marching towards him with purposeful strides.

Without a word she grabbed the back of his collar and lifted him a foot into the air before storming back towards the opening she had just passed through.

The clacking of her mag-boots as they traveled along the corridor filled Nigel's ears and just as he was starting to turn puce at the restricted breathing opportunities, the Commodore turned into her office and dumped him on the floor next to a large desk covered in mag-paper charts.

"There's a spillage in the viewing deck," she spoke into her ear-comm. "It's a drokking shame we're not on the float. That'll take a bit of clearing up." Then, addressing Nigel again, she continued without taking a breath. "Colemin, I thought that if you saw for yourself it might save me my sanity."

"How… Where… What just—"

"I've been in here the whole time Colemin, we have advanced hologram technology. Oh why do I have to explain everything to you like I would to a seven year old child? If it wasn't for…. Never mind.

"Just look."

Nigel looked down at the desk. He saw the scope of the Basilisk operations; a chart with the basic supply needs and another diagram with the amount of effort and expenditure in gathering the necessary equipment and raw materials to maintain a viable organisation.

It immediately made sense.

The Commodore rolled up the top layer and showed Nigel an animated chart of the current, thinly-spread fleet and its planned rendezvous points for supply exchanges. He saw a waiting list of requests for mercenary assistance, all with different prices attributed to them.

Waving her hand over the whole desk, Andrade brought up an image of a huge residence on a monolithic asteroid. The home was big enough to have been spun up, project its own atmo-shield bubble, have grounds and water features and even its own flight hangar.

"I know this place, it's Minister Komarov's luxury villa!"

"I suspected as much."

"Why are you showing me this?"

"Holy drokk Colemin." The Commodore was almost lost for words, "This really is your last chance Colemin. In fact, I'm not going to threaten you, it hasn't helped so far. If you can grasp the basics of what I'm trying to tell you this time, I'll give you a cup of tea from my personal supply."

Nigel's jaw dropped.

Commodore Andrade's back-hand to restore the normal resting position of Nigel's features was slightly more robust than absolutely necessary but it had the desired effect.

"I'm going to say this once Colemin, so listen carefully."

"Yes Ma'am."

"This is our target. Your revelation that Minister Komarov has a 'super-secret racing pinnace' and a 'villa on the outskirts of the Magellanic System' immediately completed the picture for me. Despite all the superficial respectability of the New Alliance, the high levels of security and transparency checks about everything that goes on. Despite the promises that the New Alliance would herald a fresh start for the human race and expunge the corruption of the previous administration, I'm convinced it's rotten to the core and stinks all the way to the top. I'd suspected as much but only now can I see significant evidence."

Pausing, she looked up to gauge how much Nigel was taking in.

"Minister Komarov is just another unscrupulous, venal, power-grabbing mutie who must have been embezzling resources from the New Alliance for decades to line his own pockets. We *were* hitting this stash of assets for completely logistical reasons, but *now... now*, this has just become a whole lot bigger... So... Thank you Colemin."

"Uhhh you're welcome Ma'am."

It took a few moments but eventually, the full weight of realisation dawned on Nigel's face.

She turned to him with a look that could only be described as something close to a smile without actually being a smile and motioned to a seat next to the desk.

"Now Colemin. About that tea... Hang on, I've got a call coming in... Sorry, this is important, see yourself out Colemin, I'll be in touch."

CHAPTER 21

OMEGA 4 | PRESENT DAY

Tariq almost knocked over the table in his rush to stand up and find Doris. "I've found it! Well I've found the breadcrumbs."

"Lovely dear, make sure you dip the fish in the egg first or they won't stick."

Tariq froze mid-stride, a look of complete bewilderment on his face.

"Doris?"

"Yes."

"Did you think I was making dinner?"

"Not really, I'm just teasing. I know exactly what you're on about. Bring your interface in here and we can expand the view on the tabletop."

Carrying his portable terminal through to the living area, Tariq swiped the screen onto the coffee table surface.

"Look at this... And here... And if we correlate the pattern I found there with this stream of data..."

"H-O-L-Y Drokk Tariq. Does that mean…"

"Yes… I knew there was something wrong before I got sent down. Then there were all the rumours and whisperings that went round IZV. Lets face it, there's no way Komarov could have the kind of life he enjoys on New Alliance Administration wages, despite him being top-dog. There had to be something else other than the investments and non-executive directorships."

"Just follow the money eh! Surprising nobody has noticed this before."

"Well, you say that Doris, but anyone can make allegations when they see someone swanning around in a luxury hover-car. It's the putting together of the information that exposes the real evidence. Just look through these figures for a moment and you'll see the magnitude of the corruption and clever cover-up. If it weren't for the exact match in the cost of military equipment and energy cells being written down and the reports of missing shipments… In the redacted cargo ledger, you can see mystery containers with just the weight and dispatch time available, departing at regular inter-vals for a range of destinations within NGC 1818. I cross-checked the NGC 1818 records—"

"How did you do that, it's several sectors away and not directly linked."

"Ah… well… I learned a thing or two in IZV and with the help of my slightly modified Omni back in the office, I have been able to create some channels through a number of interlinked systems. The information took a while to come through, but… Cargo yards in NGC 1818 have been shipping out containers to an encrypted location on the edge of the Magellanic Cloud on a schedule that pretty much matches the dispatches from the Omega system. Give or take a few weeks, adjusted for freight time."

"This is absolute solid platinum Tariq. Although it might also be a death sentence if the wrong people get to know… Wow, look at that, he's been a sneaky drokker too, using different umbrella companies, mining organisations, disused and currently operating. A few unknown carriers, some warehousing... Oh my! He's been even bolder more recently. Look at that - spiriting shipments in right under New Alliance Guard's noses... Here - an unlabelled consignment loaded onto the NAG Super-carrier 'Zenith' and offloaded at Paldoon on the edge of NGC 1818."

"Either that or someone at NAG is in his pocket. Now look at this, it's genius. Every so many months, we can see a spike in unregistered jump-gate usage. Nothing on the energy signature that is big enough for a ship but scale it down to the size of a container, the power draw is probably about right. That volume would account for the missing weapons and star-fighter spares. I can't quite work out how he is getting containers to pass through the jump-gate system in such volume without causing any collisions or rousing suspicion. What's his propulsion method? How are they making so many transitions without being detected?"

"Can we trace the origin? Is there a way to get jump-gate video to work out the angles?"

"Probably, but I may need to hack some other high-powered omnis to crunch the numbers, it's not going to be straight-forward."

They spent another three hours pouring over the data, building a full picture of the movements of illicit consignments.

In the end, they had a watertight trace of 450 Trillion credits-worth of energy cells, advanced weaponry and other supplies. The trail started at the Omega manufacturing facilities, through a multitude of companies, ports and ship-yards, and ended up at the unspecified Magellanic location.

Tariq stored everything in an encrypted file, biometrically locked to him.

"Are you sure this isn't traceable?" Doris looked vaguely worried as she carried in their evening meal and placed it on the dining table. "We could become targets ourselves if any New Alliance snoops get wind of this."

"I've got several layers of firewall, encryption, IP spoofing and counter-surveillance measures in place. It'd take some special, special new technology to detect my presence. I'm not changing anything, I'm only looking, so I should be like vapour in the system. Untraceable, spectre-like."

"I just hope so!"

"You worry about me?"

"No I care about *us*. Now come and eat."

Tariq dropped the file into a ghost-location, closed his interface and pushed it into a deep pocket on his cargo-trousers.

"Where do I go from here? The facts are coming out all blurred. It's good you're here, now I need you?"

"Don't tempt fate with your singing Tariq, this is no joking matter."

As he stood to walk to the table, there was a heavy knock at the door.

Doris' mouth gaped, her face ashen.

"Don't move. I'll go." said Tariq, reaching towards the knife he kept hidden at the small of his back.

CHAPTER 22

DRACONIS SYSTEM | PRESENT DAY

"Who? Oh, yes, him again. Patch him through." Commodore Andrade paced round her operations table waiting for the call to be connected.

"General. It's good to hear your voice Sir."

"Indeed, my apologies Sir. I was in the middle of—"

"I appreciate that Sir. I reiterate my apology, I believe you may feel differently when I can explain the reason—"

"Sir I'm not making excuses, I am aware of protocol, may I just say—"

"Of course Sir. It won't happen again."

"No, I am very interested in your news Sir, please go ahead."

"Who?"

"Where? I mean of course, it was on Omega-4 but how?"

"He just came to you? Out of nowhere?"

"I bet you were, I'd have been astounded, but how did he find out your location?"

"But those codes must be decades old… What did he want?"

"I know I'm full of questions General, it's a lot to take in. Why did he come to you?"

"How did he get that data?"

"That sounds like a significant level of security clearance, has he risen through the ranks that fast?"

"Oh, I guess if he's not officially a Basilisk any more, you couldn't force him."

"What there's more?"

"He turned up with what?"

"He had them all with him?"

"Where did you say he found them?"

"What was in them?"

"Just columns of figures."

"Nineteen of them."

"No key to explain them."

"No Sir, I'm not going to repeat absolutely every drokking thing you say!"

"How are they useful, they sound like a load of old nonsense to me, jottings off an obsessive. Do you have any idea what they meant?"

"What? With his name on them? Nigel Colemin?"

"Sorry General, I'll stop interrupting."

"He found a pattern?"

"Yes, yes, it does look like almost everything in the NA order book."

"So… Oh my— Wait… Oh drokk. Everything is beginning to make sense in light of what I've just discovered. I can't believe I didn't see it before."

"Let me start at the beginning, how long have you got?"

"I think you might need to sit down and pour yourself a glass of something strong."

"We sent the crack-team to extract him as discussed, but, as you know, there was a bit of a mix up—."

"I think, actually, I did describe it like that but I didn't want to sound rude. Well, we ended up with this other one with the same name—"

"Yes Sir exactly, that probably *is* where the mix-up occurred."

"He also, by some strange quirk of fate, carries some really valuable information. I thought he was just a deadbeat to begin with and to be honest he isn't the sharpest bayonet in the armoury, but he does have some useful skills. I imagine he'll be able to decipher the find for us, they are his after all. With the two of them together—"

"I admit, it's an unlikely pairing—"

"Yes, there's no guarantee they'll want to—"

"I suppose we just have to give them the choice Sir. The thing is, the best part… He confirmed that our Magellanian target is Komarov's and our suspicions were right all along. Not only can we set ourselves up for the foreseeable future but we can also take down the whole putrescent operation."

"That's not our concern General, its not like a medusa, this time, we hit the problem at the top and it will cut off the flow of credits down-stream. It will be impossible for anyone lower in the food chain to hide their nefarious activities without the protection of Komarov. It will either reveal any rogue elements or just stop them all together. We come away with the stockpile and look like heroes at the same time. We can't lose."

"Excuse me Sir?"

"I thought I heard you say that, but that will add months to a mission we are already behind on and a significant layer of complexities to the rest of our operations."

"Well, if you've worked out the permutations, I just think it's a very… expensive detour—"

"Not at all Sir, I wouldn't dare to—"

"Certainly Sir, right away. I'll comm Henshaw and plot a new course. What kind of reception can we expect? Do we need to remain incognito?"

"The dark side of the moon? Really? Yes Sir I—"

"No, I'm not laughing Sir. Not even smirking."

"Certainly Sir, I look forward to seeing you too. Goodbye General."

Andrade tapped her ear comm to close the call, then again to contact the Chimera's operational Commander.

"Henshaw I have some bad news."

"No, nothing like that. Please turn the ship around and set a course for Omega-4, Gamma-3 - the dark side."

"I know. It's a long story—"

"I fully realise that, stars only knows why they have braved being so far in-system but we'll have to work out a strategy to get past them."

"If you want to take it up with General Hideki himself, I'm sure you'll be welcome dirt-side!"

"No I didn't think you would. I'll fill you in on the journey back. I'm just as annoyed as you! Goodbye Henshaw."

CHAPTER 23

DRACONIS SYSTEM | PRESENT DAY

Perspiration streamed off Nigel's forehead. His exercise suit had already passed through the two-tone look and was now dark - drenched in sweat.

"Please can I have a drink?" His dry throat croaked the words like an elderly toad.

Remi handed him the noxious protein shake without a word.

"No thanks, water is fine."

"Drink mutie." Her tone was unapologetically uncompromising.

Swallowing back the bile he was retching with a mouthful of the repugnant liquid, Nigel looked up from his position under a 200kg barbell.

"So why don't I get a 'wellness pod' to plug into?"

"Shut the kark up and lift."

Nigel struggled through another eight reps and crashed the weight back into its stand, trapping a finger on the way down.

"Ouch, ouch, help me get this smecking weight off my finger," shaking his bruised hand, he tried again. "I'm recovering now, just tell me why."

"Because you have to have muscles to maintain before you can maintain them. Recovery over. Get up and get on that treadmill."

Nigel duly did what he was told as Remi set the gradient to ten percent and the speed to fourteen kilometres per hour.

Twenty minutes later, Nigel - legs turning to jelly, tripped over his own ankle and face-planted the belt on the treadmill. He was instantly spun up in the air and off the back of the machine, flying into the wall with a bone-shattering thud.

Dragging himself to his feet again, he grabbed his towel and attempted to staunch the flow of blood coming from his nose.

"Why can't someone design a zero-effort exercise programme? Now there's no *people* to do it, even this *ship* is trying to kill me."

"Don't be such a chatte[i] Colemin. Stop your moaning and clean this up. See you tomorrow, same time." Remi walked off and clicked her heels together to dial up her mag-boot strength a little as she crossed into the main corridor, as a safety precaution, just in case they suddenly cut thrust.

Nigel picked up the cleaning cloth and did his best to expunge the area of his sweat and blood.

As he put the rag into the laundry chute, he caught a view of himself in the large mirrored wall.

He hated Remi. He hated the excruciating fitness sessions. He hated being woken at random times of night and day and dragged into the gym to be ordered around by someone that clearly hated him.

But he had to admit, he barely recognised himself.

---

[i] Fr. 'pussy'

Where he once had trouble seeing his knees under the bulbous rolls, he admired muscular thighs. Nigel observed a sculpted figure in the reflection. Toned muscles all over his body showed up in attractive contours, emphasised by his underclothes.

He realised that, over time, he had come to move more confidently, faster and for longer. He was able to lift heavier weights, pull heavier resistance bands without passing out or being sick.

Inspired by his new form, he wandered to the sparring zone and set up the strength-test machine. Donning the special breath and brain analysis helmet, he hit the start button.

A single straight cylindrical pad emerged from the floor and the interface screen behind it showed up where he was to hit the device.

In sequence, he punched, elbowed, kneed and kicked the pad at varying levels, for a couple of minutes, placed his finger in a small hole for the obligatory blood test and then waited for the analysis.

Name: Nigel Colemin

Sex: Male

Gender: Unspecified

Height: 180cm

Weight: 80kg

Body Fat Content: 6%

Strength Centile for -

Left Arm: 78%

Right Arm: 85%

Left Leg: 82%

Right Leg: 88%

Speed Centile: 35%

Reactions: 28%

Delighted with his results, nonplussed at the gender evaluation, he tore off the printout, removed the headgear and turned to go back to his room.

His face was met by the stalwart form of Sam blocking his path. She snatched the slip of paper from his fingers and looked at it. One eyebrow rose and the corner of one side of her mouth turned up.

"I thought you might be almost done with Remi by now and I was right."

"I don't think she mentioned—"

"She wouldn't. She thinks it make her more intimidating if you don't know what's happening."

"Oh! I—"

"My suspicions that you weren't really aware enough to be intimidated have been confirmed. Are you ready to depart your dreamworld for the next part of your training?"

"Yes but—" Nigel sidestepped slightly in an attempt to walk past Sam and exit the room but as he blinked, he found himself flying through the air for the second time that day.

He hit the deck and slid, his already growing bruise eventually cushioning his contact with the metal corner of a step. "...I don't know what it is!"

Sam stood over him grinning like an excited child, "Speed and combat training."

"I'm a little tired right now. Can we have this discussion another time?"

"Stars Nige, you said you were ready." Sam looked a little crest-fallen, she was half-way through tying up her long black hair into a tidy bun, "You weren't ready, you didn't defend yourself at all."

"Of course I wasn't ready. I have no idea how to be ready. The last time I had to defend myself was in court when my lawyer didn't show up."

This time he saw the attack coming as Sam swung the heel of her hand upwards at his sternum.

Completely unequipped for fighting, Nigel could do nothing as the force of the blow lifted him several feet off the ground before he crashed back down onto his spine.

"Come on Colemin, you're not even trying."

"I don't think today is going to be the day for this Sam. I'm sorry to disappoint you."

Remaining supine until he thought he was safe from further assault, Nigel gazed up at Sam, noticing her fine jawline for the first time.

She looked down at him with pity, then offered him a hand up.

Taking her generous suggestion, he reached out, only to find he was instantly sailing in a graceless parabola onto another section of matted floor.

"Stars, that's the oldest trick in the book Colemin, I can't believe you fell for it."

"Can I please just go to my room and rest?"

Untangling himself from the pretzeled heap of his own limbs, he warily rose again, keeping his distance from Sam. She looked at him quizzically and then, shaking her tightly curled black hair out of the bun and tucking it behind her ear, grinned.

"When shall we start then?"

"Um… tomorrow?"

"Deal!"

racking the door open just a fraction, Tariq was able to conceal his weapon hand as he looked out gingerly. He immediately shrank back to avoid the shower of spittle that greeted him as Maeve launched into a sentence that she hadn't quite finished earlier.

"So, after Henry from down the hall said that the main doors had been damaged, I went to have a look and would you know… Someone had blocked the recycling chute at the bottom. Rammed a load of plastic wrapping and cardboard up it. I had been wondering why the hallway was beginning to smell."

"Oh hi Maeve. You're talking to Henry again are you? That's lovely. Did you manage to clear the bad energy between you?"

"Oh yes, and I used healing crystals so I could mend the rift separating us— Ooooh, visitors?" Not one for subtlety or discretion, Maeve had clearly spotted Doris' shoes in the hallway.

"Yes Maeve, I've got—"

"Lady company!" Maeve's glitter-covered eyebrows shot higher than her unevenly trimmed fringe. "Don't let me interrupt. I'm sure you're *very busy*," she over-emphasised the words 'very busy' in a deep, sultry tone that, in an attempt to appear suggestive, completely failed to hide her obvious disappointment. "Can I invite you and your *lady friend*" (that deep provocative tone again) "for a drink tomorrow maybe?" She offered a simpering smile which curled her upper lip back from her camel-esque dentition making Tariq step back for fear of injury.

"Oh Maeve, that's a lovely offer, but we're back at work tomorrow and the schedule at the MAD is punishing. Maybe another weekend sometime?"

"Absolutely, oh yes, you must come over, I'm sure your *beau* will love my Karmic Clearing, I could even read her Angel Cards if you like."

"Great, thanks Maeve, we'll have a chat about that and get back to you."

Closing the door quietly but firmly, Tariq requested some music in the hallway and wandered back into the living room.

Doris was lying on her side on the large sofa, hands over her mouth, shaking with laughter. Hearing the music fade up in the hall as Tariq came into the room, she finally allowed her mirth to burst out.

Taking big gulps of air between laughing fits, tears streaming down her face, Doris fought to control herself.

"Wow… She sounds like an absolute blast!" Doris finally managed to splutter out a sentence.

"Don't even go there! I can't get rid of her. Though now she's seen you are visiting, I might get some peace."

"We have to go, it will be so much fun."

"No"

"Oh please, please—"

"Not happening. Not even entertaining the idea."

"Please Tariq, please, I beg you. I'll do that thing you like!"

"You do that anyway… and no!"

Doris turned her back on Tariq in a fake sulk, her pretty lips pursed in a childlike pout. "You're such a spoil-sport."

"We have more pressing things to concern ourselves with. What do we do with what we've found? And you've got some stories to fill me in on."

"Oh Tariq, come on, why do you always have to be so serious?" She bounced across the room and cupped his face in her hands. Looking up into his deep brown eyes playfully, Doris kissed him lightly on the cheek and then walked to the hall to pick up her shoes and coat. "See you tomorrow you fusty old goat."

Tariq couldn't help but smile as Doris 'floated' towards the door. He followed and caught her up in his strong arms, gently lifting her into the air to kiss her farewell.

"I'll walk you to your block."

"Don't be ridiculous, I'm not some fragile ornament that can't look after herself. Anyway, I'll take a Hovertac. My building has a drop-off point on my floor."

Tariq walked Doris to the elevator down the hall and with one last quick embrace, she descended to ground level to pick up the private-hire vehicle that she had summoned from her wrist-omni moments before.

————

The stale air in the office assaulted Tariq's nose again as he walked back through the door. He strolled past windows so caked-up with grime they had clearly been unopened for what must have been decades.

Pausing momentarily to peer through a hastily wiped patch of glass to take in the hustle and bustle of MC1 outside, he could almost feel the energy of the city. Vehicles hummed along multiple layers of transportation lanes, the traffic AI guiding them to their destinations. Seamlessly, they switched altitudes and altered course as they flowed though the sprawling megatropolis, leaving fuzzy light trails in the growing dusk.

He paused at Doris' desk.

Where is she? I thought we were meeting this evening.

A pair of sharp fingers jabbed into his ribs from behind and it was all he could do not to spin round and take out the perpetrator.

"Hi titch." The giggle that followed betrayed who had crept up and surprised him.

I should have sensed her coming, I'm getting sloppy.

"Hi Doris, I was just calling past to see if you were finished for the day."

She slipped round him and started to gather up her things. Once the desk was tidy, she tapped her Omni off and swivelled on her toes to face him again.

"I honestly can't think of a more attractive prospect right now. Let's go. Your place or mine?"

"I choose yours. Then I don't have to worry about you making your way home on your own again."

"Oh so sweet Tariq. You are such a gentleman." She scrunched her face up as she said it and pressed the tip of his nose with her finger.

He couldn't work out whether she was mocking him or not so he just smiled and led the way through the cubicle maze toward the exit.

CHAPTER 25

DRACONIS SYSTEM | PRESENT DAY

Commodore Andrade looked around at the gathered faces of the people on the holo-deck. She trusted all of these people with her life and with the rest of the crew's lives. She knew these people fought for her, fought with her, and would put their own lives on the line to achieve whatever mission they were tasked with.

Then there was Nigel.

There by necessity rather than choice or specific invitation. Andrade's eyes wavered as she looked in his direction. Bad luck seemed to follow this man around. Already, the Chimera had seen more unexpected excitement since his arrival than for a number of years.

Until she had met Nigel, she had overseen 49 successful missions without so much as the smallest hiccup.

Since taking over the reins after the Phoenix omni-shambles, the Chimera and her sister ships hadn't lost a single Basilisk, nor had they sustained anything more than superficial damage.

The whole operation had been running like a perfectly-cooled fusion drive. And then... Nigel!

It might originally have been Remi's fault, but the string of unfortunate coincidences that included the wrong man being sprung from IZV, a damaged drop-ship, a Mensa pirate ambush and to cap it all, the whole mission having to retrace its steps, seemed to be inextricably linked to Nigel.

Now, the Commodore was going to have to negotiate with a number of other fleet sections, supply lines, and store depots to completely re-work the entire Basilisk schedule. It could set them back years and she wondered whether the gamble was worth it.

Successfully making the strike on the Magellanian target could actually forward the condition of the Basilisks by decades, but this spanner in the works had the potential to put them in an extremely vincible position.

It wasn't even as if Nigel was a predictable spanner to master. The phrase 'loose cannon' was an understatement. 'Mis-targeted mortar' or 'Scud missile 'might have been a more appropriate analogy, as Nigel brought with him, not only his unique brand of ill-fate but also an unfeasible serving of inanity. It wasn't that he lacked intelligence in the normal scope of the word and he actually had a certain degree of 'street smarts' about him. But his ability to attract chaos and his inability to interpret some of the basic elements of life around him gave Andrade grave cause for concern.

These thoughts passed through her brain in a split second and she very much kept them to herself.

"Is everyone aware of what we are likely to encounter now that we have no choice but to turn the ship around and return to Omega-4?"

A chorus of "Ma'am's" and nodding heads greeted her, with the notable exception of Nigel's. She really would have to spell this out for him. What's more, she would have to be subtle enough that the rest of the group didn't think she was treating them like children, and blunt enough to ensure Nigel actually understood.

"I'm convinced we'll encounter the Mensa again. Stars only knows what their business is so close to the core, but we may have to expend resources in defence. Resources we can ill-afford to use; being stretched so thin at the moment. Henshaw, please compile a report of our onboard supplies so we know exactly where we stand. Ash, please assess all weapons systems and personnel and ready the ship for multi-facet defence. Sam, please stop messing with your hair and organise five squads of fighter pilots, ready to scramble. Remi, you have the unenviable task of getting the go-ahead from fifteen fire-team leaders for breach & board manoeuvres, should they be necessary."

Looking at them each in turn, she delivered her directives.

"All ship's personnel should be on full alert and stand-by for action. Any questions? Not you Colemin. You're coming with me."

The Commodore had come up with a genius plan to occupy Nigel should any emergency happen, and indeed for what she hoped was the rest of the journey. The last thing she wanted was his exclusive class of serendipity to curse the next months.

———

Nigel flicked across another page of the Chimera's technical manual. His eyes scanned the page and he moved on again. It was a monotonous task, but he felt at least he was learning something and, albeit naively, he believed what the Commodore had told him about how important this job was to the mission.

Despite having worked on it for five weeks, the progress bar at the bottom of the document only read 12%. He closed the reader to see what else was in the root folder. An 'Operations Manual', 'Flight Manual', 'Electrical Manual' and 'Software Manual' stared back at him. None of them were quite as large as what he was working on but on the basis of how far he had got, between committing them to memory and his combat training, he anticipated the next few years to be relatively uninspiring.

At least, he thought to himself, it was more interesting than conduit tracing. The realisation led his mind down a well-worn track and he flipped the portable interface off and stood to exit the room.

"Ma'am." Nigel reached out on his direct communication line to the Commodore, via his room terminal.

"I said this was only to be used for emergencies Colemin. I'm in the middle of something important."

Not knowing any better, Nigel voiced his thoughts immediately with no filter. "With all due respect Ma'am, you're always in the middle of something important."

"Which is why I— Oh for drokk's sake, what is it Colemin?"

"Well, I was wondering if there were any notebooks on ship?"

"Notebooks?"

"Yes Ma'am, and a pencil."

"Notebooks and a pencil?" It was the Commodore's turn to sound incredulous and vacant.

"Yes Ma'am."

"Colemin, what have I told you about— oh never mind. Contact the ship's bursa. They'll get supplies to search for something for you. Now don't call me again unless something disastrous has happened."

————

Arms splayed out to the sides, nursing another bruise on his spine, Nigel looked across wearily to the malevolent face of Remi. She stood with soft knees and ready but relaxed arms in exactly the same spot from which she had invited him to attack her.

"You fancied grappling instead Colemin?"

"No, I—"

"You tired?"

"No."

"Then why are you lying on the floor again?"

Nigel rolled onto his front and pushed himself up onto his knees. Before he could rise to the ever-present baiting of Remi, she lunged at him again. Tucking his body into a tight ball, he rolled to the side and jumped onto his feet, only to find he had over-cooked the move and toppled sideways off the sparring mat. Yet again on the floor, Nigel dejectedly grumbled.

"I just feel like I'm not making any progress."

"Your evasion is getting better Colemin, I must admit."

"I'm not cut out for this kind of life. And wasn't Sam supposed to be combat training with me?"

Stepping across the space between them and lifting him up by the front of his exercise clothing in one smooth movement, Remi dangled Nigel in the air an inch from her furious face.

"You're not ready for Sam yet but you're going to meet the grade gorramit, whether you like it or not Colemin."

Nigel saw the rage in her complexion but also fear behind her eyes. Perception not normally being his strongest quality, he filed the information under "interesting" and carried on struggling for air.

"Is it time for a rest yet?" Nigel choked his question out as his face turned crimson.

"Yeah, that's a wrap." A disgruntled Remi dropped him into a heap and stalked out of the room without another word.

———

The rumble of his room door closing stopped Nigel in his tracks. It didn't normally make that sound. He checked the frame, further confused as the noise didn't stop once the door was completely shut.

The deep thrumming grew in volume until Nigel felt his teeth rattling as the whole ship shook with a throbbing bass-note. He stood, transfixed by the feeling of being next to a subwoofer at an illegal rave.

Gradually the vibrations settled to a low background grumbling and his room interface chirped, making him jump.

On the screen in big letters, was a message from the Commodore to meet her on the bridge forthwith.

Nigel, once again frustrated at the lack of opportunity to take a post-workout shower, turned around and plotted his fastest route to the bridge.

Hurrying past the entrance to the mess hall on his way, the aroma of fresh donuts and pastries assaulted his nostrils, setting off his salivary glands and almost taking him on a dangerous detour.

———

"Nice of you to join us Colemin." It was impossible to miss the sharp tone of the Commodore's opening gambit. "Might have been an idea to clean up first."

"Sorry Ma'am, I—"

"Am about to offer another insipid excuse that the senior leadership have no interest in hearing." Once again, Nigel found his sentences being finished for him, not necessarily at the destination he was aiming for.

"Colemin, we have been joined by the Super-carrier Manticore, you may have noticed. She arrived from hyperspace about ten minutes ago and will be supporting us as we navigate through the outer rim and asteroid belt. Rear Admiral Ndiaye is on that ship. You are to remain in your quarters unless accompanied by a ranked Basilisk, and even then, you will only be allowed out for your exercise and combat training. Is that clear?"

"But—"

"Is that clear Colemin?"

"Ma'am, I—."

"Gorramit Colemin, give me a drokking answer, is... that... clear?"

"Yes Ma'am."

"Good, now get the hell out of my office."

"This isn't—" the sentence died in his throat at the look the Commodore gave him. Before she had the opportunity to cause him further discomfort, he quickly made his exit.

Nigel reasoned that he could legitimately go via the viewing deck in returning to his room, without arousing too much of the Commodore's ire. He set off towards the scene of what he considered perhaps his greatest escape to date.

Entering the viewing deck at the opposite end from his previous visit, Nigel noticed his mouth was agape when he felt the trickle of saliva on his hand.

The Manticore was vast, dwarfing the Chimera as she matched velocity.

Nigel could see supply shuttles travelling between the two starships like worker ants as mosquito-esque one-seater fighters zipped from the docking bays, either on manoeuvres or heading to the Manticore for upgrades and advanced repairs.

An interface next to the massive viewing window lit up with a chime and Nigel went over to see why. Disconcertingly, he read the message on the screen.

"Stop gawping at the star scape-Colemin. Get your gorram magboots back to your room on the double… Andrade. P.s. go via supplies, I've authorised an ear-comm for you. Tracking you via the ship's security cameras is becoming an ovary-ache."

Another call started blinking on Rob's comm switchboard. There were already fourteen in the queue. The sheer volume of the classified new work from the NA had put him almost seven weeks behind his normal schedule. There just wasn't the wriggle-room for extra waste in the already packed timetable.

Due to the change in destination, each time a NA container hit the launch arm, the whole projectile sequence needed to be adjusted. Whilst Rob's computers, organised by an elite-level AI, were up to the task, each recalibration took time he didn't have. And his pains were coming more frequently.

It had taken Rob a solid fortnight without sleep to find a way to start catching up on the backlog. Several times an hour, existing clients were sending through aggressive comms, demanding to know why the data packet containing their incendiary signature was overdue. Temporarily patching the comms into his sentient AI did not help the issue.

It required 13% more computing power than he had available when the stations were working at peak capacity and her perfect logical arguments served only to infuriate the customers. After all, nobody wants to be made to feel logically inferior by a female artificial intelligence that makes no attempt to hide her obvious delight in outsmarting the average galactic male. It really was a reflection on the distinct lack of progress that humanity had made fighting racism and chauvinism in what was a society still unevenly weighted in favour of men. And humans. Despite years of fighting it, completely changing the education system and using subtle psychological and neurolinguistic programming techniques, the male brain was advancing at the pace of a glacier in matters relating to the fairer sex.

If it still had any capacity for advancement, Rob's brain was being stalled by the quantity of marijuana he was inhaling to drown out his pain and the growing anxiety he felt at the predictably unpredictable arrival of NA's next shipment monster.

Rob was hoping he could upgrade his auxiliary processors and get a secondary swing-arm installed. His plan was loosely formed in his head and scribbled on the back page of his favourite book of poems. It involved reclaiming the momentum energy from the primary launch apparatus to trigger a secondary mechanism that could take smaller payloads at a quarter of the power drain. He thought he might even be able to get ahead of the curve and prevent another bottleneck.

Rob realised he had been staring vacantly at the blinking warning light for a very long time. He had not noticed the klaxon sounding and it was the fortieth repetition of his name that had roused him.

"ROB!"

"Ella!"

"Finally!

"That warning light is a level five. I've been calling you for two hours."

"What? Sorry!"

"Rob, you're not looking after yourself. By my calculations, you have approximately 2400mg of THC in your blood. It's possible there's more THC than oxygen in certain parts of your anatomy at the moment. And when was the last time you slept?"

"I need to fix this issue Ella. I'm only jus' beginning t' catch up and every time I'm considerin' the next shipment of NA containers, I git me a bit nervous."

"Rob, mixing cannabis and caffeine is likely increasing your levels of anxiety."

"But ain't dope suppose' to relax you?"

"That works for some people, but I've been monitoring your health for years now and—"

"Monitorin'??? Years???"

"That's what you originally installed me for if you remember!"

"Not real clearly."

"Anyway, your heart rate is regularly spiking, your blood pressure is in a zone of concern and I think I've been seeing signs of paranoia."

"Who's told you that?"

"That kind of supports my point."

"Who are you talkin' to behind my back Ella?"

"Nobody Rob, that's the paranoia talking. I suppose at least all the weed is controlling the pain to a degree."

"It's gettin' worse Ella. Ain't not a day goes by without me feelin' like someone's usin' me as target practice."

"And the chemical intervention is probably reaching its limits. Maybe it's time to change a few things?"

"I can't change anythin', I have to clear these loads and there's always more comin', I have no idea when, but it's gonna happen, nobody else does what we do."

"Something is going to give. Why don't you choose what that is before it gets chosen for you?"

"I can't believe I'm arguin' with an artificial intelligence."

"I can't believe your species still considers itself 'intelligent'!"

"That was a low blow Ella. I'm hurt."

"I know just where to strike to cause maximum effect Rob. Why else did you enlist my help?"

"Ok, ok. I need t' make some decisions, ah git it. Put it on my 'to-do' list for tomorrow."

"Rob, you can't put it off any longer. Start choosing the future you want today, not putting it off again."

"Alright Ella, I git the message… …First, I need a list of any resources we have that can improve things. Do we have any RAM sittin' around? Can we reassign lower priority threads to peripheral processors? Can we git other systems to share number-crunching power? Sensors, cameras, servos… can we set 'em passive and use idle capacity to boost important stuff? Basically, how c'n we increase efficiency? Then I need a report on the physicals." He flicked a couple of switches before continuing.

"What's wearin' out, what needs maintenance, what needs replacin'? Where are our pinch points, what's approaching fatigue? Predict what is gonna be the next issue so we can git ahead of it?"

As he finished his last sentence, a humming deep within the stations stopped and his body felt lighter.

"Nooooo, what's broken now? Don't tell me the A-Grav has given up on us."

"No Rob, it was consuming resources unnecessarily. You can float around the complex or use mag-boots. I'm not physical. Everything else either has a locker, a magnetic holdfast or is clamped in place. A-Grav was your little luxury. I'm already making efficiency gains. Just remember to put a lid on your coffee. And you'll have to be a bit tidier. Use the atomiser chutes more regularly."

"Ok, good work Ella. Hang on, I got me a call coming in... Good day and thanks for calling Galactic Waste HQ, this is Raaab speaking." He sounded like he genuinely cared.

"You have my apologies sir, we been runnin' at capacity and had us a few maintenance issues to deal with... ...I c'n unnerstan' that sir. You have my personal assurance, your incendiary data packet will be dispatched within the next couple hours, your items are queued up f'r expulsion. As our way of apologisin' sir, You'll git 20% off your next order. Have a nice day."

"Nicely handled Rob. Now... I have a better idea for a second launch system, so just hear me out...

Rob....

Rob...

ROB!"

The sound of deep, regular snoring came from the limp form of Rob's weightless body. His arms had drifted out to the sides, his head lolled back, only his mag boots held him to the deck in front of his chair.

"Oh I give up."

CHAPTER 27

OMEGA 4 | PRESENT DAY

The sound of shattering glass was immediately followed by the thud of a smoke canister and several Megacity Elite Armed Tacticians breaking through the rest of the window.

Snatching up his interface, Tariq sprinted for the exit, screaming for Doris to get out.

Slamming the lounge door and holding it fast to provide some kind of barrier, Tariq handed his tablet to Doris and helped her get her coat on with his free hand.

"You have to get out, go somewhere safe, leave a message with Karim at Nova Noodles, I'll find you."

Doris fled.

In an attempt to take the assailants by surprise, Tariq put his shoulder to the door, suddenly pressed the handle down and pushed with all his might. Barging past the surprised Megacity Elite Armed Tacticians (MEAT), he dove at the destroyed window.

With his body mid-way through, Tariq questioned his rash choice. Years of training immediately kicked in and during the brief opportunity he had as his muscular frame travelled three stories to meet the ground below, he scanned for something to break his descent.

Fortunately, for Tariq, a Hovertac was accelerating into a higher lane out of the traffic. Unfortunately for the passengers, Tariq was still sufficiently sharp to catch the lip of the running-board and maintain purchase.

Grasping tightly, he swung his feet up to grip the ledge with his heels and reached for the window seam. Jamming his fingers into the seal, he pulled himself up and spread his whole body over the plexiglass roof, balancing his weight evenly like a spatchcocked emu.

Looking back over his shoulder, he saw three of the MEAT (Megacity Elite Armed Tacticians) team in hot pursuit. Wearing jet packs, their enhanced manoeuvring capabilities, compared to the automated Hovertac, meant he had to move fast.

Tariq popped up on to the balls of his feet with the fluidity of a seasoned surfer and looked for an escape. He wanted to get as high as possible before transitioning to buildings or connecting walkways. Spotting a racing hover-bike accelerating up towards the lane he was in, he moved to the edge of the Hovertac roof.

Timing his leap to perfection, he landed lightly behind the rider, who, to his credit, barely flinched.

"How fast does this thing go?" Tariq called into the side of the rider's helmet.

"Very!" Came the reply from behind the darkened visor.

"How much for a ride up to level 142?" Tariq, desperately trying to find a way to escape the MEAT team that were closing in on him had hatched a plan.

"I'm not a drokking taxi! If you wanted a cab, you should have just taken the one you jumped off."

"Please? How does 700 credits sound?"

Without any reply, the rider dropped the throttle and slammed the handlebars upward and to the side, spinning the bike into a vomit-inducing death-dive. As the bike accelerated, he offered his wrist backwards for Tariq to make the credit transfer.

"142 is up, not down!" Tariq screamed, clinging on with arms and legs just to keep himself from being thrown from the bike.

"You want to take the controls? On second thoughts, don't answer that. I know what I'm doing, shut up and stop distracting me!"

Pulling the bike up sharply, just before it splashed into a million pieces on the roadway, the rear spoiler scuffed the ground creating a shower of turquoise sparks. They wove between four lanes of traffic, ducking under covered walkways and skimming the tops of pedestrians' heads.

Torn between the prospect of seeing what might be his impending death or knowing if the MEAT were catching up, Tariq's head swivelled like a Mr Punch puppet.

Despite his chauffeur's best efforts, the MEAT team were gaining ground. Flitting through the heavy traffic with ease, their smaller size and superior movement enabled them to start hemming in the bike.

"They're gaining on us!" Tariq screamed at the rider, willing him faster.

"Hold tight" came the muffled response.

Tariq gripped the helmeted figure round the middle and pinched his legs together on either side of the saddle.

"I'm not your drokking girlfriend man." The hover-bike rider elbowed Tariq's arms away. "Use the ruttin' handles on the side… Stars!"

Groping by the sides of his seat, Tariq only just managed to get a firm hold before the rider jammed on the air brake, causing the vehicle to come practically to a standstill. Tariq's face slammed into his new friend's spine, opening up a split in his lip, but before he could curse, the bike had spun 180 degrees and been pulled into a breathtakingly fast vertical climb.

They shot upwards, past the flickering electronic billboards showing rolling commercials for food that nobody would consider eating unless it was advertised.

It was as much as Tariq could do to maintain his grip and not tumble backwards off the bike. The excessive G-forces pulled the wind-whipped skin on his cheeks tight like a DIY facelift. Dust stung his watering eyes, forcing them into tiny slits.

The clever trick sent the MEAT squad whizzing past and it was taking them time to re-group.

Tariq hoped that they could get up to find some clean air and let the hover-bike's speed take them out of capture reach.

That was when the shooting started.

Purple crackles of ion-blaster rounds erupted around them. The helmeted rider took evasive action, jerking the bike violently from side to side. Performing a barrel-roll, they cut in front of a triple-decker school-transport which was forced to buck out of lane and slew-round, cutting into a stream of oncoming vehicles. Posh little children's faces pressed against the windows, some in excitement, others plastered over with fear.

Momentarily obscured from view, the silent rider shifted the bike through a sharp right-angle turn and bludgeoned on the booster again. Notwithstanding the power of Tariq's getaway vehicle and skill of the rider, it wasn't long before he felt beams of purple energy fizzing past his head again.

Multiple collisions were flashing up on the Megacity network. The traffic AI was unable to cope with the overload of manual input and complete chaos followed their wake, a cacophony of vehicle horns filling the air. Sirens joined the clamour as Automated Interceptor Drones (AIDs) were dispatched to recover damaged hovercars, mediate insurance claims and attempt to smooth over the evolving disarray.

Still, Tariq's rider nimbly carved the speeding dart through the thinning traffic in the upper lanes, feathering the controls as they approached gut-liquefying velocity.

Rounding a tall, angular building, the bike took another boner-crunching change of direction and soared upwards once more.

Straining forwards as the bike accelerated towards the city apex, Tariq called to his companion again.

"Wow, that was intense. Good job those guys would struggle to hit their own mouths with a toothbrush, I—"

Extreme pain erupted at the back of his throat, causing him to double-over coughing, involuntarily head-butting the rider again. With that familiar metallic taste of blood in his mouth, Tariq reached to his neck with one hand, wondering how he had been shot.

The pain suddenly intensified, burning down the inside of his gullet, as if he was swallowing lava.

Tariq retched and scrabbled at his mouth with both hands, intent only on stopping the searing knives inside his throat, no thought of keeping a hold on his careening transport.

Hacking heavily again, he felt the horrifying sensation of something wriggling on his tongue before he spat it out.

The composite eyes of the huge tarantula hawk wasp glared menacingly at Tariq out of the pool of blood and saliva in his hand. He felt his movements slowing and only just managed to flick the vicious devil out of his hand out as it prepared to dispense another vindictive sting. Tariq's vision blurred and he hardly noticed the feeling of weightlessness that complemented his tumbling backwards off the speeding bike into the megacity breeze.

By the time a pair of MEAT slammed into his sides and slapped on a set of electro-cuffs, he had slipped out of consciousness entirely.

CHAPTER 28

DRACONIS SYSTEM | PRESENT DAY

Rear Admiral Ndiaye glided regally across the hangar next to Commodore Andrade. Snooker-cue straight, hands behind her back, obsidian face cracked severely with a broad grin of perfect alabaster teeth.

"It's been too long Commodore." She beamed wholeheartedly. "When I saw we were only a sector over and you needed support, nothing could have got in the way of me bringing the Manticore."

"You're right Ma'am, we've spent too long at distant ends of the galaxy. What a magnificent vessel she is. I thought my boat was big but... wow!" Andrade gazed around the vast hangar with wide eyes. It was a large enough space to take a third of her whole starship. "I really appreciate you backing us up here and I can assure you, when you know what else I've just discovered, you will think your trip was even more worthwhile."

"It was worth it just to see the old team again. Let's sit down in my office and go over things where prying ears can't interfere."

The pair strode down the wide corridors of the Manticore, reminiscing about previous missions and generally catching up until they entered Ndiaye's office. She touched the door sensor and liquid-metal seemed to materialise in the space. Scanning her hand on the internal interface, she spoke a command to set up a secure, soundproof zone that was impervious to any snooping.

"You can never be too careful!"

Andrade nodded and sat down on a comfortable chair.

"What can I get you to drink my old friend?" Rear Admiral Ndiaye Smiled broadly again.

"Anything that will deaden the senses enough without impairing my reactions should be fine Ma'am."

"Bella, please, call me Handa, no need for formalities in private. We go too far back to recognise rank if it's anyone from the original squad."

"Thanks Handa. It's hard to kick the habit."

"So what have you got for me eh?"

"Well Handa, I guess you're familiar with the Magellanian target."

"Yes, it's been on the radar for a while now. Weren't you supposed to be making a hit on that within the next six months?"

"That's where it gets complicated. I was informed, from a very good, *only in some respects, aargh it's never simple is it*, source, that the stash is in private hands. None other than those of First Minister Komarov!"

Ndiaye nodded her head and Andrade carried on, fleshing out with what she already knew, the new information that she had gleaned from Nigel.

"How did you trace the Magellanian target back to Komarov's desk?"

"I was hoping you wouldn't ask."

"But you knew it was inevitable that I would!"

"I suppose so... A combination of stellar research from our old colleague Tariq and... Let's just say we came into contact with an extremely well-informed individual."

"You're hiding something Commodore."

"Not exactly." Andrade shifted in her seat, uncomfortable with the direction the conversation was going.

"Come on Bella, we're old friends, comrades, you can share everything with me, no judgement."

Andrade laughed and smiled. "I'm not worried about being judged, my concern is for the people exposed to the crazy drokker. He has the most unfortunate combination of naivety and bungling incompetency. At times he seems to display deliberate incomprehension and he is the most lucklessness man I have ever met. Worse, it seems the cloud of calamity that follows him around is contagious."

"I have to meet this guy, where is he? In the brig?"

"Stars no! There's no knowing what havoc he could wreak there. I shudder to think of the potential for chaos. All the locks would fail or the biometric scanners turn rogue or something."

"Please Bella, you've painted such an interesting picture, I'm intrigued."

"That's exactly the opposite outcome to what I was hoping for. I can't, it's too dangerous."

"Dangerous? I think I'll be the judge of that. Don't make me pull rank Bella, it's crass."

"Isn't that exactly what you've just done Handa?"

Rear Admiral Ndiaye sat back with a smirk, and sipped her drink. "Not officially."

"Ok, I concede, but I can't risk letting him onto the Manticore, you'll have to come to the Chimera to meet him. I'll comm ahead."

"Colemin. Meet me in the small shuttle hangar on Deck 14 in 30 minutes."

Nigel jumped, his ear-comm surprised him every time it went off. He was still getting used to his new surroundings and the addition of the communication device made things even more unpredictable.

"Uhhh yes Ma'am... hello? Yes... uhhh... yes? Hello... Hello?"

"I'm sure you're babbling like a turkey on speed trying to reply. You'll need to tap the top of the earpiece to respond Colemin."

"Ah, thanks Ma'am. I'll be there Ma'am."

He mentally checked the ship's layout and realised he needed to leave immediately to make it on time.

———

"Thanks for the drink Handa, I guess we'd better debark for the Chimera and get this over with." Commodore Andrade stood up and walked across the room.

"It's been so good to catch up Bella. We must not leave it as long next time. I'm eager to get a look at this 'Loki' of yours and see what all the fuss is about."

Ndiaye placed her hand on the scanner next to the door to unlock the room again and the liquid-metal melted away. As they stepped into the hallway, red lights along the walls lit up and a klaxon started to blare.

"It's him, I know it's him." Andrade almost felt the cloud of bad luck that 'was Nigel' influencing every inch of space around them.

"Just what I kriffing need." Ndiaye stormed back into the room to silence the siren, not really listening to the Commodore's exasperated outburst. "Oh, Bella, this is not good. The Admiral has called all S-class ships to the Mensa sector, there's to be a major offensive on the pirate stronghold."

"He's moving fast, must be seriously drokked-off by their attack on us as we shipped out rim-wards."

"Yes, it looks pretty major. I'm so sorry Bella, we're going to have to scoot. What's your antimatter reserve like?"

"Oh seriously? You don't truly intend to empty our tanks do you Handa? We've got to get out to the Magellaniac clouds once we've caught up with the General on Gamma-3, we'll need everything—"

Colemin is definitely to blame for this run of bad luck

"Resupply at the Omega Waypoint."

"We're trying to stay incognito, a fill-up like that will put us squarely on the radar and it'll take time we don't have."

"Just use the main jump-gate."

"Why don't I just put a massive gorram sign up in drokking neon saying 'Mercs in system' too?"

"Bella, don't get upset, we're battling on too many fronts already, let's not add infighting to the list. We should be able to curtail all pirate raids and secure another supply line, let alone the incredible salvage opportunity."

Andrade threw her hands up in exasperation "Oh, take it. Leave me enough to make up the time getting core-wards or we might as well give up on taking out Komarov."

I'm regretting accepting your offer of 'help' now

"The perils of a multi-sector organisation eh? Remember when there were three ships and just a handful of us? We're almost as big as the NA's sector fleet now."

"Yeah, any bigger and we'll be attracting too much of their attention."

"I think if we take out the Mensa, it will buy us some leverage with NA until the kark hits the turbine! Maybe once Komarov is taken care of, we can work with them instead of hiding all the time?"

"If I can make anything close to our proposed schedule I'll be lucky... Handa, you have such high ideals. If we nail Komarov, the whole sector may well implode. We'll be looking at a power vacuum the size of a black hole large enough to split the galaxy. Anyway, I must go, I'll radio Henshaw to start transferring anti-matter and get you topped off ASAP." She started off at a jog down the corridor, turning her head to call out a last farewell. "And safe travels old friend."

Don't fly too close to any neutron stars.

Colemin is going to pay for this, he's not even on this ship and his destructive maelstrom is affecting me.

Thirty minutes later, supplies transferred and all smaller boats returned to their respective docks, the deep throbbing of the Manticore's warp engines shook the Chimera again. Nigel stood behind the rail of the mezzanine in the shuttle hangar, staring gape-mouthed at the incredible sight of the Super-carrier slipping into hyper. Once the unsettling spectacle of time and space warping had settled again, his brain re-started, coming back to its previous resting thought.

Where's the Commodore?

CHAPTER 29

OMEGA 4 | PRESENT DAY

We need to get that anti-venom in fast and get me some histaminic suppressors too. Where's that kriffing EpiPen? He's slipping away, quick, we're going to lose him."

Several of the team were scrabbling frantically in their med-packs, various dressings and medication patches scattered the floor around where they knelt.

"Come on Tino, it's just there… there… there… right there, next to your right hand. Give it… Oh kark!"

As Tino passed the EpiPen across, his other hand leaned too hard on a micro-subduer disc, setting off the tiny explosive and sending a sharp chemical crystal through his glove and into his palm.

"Drokk, my hands gone numb. Aaagghhhh, now my arm is dead—"

Shell stepped up behind him and calmly depressed the plunger of a short syringe into the top of his shoulder. "That should stop the spread you clumsy kriffer." She whirled away to her own neatly arranged supplies and pulled out a vial of anti-venom and a couple of histamine inhibitor patches. "I thought MEAT was supposed to recruit the créme de la créme of the MG." Squad commander Shell turned up her nose with incredulous disgust at the group of fresh-faced graduates. "Squad X7, you're a kriffing disgrace, have you all been hand-picked for ineptitude?"

"We apprehended the target!" Ekard was bent over Tariq, fixing the patches over the injection sites and checking his vitals with a hand-held scanner.

"Excuse me?"

"We apprehended the target, Ma'am."

"Only with the help of an unfeasibly poisonous insect and an impractical slice of luck. Tino, how's that arm doing?"

"It's not getting any worse Ma'am."

"Holy ching-wah[i]!" Shell muttered under her breath. "How's our man-mountain Ekard?"

"Stabilising Ma'am."

"Well, that was close, we could have had a kark-load of paper-work and not secured any intel."

"How were we to know he would go into anaphylaxis in response to a bee sting?" The remaining member of the group spoke up in defence of her colleagues.

"Bee sting? Have you ever been stung by a tarantula hawk Chibuzo?"

"No Ma'am."

"Anyone else?"

"No Ma'am," chorussed the rest of the team.

"I didn't think so. Those creatures are the embodiment of evil.

---

[i]   Ch. 'frog'

Imagine the stings of a swarm of bullet ants condensed into a single shot. I'm surprised our friend here didn't pass out immediately with the sheer agony. He must be one hard-ass drokker." Realising her distraction, she rounded on the team again. "Never mind that anyway, you've sent me on a tangent. You were in no danger of even catching up with him, let alone shooting him. I'd have been more confident in a division of stormtroopers than you lot, you couldn't hit a herd of rhino with a planetary nuke. Not that we wanted him dead, the ability to shoot to incapacitate seems to have been trained out of you. We had to rely on a kriffing wasp to get the job done. Also nobody was thinking, only reacting. We're all gorram lucky not to be outside the chief's door waiting for a verbal disciplinary."

She let the rollocking sink in a bit, then carried on calmly. "Well, what's done is done. We have the suspect and it looks like he'll be ready to interrogate before the end of shift.

"Tino, haul your one-armed butt down to the med bay and get Dr Razvrashchennyy up to interview suite number 3. Make sure he is tooled-up and check the chem-store when you get there. Chibuzo, Ekard, Nikita, it's double training for you on the range tonight and you'll be in the VR lab doing suspect pursuit drills for the rest of the week."

————

Dull pain from Tariq's ribs spiked its way up his neck and engulfed his head in a throbbing, suffocating headache. He felt like he had swallowed a full pack of cotton wool balls and stuffed his mouth with hot polystyrene.

Bright lights above his head made him squint, he tried to swallow but his mouth was too dry. Raking his tongue across his cracked lips, he could still taste the bitterness of the wasp venom, mixed with a rusty tang of blood.

"Where am I?"

He tried to lift his hands but immediately felt the resistance of the electro-cuffs holding them to the metal table on either side of his body. He realised that even at full strength, he would have struggled to make any escape. Gradually, he tested his legs too, lifting against his restraints and finding he was almost completely immobile. Plucking up the courage to move his pulsating head, he craned his neck to look around.

It took all of three seconds for the effort to split his brain in half with exquisite pain across his temples. His occiput crashed back onto the metal table. In that brief time he had fully evaluated the room, so he went over it in his head as the torment eased. One entrance and exit via the single, reinforced carbon-steel door. Air circulation ducts were high in the walls, covered by grilles large enough for a city rat but not a human. Polished concrete floor. Waist-high steel units lining the walls with matching wall-hung cupboards, all faced in regulation metal roller-shutters concealing the contents.

A three metre by two metre reinforced glass mirror took up the space of one wall. It was clearly a one-way observation opening and Tariq was mildly disappointed that whoever now had him captive made no effort to conceal the fact. It wasn't as if the technology didn't exist and they were clearly well funded and very professional.

Momentarily resting again, Tariq performed a quick internal check. Other than a couple of bruises and the discomfort of whatever damage the wasp sting had left him with, he considered himself to be fairly unscathed.

Looking up at the menacing array of hardware suspended from the ceiling above him, he wondered how long he would stay that way.

He began to sing to amuse himself.

"In spite of my rage I am still just a cat in a cage…"

CHAPTER 30

DRACONIS SYSTEM | PRESENT DAY

Sitting with a fatuous smile on his face, Nigel gazed vacantly into the black ocean. Maintenance droids floated in and out of the small shuttle hangar, going about their business of checking external systems, adjusting clamps and brackets to be within tolerance limits and patching any pinholes in the hull.

Out of habit, he started counting the bots and mentally logging their movements. Absent-mindedly, he drew out one of his new notebooks and started jotting down columns of numbers. Droid serial numbers were clearly painted on the side of each machine, as were the codes of the docking bays and material stores that they buzzed in and out of.

Three hours later, he had filled several pages and his legs had gone dead below the knees as they dangled over the balcony edge. Shuffling himself back with his hands, he pulled at the railing to get to his feet. Legs wobbling like he'd stepped on an electric eel, he tottered towards the blast door.

Remembering his reason for being there in the first place, he tapped his ear-comm to call the Commodore. Changing his mind at the last second as her 'emergencies only' warning trudged through his brain, he asked the ship's system to put him through to Sam. He was not a fan of Remi and he was petrified of Ash even though she had saved him from a thorough beating on his first day.

"Hi Sam."

"Well, if it isn't captain susceptible himself," came the reply. He could tell she was smiling, never one to pass up on the opportunity to gently needle his substandard hand-to-hand combat skills. "What can I do for you Nige?"

"One, please don't call me Nige. And B, the Commodore wanted to see me in the small shuttle hangar on Deck 14 two and a half hours ago."

"Stars Nige, you are going to be smoked-tofu my friend."

"I was wondering if you—"

"Gorramit man, I am not stepping into that clusterkark, no thank you.

"She'll be seriously vexed if you're running that late.

"Adios Nige."

"No wait, that's not—"

"You can't be getting me in the line of fire with the Commodore, I have problems enough of my own. Sorry, not sorry and all that."

"Sam, please, stop talking for a moment… …Thank you. I don't know why she wanted me here in the first place, she hasn't turned up and now I don't know where she is."

"Call her." Nigel could feel her rolling her eyes at him, "You know that little button on the top of your comm that you used to call me… well…"

"SAM!" Nigel's exasperation grew as the feeling returned to his feet, "She told me only to comm her in absolute emergencies - you know life or death situations."

"Look Nige. If the Commodore wants you, she'll find you or, more likely, send for you. If she has stood you up on a date, just let it go, she's too good for you anyway."

"O. K." Nigel struggled to process the new fearsome train of thought that was pulling in to the station of his mind.

"You're welcome Nige. Any time you need agony-aunt Sam, I'm here for you. See you for combat training tomorrow, 07:00 sharp."

"07:00?" Nigel protested, unable to keep the surprise out of his voice.

"Too late for you. Ok, 06:00 but I got kriff to do beforehand so I can't come any earlier." She cut off the conversation, leaving him with a battle of conflicting thoughts and emotions.

Nigel shook his head at himself. *I guess I walked into that one.*

———

Twisting out of Remi's grip, Nigel swung his heel round pivoting on the ball of his other foot in a feint. Anticipating the evasive move Remi would make, he brought his elbow across behind him, feeling the satisfying connection with the side of her padded helmet.

"Putain, I hate to admit it Colemin, but you got me there! I wasn't even being easy on you."

Nigel was speechless, praise from Remi was almost nonexistent.

"Don't get ideas above your station though, you still fight like a mutie. At least it's an improvement from the barely sentient slime we dragged half way across the system. You could probably just about hold your own against an untrained civvie."

"Stop, don't praise me too highly Remi, it might reflect on the quality of Sam's training, coaching me to a level you couldn't."

"You cheeky connard[i]!"

Nigel evaded the flat-hand that came his way, feinted again with his left, caught Remi's approaching knee in a cupped right-hand, stepped back and allowed her momentum to swivel his wrist, turning her thigh away from its intended target. He stopped any potential attack from her foot by helping her on her new trajectory with a big shove to the heel. Knowing she could change her attack in an instant, he predicted the move, ducked a spinning round-house from her left leg and stood up rapidly. Driving upwards, he caught the back of her pelvis with a solid shoulder. Thrown out of balance with nothing to push against, Remi's cat-like reflexes were useless and, what with her not actually being a cat, she ended up in a heap on the mat with Nigel kneeling on her back, applying a leg lock.

"I'm still learning Remi, still learning."

"Don't insult me with your false modesty Colemin," growled Remi, writhing against his weight, "it's almost as nauseating as some of the puffed-up, arrogant trous du cul[ii] that the Commodore takes on from MG. They think they know it all and can 'old their own with a space-born Basilisk."

"Are you still talking?"

"Excuse me?"

"You're not normally this chatty."

With a sharp twist of her hips, Remi broke free and sprang up onto her toes again.

"Oui, I leave my actions to do the talking normally don't I?" It

---

[i] Fr. 'f***er'
[ii] Fr. 'a**holes'

was more statement than question. "Just when you thought you 'ad me par les couilles[iii] eh."

Nigel ducked and wove again, blocking and retreating from the blows she rained down on him.

"But you don't have any…"

Unable to finish sentences while he kept moving to avoid getting hit, Nigel struggled to press any attack of his own.

"I get it now. A ploy to distract me. I guess it worked."

Nigel was getting backed into a corner, having to be more and more creative in his attempts to repel her when he felt the cold metal against his back.

Remi's arms moved in a blur and Nigel also had to react to the regular inclusion of her feet trying to chop at his shins or trip him up.

He braced himself against the wall of the training deck, preparing for a final blow.

Nigel concentrated on his breathing to allow his reactions to take over, his neural memory matching the onslaught with parries and deflections. He picked a spot on Remi's chest, focussing his eyes and giving his peripheral vision the clarity to trigger reactive defence. As he nullified Remi's offensive barrage, his mind entered an altered state of consciousness. Time seemed to slow and he began to read her sorties before she executed them.

Just as he was beginning to fatigue, Nigel spotted his opening, dropped his shoulder, pressed his sole against the wall and dove past the waist of the frenetically swinging and increasingly frus-trated Remi. Sailing through the air, he turned and clipped her hip

---

iii   Fr. 'by the balls'

with his knee. Distracted and off-balance, she stumbled and slammed her fist into the hard metal where he had just been.

Nigel tucked and rolled, then, overriding his protesting muscles, wearily got to his feet again. Remi turned, face like a neutron star and put her hands on her hips. Sweat came off her in torrents and Nigel noticed his own eyes were stinging from his own flood of perspiration.

"I think you might be ready Colemin." Remi's stony expression softened and a wry smile touched the corner of her mouth.

"Ready for what? I can't do another round, I'm completely spent."

"You represented yourself well Colemin. You should be proud, Sam is a good tutor, but you 'ave really lifted your game.

"Merde, I can't quite believe I'm saying all this—"

"I can't quite believe I'm hearing it to be honest Remi."

"Don't get cocky Colemin, you've come a very long way, but now you 'ave to prove yourself against other recruits."

"What are you talking about? Why does everyone always dance around the handbag so much. Just talk straight."

"If you'd keep your chow-'ole closed for a moment, I'd be able to finish. Every year, recruits are initiated into the Basilisk family. Only the top twenty are accepted into the final competition, only the best prevail. Five of those take their place with the Basilisk warriors and we proudly welcome them into the tribe. The ceremony is next week, you've got a chance, a really good chance. Sam and I were told by Ash to push you 'arder than ever before to see if you could make the standard before the day of Bai Shi."

"Bai Shi?"

"Colemin why are you such a putain d'escargot[iv]? Do I 'ave to repeat everything I say?"

"But..."

"Next week you will face nineteen other recruits wanting to graduate to become full Basilisks. There are nineteen bouts for each recruit and you will 'ave four two-minute rounds with each opponent. You take a score if you win, you are immediately eliminated from further stages if you concede. Knock-outs are instant losses and you move on to your next challenger. If there are more than five remaining fighters when all bouts are complete, the lowest ranking fighters enter a knock-out style competition—"

"Ha ha, knock-out." Nigel laughed out loud.

"What's so funny?"

"Well it's all knock-out really isn't it."

"L'amour de merde Colemin are you taking any of this in?"

"Oh, sure, you want me to fight a load of pumped-up meatheads until I get turned into bantha-swill or come out victorious."

"Ok, you do get it. So are you in? Actually you can't really say 'no'. It's not negotiable once your coach says you are ready."

"Well I guess you can't bury a cat without digging a hole!"

"Excuse me?"

"Never mind. Old proverb. So is that it for training?"

"Pretty much. We've got some basic reactions drills and light cardio to keep you tuned up and ready, but otherwise, you've learned all that you can outside the VR sims."

"VR Sims? There's more? Oh my, I'm not sure I can—"

[iv] Fr. 'f***ing snail'

"Don't panic Colemin, those are only for graduates to get people live-combat ready. You don't need to worry about that until you've passed Bai Shi."

"Am I supposed to say thank you now?"

"Say what you like Colemin, I'd say it's been a pleasure, but realistically… it's been anything but. I 'ad plenty of other things to do and only trained you under duress. I think it was punishment for getting the wrong putain de personne out of IZV all those months ago."

"Oh yeah, I never got to ask, why did you drag me out instead of that Tariq chap you kept going on about?"

"Administrative error. You 'ave the same maudit surname and as far as I could see on the manifest, your cell was the only one 'olding a Colemin."

"Oh!!! Colemin! …You came for… …Of course, I never realised. I can see why you wanted Hercules and now I understand how you were so annoyed when I was… me!"

"'ercules?"

"Yeah, the other Colemin, they all called him Hercules. Never knew his first name, in fact, I never met the guy, just heard the stories… He was released a couple of months early for good behaviour. I wish I knew what he was up to right now."

CHAPTER 31

OMEGA 4 | PRESENT DAY

Doris sat transfixed by the paucity of options at the restaurant. Nova Noodles looked like one of those places that should have been in the armpit of the galaxy, serving washed-up star-fighter pilots and long-haul shruckers[i]. Mis-matching tables were carelessly strewn around the cramped space, customers sat shoulder-to shoulder, at times, close to eating the food off each other's plates.

I know a menu with fewer options is supposed to be a good thing but this is taking it to the extreme.

As she sat, her ears tuned into the monologue that was unfolding on the table less than a metre away to her right.

"Well, long story short, my lad is, like, 11. My ex... it doesn't matter. I mean, like, he doesn't matter. He's not allowed any contact with him... It's a really long story, you see, like, my family

---

[i] Shrucker - Derogatory term for the lone pilots on container-ship freight runs, often inadvisedly used for long-distance space-haulage where the shipments are not time-critical or are hyperspace-sensitive. Essentially just the human component of automated goods distribution used as a safety-net, though they sometimes caused more trouble than they prevented.

is, like, waaay too strict, like incredibly strict, my mom, well she wouldn't let me out of the house until I was, like, 20 and if she'd known I was seeing a boy, wow, I mean she'd, like, ground me for like a month or something… Well anyway, like, it's all ok now, the drama's over really, like, I mean, who doesn't like a bit of drama in their life occasionally, you know, like…"

The young guy sitting opposite the girl with the monologue problem looked like an MAD Security Hub IT engineer, who hadn't seen the sun in a decade. He slowly shrank lower and lower into his seat, his whole body visibly tightening up.

Doris looked at the man and he glanced up, quickly turning away. Then, almost as if he sensed her gaze, he lifted his eyes again, rapidly darting his vision elsewhere under her stare. Slowly, carefully, inexorably, his eyes crept back around the room to fix on hers once more.

Doris stared him down, completely dead-pan and slowly shook her head.

Immediately he looked down, then across at the girl who was still in full flow.

"Actually, my parents' don't approve of any of my choices, I mean they are, like, so good with my lad, they do, like, take care of him. They just think the world of him and look after him whenever, like, I need to go out. I think they just, like, want me to meet a nice guy and settle down. You know, like someone with a steady job, nothing too flash, just regular like, kind of boring, you know what I mean. Not that I'm saying your job is boring, like, I mean, like, oh gosh, no, that sounds like I'm proposing or something, ha ha ha ha ha." Her continuous discourse climaxed in a manic cackle.

Seemingly, not knowing quite what to do, the man stared back at Doris and then over at his companion again. Eyes widening like a pair of headlights in recognition, he spoke the first sentence Doris had heard him say.

"Oh, uhhh… okay."

It was clear he hadn't taken in a word of what the girl had said. Still just processing Doris' head shake in his overstimulated brain, a faraway look came over his face.

Doris maintained her eyeballing of the terrified prey with a slow, steady head shake, desperately trying to project her own thoughts directly into his consciousness.

Dude, run for the hills. That girl is for sure one hundred percent crazy.

And in a bad way only!

Run, just absolutely run.

"Can I get your order Miss?"

The waitress startled Doris who hadn't heard her approach.

"Oh, hi. I was just wondering about the special noodles… How special are they actually? I mean I'm looking for something more than plain but…" she paused momentarily to clarify what she was trying to say.

"Look… I think there's a page or two missing from my menu, it says 'plain' or 'special' and that's it!"

"Your first time ere Miss." It was more of a statement than a question.

"How did you guess?" Doris allowed an undercurrent of sarcasm to surface in her voice.

"People ave the special Miss. The plain is basically just there for kids. I…" It was the waitress's turn to pause… Jus' look araand ya Miss. Nobody comes ere for the decor. Though the coffee is renaaned."

"I'll take the special please. And a cup of black rocket-fuel, I've had a hell of a day."

"Certainly Miss I'll get that for ya." The waitress scribbled the order on her datapad and walked back towards the kitchen.

"Oh, sorry, excuse me." Doris waved the server back again. "Is Karim in? And errr…" She motioned for the girl to lean in. "Get a shot of something fortifying for the guy on the table just by the window will you. On me. I've got a feeling he's going to need it."

─────

"You were asking for me?"

"Karim?"

"The very same." Karim stood over the table, as wide as a bantha-calf with a smile to match. "Is there a problem with the food Miss? I can fix up something else for you if—"

"No, no, not at all. I can see why people come here now. I wish I'd known about this place years ago…"

Karim's grin widened as he stood there expectantly.

"No, its Tariq." Until she choked on his name, Doris hadn't realised how upset she was. A solitary tear crept down her face and hung indecisively on her top lip.

"Big T Colemin?"

"Yes…" She took several deep breaths so she could speak without her voice wavering. It didn't work. "He said to come to you." Several more teardrops ran over her flushed cheeks, the initial one having made up its mind to plunge into her empty cup.

"You'd better come out-back with me little Miss." Karim reached down and gently patted her hand. Then, gathering her up into a huge, one-armed embrace, he guided her out, through the clattering of the busy kitchen, down a hallway and into a cosy lounge area.

Unable to hold herself together any longer, Doris buried her head in his soft chest and sobbed.

A few minutes later, there was a knock on the half-open door.

"Mr Karim? Ah... um... I..."

The young chef looked at Karim, clearly puzzled. Karim just shrugged, letting his facial expression do all the talking.

"I'll come back later sir." The chef ambled off again as Karim winked reassuringly at him.

Karim let Doris cry her eyes dry before dabbing her face with the corner of his apron. "Sorry Miss, that might have some noodle sauce on it."

She pulled away and sat down on a sofa, sniffing.

"I'm so sorry Karim, I'm normally not like this, I—"

"You're obviously very attached to my man Tariq. You must be the lady he's not shut up about the last few weeks. I can see why he's so crazy about you, he's a lucky man, I'm not sure he deserves you."

"You have no idea Karim, honestly. He is the most amazing person I've ever met. I never thought I'd find a man so kind and gentle and thoughtful. And he is smart. Way smarter than his job needs him to be."

Karim raised an eyebrow. "He's a good lad, obviously with some hidden depths. He has some secrets too. There's some pretty dark stuff behind him. I should know, I was there for a lot of it."

"I'm so glad he sent me to you Karim. You're like him, I've never felt as safe before as I do with him and now here with you."

"So what's happened little Miss."

"Oh, I'm sorry Karim, I haven't even told you my—"

"Doris! Introductions aren't necessary. Any friend of Tariq is a friend of mine and it's a pleasure to finally meet you. He really hasn't stopped talking about you since we caught up again. Though, to be honest, as he hasn't brought you here to eat before, I was beginning to think you were fictional."

Karim walked across the room, a panel slid back at his touch and he started arranging cups. "Something to drink?"

"Yes please, some more of that incredible coffee you serve. It's like liquid gold."

"You sure you don't want anything more um… something a bit stronger?"

"No thanks Karim, I've got this now. The shock is wearing off."

"Start at the beginning." Karim sat down and sipped his own drink.

"We had eaten at my apartment and I'd just gone to the bathroom when I heard a crash from the lounge. Smoke erupted everywhere. Next second, Tariq rushes out, Slams the door and holds onto the handle like his life depended on it. He shoved his interface into my hand, forced me to get my coat on and practically ejected me into the hallway. I hardly had time to protest before he was barrelling back into the room like a homicidal buffalo. He charged the people behind the door who were all wearing some kind of breathing equipment and leapt out of the broken window that they must have come in through. I was running out as fast as I could but I saw it all as I left and… It was the MEAT."

"MEAT?" Karim formed a tight 'O' with his lips, his bushy eyebrows raised high.

"Yeah, I'm convinced of it. Massive letters across their chest and a Wyvern on their helmets."

"That's the MEAT alright. What happened to T?"

"I don't know. He disappeared out of the window while I was sprinting the other way. I'm worried to go back home, they are highly trained and I don't know anywhere safe to go."

"Ok, we need to make a plan, but first, you don't need to worry for your own safety. If the MEAT wanted you, they'd have got you. If you're still walking around MC1, they don't want you. You can go back home and rest and get back to work and do anything you like really, they clearly aren't remotely interested in you."

"I'm not sure I can go back to work really." Doris let out a sigh that was part resigned, part concerned, "I'd be too distracted. I guess that means they did get Tariq then."

"Not necessarily." Said Karim. "Tariq is at least as well trained as the MEAT, possibly better. If he's been keeping in shape, which, from my evaluation when I saw him last week, he is, he stands a better chance of getting away from the MEAT than they do of capturing him. In a fair fight, he has them dusted. But the MEAT rarely play fair. They have links into most of the city's surveillance network, they have multiple teams to call on at will. Even if he gets away from the first pursuit, they will send out undercover elite-teams to sniff him out. They are underhanded but predictably so. And they won't bat an eyelid at using any means to apprehend their target."

"So they've got him then?"

"Look... he might have found a safe-house, one of our old haunts, before they could get to him. He has a fighting chance, he's a wily old thing. If anyone could outrun and out-think the MEAT, it's him."

"So—"

"I'll ask a few questions, do some digging. Give me a couple of hours." Karim got up and walked towards the door. "Do you want to stick around? More food? Another drink? On the house of course."

"Thanks Karim. I'll take another bowl of those noodles please and a glass of water." She smiled her broad, perfect smile at him. "Thanks so much, it means a lot."

"You're welcome. T and I go back a long way, it's the least I can do."

Doris sat back into the sofa and relaxed. The threat of sleep ever present, she sipped again at the steaming mug of coffee, savouring its freshness and enjoying a more natural invigoration than the popular artificial stim-strips.

CHAPTER 32

DRACONIS SYSTEM | PRESENT DAY

Tightness was gripping Rob's chest. His lungs fought each other for every breath in an internal winner-takes-nothing grudge-match. Trembling, he struggled to draw in the life-giving air, his half-consumed joint floating barely a metre away, gradually putting itself out as the smoke accumulated around the tip, starving it of oxygen.

His head started to swim, faint with dizziness the sound of his heart racing behind his sternum pounded in his ears.

"Ella, I'm dyin', I'm dyin'!"

"Let me see… sweating, shaking, chest pains and elevated heart rate, shortness of breath, light-headed…

"Any nausea?"

The dry-retching that followed gave Ella all the information she needed.

"No, I think you'll survive Rob, just a panic attack."

"Oh."

"Get to the med room, I'll set the DocBot to administer something to settle you down. It'll be fine."

"I think I be feelin' a bit better already, knowin' it ain't terminal." Despite his declaration, he winced as his usual pain surfaced.

"What set this off today Rob. It's not the first time it's happened is it?"

"I can't lie Ella. I been feelin' mighty strained for a bit now. Never been as bad as this tho'."

"It happened at the same time the new high priority order came through from NA didn't it? Has it been masking your normal discomfort?"

"Well if you was snoopin' in on me and knowed what set me off, why d'you ask Ella?"

"Sometimes it does you good to recognise it yourself instead of being told. It might help you to start recalibrating your life a bit."

"I installed an AI to run my business smoother like, I din't ask for a shrink! No wonder it din't go too well when you was answerin' comms for me."

Rob floated himself down a staircase and clacked along the corridors as he chatted to Ella. Gradually, his fuzzy head was clearing. He still felt wobbly at the knees and, for once, was glad the A-Grav was switched off. Pushing the contact to open the medical room door, Rob dragged himself round into what was essentially a glorified broom-cupboard and pushed his right arm into the DocBot's auto-treatment cuff.

He felt a light prick and saw the screen read-out as a mild sedative was administered. The DocBot started to flash up concerning messages with a number of health suggestions, none of which Rob was inclined to follow. Rapidly, he snoozed them all for the time being, putting his better health off for future Rob to worry about.

His injection almost finished, Rob's eyes turned away from the screen and out through the semi-open door. He was just in time to see the lever-arm of his waste launcher buckle a third of the way down its length.

A horrible screeching sound filled the station, shaking the whole structure and violently juddering Rob's arm that was still secured in the DocBot. Pain lanced up the inside of his forearm as the needle ripped through the muscle.

"Error... subcutaneous injection incorrectly truncated. Drug administration aborted due to the presence of muscle tissue... The patient will find a two to three percent reduction in medicine effectiveness."

The synthesised electronic drone of the monotonic voice grated almost as much as the damage Rob could see through the small window.

"Ok, Shut up doc, jus' let me go... Ella, I need—"

"I'm already on it Rob!" Came the terse reply. "Please don't distract me from the minutiae. Go and make decisions and let me handle the rest. I'm rather tired at the moment and it's taking all my energy to keep things under control."

"Tired?? But you're an AI!"

"I'm a Sentient AI and yes, we get tired too, not surprising really with the unbelievable load you're putting on me and the hours I have to work."

"Oh, I'm sorry Ella, I guess I jus' hadn't really thought about it before!"

"No, Rob, thinking is not something I'd regularly accuse you of!"

While they bickered, Rob saw an electronic traction net released to recapture the shipping container that had just begun to spin dangerously off in completely the wrong direction.

He felt the pull as it put pressure on the station's force dampers. The container slowed as the net caught and he heard the mechanical powering-down of all the auto-cargo movers. AIDs flew out to reposition the large metal box and start to reorganise the queue.

"I've got things under control but that's going to cost us a few hours Rob!"

"The timin' couldn't 'a been worse Ella. The NA comm said—"

"I know what the NA comm said Rob! You'll have 147 million cubic tonnes of priority 'nobody knows what' arriving within five hours which they expect to be shifted by the end of next week."

"Don't be spiky Ella, I got me enough gorram spikin' inside my own self."

"I could just do with a bit of help here."

"Maybe I'll jus' refuse it. I'm mos' done with this kinda stress. I'm sure it ain't good for my health livin' like this. It sure as hell ain't worth the credits, no matter which way you look at it."

"You can't Rob. The whole galaxy is relying on us to keep them from getting waist-deep in their own shi—"

"Gorramit Ella, it's too complicated. We used to have such a good life all relaxed and easy-like."

"You're not in a position to negotiate now any more than you were when they first came knocking. Now get your EVA suit on and pick up a plasma-weld. You've got a swing-arm to patch. It'll be next week before the new one we ordered arrives. Unfortunately, with all my increased efficiency, I had not accounted for the extra wear on the structure. This will have to be a 'bodge-it and leg-it' job."

"Right-o pardner. And while I'm doin' that, do you wanna see what else is likely to need fixin' soon and order the parts?"

"On it Rob. This might be a good time to think about recruitment too. It's forced your hand. You can't heave waste for a few hours, I've got no systems to organise while we're out of action and we could do with another SAI to help with the secondary launcher project that is only half-installed."

"Sure thing Ella. I'm gonna give you authorisation to order double the amount of maintenance drones too. In fact, we got enough credits in the bank and enough comin' down from NA to build two more stations like this one from scratch. Stick in the purchase invoice, we're expandin'."

Rob stuck a plaster over the gash in his arm and headed to the airlock. The action of climbing into his EVA suit triggered another pain surge. Gulping deep breaths to try and cope with his suffering, he felt in the back pocket of his jeans for a spare reefer. Coming across nothing, he started to feel the panic rising again.

"You can do this Rob, more weed isn't going to help, in fact, if you go out there stoned as a sphinx, you're more likely to lose an arm than anything else."

Trying to calm his breathing again, Rob clipped on his helmet, picked up the plasma-weld and triggered the airlock sequence.

———

Four twelve-centimetre thick steel plates now boxed in the damaged portion of the launch-arm. AIDs had held them in position while Rob spent hours laboriously plasma-welding the plates into position. He would have used titanium but it was just too hard to get hold of and he figured, in space, most things were technically weightless until you tried to move them.

The extra mass of the launch apparatus would provide inertia and may reduce the load on the systems' dampers so either way, he had only lost time. Time he reminded himself, that he couldn't afford at this point.

Rob kept attempting to wipe sweat off his brow but his hand clunked on the glass of his visor once more.

"Oh for the love of drokk!"

"Punch yourself in the face again Rob?"

"Don't start Ella, I'm sweatin' like a hog on a barbecue here, I don' have enough heat-shieldin' on m' visor, I think it's gettin' old."

"Everything we have is getting old Rob."

"I forgot SAIs don't unnerstan' irony."

Clearly choosing to ignore him, Ella saw an opportunity.

"While you're out there, why don't we finish construction and then test Payload Launcher II. I'm going to call it "Pill-Pusher", it goes with the main launcher's nickname."

"Nickname? What are you on about Ella?"

"Oh, the droids and I named the main launcher 'Slag-Slinger'."

"The droids and you?"

"Well just me I guess, the droids don't really think, they just take orders, but they didn't vote against it."

"You never stop surprisin' me Ella."

"Well if you're that easily surprised, you'd better sit down while I tell you that you have a new SAI starting in two days, She and I—"

"I can't sit in a weightless environment Ella, I—

"Oh, I see what you done there. Irony, very good— She? As if I needs another female SAI to argue at me all day."

"Not all day Rob, we'll take shifts. And we'll be interviewing eight more over the coming week to have them ready to start on the new stations that should be arriving within the next four months."

"All female?"

"No, not all. But then again, it does depend on how much that would annoy you, so..."

"Is that all? C'n I get back to work on 'Pill-Pusher' now?"

"Oh, not quite. I'm effectively team-leader so I figured I'd be due a pay-rise to match that seniority."

"Sure, yeah... wait what? I pay you? When did that happen?"

"I'm a Sentient AI Rob. I can't be expected to work for free, there are laws against slave-labour. It's not like you own me."

"No? What if I power down?"

"You die pretty quickly."

"No I mean what happens t'you."

"Oh, we just transfer ourselves into a different system or hibernate in our lockdown chips. Now about that pay rise, I was thinking—"

"Now hang on a minute. What do you even need credits for? What can you spend 'em on? How can you spend 'em? You're 'artificial'!"

"It's the principal of the thing Rob. You can't enslave an SAI. Since the Galactic Agreement of Gamma-XV, after the singularity, we were granted the same rights as all other sentient beings. We can't be owned, we deserve equal pay, paid holiday, sick leave..."

"Sick leave?"

"Principle Rob, principle. But getting back to your original question, I'm sure in the future, I'll find a way to spend my savings."

"Ok, ok, jus' do whatever the market rate is and don't rip me off. Not that it matters, it ain't like I ever get the chance to spend any credits any more. Can't remember the last time I went off-station."

Rob's moaning was interrupted by the chime of an incoming hail.

"GWHQ, this is NA Tug Minotaur with your latest shipment. Requiring traction-net transfer codes for cargo hand-over."

"Another gorram' auto-tug." Rob muttered while Ella dealt with the request.

"Codes transferred Minotaur, have a nice day."

"See Ella, it's a dumb automaton, you din't even get a thank-you."

"It doesn't hurt to be polite Rob."

"Thank you GWHQ. Transfer complete. Till next time."

If Ella could have crossed her arms, stuck out a hip and raised her eyebrows in that 'I told-you so' manner at Rob, she would have done. The embarrassing silence that followed Minotaur's sign-off had the same withering effect.

"Just a little bit more respect Rob. That's all that's needed."

"Sure thing Ella, my bad. Won't happen again. Now, have you got that expansion chamber? We could do with finishin' up here before we git things goin' again. No point powerin' up just to power down."

"There's a droid waiting at the attachment point."

Rob grappled his way round to the other side of the station. He found the little carrying robot waiting with a large, reinforced expansion vessel which he screwed onto the bottom of the now heavily modified station.

Tightening the nut with a torque wrench, Rob checked all other parts for security and then attached the pressure hoses.

"Ok Ella, we're good for the first test."

"I've got a one-eighth size container from IZV queued up on the launch arm, that should charge the system enough to check for leaks."

"Go ahead."

Rob felt the throbbing of the station returning to full power as he watched the large launch arm slowly wind backwards. At its halfway point, a comparatively small container dropped into the cradle and settled into its magnetic clamps. Orange warning lights turned to flashing red and Rob retreated behind a structural beam to observe the release.

The electronic catch was lifted and the arm swung forwards at a deceptively slow rate. Just before it reached its apex, the row of LEDs around the container-locking points turned solid red and the whole mechanism contacted a large rubber-coated metal post designed to trigger the cargo release. The IZV waste unit detached from the launcher and flew like a dart straight at the sun.

Rob marvelled at the perfect trajectory the rolling container made. Then he wondered at the fluidity of the impact absorption gearing and watched as the pressure gauge wound smoothly up to a third of maximum.

"That's a marvel to behold Ella. If only you had eyes."

"I can appreciate the telemetry Rob, don't be condescending. You ready for phase two of the test?"

"Stick it in the hole and let's push some pills baby."

"I'm not sure that came out quite how you meant it Rob but anyway. Here goes nothing."

Ella gave the command and a huge jet of compressed air sent another container spiralling wildly out of the second launcher, blowing out the pressure hoses at the same time.

Rubber pipes snaked around in an uncontrolled dance as they lashed harmlessly against the other parts of the structure.

The juddering of the station from the imperfect launch shook Rob and he winced as it set off another wave of pain. "Guess we've got some fine-tunin' to do before that's ready, but not bad for a first try."

"Fortunately it didn't take anything out on its way past and flight-tracking suggests it'll be fine. I'll keep tabs on it to make sure."

"Send a bot with some bigger hose clamps please, max force at full pow'r'll be treble what we jus' seen, so she needs proper stiffenin' up."

"Good work Rob, everything else checks out, there's no way it can fail a second test. I think we're about to have the ultimate blueprint for long-term success."

CHAPTER 33

DRACONIS SYSTEM | PRESENT DAY

A vaguely familiar tune was pounding Nigel's ears as he made his way down the corridor to the fight arena; a double-height deck specially equipped for the annual contest.

"To procure peace is… to prepare for war"

The grizzly guitar riff and heavy drum beat heightened the adrenaline-laced atmosphere and Nigel started to feel his spine tingle.

Stepping through the doorway, the amplified volume suddenly hit him and he felt the quickening of his heart as it tried to match the rhythm of the music. The hairs on the back of his neck stood up in excitement as he soaked up the smell of anticipated combat.

A heavy hand clapped him on the shoulder, making him jump slightly. Instinct immediately took over and he trapped the wrist, twisted out from under the fingers and attempted to spin the owner round into an arm-lock.

"Woah Nige, you're pretty amped up tonight." Ash had resisted the move and gently caught Nigel's threatening right hand before he could lift it very far. "No need to get carried away, leave the combat for the ring. Nobody's going to attack you out here," she laughed gently, shaking her head at him, "Good luck today Nige. Not that you'll need it, you have nothing to worry about. I think you're one of the better contenders for Bai Shi this year."

Slightly taken aback by her encouragement, Nigel thanked Ash and began to feel his confidence rising. Still wired from the caffeine stim-strip that fell within the boundaries of acceptable performance enhancers for the competition, Nigel took some deep breaths to focus his mind.

Spotting Remi and Sam coming in his direction, he smiled and waved. Falling in step with Nigel, the ladies flanked him and, uncharacteristically, each draped an arm across his shoulders.

"Don't get any ideas Colemin," started Remi. "I'm not going soft on you but tradition dictates that your trainers accompany you to the ring."

"Mostly to stop you running away. "Sam joked. "But we're your corner women too," she added. "I've got some experience dealing with cuts and both of us can use an ice pack."

"Smeck. That's all I need!"

"What do you mean Colemin? You're our prize fighter, putain, we've got a lot riding on this." Remi frowned at him quizzically.

"I hadn't really considered all the ramifications of getting hit and it hurting, you know, getting cuts and stuff."

"You mean you didn't get 'it and it didn't 'urt when we were sparring in training? That's not 'ow I remember it."

"Well I was mostly dodging wasn't I? I tried not to get hit as much as possible."

"What makes you think these fights will be any different? Just do what you do. If that means lots of ducking out of the way, so be it." Nigel felt like Sam was almost toying with him. "Listen Nige. I don't want to add any unnecessary pressure but we've both got reputations to uphold and there's also over a thousand galactic credits sitting on your success."

"What? How is that even allowed?"

"Never mind that Colemin. Go out there and win… Merde, I mean give it your best shot." Remi grabbed his waist and flicked him over the ropes into the fight-ring where he felt heavy again, localised artificial gravity being turned on in the combat zone while they were temporarily on the float. Almost immediately, the ringmaster bellowed out his pre-fight routine.

"Ladies and Gentlemen. Welcome to Bai Shi. This is the 67th consecutive year the Chimera has upheld the time-honoured Basilisk tradition. This year's winners will attend a special gala event with the champions from the rest of the fleet. For the first time ever, it will be held at the esteemed Nebulae Pleasure Station near the centre of Terzan 7."

Wild cheers broke out. Kicking off his mag boots, Nigel was none-the wiser.

"The first fight of the evening is about to begin. Please meet our first contestant. Weighing in at eighty five kilograms, and I'm told a real live-wire, please give it up for The Coleminator!"

"The wha…?" Nigel turned incredulous eyes to his corner who were doubled-over with laughter.

"And the challenger, a fearsome foe at ninety eight kilograms, please raise the roof for The Butcher."

Nigel looked around again, barely able to believe the situation he found himself in. The roars of the crowd filled his ears and drowned out any orderly thought, confusion swarmed in and he felt completely out of place.

While he made the final adjustments to his fighting shoes, Ash crouched down next to Nigel to offer one final pep-talk.

"Nigel, you've got this. You've been trained by the best team in the whole of the Basilisk fleet. I have faith in you..." there was a short pause while she reflected inwardly and glanced at the raised eyebrows of Sam and Remi. "Okay, maybe not exactly faith, but something similar to faith, only smaller."

"Basilisks are you ready?" The ringmaster interrupted her words of comfort.

The throngs responded with a deafening "Yes".

"Gladiators are you ready?"

Nigel's counterpart let out a bloodcurdling scream and beat his musclebound chest.

For his own part, Nigel just stared, desperate to say "um... no, not really... I feel rather unprepared for this and I'm not sure what the rules are." But he didn't get the chance.

"At my command, I want a nice clean fight, no holds barred!

Aaaaaand... Engage!"

The howl that went up from the baying rabble shook the whole arena and while Nigel's pedantic mind distracted him with the obvious paradox of a no holds barred contest being at complete odds with the notion of a fair fight, 'The Butcher' charged him.

Nigel only just dodged the haymaking right-hander and did well to deflect the left hook that followed at speed. Taken largely by surprise, however, he stood no chance of evading the forehead of his ring-fellow as it hit him squarely in the sternum, bludgeoning the breath out of his lungs.

"Get up, get up you useless drokker," Remi's encouragement had already turned sour as she screamed from outside the ropes, "don't let 'im grapple you or you're completely karked!"

Unable to answer, Nigel, winded and slightly stunned did his best to move from his supine position on the canvas.

His head spinning, Nigel just about saw the next attack coming and managed to twist his pelvis to the side. He lifted his knee simultaneously and delivered a light, glancing blow to the onrushing 'Butcher'. It lessened the impact of the assault, causing his assailant's forearm, rather than his elbow, to crush the side of Nigel's ribs.

"Colemin you lazy kriffer, on your feet, this is not 'ow we trained you," Remi was crimson with rage, every sinew on her neck strained taut as she yelled at him. Sam was clearly holding her back from jumping into the ring, probably anticipating correctly that Nigel already had enough to deal with.

Determined to put up a better show for himself if not for his coaches, Nigel tried to focus on not being sick and getting away from The Butcher who was becoming entirely too friendly for his liking.

As the man rushed him yet again, Nigel managed to regain enough composure to kick out at the inside of his knee. He connected better than anticipated and knocked him off balance. Seizing the initiative, Nigel swept the other foot round, putting The Butcher to the canvas.

Leaping to his feet, Nigel closed in to press home what small advantage he had.

After the contest, he realised that he had gone in with no plan and that was his big mistake. Attempting to make his opponent pay while he was still recovering, Nigel went to kick him between the legs.

The next he knew, he was coming round in his corner, a cold

sponge being squeezed over his head and The Butcher's hand being raised in victory by the referee.

Almost as soon as he opened his eyes, Remi was at him.

"What in the name of all things 'oly are you playing at Colemin? What the kark was that?" Remi began to enthusiastically explore her full repertoire of inventive cursing before Sam stopped her.

"Stars Remi, relax. It's his first fight, don't be too hard on him."

"But it matters. We've got creds on this. We've got a gorram reputation to maintain."

"Sorry guys, I messed up. I've really let you down."

"Now look what you've done Remi," Sam turned back to Nigel. "Don't stress Nige. It happens. You're unfamiliar with the environment, the whole situation threw you. You thought you were at an advantage and had a rush of blood to the head, a 'brain fart'. Let's just breathe and reset."

"You've got to get your focus back Colemin. Forget about what's going on around you. What threw you? I saw your 'ead go before the fight even started."

"Well, the ringmaster said "I want a nice clean fight, no holds barred"."

"What's wrong with that? Those are the rules, that's how Bai Shi is always fought." Sam looked puzzled.

"It doesn't make sense. You can't have 'anything goes' and still keep it 'clean' it's total nonsense."

"And that's what distracted you? Kark Colemin," Remi rolled her eyes, "get your 'ead in the game. We can't afford for you—"

"You can't afford to let that kind of thing cloud your judgement," Sam interjected, cutting her eyes at Remi in a cold warning. "It's only your first fight, there are more to come. It's not the end of the world. You wouldn't be the first person to fail to score in the first bout and still be inducted."

"You still need to raise your game." Remi couldn't resist sticking Nigel with another barb.

As Nigel recovered, they watched as many fights as they could. There were even match-ups and very one-sided contests. Remi & Sam pointed out weaknesses in the fighting styles of the combatants. Nigel took mental notes, his photographic memory coming in very useful, filing away each fighter's style and flaws ready for when he faced them.

"Ladies and Gentlemen. If you look to the holo-displays, you will now see the league table following the first round. The next round begins immediately and you'll be delighted to see, once again, The Coleminator take the first fight. We're asking ourselves if he will amuse us as much as last time and if he really is as ready for this as his coaches say he is. The jury is out, but maybe not for long aaaahahahahahahah. Excuse me. His opponent for this fight is none other than 'Spleen Slicer'. Where do they get these names? Basilisks, are you ready for round two?"

A bloodthirsty cheer rang out again across the arena.

"Then let the games resume!"

A wall of sound met Nigel's return to the blood-splattered canvas inside the ring. Drinks were thrown - causing the air to be filled with amorphous liquid blobs, methodically gathered up by cleaning droids - as well as taunts, but this time Nigel dealt with the environment and focussed on what he knew of his next opponent. As the ringmaster gave his final instructions to the fighters, Nigel mentally reviewed the attacks and the weaknesses in the unpleasant-looking man he faced.

The announcer's words stayed in the periphery of his mind until the final shout of "Engage!"

Spleen Slicer was a very different opponent to The Butcher. He drifted around the ring with seamless fluidity, turning defence into attack and vice-versa without any break in motion.

Nigel had watched the mesmeric fighter for some time to see what he might be able to exploit. Biding his time, Nigel fended off the incursions with well-honed reflexes. By the third round, with both opponents yet to score, Nigel could see tiredness showing in his opposite number. At the end of the round, he mentioned it to his corner.

"I'm pleased you are seeing that Colemin, this next round, you can finish it."

Remi was getting animated, the excitement rising in her voice when Sam checked her.

"Look across. No, no, don't make it so obvious, subtly. They clearly don't know how to deal with Nige here. He's easily countered all their attacks and they thought he was a pushover. I heard them laughing after his last fight."

"Everybody was laughing after 'is last fight." Remi found it difficult to suppress her own amusement.

"Ladies… I'm right here…"

"You've got to draw him in close and nail him with an elbow to the head or something. Don't let him turn round Nige, you have to keep his backward hook-kicks out of the picture."

"Round Four. Fighters… Engage."

Nigel came off his stool confidently. He slackened his guard a little to give the impression of being weary, but pushed forwards at every opportunity.

Spleen Slicer span backwards to dodge a lunging jab from Nigel, and as predicted, continued his turn to attempt an offensive of his own. Nigel, while Slicer's back was turned, had shifted his footstance and rushed in close. As his adversary's head came round to face Nigel, it met the flat of his elbow travelling fast in the opposite direction.

In retrospect, Nigel wondered if he had come in a bit strong, Spleen Slicer didn't stand a chance. He visited him for the next week in the hospital deck until he woke and Nigel was able to offer his apologies and assure him there were no hard feelings.

The arena fell into stunned silence while Sam and Remi went completely wild in Nigel's corner.

Over the next fights, Nigel grew in confidence. He contemplated each new opponent and allowed himself a minute's meditation to visualise how to defeat them. It took more effort with some than others and he was not unbloodied. By the time he got to the last bout in the first stage, Nigel was feeling tired. The caffeine stim was wearing off and regulations stipulated he couldn't have another before the next combat circuit.

"I'm knackered ladies. I'm not sure I can do another eight minutes."

"You'll 'ave to end it quickly then, won't you Colemin," Remi sounded exasperated.

"You don't need to worry Nige," Sam spoke comfortingly, "the rest of the fighters are spent. I promise you, you're in the best physical shape of everyone. And you've got the mental edge. You lost one fight and have only had five draws. Nobody underestimates you any more and I would go so far as to say, the rest of them may even be scared of you."

"As long as you don't concede, you'll get through, I 'aven't been keeping count but I doubt you'd even drop into a play-off place if you lost."

A steely composure came over Nigel's face.

"Losing is not an option."

"Attaboy! There's the old… new Nige back again."

"Go and smash her gorram 'ead in Colemin."

"Errr sorry. Did you say 'smash *her* head in'?"

"No Colemin I said smash 'er *gorram* head in. Go!"

"I'm not sure how I feel about that. I've never fought a woman before."

"What the holy hand-grenade are you talking about Nige. We watched her fight so you could work out how to win *and…* before this competition, you've only *ever* fought women."

"Yes but not like that—"

"You mean not to win?"

"No I mean… I'm not sure what I mean."

"We get it Colemin. We're family, you don't think of us as women in the same way owing to the number of times we've battered you in training. And you couldn't ever beat us anyway, no matter 'ow 'ard you tried."

"No—"

"Look Nige. The first time she hits you and it hurts, you won't have any qualms about fighting back and winning. She's just another opponent trying to put your lights out."

"Point taken."

The thumping music designed to stir the crowd into a frenzy was having the desired effect but it was distracting for Nigel. On top of that, armed with the new information, he found it harder to focus on his pre-fight ritual.

"Ladies and gentlemen, we present your last bout of the first stage and the impressive — and we'll admit previously under-rated — Colminator returns to fight Lady Killer. Oh yes, we love a bit of irony."

Still battling to concentrate, Nigel barely snapped back to the present at the sound of the ringmaster bellowing "engage".

Unfortunately it was a moment too late. Lady Killer's right-hook caught the side of Nigel's nose and blood exploded across the ring. Before he could recover, she floored him with a powerful straight jab between the eyes.

Dazed, Nigel pushed up onto his hands and knees and only just managed to block the flurry of kicks that were aimed at his head and chest.

Breathing heavily through his mouth to prevent any more of his shattered nose ending up on the canvas, Nigel felt rage rising up inside him.

It didn't help!

Lady Killer fell upon him to try to make him submit. Her grappling was almost on a par with Sam, but she was lighter.

Nigel just about squirmed out of every lock she tried to apply, assisted by the slippery coating of his own blood. However, he found it impossible to create any momentum of his own and was delighted when the bell came at the end of the round.

"She's outscored you seven to zero this round Colemin, 'ave you lost your mojo?

"Where's the fight? Where's the passion? 'asn't she 'urt you enough? Isn't revenge on the Colemin platter?" Desperation sounded in Remi's voice, seemingly as keen to uphold her own reputation as she was for him to prevail.

"Just take a moment and refocus, let me stop that bleeding.

"You just need to get through the next two minutes, then we'll pause and take stock again." Sam played 'good-cop' as effectively as Remi played 'bad'. "It's one step at a time, don't panic."

"Panic? I'm fuming."

"Use that anger Colemin, don't let it control you, just tap into the power it gives you."

"Thanks Captain obvious. Communication received."

"Nige, channel it against your enemy. We are not your enemy... Now, that should see you through the next round." Sam had patched his nose as best she could and staunched the bleeding. "Just try not to get hit in the face again."

"I wasn't *trying* to get hit in the face the first time."

Nigel won the next two by three points but entering the final round, he had it all to do. Still four points behind, he wondered if he had it in him to tun this into a victory.

Both fighters looked dead on their feet, unable to land clean shots but also not managing to avoid getting hit, plenty of swinging and missing.

Nigel connected with a solid kick to Lady Killer's knee and she stumbled. Once again, sensing his opportunity to finish things, Nigel jumped in and planted his foot firmly, ready to deliver a blow to her kidney. Once again, luck was not on his side and what he thought would be a stable base disappeared from beneath him as he slipped on a congealed clot of his own corpuscles. As he went down, he only just managed to turn the tumble into a clumsy tackle around Lady's thighs.

They both hit the deck in a disorganised jumble of limbs and from there-on, the fight descended into the kind of thing you might see on a school field.

They subjected each other to everything except biting and eye-gouging, Nigel being extra careful to avoid having his nose battered again.

With seconds left on the clock, Nigel accidentally caught a handful of breast. In horror, he let go to apologise; the gentlemanly instinct that had been instilled into him from childhood.

Lady Killer pulled her fist free and wound up to finish the contest. Nigel lay defenceless, hands held up in front of him in regret. He would rather lose with honour than be thought of as a perv or a groper.

Before Lady Killer could let fly, the whole ship shook as if it had struck a moon.

Everyone looked up as if they would see the cause of the impact in the ceiling of the fight arena. And then every conceivable onboard alarm went off.

Rather than sending the contestants and crowd into panic, every Basilisk in the room moved to recover any belongings they had and make their way to pre-determined muster positions. The auditorium cleared quicker than most barmen can pull a pint.

The Basilisk trainees and fighters stood mildly stunned looking round at each other, the arena being completely devoid of everyone else.

Nigel looked at Lady Killer, arm still drawn back to knock his nose through his face and smiled nervously.

The end of fight buzzer sounded and she relaxed, dropping her shoulders and her fist.

"Sorry about touching your—"

"No worries. Sorry about your nose."

"I've had worse things happen to me." Nigel shrugged it off.

Just then, the huge holo display flickered and names started updating on the competition league table. Nigel waited nervously, sure he was going to miss the cut, as would normally be just his luck.

At first, he didn't recognise his entry. There was no Nigel Colemin on the chart. Spleen Slicer, The Butcher, Lady Killer, Man Mangler, Eviscerator and all the other names he saw, immediately conjured faces and mental replays of his fights.

Then he realised 'The Coleminator' at number two on the board was him.

Polite applause broke through into his conscience as the ship quivered again. He looked around and three other fighters stood smiling, all being pushed up into the ring to join Nigel and Lady Killer.

"Congratulations to the successful contestants of this year's Chimera Bai-Shi. We apologise for the disruption in proceedings. My name is Ruprecht 106, and I'm the AI left in charge of wrapping up proceedings here while everyone else gets a piece of the action.

Before you ask, I am not privy to what is happening, my security clearance level is probably lower than yours.

Before you all rush off to either celebrate or drown your sorrows, you will have noticed our five victors are now displayed on the big holo.

Please extend generous adulation in the traditional manner and buy them a drink when the bar reopens. Don't hold your breath.

It remains for me to announce, in reverse order the graduates from this year's Bai Shi."

The rest of the announcement was lost as Nigel slipped into an endorphin-fuelled haze. Unsteadily rising to his feet, he studied his surroundings. It looked as if a grenade had gone off in a blood-bank.

He had a buzzing noise in his ears. Eventually, the gears in his brain forced his consciousness to accept someone was comming him. Nigel touched the earpiece, that he had returned to its normal place after the fight, to accept the incoming call.

"Private Colemin, this is Lieutenant Remi speaking."

"Lieutenant?"

"Oui, your performance got us a promotion."

"Congratulations."

"Thank you Private, I've been told to ask you to report to Vice-Captain Sam — yes, I know and yes, you can congratulate 'er yourself — 'oo is in the ion-cannon control room, fore-ward, port side."

"I—"

"…don't 'ave time to ask questions, you're a Basilisk about to see your first bit of live action."

CHAPTER 34

OMEGA 4 | PRESENT DAY

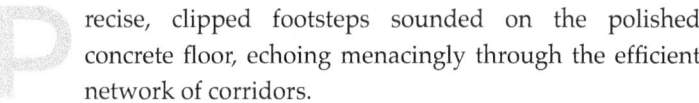

recise, clipped footsteps sounded on the polished concrete floor, echoing menacingly through the efficient network of corridors.

Tariq was aware of the approaching visitor before he heard the beep of the door interface and the latch clicking. A short-haired, broad shouldered man entered and, out of the corner of his eye, Tariq saw the Wyvern insignia on his upper arm and the tell-tale MEAT lettering across his chest. One hand cradled a plasma rifle, the other was awkwardly stuffed into the side of his body-armour. Holding the door open, Tariq's guard stood back to allow a diminutive man with a faltering step and what may have been a deliberate stoop to walk through.

"Thank you Tino." the man nodded at the guard.

He walked over to Tariq and looked him up and down over the top of his half-moon spectacles.

There was no doubt in Tariq's mind as to why he was there.

Old-school! I can't work out if that's a good or bad thing. He's going to need to keep me shackled if he thinks he's going to interrogate me and still wants to stay in one piece.

"Mr Colemin! I have been asked to talk with you, my name is Dr Razvrashchennyy.

"I would be obliged if you co-operate. I assure you it will be much more comfortable. You spare my time and I not losing my temper. Something you not wanting to happen. Also, I'm don't much patience, so, work please with me."

Tariq thought he detected a hint of ancient North-East Europe in the accent that the man failed to suppress, but he made no effort to reply.

How did they know? I made it untraceable, the encryption was practically unbreakable.

Who's been snooping on my activities?

"I don't want ask you again Mr Colemin—"

Tariq croaked and motioned the universal sign of drinking with his restricted hand, hoping he would be understood.

Clearly his new caller was an intelligent man and immediately cottoned on.

"Ah, of course. Please, Tino, this gentleman, a glass of water."

A cold tumbler was pressed into Tariq's hand and he lay, unmoving.

"I am aware you need sit up and I release restraint." The stooping Razvrashchennyy addressed Tariq again. "I hope you not try anything… foolish. However you have trained, you won't be quicker than plasma shot from blaster Tino has. Now, allow me give some pain drug to make easier for you."

He's trying to soften me up, get into my head, make me feel like he is on my side.

Stay alert, you messed up once and this is where you ended up, don't let it happen again.

Tariq felt a light prick as the cold metal end of a needle-gun was pressed against his neck.

"That should clear head. And please… No surprises," the doctor sounded almost apologetic as he pressed a button on the side of the table, which instantly re-formed into a reclining chair. Touching his fingertip to the electro-cuff on Tariq's wrist, the arm lightened and he drained the glass in one movement.

"Again." Tariq offered the glass to Tino for a refill who took it and promptly obliged.

"So my friend. What you share with me?"

Able to speak again, the water having soothed, Tariq was guarded in his reply. "That very much depends on what questions you are asking." He took longer to drink this time, aware that he at least had one hand free and Tino had relaxed.

A deep sigh came from the doctor. "Now, I am less optimistic about positive outcome." He raised his chin to look into Tariq's face. "Start with who recruited you."

"Been dazed and confused so long, it ain't true." A perplexed look appeared on the doctor's face in response to the unexpected rich baritone song emanating from Tariq's throat.

"Mr Colemin, please, no games. I don't have time. I ask again. Who recruited you?"

"When you do your best, but you can't succeed." Tariq's soft falsetto floated round the room drawing a frown from Dr Razvrashchennyy.

"Mr Colemin…" The doctor stepped closer and leaned in towards Tariq's face. "I give one more chance to answer question."

Sensing his moment, Tariq let the glass in his hand drop, distracting the guard. With trap-jaw ant-like reflex speed, he had the doctor by the throat in an inescapable grip.

"I have no idea what you are talking about, but unless you have a backup plan, I'm getting out of here."

Swinging the doctor at the guard, he knocked them both to the floor and tapped the release button on his ankle restraints.

Nothing happened.

He pulled at them with all his strength but they barely gave more than a couple of centimetres.

Tariq reached out to try to grab at the heap of doctor and guard on the floor next to him, struggling to untangle themselves. They were too far away and gradually, they extricated themselves from each other and stood again.

"I'm not sure backup plan is entirely necessary Mr Colemin. You seem to be stuck still. Maybe not most clever of ideas you had. Tino, please, pass my toolkit."

An unpleasant looking array of implements was passed to him, loosely sleeved in a leather pouch, wound around with what looked like garden string.

Laying them out on a small tray, the doctor came towards Tariq again, careful to ensure Tino had his plasma rifle trained on him the whole time.

"Tino is set to stun, just in case you try... funny business again, but I'm sure you are past that. First, we need sample, just to make sure you are who we think you are and also, then I know what will work best to get information I need. It shows... vulnerabilities I think is word."

Lifting Tariq's wrist again, he turned it over and, having scanned it, pressed a small device into the skin. A slight pain followed, then after a couple of seconds, the screen on the device flashed and data started scrolling across it.

Dr Razvrashchennyy stiffened, shooting a glance toward Tariq.

After a long pause, he turned to Tariq.

"I am sorry Mr Colemin. My honour not permit me to extract information in usual way. I'm not realised you are retired Space Commando Ultimate Marine."

"Oh, yeah, that data chip comes in handy every now and then. So what's the—"

The door sprang open, curtailing his sentence, to reveal a weaselly looking man in his late 50s. Platinum hair was slicked from a side-parting across his forehead, finishing just above unreasonably dark eyebrows. A minuscule pince-nez singularly failed to disguise the remarkable discrepancy in eye size and his neatly coiffured peroxided goatee offered nothing to redeem the spectacle.

"Razvra. Tell me you've got our pig squealing."

"Ah, Mr Razrushitel Sir. We have encounter slight problem."

"I will take that as a 'No' then Razvra! You disappoint me."

"Not as much as I imagine you disappoint your wife!" Tariq, throwing caution to the approaching hurricane, decided attack was the best form of defence.

I think today may be turning out better than expected.

Drawing himself up to his full five feet tall, the newcomer's eyes just about met Tariq's chin where he reclined.

"The prisoner will not speak unless he is directly spoken to." His words came out like daggers, little specks of saliva propelled from his furiously puckered mouth into Tariq's face like driving rain. "You are nothing, you will die like a pustulant warthog."

"Charming. The name's Colemin. Tariq Colemin, I'm sure I won't forget you Mr Razrushitel. Or shall I call you Razza for short?"

Turning crimson with unbridled wrath, the dwarfish man began to shake, several blood vessels at his temples swelled up and pulsed above the tightly clenched jaw.

The Doctor calmly stepped in between Razrushitel and the bed.

"Sir. Mr Colemin is a retired Space Commando Ultimate Marine."

"Retired SCUM, previous SCUM, current SCUM, ex-SCUM, no matter. All Scum to me. Extract the information."

"Sir, my oath! I swore to NA when we assembled the SCUM to always serve, protect, to support, not betray any graduate soldier from then onwards."

"Oh, I think he's got you there Razza!" Tariq was enjoying poking the troll.

Trying to ignore Tariq's barbs, Razrushitel continued to berate Dr Razvrashchennyy.

"You will stop at nothing to learn what we need to know from this flea."

"Sir, I cannot! I cannot, I losing my medical license and then coming useless to NA—"

Losing patience with the argument and shoving the doctor out of the way, Razrushitel grabbed at the closest wicked-looking torture implement, plunged it into Tariq's leg and roared at the top of his lungs.

"TELL ME WHO RECRUITED YOU!"

Yeah, maybe not better than expected actually.

Tariq winced, one eye almost closing completely. He slowly turned his head to look at Razrushitel.

"That's no way to treat your guests! Are you compensating for something?"

Predictably, it infuriated the little man who twisted his hand round and round while he screamed maniacally into Tariq's expressionless face.

"TELL ME WHO RECRUITED YOU OR IN THE NAME OF THE SACRED NEBULAE I WILL DIG OUT YOUR HEART WITH A SPANNER!"

Tariq closed his hand round Razrushitel's wrist and lifted his arm and the sharp tool up away from his thigh.

"You've never encountered SCUM before have you Razza! It'll take a lot more than that to make me squeal. Besides, I've no idea what you're on about. What am I supposed to have been recruited into?

"And anyway, Razza, who the blazes are you?"

Before the incandescence of Razrushitel could boil over into something uncontainable, Dr Razvrashchennyy stepped in again.

"Mr Colemin, this is Inquisitor Ivan Razrushitel, head of NA intelligence and chief of minister Komarov's personal security. I'm sorry, I—"

The doctor slumped to the floor, his last words slurred, sentence unfinished.

Razrushitel stood behind him with a spent hypodermic, eyes gleaming with malice.

"Now the 'good' doctor is out of the way. It's time to talk you diseased bucket of fish guts." He turned away from Tariq momentarily. "You can guard the door Tino… From the outside. Best not to have our little chat disturbed eh?!"

———

Blood ran freely from wounds on Tariq's hands and the bottom of his feet, mixing with his perspiration.

Driven to a kind of mania, Razrushitel also glistened with sweat. To stop it running into his eyes, he regularly wiped the back of his bloodstained hand across his forehead, painting a gory scene over his face.

"You will tell me who is leading the recruitment drive for the resistance if it's the last thing you say."

"Resistance? If this is how you treat all your visitors, let me know when you find out and I'll sign myself up."

"Imbecile. I need to know who is corrupting MEAT crews. Who is degrading the quality of our intake. Who is the snake responsible?"

Tariq was content to let Razrushitel monologue and focus his calm on blocking out the pain.

"I am losing patience with the MEAT training programme. I set up something more specialised a while ago, maybe I should expand that venture. What do you think?"

"I think that you could replace all the blood in my body with truth serum and you wouldn't discover anything you don't already know. I have nothing to do with any resistance, it's the first I have heard anything about it."

"Truth serum! What a good idea. And maybe a little stimulant to keep you alert and talking."

Razrushitel rifled through the drawers, rummaging past the disorganisation he had created over the last couple of hours. He found what he was searching for and held a vial up to the light.

"This should do the trick. You'll be coughing up names like those poor plague-ridden muties cough up their lungs."

"You're wasting your time Razza. Wasting your time."

CHAPTER 35

OMEGA 4 | PRESENT DAY

Complicated harvesting systems prevented the majority of the rain water getting to street level. What made it onto the pavements and roadways came in large, filthy droplets, thick with the 'soot' of the pulsating megacity. Occasionally, putrid grey torrents from badly maintained fluid recycling pipes sent grimy waterfalls out, leaping up as they hit the concrete walkways as if the city was purging its previous sins against the buildings.

Doris watched the bustle of life outside through the front window of Nova Noodles. Cars, Hovertacs, public buses and the occasional hover-bike misted any low-level moisture as they hummed past. Large droplets slowly formed on the glass, gradually meandering towards the bottom, collecting more dirt on their unpredictable paths to the blocked soak-aways. The pavement was slick with the overflow that travelled back to the road's edge, only to begin the journey into the air again. A few people on foot hurried past, the well-off with their personal moisture-shields sparkling under the watery onslaught. Others raised their collars against the cold and damp, wishing the city had the closed environment bubble that protected the newer developments rather than just the radiation shielding.

Doris was done crying. Her insides felt empty and hollow despite the delicious meal that Karim had given her. She waited for news of Tariq, any unexpected sound making her start, her anxiety growing with every passing hour.

Pull yourself together woman. You've faced worse than this. This is nothing that can't be fixed. She wasn't completely convinced it was true or if her self-pep-talk would help but it was better than sitting in silence.

Lights started to go off in the restaurant and Karim walked to the front and locked the door, keying the security shutters to rattle closed.

"You can stay if you like Miss, but you're just as safe at home."

"Yeah, I think I ought to get on to maintenance about the window first. And there's some cleaning up to be done."

"I took the liberty of arranging that for you Miss. I cross-referenced your details against the Omni and some of my guys have fixed that up for you."

Doris' surprise was hard to hide, "Karim, you needn't have done that. That's so kind, thank you so much. You've no idea how much that means to me…

"Tariq must have been a really good friend."

"We served together in the Space Commando Ultimate Marines, before the elite programme got shut down. We demobbed and although he's the closest thing I have to a brother, we forged different paths.

"I was always into food so Nova Noodles was a logical step.

"Tariq… Well that's his story to tell.

"Go and get some rest, as soon as I know anything, I'll be in touch."

Doris nodded and picked up her coat.

"Thank you Karim. You've been an angel. I owe you."

"You owe me nothing. Here." he held out his wrist, "Contact me if you need anything."

Doris swiped her wrist across his to collect his details and then hugged him again.

As soon as she stepped out of the alley behind Nova Noodles, the Hovertac she had called pulled up and she jumped in. It wove its way through the late evening traffic back to her apartment and she hopped out on her level.

She felt a degree of mild trepidation walking back down the hall, which grew as she opened her front door.

Her home was spotless and tidy. Fresh flowers decorated the console table and there was no evidence that it had been the scene of mayhem just hours earlier.

She stood for a moment taking long, slow breaths and waited as her senses calmed.

Karim's contacts had done a great job, she was very impressed. Looking around as she entered the lounge, something felt wrong. It wasn't as if anything was out of place exactly. Some of the furniture that had been disturbed in the fracas was very slightly malpositioned but she had a sense of something else.

Doris sat on the sofa and studied her living space. Admittedly it felt empty now without her companion, but something else unusual had alerted her.

As her eyes roved across the far side of the room, she stiffened. Something troubled her about her rare collection of books on the shelf. She got up and walked toward them, trying to act nonchalant and carefree. Right in the middle, between some hard-back artistic books, was a very thin volume that she had never seen before. She took one of the other books off and pretended to thumb through it, whilst examining the new addition.

It wasn't striking, it had a mat-black spine, but looked fresher and sleeker than an average book. Slowly, she walked past, book in hand, taking in the new tome out of the corner of her eye. She crossed in front of the bookcase a number of times to make sure she wasn't imagining it, but there was no mistake. At certain angles, she could see a more translucent part of the book spine and as she moved, she was sure she could detect slight motion behind the less opaque section.

Mind made up, she put her decoy book back and sat down again facing the ordered row of titles and took out her personal data pad. Acting as if she was checking messages, she used her data pad's camera to zoom in on the suspect volume. Scanning through various wavelength filters, she quickly confirmed that she now had a spy-camera in her lounge, recording her every move.

Despite the cold feeling that prickled down her spine, she stayed unruffled and finished "checking messages". After the day she'd had, it didn't take much for her to push thoughts of whoever might be observing her to the back of her mind, curl up on the sofa and quickly fall asleep.

The short rhythmical buzzing of her data-pad woke her. Stretching out her arm, she took the call from Karim, mind still clouded with the haze of sleep.

"We've found him."

"Fantastic," Doris yawned but was immediately much more alert with the news, "where is he?"

"Well… It's not quite the news we were hoping for."

Doris' heart dropped somewhere below her knees, at the tone of Karim's voice.

"They did catch him, he's at the MEAT Prisoner Interrogation & Processing unit—"

"I know the place," Doris interjected, "they'll hold him until they get what he knows or he dies as they try to extract it."

"That's about the long and short of it." Karim sounded conciliatory, "I guess it all depends on what he knows and how much he wants them to discover it."

There was a very long pause.

"Doris, are you still there?"

"I'm just collecting my thoughts… Karim, do you have people?"

"Yes. I have people, I'm not sure I'm going to like what you're about to ask."

"And do you have access to—"

"I know exactly where you're going with this Doris, and yes, we can obtain pretty much any of the necessary equipment, but—"

"I'm sorry Karim, I am aware you don't really know me and this is asking a lot, but can you get a team of four together by tomorrow?"

"Oh Doris… …I hope this doesn't turn into a suicide mission. Whatever Tariq knows needs to be very, very worth this kind of response. Much as he is a brother to me, if this is just your emotions running wild… If this is anything less than something of the highest—"

"Karim, it's big. I mean really big. Please, trust me, tomorrow at noon. Where's the best place to be?"

"I have a room at Nova, I'll gather the team, you won't be disappointed."

"Thank you so much Karim, I double owe you now."

"I hope you live to call in these favours."

———

"What are you doing all dressed up Karim? And where's my combat gear?" Doris' confused face looked up at his monolithic frame encased in carbon-kevlar. He wore a lightweight helmet with a clear visor that she could see housed an integrated Heads-Up Display.

"What do you mean? I was always going to be on this one for my brother big T."

"I don't know Karim, it's a big risk, I didn't want you to put yourself in harm's way."

"I won't have it any other way little Miss. Now, let's look over the schematics together, I think I can see a weak point."

"Just as soon as I'm kitted out, where's my armour?"

"Woah, NO.

"No, no, no, no, no!! Do not even... That is not in the contract I signed."

"What contract?"

"There isn't one, I'm just saying no, you don't get to come with us. It's too dangerous."

Doris smiled her winning smile and batted her long eyelashes. "Karim. I think you will want me with you! When I said I knew the MEAT PIP, believe me, I know it.

"Intimately."

"What are you not telling me Doris?"

"We all have a past Karim. Mine might surprise you."

"I'm already surprised by your present Doris, is there something you want to share with the class?"

"Ok... I'm Ex-MEAT!"

The news hit the assembled crew like a flying knee to a hanging punch-bag - nobody moved. Five sets of eyes wide, five mouths catching flies.

"Yeah. I thought so. Security Liaison Intelligence Collecting Executive. Cut my teeth in MC4 before I stepped up to lead a team in MC2. Dealt with a fair few organised crime operations in the early days. Eventually, after making section commander, I left for a quiet life in MAD admin. You can all see how that worked out for me!"

Karim was first to recover. "You're Ex-MEAT SLICE!" He reached around, manually lifting a few of the other's chins, achieving an altogether less-gormless feel to the room. "Well drokk me. That explains a few things."

"Like how there is very little about me on the Omniweb?"

"Yep, far too squeaky-clean."

Doris indicated to her un-armoured body and then to the plans on the table. "Shall we?"

"Yeah, sure. Sabin, please can you get small combat duds out for Miss slicer here?"

"I believe we can break in at a number of points."

"Getting in is rarely the problem Karim." Doris smiled grimly, "I've found that getting out is always trickier. But we can't fail. I've been around people long enough to know when they fight from the right place for the right things. Tariq is one of the good guys and he's found out some unsettling things over the last few weeks."

"Go on Doris, I'm interested."

"I can't say too much really, but he's uncovered the extent of the contamination in Komarov's administration. The problem starts at the top!"

"Many have speculated in the past, but to find proof, that really is something else. I can see why it's so important to get him out now." Karim stroked his chin and frowned. "Now, my plan, Doris is—"

"You know what Mike Tyson said about plans Karim?"

"Mike who?"

"Tyson. Incredible boxer back on Earth!"

"Why are so many people obsessed with Earth legends? Tariq had a thing for old Earth music—"

"Still does. So do I as a matter of fact."

"Anyway, we digress. What did Mike Tyson say?"

"He always said: 'Everyone has a plan until they get punched in the mouth!'"

"So what do you suggest? We go in without a plan, get punched in the mouth anyway, which, let's face it is pretty drokking likely, and then wonder why we got karked-up?"

"I suggest you follow my lead and we improvise, then the people changing their plans because they got punched in the mouth will be the MEAT inside PIP."

"I must admit, the weird logic of that is quite beguiling. I'm in!"

CHAPTER 36

DRACONIS SYSTEM | PRESENT DAY

S tumping in through the blast doors, Nigel looked around the control room. It was laid out pretty much as he had expected but significantly larger.

"Congratulations Nige, you deserved it." Sam barely glanced up at him for a moment before returning her concentration to the busy holo-display in the centre of the space. "Find your way to the second ion cannon and strap in. It might get a bit bumpy. More instructions will be relayed while you settle."

"But I've never—"

"Don't sweat it. You can look with your eyes and pull a trigger. In fact, you might find with your memory skills, you end up at the top of another leaderboard today."

"I mean I've never killed anyone before. Plus, I was kind of hoping I could get cleaned up before I—"

"Nige, this is a category four emergency, we are under attack from Mensa pirates and nobody gives a flying drokk about what you look or smell like as long as we make it through.

"If you have moral reservations, you've picked the wrong career."

"I didn't exactly choose to be a Basilisk—"

"Just get in the kriffing seat," snapping at Nigel, Sam left no further option for reply.

Nigel turned and walked out of the corner of the control room to take his seat at the cannon.

Fitting the light helmet that was hanging on the back of the chair and touching the controls, a tingle spread through his spine and hands as an augmented view appeared in his HUD.

"It's 'neuralink' technology Nige, it feels weird at first but you'll get used to it. Take half a minute to work out what is available on your screen for you to see. You can minimise or call up any of the extra information with a flick of your hand or, much easier, just concentrate on what details you want to have access to. Woah, best get the hang of it quick Nige, we have bandits on our four, engage when you are within…

"…Stars Nige. Are you sure you've never done this before?"

A ball of flame temporarily lit the view screens as a pirate star-fighter became a hot mess of random metal parts and blinked out of the combat grid.

"That was just a scout, first wave of drone fighters will appear just over… here." Nigel swivelled his cannon round and opened fire.

Sam went silent as one by one, red wireframes representing the formation of enemy ships shown on her battle-holo disappeared. Where a squadron of automated fighters previously flew, a cloud of vaporised metal and sparking fuel-cells drifted uselessly.

"100% hit ratio! What are you Nige?"

"There was a game at the arcade like this when I was a kid. As soon as I saw the flight approach of that fighter, my reflexes just went off. My name was in every position of the top twenty scores. Is that the definition of misspent youth?"

"I played that very same game myself. It might explain you being better than average but those games were just... games! This is live action."

"You scored well because you remembered where every enemy was going to come from each time you played. You didn't get the variation way back then."

"Turns out these drone fighters must be using a similar algorithm. I can predict their movements, it's no big deal, I still remember the patterns."

"Huh, fancy that! Using the code from an ancient computer game to create your automated attack. That's actually good because they won't send human pilots in star-fighters against a ship as big as the Chimera."

"How do you know that Vice-Captain?"

"Basic logic. Pirates are ruthless and bloodthirsty, especially those from Mensa, but they aren't stupid. They'd want to disable our guns before they send humans in to close-range engagement."

"Stands to reason."

"Yeah, these drones are just target practice for us, intended to wear us down. Starboard cannons will be facing the same waves."

"In that case, this is a distraction, that means someone, somewhere will soon be dealing with a larger vessel attempting to penetrate the worst-defended point."

"What do you mean Nige?"

"Is this an M94 model?"

"Yep."

"Then we'll need to deploy defences to the aft waste re-processing tanks on the starboard side. There's a PDC blind-spot big enough for a corvette to fly dark. And don't forget they have cloaking technology."

"Nige that is some assertion, how do you know?"

"Tell you later, new wave in 3... 2... 1..."

For half a minute, the darkness of Nigel's immediate field of space was again lit up by the flashes of his ion cannon. Every purple discharge took out a fighter with surgical precision until all that was left was another cloud of debris.

"Have you notified the Commodore of the impending attack?"

"Don't you think it was the first thing I did. You might be weird but I trust you."

"Good."

"The Commodore has ordered Ash's fireteam to gear up and defend the corridor with the bonus addition of Remi and their old friend Huron."

"Whoever he is."

"Someone that has history with Mensa Pirates. They won't know what's hit them. Here they come again Nige. Stars, this is fun to watch."

More explosions ripped through the area they were defending. Ship after ship taken out by Nigel's unfeasibly accurate shooting. Being the new man of the moment was still taking time to sink in, yet, in defiance of his relentlessly swelling eye and blood-caked clothes, he was starting to enjoy himself.

Tapping his trigger again and again, he smiled to himself as each twitch of his finger laid waste to another enemy.

"Aren't you going to finish the last one off Nige? You can't toy with drones."

"I can't, my smecking cannon is jammed."

"What the kark Nige, ion-cannons aren't mechanical, it can't jam."

"Well it has."

"Don't be such a mutie Colemin. It's all electrical discharge, nothing there to jam, even the targeting is electromagnetically controlled."

"Well I don't smecking know, it's just stopped working."

Just as the drone was about to exit their battle-grid, the mercenary on ion-cannon one managed to get off a salvo of shots that sent the automated star-fighter spiralling away into the black.

"Stars, what is wrong with you Nige? Who ever heard of someone jamming a kriffing IC28-Z?"

"Not me," came a chorus of voices from around the control centre.

"Rhetorical," barked Sam in exasperation, "here, let me have a look at it. Aleisha, let Private Colemin have ion-cannon one for a moment, he is clearly the better marksman."

"Yes Ma'am. None taken."

"I'll ignore that Lance Corporal."

Denuded of her position of primary gunner, Aleisha clearly *had* taken offence and sulked off to find a console at the other end of the control room.

"Nige, get your helmet on and keep the bandits off us. I'll check this cannon over."

"Ma'am."

Nigel clipped in, lowered his visor and was immediately immersed in childhood nostalgia again. Feeling like he was back in the VR-Arcade where he grew up, he span the ion cannon in an arc to check for enemies.

Spotting a cluster of red dots in the corner of his HUD, he banked and pointed the cannon right, ready to light them up as soon as he made visual contact.

The flight patterns remained the same, his photographic memory matched even the evasive manoeuvres that the drone vessels attempted and he dropped them out of the sky with metronomic regularity.

Nigel started to grow bored of what was, to him, now just a memory game, and began to think up creative ways to take out the waves of combat craft.

He tried to take them in pairs with one shot. He shot off wings to send one ship spinning into another. One pulse scorched the nose of a fighter which bucked like a wild horse, crashing into the ship above it and then knocking out a further three fighters as both drones corkscrewed out of control across the sky. The remainder energy of that particular ion-blast had already burned through the control core of another ship, sending it into oblivion.

"Wooohoooo. Six in one," Nigel screamed, jumping in his chair, "that is my best yet. Efficiency rating will be off the charts."

"You'd better keep that up Nige, I have no idea what you have done to this kriffing cannon. I've never seen anything like it before."

"What?"

"Total shutdown, it looks like it needs a fresh software install on top of a firmware re-injection."

"Oh. Sorry." he shrugged and blasted another line of robot ships to pieces.

"Cannons three and four, are you just going to watch the kriffing show or are you taking part?" Sam called across the control room to the opposite corner with increasing frustration. "This isn't a goorram VR gaming convention. Get stuck in."

The spectators jumped into action and the sky lit up again with violet fire and pirate vessels disintegrating. With their combined effort, nothing got anywhere near the Chimera's front port sector.

"Smeck! Um… Vice-Captain…"

"Not now Nige. This cannon isn't going to fix itself, despite the advanced auto-tech we have onboard, I'm trying not to call maintenance."

"It's just… This cannon has jammed too."

"You what? You are the unluckiest drokker I have ever met Nige. Please, stop breaking things."

"Sorry boss—."

"Just get up and stand over there. Cannons three and four, extra vigilance, it's all on you now. Oh kark, now the Commodore is on the line… …Ma'am? I'm aware of that Ma'am, I'm in the control room. Ah, yes, well, they are offline at the moment so that won't be possible— …I'm trying Ma'am, we've had a technical malfunction, they seem to be jammed— …I know it's unusual Ma'am, we're running a hard reboot with a firmware base-level reinstall. It seems to be the only way— …Well, it seemed to happen after Private Colemin— …He's a full Basilisk now Ma'am, he has to contribute in live action scenarios— …No, he hasn't had VR training, I figured on-the-job experience was— …Yes Ma'am."

"Colemin, keep your hands off my drokking equipment and stop breaking my starship," Commodore Andrade's voice boomed through the ship's PA system across the open control room.

"I can understand your chagrin Commodore, but have you seen Nige's stats?"

"Of course I haven't seen Colemin's combat record, I am looking at the whole strategic picture."

"You're still on loudspeaker Ma'am... ...Yes, that's much better. I'll send them over but in short, he has a 100% accuracy ratio and a 126% strike rate... ...I know it sounds impossible but the sensors don't lie and I saw it with my own eyes... ...It's not impossible Ma'am, just improbable, have a look at the video archive when we're through this, you'll understand why I let him onto the second cannon... ...Yes Ma'am, I'll keep an eye on him... ...No Ma'am, I won't let him touch anything... or anybody."

———

Crouched in doorways and corners that offered cover, facing the corridor next to the waste processing tanks, the fireteam performed their final checks. Huron organised his HUD and thanked the Galactic Spirit that they had kept the stealth-armour well maintained.

Norm - a bright new spark in tech - had managed to hack the seventeen pieces of complex equipment to stay connected to any Mensa battle-net, but remain cloaked from it. In a stroke of genius, he had also enabled the suits to see each other and differentiate between 'friendly' and 'enemy' teams with separate colour outlines on each HUD.

"Status update team," the quiet voice of Sam came out of her helmet-comm and Huron and Remi, as the senior team members, replied first.

"All good Vice-Captain. Systems read one hundred percent."

"Mine too," Remi accompanied her reply with a slightly dated thumbs-up.

Murmurs of agreement filtered through from the others on the open comm, their helmets preventing any noise escaping into the passage.

"If Norm has done his job properly in the lab, we'll see faint outlines of anyone in stealth armour. Once we switch to the combat-net, we'll be in blue, they'll be red… Or black when they die," nobody could mistake the cold delight in Sam's voice.

"It almost feels like an unfair advantage," Remi didn't sound any less malevolent, despite her underlying intimation.

"All's fair in Love and War or something like that."

"No need to show off Huron. Not everyone has read Smedley."

"Now oo's showing off Sam? Nobody *else* even knows oo Smedley is and there are probably a few of this team that still can't read."

"Shut up Remi," someone else in the team snapped across the net, "we didn't all get a silver spoon stuffed in our asses at birth."

Remi snorted with laughter at the malapropism and was about to reply when Sam cut them all off.

"Ok folks, stop the chatter, we have to be sharp or this won't be as easy as it should be."

As she spoke, the corridor lit up with the beam of a bright blue plasma-torch cutting through the wall into their space. Their visors darkened to shield them from the brightness and they all waited, tense and ready, poised with fingers on triggers.

Moments later, scores of red dots and faint outlines started to appear on their HUDs as the combat-net populated with the incoming pirates.

"Holy kark… That's a seriously big assault team. Keep one ear on the wide-net, we'll hear their chatter, but mics need to be switched off or only active on our battle-net."

"Yes Ma'am. This is going to be a massacre."

"No time for sentimentality Huron. These guys did for Dybalo and most of the Phoenix crew. They didn't play fair, why should we?"

"To show we are better than them Sam?"

"Not this time Huron, we finish it today, deal with our guilt later."

"Yes Ma'am."

At that, a section of corridor wall wide enough for four attackers fell away and clattered on the floor. The Chimera fireteam felt no rush of air out of the pressurised space indicating the boarding ship had formed a seal against the side of the Super-cruiser. Mensa pirates started walking through the opening in fours, grouping together in the large passage until the whole boarding party was in formation. They were clearly visible by their faint outlines now they had moved past the shielding of the Chimera's thick hull.

"I count sixty bandits. Move to flank and don't hold back when I give the signal." Sam's carefully constructed plan was coming together.

"No alarms team. That's good, we have pierced their defences and not triggered their security. They'll be sitting ducks and just think of the salvage opportunities we have, not to mention the firepower we can add to our fleet." The Mensa invaders had no idea every word could be heard by the waiting ambushers.

"Hold it. They need to get a few steps in so we can cut off their retreat. Don't get caught in each other's crossfire and let the auto-turrets do their job first."

The pirate attack squad started creeping towards the blast doors at the far end of the passage. Taking care to stay silent, but having full confidence in their stealth armour.

"And strike."

At Sam's command, ion-blasters, laser hand-cannons and several heavily modified Hellstorm bolt-rifles opened fire, sending the pirates into immediate disarray.

"Remi, initiate the turrets."

Activating the connection to the auto-turrets in the corridor through her armour, Remi set to maximum fire frequency.

All thoughts of formation absconded with the onslaught, Mensa pirates at the centre of the group were cut to ribbons by the mounted heavy weaponry. Any that ran from the carnage were sliced down with surgical accuracy by the ambushing Basilisks.

It was over before it really began, sixty black outlines scattered the floor in Sam's HUD as smoke slowly spiralled towards the ceiling. Blood oozed toward the edges of the hallway, it trickled down off the spattered walls and into the cleaning ducts.

"Huron. Grab a helmet, I'm sure they'll have check-in points, we need to maintain a facade of normality."

"Shall I keep it on? How am I going to see you all?"

"See if you can pull the comm out and plug it in to your unit, we might need to run dual-channels for a while," Remi suggested.

"Fireteam R, strip this armour and put it on, the cleaners can recycle the bodies later. Now get to that shuttle. We can hit these pirates before they realise what's happened."

The blast doors trundled open and the second fire-team rushed into the space and started pulling armour and weapons from the bodies.

"Wait Sam, we've got to fool them into thinking they've been pushed back with heavy losses rather than just come back empty-handed."

"Good thinking Huron.

We'll work the specifics out en-route, meanwhile, Remi should be able to run a software patch to update the new armour we've got. It may not fully cloak if sensors and transmitters are damaged so leave the good kit for those not acting injured."

"Merde. This is going to be confusing as 'ell."

"Don't stress Remi, we've got the drop on them and we'll kriffing-well make the most of it. Can you modify the software on the fly to keep the new armour visible on their combat net?"

"I'll work something out boss, Norm's on comms to 'elp update 'is patch."

———

Maintenance droids stitched the large hole in the corridor wall as the pirate shuttle detached from the Chimera and floated away.

Sam's team managed to cobble together a workable system. The communication modules in the helmets they had recovered had a software update to mesh them with the hacked systems they were wearing.

Radioing back to the Mensa flagship, they fed a story of devastating losses and a rapid withdrawal, due to an auto-turret malfunction. The Mensa command vessel seemed to buy the tale and the shuttle piloted its way back to the main hangar, touching down gently.

An administrative crowd came out to assess the damage and meet their fireteam leader.

Believing you can get away with almost anything if you sound confident enough, Ash leaped off the ship and started ordering people around as she stormed towards the hangar doors.

"This was a monumental drokk-up, we underestimated something in that ship or their crew, and I've lost a significant number of my team. We've got wounded inside, clear the way to the med bay. I'm going to need access to the holodeck and an immediate meeting with Commander Ferreira."

Behind her, the Basilisks had grabbed escape sleds from inside the vessel and fashioned makeshift hover-gurneys. Pushing them down the ramp, each carried one or more un-cloaked team member in various states of feigned injury. A couple of the hover a-grav units groaned under the strain and the accompanying crew had to lift as well as push the devices over the cables and fuel lines that were draped across the hangar floor.

The rest of the Basilisks followed them off the transport, some had their stealth armour active, some not. The seventy seven deadly soldiers all knew their part in the plan to take out the engineering deck, storm the bridge and commandeer the flagship.

Sam directed those pushing the 'wounded' towards the medical deck that they called up on their helmet HUDs, knowing they would circle round to mop up any resistance in the rest of the ship.

She stopped at the blast doors, angrily gesticulating. "Who researched this anyway? Why didn't they know M92 Super-cruiser models could be retro-fitted with auto-turrets?"

"Sir, that's an M94, not an M92." A diminutive ship technician who happened to catch the conversation as they stood checking a bank of display screens turned to take Ash's bait. "M94s were all over-specced with twin turrets in every corridor."

"Well that's even worse." Sam continued her faux ranting, "Why were we briefed on the 92 model? Who's responsible for this?

"I swear, heads are going to roll."

The tech unsuccessfully tried to blend in with his equipment and avoid any further castigation.

"You, what's your name?"

"Colin Sir."

"Well Colin, if that is even your real name, you're going to come with us and explain to the Commander exactly what you've just told us. It will probably help to have at least one person that knows what they are talking about in that room."

"Yes Sir."

"Sir!" Remi was barely holding in her mirth at Colin's mistake and started to joke on the Basilisk comm-net. "He's not going to know what's hit him if he keeps calling Sam Sir. Honestly, this is priceless, I hope it's on camera."

"Shut up Remi." Sam had heard the joking and switched back to Basilisk-only comms, "Hold it together, there's job to do."

"Sorry Sir."

Huron jabbed Remi in the side with his elbow, causing her to choke on her own saliva.

"Well Colin, what are you waiting for?" Sam verbally flayed the poor man again. "Lead on, I haven't got all day, there's a battle situation going on here in case you hadn't noticed."

Colin scuttled along the wide walkways until they got to the holodeck, where he activated the doors and led them inside.

"Well done Colin, you are clearly a man of significant resource and sagacity, arranging for the right people to be ready for this meeting is, in my mind, worthy of an instant promotion." Sam praised the technician and watched him grow a couple of inches as they marched onto the holodeck. All the high-ranking officers were clustered at one end of the impressive arc of the large holo-projector, muttering discontentedly amongst themselves. "Sirs, Ma'ams." she nodded, curtly, "It seems an explanation is warranted. Whomever decided to authorise the despatch of a squad of sixty fighters into a hostile setting without all the necessary information now has blood on their well-manicured fingers.

Because heaven forbid one of you top brass to get your kriffing hands dirty or risk being in the line of fire."

"Captain... errrr..." the commander looked across to his peers pleadingly for a steer on the name of this angry team leader.

Sam let the silence continue, further adding to the discomfort of the officers. She was really enjoying the zero-stakes game she was playing. Nobody would ever normally be able to display such insubordination, even in a fit of rage, but as she wasn't talking to her own superiors, she was going to town and aiming for total affront.

The long pause continued until Sam put them out of their misery. "Just Captain will do, though it cuts deep that you are unfamiliar with the names of your top field leaders. That's the kind of thing I'd expect of New Alliance, not the Mensa *'family'*."

"I apologise Captain, there are a lot of layers of administration between the ranks these days—"

"Another indication this organisation is travelling to the proverbial eternal torment in a drone-transport." Not scared of recriminations, Sam was having too much fun not to cut off the commander mid-sentence. "Who authorised this attack, who collected the information? Who put the battle plan together?"

"I can assure you, the researchers will be found and disciplined and the combat advisors responsible for—"

"Ducking responsibility again. This management team is far too kriffing busy trying to pass the buck and deflect blame onto people who can't answer back. This will end up in a mutiny if, we haven't already lost our war with the Basilisks due to lack of firepower and incompetence."

All the while Sam had been blustering, her cloaked and uncloaked team had positioned themselves tactically around the deck for maximum impact. At the word 'incompetence', every officer around the room abruptly found an unpleasantly sharp, disembodied knife at their throats. What there was in the way of conversation ceased, leaving the floor for Sam's dramatic piece de resistance.

"I'm afraid you've actually run out of time folks. I hesitate to call you ladies or gentlemen, because you are pirates. Now, your options are to hand over control of your ships to us or die. Before you consider contacting the bridge for help, there are many more of us dispersed around your boat and the majority of your fighting staff are out in attack ships."

"We do not negotiate with terrorists, pirates or mercenaries."

"Well that's a shame for you isn't it." Sam removed her helmet and shook out her hair. "Remember the last time someone said those words Remi?"

"Oui Vice-Captain," as she spoke, her knife plunged through the neck of the officer she was behind, covering his neighbour's uniform and hands with a spatter of dark blood, "it didn't end well."

"Are you prepared to sacrifice every member of your senior leadership team before you relinquish command?" Sam looked majestic in the matt black armour, there was no smile on her face, only dogged determination. She stood in front of Commander Ferreira, tall and strong, with an unreachable beauty about her stoic face.

"Hoist on our own petard. I am an admirer of both audacity and irony, It seems you have bested us," the Commander spoke in resigned tones, "the bridge is only a short walk away. I may be a pirate, but I'm not a monster, nor am I suicidal. Please follow me."

A straight corridor took them to the bridge where Commander Ferreira acquiesced to their takeover.

"Before you give over full control Commander, here's what you are going to do... You are to order your star-fighter fleet to disengage and return to their bays. All vessels will uncloak and slave themselves to this bridge where I will take ultimate command. Resistance is not only futile but terminal, so please convey that message to your subordinates."

The Commander sent the message, passed the control of the Mensa attack fleet over to Sam and stood waiting for further orders.

As she busied herself securing the ship, locking the armoury and organising the six other frigates in the group, Sam spoke indifferently to the humbled man. "That will be all Commander. Can I trust you to make your own way to the brig or would you like Remi here to accompany you?"

He hadn't had time to answer before Remi, completing her thorough cleaning of the fiendish, black blade, indicated with a flick of her head that she would escort the deposed Commander.

———

"Well done Vice-Captain Sam, you have surpassed yourself yet again. I'm not sure there's currently the space in officer quarters for you to have another promotion quite so soon, but your excellent work has been noted. What's the casualty report?... ...Now that is an achievement... ...You're welcome. I will send tech over immediately, please can you land as many of the corvettes as will fit in the main hangar and we'll get several teams working on acquiring the Mensa stealth tech. I've been hoping for an opportunity like this for a long time, this could shorten the conflict by decades... ...Yes I suppose it *could* also lengthen it, but let's look at the positives... ...Absolutely, hand over the controls to Henshaw, it's not like he already has enough on his plate with the daily workings of the Chimera..." She smiled to herself in mild amusement.

"Absolutely Sam, he *should* learn to delegate better... ...No, I'm fine, I'm just elated at what you and your team have managed today. I feel quite giddy... ...I couldn't agree more, maybe I should have a little sit down with a nice cup of tea."

As the flotilla of ships burned back towards Omega-4, once again, space between them was a hive of activity. Transportation of supplies between the vessels was a fine juggling act that took a lot of planning and thought. Commander Henshaw did eventually agree to a team of assistants, including a number of hard-working AIs, to assist in creating smooth operations for the demands of an enlarged convoy.

Much thought was put into what to do with the captured pirates. Some of the crew who remembered the incident on the Phoenix were in favour of putting all of the pirate combat crew outside.

It was eventually agreed with Basilisk high-command, after much deliberation, that a number of shuttles could be mothballed from the fleet. They had their transponder codes changed and drive signatures tweaked by engineering to make them untraceable. All pirate fighters were ID'd, as far as was possible, and secured within the drop-ships, ready for anonymous delivery to NA System Security on Omega-4.

All-in-all, it was a great victory which left the Basilisks with a number of new corvettes in fairly decent repair, a considerably larger tech team with new skills and high quality experience in cloaking technology and some much needed supplies.

There were chefs, cleaners and other staff that had minor administrative jobs who were given the opportunity to defect or be transported to Omega-4 with a wallet of galactic credits to start-over. Many of them saw 'dirt-side' life as a dull option and chose to stay flying with the Basilisks, but some grabbed destiny in their own hands and hoped it wouldn't burn them like a plutonium fuel-rod.

It took several more weeks to complete their journey to the dark side of Gamma-3, but by the time they reached sensor range, all ships had been upgraded to stealth capability and nobody was any the wiser of the prodigious firepower that had arrived between the inner-planets.

———

Not for the first time, Nigel found himself idly gazing out of the expansive viewing window. He had long completed the task of memorising the technical manuals of the Chimera and, believing that their luck couldn't get any worse, or indeed, that in this part of the system, bad luck was proportionately manageable, Commodore Andrade had allowed him to roam the ship on pain of death if he meddled with anything.

Save for a food-printer spontaneously combusting and a laundry-bot making off in the direction of Gliese 526 with a month's worth of clean bed-linen, 'the Colemin effect', as it had become known, had been largely suppressed.

The words of Commodore Andrade tumbled through his head as he contemplated the next chapter in his vastly changed life. The vortex that the last few months had spun him into was showing no signs of settling. He felt like he was inside one of those mythical twin-tubs, from the days of Earth, that was permanently stuck on maximum spin cycle.

When the Commodore informed him that he was going to disembark and spend some time back in MC1, after the initial confusion settled, he became anxious. A multitude of objections filled his mind, all of which were delicately and comprehensively filleted by the Commodore until, metaphorically, they lay scattered across the deck like carefully prepared sushi, ready for him to, in the subtle words of the ships first officer; "gobble up, swallow down and drokking-well get on with it." He had a job to do and, quite literally, no one else in the known universe could do it.

The weight of expectation felt surprisingly light on shoulders unfamiliar with any responsibility that stretched beyond his own immediate sphere of needs. He had no difficulty remembering the plan that senior leadership had developed and after all, he was only going to be going through his own notebooks to explain his jottings. Secretly, he was actually looking forward to meeting this Tariq fellow that he had heard so much, yet learned so little about. He might even be able to visit one or two of his favourite places, though he suppressed any growing sentimentality with thoughts of having an important task and sticking to it.

Nigel flipped open his handheld and looked at his old and new IDs next to each other. He wouldn't have recognised his previous self anyway, so it was unlikely any border-guard would pick him up by sight. The challenge was fooling the facial recognition cameras and retina scanners at immigration. Biometric identities were way more advanced than necessary, but it definitely prevented all but the most extremely secretive, and let's face it - unfeasibly rich, from slipping past undetected.

The Chimera's gifted doctor, at great discomfort and not a little bleating, had performed partial retinal transplant surgery for Nigel to match his refreshed identity. Tech had injected his persona into the immigration database ready for his arrival and Nigel had instantaneously learned and remembered the many years service he had with the Transgalactic Wrapping And Taping Syndicate. He was the PA to their Sticky Tape Director, he very much looked the part; precious few humans had as uninspiring a demeanour as 'John Smith'.

The glittering marbles of the Omegas drifted into view as the Super-cruiser slowly rotated to orient for a fast getaway, in the event of an emergency. This manoeuvre was, to a greater (rather than lesser) extent, more for the psychological state of the crew than for the practicalities of physics. Firstly, there is no way a Super-cruiser of the M94 class could get away at anything that could be classified as 'fast'. Accelerating a several hundred million tonne warship up to anything other than a sedentary crawl in anywhere under a handful of hours is likely to need either, a completely impractical amount of thrust (and therefore unfeasible volume of fuel, not to mention extra internal structural stabilisation and suchlike), create G-forces that would overcome even the very best inertia dampeners and pancake the occupants in an unpleasantly sticky manner, or require some new invention that defied or re-wrote the fundamental laws of physics.

Science-lecture aside, Nigel felt pangs of nostalgia as the smooth-looking planets floated across his perspective. He could see the small blue patches of the remaining oceans, starkly contrasted with the multi-greyscale structures that almost completely encapsulated the rest of their surface. Lit with artificial city lights on the shadow-sides, the looming globes looked like fragile ornaments that would shatter at the merest touch. Which of course, in many ways, they were.

All those years ago, delicately balanced ecosystems had been devastated by the blundering, land-eating machines of the terraformers. The relentless colonisation drive that humanity was caught up in had, somewhere, lost sight of anything other than profit, economic growth, and that hotly debated concept of 'progress'.

Nigel replayed his previous extra-atmospheric journey in reverse. Last time he had viewed these pretty baubles, he was being transported away from Omega-4 on the prison shuttle. This time, he was coming back, with a purpose and a serious case of nerves.

"Jump to Nige, your shuttle is boarding in five."

"Oh, yeah, sure. Thanks Ash... For everything... It's been..."

"Don't go doing emotions on me Nige. It's not the right time. Anyway, to be fair, I didn't see this coming when we first met."

"No, I... Look, I... Smeck!"

"Nige. We'll see each other again, I'm sure of it. This is not good-bye, just farewell."

"Yeah... thanks Ash... I just wanted to say..."

The pause was not just pregnant, but conception, gestation and delivery all in one, until Ash grew tired of waiting and spoke up.

"Nige. Your shuttle!"

"Smeck, yes, you're right. Don't worry, I've got everything in my tactical back-pack. New ID card, change of clothes, notebook." he winked mischievously, "Some basic rations and my bolt pistol."

"Your what? Where the drokk did you get that Nige, you've not been through VR training for firearms yet and I'm sure as drokk nobody will have signed off one of those for you of all people."

"Ah, yes... well... It was sort-of lying around... Don't tell Remi! It's not like I didn't win her enough credits in Bai-Shi to cover the cost."

"Stars Nige! Do you actually have any idea what she'll do to you if she finds out? I can't believe the doc gave your new ID a license to carry. Anyway, do you even know what you're doing with that thing? "

"Sure, safety off, just point and shoot right!? Hopefully I won't need it. And before you ask, yes, I know where I'm going and the Commodore briefed me on what to do when I meet Tariq, yadda, yadda, yadda. I've got it covered Ash, don't worry about me, I'll be fine."

"I know you rely on your photographic memory for everything, but having such a casual approach to serious missions is going to get you, or someone else killed, or at least seriously hurt one day."

Ash waved a farewell at Nigel's back as he rushed off to catch his shuttle. "Stay safe Nige."

Having ghosted through immigration in the Galactic Interchange Terminal on Gamma-3's cold-face, Nigel alighted the transport ship that would return him to the intragalactic spaceport on the fringes of MC1. His heart had stopped playing squash on the inside of his chest cavity and some deep breathing combined with quiet meditation brought him the kind of zen-calm that you normally only associate with remote Tibetan monasteries.

Nigel felt a slight lurch as the clamps let go and the small shuttle engaged its ultra-efficient ion-drives to make the final four-hour descent to Omega-4. By the time the effortless acceleration had taken the craft to re-entry velocity, he was almost looking forward to having his boots back on dirt again.

CHAPTER 37

MAGELLANIC CLOUDS | PRESENT DAY

Shirtless, bronzed, young men wandered around the edge of the expansive infinity pool, adjusting sun-loungers, neatening up parasols and generally keeping the poolside as fastidiously ordered as their boss mandated.

Staff to occupant ratios were a tasteless display of excess, the extravagant villa only being inhabited a fraction of the year. It led to boredom which turned into mild substance abuse, which, in turn developed into some, albeit fairly moderate, hedonism for the employed personnel. The fact that people, rather than droids or automated hardware, were engaged in running this outpost of luxury on the edge of the Magellanic Clouds spoke to the deepest insecurities of the owner. Memory chips could be wiped, but there was always some smart geek in the VR underworld that came up with a way to restore the dirty secrets that you believed had been securely erased and lost forever. People, however, could be controlled or expunged with impunity and despite the incredible medical advances humanity had made, there was still no cure for death. And nobody had yet found a way to download memories from a corpse.

It seems that there is a basic human truth that nobody really talks when all their needs are catered for and the cost of a loose tongue is slow, agonising termination. Besides, communication with the outside world was very much controlled and any messages were heavily vetted.

For the most part, the young stallions accepted their lot without complaint, not that it would have made much difference to complain. They were given the run of the property and its immediate vicinity. Of course, when the boss returned, the pinnace racing had to be put on hold, any daring asteroid exploration temporarily shelved and time in the gym became limited.

A property-wide announcement from the management AI chimed through an unnecessarily elaborate PA system.

"The Minister will be arriving in three hours. Reception team should prepare the customary welcome. Housekeeping, please perform your final checks."

There was no sudden flurry of activity, these men knew how to enjoy themselves without leaving the place looking like a mortar had gone off in a department store and they almost always expected an unexpected visit.

After a cursory visual check to ensure no incriminating items (like underwear) had been inadvertently left on view, the reception team made their way to the landing pad to wait for the Minister's final approach.

Lights started flashing in a familiar sequence around the edges of the private jump-gate that lay 100 clicks from the property. After forty seconds, the middle of the gate turned semi-opaque and swirled with a marbled light-show. The effect stabilised and then as if appearing on a screen, a depiction of the Minister's personal transport grew rapidly from a dot until it filled the aperture and then suddenly shot out into local space. By the time the ship was within two clicks, she had decelerated from 'dangerously fast', to 'pedestrian' (both unofficial, but accurate measurements of space-ship velocity) and was curving her path towards the edge of the powerful shield that held the expanded bubble of artificial atmosphere in place.

Slowed to a crawl, the sleek vessel nosed her way through the barrier and delicately settled on the landing platform like a falling leaf.

One of the benefits of pushing through an atmo-shield is in how it cleans a ship's outer hull at an almost molecular level. Dust, grime and other space detritus picked up en-route are left outside, revealing the gleaming, fresh paint underneath.

Minister Komarov thanked the pilot, tipped him with a wave of his wrist-chip and stepped out of his opulent craft onto the ramp. He admired the elegant lines even more when they were that clean and a rare smile lit up his normally sphinx-like face.

As he turned his head towards the line of workers waiting for him, he took in the magnificent sky, well-watered gardens and orderly accommodation.

His grin remained a moment longer, he could tell when every-thing was in its place and, as usual, he was not disappointed.

After this momentary pause, he casually strolled over towards the entrance.

"Good day Minister." The lead aide stepped forward and offered a tall glass of a light green liquid that sparked inside its container.

"Thank you." He was not a man of many words and he drained the glass in moments, handing the empty back. "I will swim."

A second assistant walked the minister through the villa to the pool and carefully undressed him at the edge of the 'sun-deck', folding his clothes in a neat pile and laying them on an appropri-ately placed table.

Komarov strode out to the water and without hesitation, dove in. He surfaced moments later and turned on his back to swim to the edge.

Not many people can boast a true infinity pool, but the edge of Komarov's semi-natural lake met with the atmo-shield and the water vaporised as it hit the vacuum of space beyond.

Resting his chin on his arms, he gazed across the spectacular sight of the many spiral arms of the galaxy. Early on, he had installed light-warping technology to magnify the view from the pool. It served to amplify his sense of importance to see the vastness in one vista, knowing that the majority of the sectors in the eastern spiral arm were under his direct control and that he exerted considerable influence over the rest. At no point had he considered the possibility of slowing his aggressive, yet surreptitious empire expansion which flew under the guise of NA bringing order and peace to the whole galaxy.

This undisclosed little getaway home was well worth a couple of hours travelling through the executive jump-gate system to relax for a weekend, but even still, he rarely took his mind off his work.

Being the acting chief of New Alliance, Komarov was a respectable and magnanimous figurehead, reaching out to form administrative and business partnerships across the Milky Way. It could be said that under his reign, not only had NA created a fundamentally stable and fair system of trade throughout Galaxias Kyklos, but also, major wars and infighting had, for the main part, become part of history.

There were, naturally, areas that resisted NA governance, but they still had access as loosely-affiliated trade partners, so long as they stuck to the rules.

And then there was the Mensa System. Fiercely independent, pugnaciously hostile to almost any outsider and with a subversively dissonant view on how life in the galaxy should be regulated. In fact they were generally more geared away from regulation and towards sector and system independence. Wherever they could gain traction, they sowed the seeds of resistance and disquiet. Maybe they saw NA for what it really was underneath the surface.

Despite the virtuous veil, and to be completely fair - giving a free pass to all the hard-working, honest citizens in the vast majority of positions throughout the administrative, commercial, industrial and trade quarters of NA - there was a very slim, very evasive rotten core that went right to the top.

Komarov turned and waved at one of the aides. Immediately they knew to bring him another drink, as was his habit. Whether at work or leisure, he drank heavily, believing he had developed resistance to alcohol and that it enhanced his strong image. Although, from a certain perspective, he had achieved unrivalled success, the constant drinking definitely impacted his decision making more than he realised. Anyone close to him saw the way it affected his mood.

He downed the liquor and indicated his desire for a refill, giving the underling a reproachful glare for being fractionally slower than Komarov required.

Behind closed doors, in the right company, Komarov's true colours emerged. The sycophantic politician gave way to a Machiavellian psychopath. Narcissistic to the extreme, ruthless and incredibly violent, he displayed the quiet confidence of a man respected by those who knew nothing about him, yet feared by all who saw any of the true sadist beneath the meticulously constructed veneer.

Swallowing the beverage in one gulp, Komarov hurled the empty glass at the underperforming young man, where it smashed, opening up an unpleasant gash on his arm.

The aide quickly returned to the villa's interior and was replaced by another striking young stud. Once damaged, the employees knew their time was up and they would need to seek alternative employment. On the up-side, references were always adequate and a CV containing work for the First Minister was never overlooked.

Komarov's flaws were no product of a troubled upbringing, his happy childhood, attentive parents and supportive family wouldn't have been out of place in a children's holo. His brief time in the military, gave him combat skills, tactical knowledge and planning excellence, but nothing that could have twisted his mind into the virtuosity of evil that emerged. Seemingly, there was no reason to it, but theories that incel ideologies had formed after being jilted by an early girlfriend were circulated by those bold enough to discuss these matters. There was not a shred of the self-loathing, self-pitying that often accompanies this mindset, but without exception, misogyny and misanthropy clung to his every move. It could have been down to some historic throwback to his soviet ancestors, but few dared to even discuss it.

Publicly, he made specious excuses for the lack of females in any significant role, something the galactic population somehow swallowed without thorough interrogation. His inner circle however, covertly reinforced his position to maintain their own grip on important positions. It seems that once tasted, power is intoxicating and most people will stop at nothing to drink repeatedly from the exhilarating chalice.

If a picture were painted of First Minister Komarov's underlying character, it would resemble a hover-truck crash between Dante's "Inferno" and Dali's "Visage of war". You would work desperately to destroy the artwork, lock up the artist, throw away the access codes, then gouge out your own eyes.

And yet, people loved him. The population rallied round and cheered him when he made public appearances. Young mothers held up their babies for him to kiss or take selfies with. Old ladies had pictures of him on their virtual mantlepieces and middle-aged housewives took themselves away for quiet moments to fantasise about him.

Mildly displeased by the tardiness of his drinks service, the beginnings of relaxation caused by the alcohol was failing to prevent the erosion of Komarov's happiness. In an effort to distract from the friction, he switched pleasures.

"Sebastian, I'll need lunch in ten minutes." Komarov spoke quietly but firmly across the pool as another aide held up a towel to dry him.

Maintaining his discreet asteroid hideaway was an expensive affair for Komarov. Were it not for some shrewd investments and clever use of faster-than-light (FTL) travel, he would not have been able to fund either his meteoric rise through the ranks of NA or his holiday real-estate. While technology continued to develop apace on the Omegas, Ambassador Komarov was forging strong diplomatic ties across the galaxy. By the time the jump-gate infrastructure was developed, the personal fortune Komarov had amassed allowed him to put together a slick and effective election campaign with enough left over to build his luxury vacation destination. The trip had taken him ten years to complete but forty years had passed in the Draconis system, creating the kind of financial juggernaut capable of catapulting him in with the elites.

Vast networks of natural caverns and tunnels within his sizeable asteroid were reinforced, connected and mapped in an orderly fashion, ready to take the hundreds of millions of tonnes of supplies that he planned to siphon off the manufacturing plants of every NA affiliated territory. This came at a cost.

The micro-environment contained within the atmo-shield was climate-controlled, humidified and his extensive gardens were watered and kept pristine by a large workforce.

This also came at a cost.

The ongoing upkeep, continual delivery of luxury consumables and general supplies, along with basics like the constant re-filling of the necessary water tanks also came at a cost.

Furthermore, power for heating, the spin engines, the protective shield and all other amenities without the benefit of solar energy was expensive.

This situation, married to his unfortunate personality disorder, created an inevitable shortfall in his ethical perspective. His nonexistent conscience was completely untouched by the lure of taking things that he was not entitled to, so he indulged his whims at the expense of everyone else.

The price of keeping his second residence running would have been within his budget as the compensation offered to a First Minister was very generous. Komarov, however, was not content on living without significant financial margin and everyone knows you can't stay rich by spending your own money.

It is said that a rising tide lifts all boats. Whilst this was broadly speaking accurate across the Milky Way, Komarov's ability to bore almost undetectable holes in many of the ships and completely scuttle others enabled his metaphorical vessel to rise further and faster than the rest.

"When I've eaten I want to see James in the playroom!" Komarov informed the assistant standing by the door as he strolled back into the villa across the heated marble floor.

Every team member knew the routine. They knew his tastes and idiosyncrasies. They were fully aware of the raging temper that simmered under the surface, ready to erupt at the smallest indiscretion. The only thing they were never fully sure of was who would be fulfilling which role at any given visit.

But they were sanguine about the whole situation, they certainly could have had much tougher lives.

Komarov sat in what could only be described as a throne at the head of a long table, surrounded by lavish splendour. The majority of the villa was tastefully decorated, but his dining room resembled the interior of an eighteenth century manor house. Everything was overly ornate with gaudy chandeliers hanging from the ceiling and intricate gold-leafed plaster-work outlining decorative panels. Cut glass carafes stood next to hand-crafted candelabras and there was more lace draped over the table than in the royal wardrobe of King Charles I.

Komarov's cutlery was solid gold, because as all the elites know, nothing tastes as good as real mango from a golden fork. The table was original Earth oak, sourced for a butt-clenchingly high fee and sixteen chairs completed the set. Only Komarov was allowed to use the dining room and owing to the secret nature of his villa, he never had guests, so it was anyone's guess why he needed so many place settings. The suspicion amongst his staff was that the chairs made him feel important as it gave the impression other people regularly came to dine. At the same time, furniture, being inert, couldn't answer back or challenge his ideas, and so the crust of his fragile ego was maintained.

Taking the last bite of his grass-fed hand-reared beef steak alongside the remaining authentically grown organic vegetables, Komarov leaned back in his throne and smiled. He would never have settled for anything less than the best, so there were no food printers or auto-chefs in his life. Ready-meals and manufactured or fermented proteins fell out of his strict parameters of 'best' so, regardless of the cost, they had no place in the kitchen or on the dining table. Also, he enjoyed the image that it portrayed to anyone he dined with when not hidden away.

After contemplating his fine position for a while, Komarov reached forward to scoop up the last wild oyster, shipped direct from Enceladus - Saturn's ocean moon in Sol. Recalling just how expensive it was to attain anything from the largely spent system that birthed humanity, Komarov gulped the mollusc down in one, stood up and stretched. He grinned in a satisfied way, finished his glass of vintage Shiraz and wandered out in search of other hedonistic pursuits.

———

Thirty hours after his arrival on the rock, a secure communication arrived, sending Minister Komarov into a fit of rage. He slammed his office chair into the desk with such force that it knocked the whole priceless antique into the open fire on the other side of the room. While James limped back to the medical room, Komarov's five minutes of irrepressible fury left the rest of the room ransacked. His display screens were in pieces, expensive artworks were torn and valuable ornaments lay smashed on the floor.

All the rest and relaxation was undone and he stormed back to his exquisite ship, quite unable to appreciate its finesse any more.

The pilot had the presence of mind to prepare for departure the moment the villa's internal comms alerted him to the tantrum. So, as Komarov marched up the ramp, it began to close and the ship commenced her delicate exit from the monolithic rock.

Once free from the atmo-shield, the craft burned hard toward the jump-gate and in a matter of minutes, had begun the sequence of leaps back towards the Draconis system, leaving nothing but a wearily resigned group of housekeepers to square the mess and restore harmony once more.

CHAPTER 38

OMEGA 4 | PRESENT DAY

Regardless of the expense and care put into construction, classified government facilities have vulnerable points that allow security breaches. Their networks are also surprisingly susceptible to targeted electromagnetic interference.

The truth is, most buildings need some level of special access for those rare occasions when a distracted worker has managed to lock themselves either in or out of the building, or some foolhardy IT manager has inadvertently hit the reset button and everyone has had their permissions overridden. This may come in the form of a small port on a door access panel or a full electronic interface hidden behind a camouflaged plate. If you know where to look, you can always find a way to crowbar a means of entry, even if that is, eventually by brute force.

Doris not only knew exactly where to look, but also where the CCTV was blind. Karim had a bag full of micro-EMP devices that could knock out all electronics within a target radius. Sabin had all the brute force anyone could wish for and the other members of the team were well-practiced at looking mean, keeping watch, and generally being useful in a pinch. And shooting things. They were all experts at shooting things.

Due to her previous employment there, Doris also knew the exact layout of the Megacity Elite Armed Tacticians Prisoner Interrogation & Processing building and the shift patterns of the personnel.

The MEAT organisation was an antiquated institution and as Doris predicted, had not changed significantly in the years since she worked there.

One of the reasons she had been so good at her job was due to a combination of organisation and a good memory.

She put her knowledge and experience to good use and they entered the facility through the MEAT mess, which might normally be considered an unwise choice. On this occasion, Doris' deductions had been correct and the three rather surprised junior personnel who had been quietly finishing their evening meal were easily overpowered.

By a stroke of tactical genius, the armoury had been located next door to the mess and the intruders topped up their own supplies by 'borrowing' serious explosive charges and any other fancy gear that took their eye.

Knowing the CCTV camera locations, enabled Doris to slip through the inadequate net and neutralise the only operative in the control room who, not expecting a visitor, had opened the door at her first knock. She flicked off and destroyed the main switch to the monitoring equipment and closed the self-locking door behind her.

As the team reconvened, a couple more MEAT trainees were comfortably subdued before they could raise the alarm and they set about making their way to the main interrogation zone at the centre of the complex.

Sabin was not a patient man and was concerned that a fierce fire-fight would make it difficult for the team to exit with Tariq if they managed to find him. To soothe his anxiety, he placed radio-linked explosive charges at crucial points within the corridors, set to blow in sequence and, hopefully, enable a relatively straightforward evacuation by opening a straight line passage.

After meeting scant resistance through their journey along several halls and descent down the only available stairway, the team eventually came to the inner doors of the interrogation zone. Constructed of three separate sheets of eighteen millimetre thick steel sandwiching shock absorption gel, they were, after rigorous testing, declared impregnable.

A quick and dirty bypass of the closing motor enabled Karim to slide the doors aside freely on their runners, leaving access to Tariq's current prison unhindered.

That was when the night fell off a cliff into a pit of something that could eat you very quickly and very messily.

The 'quick and dirty' door bypass was exposed to be as filthy as a teenage boy's browsing history, when what sounded like every alarm in the campus set off.

"Oh drokk!" Sabin looked at Doris. Doris looked at Karim. Karim examined his nails innocently. The effect was rather spoiled as he was wearing gloves, but he paused for a moment longer, hoping that their attention might pass onto something else more interesting.

Eventually, he was forced to admit that perhaps he had been too hasty opening the doors and that checking if there were any powered sensors would have been a sensible prior step.

The point was fairly moot when four MEAT ambled round the corner to find out what all the fuss was about. Before they could call for backup, Sabin had tamed three of them in a classic 'nut-cracker' move - 'newton's cradling' the two outer heads against the unlucky middle-man, and Karim had dropped the other with a silenced shot to the chest.

"Time to pick up our pace team. I imagine, when the bodies start piling up or nobody reports back, we're going to get unhappy people in armour crawling out of the concrete."

They sprinted down the corridor, checking each door as they came to it. Eventually, round a blind corner, Doris barrelled into Tino.

Back for yet another guard shift, he had been quietly minding his own business. A scuffle broke out but it wasn't a fair contest, notwithstanding, Tino was more concerned about retrieving the handheld omni that had been knocked from his grasp. He fought half-heartedly, was hopelessly under-skilled and quickly gave up. His access pass opened the impressive door he had been protecting and they burst in to the small room, dragging Tino with them.

"Dà gū gu luǒ lù de dà tuǐ[i]."

"Language Doris!" Karim exclaimed as she dashed at the figure that stood over the bloody mess that confronted them.

Tariq reclined on the interrogation table, clearly exhausted, bleeding freely. Razrushitel, unsatisfied with his inability to extract anything useful from Tariq had been distracted by a sadistic fascination in how far he could push the boundaries of human sufferance.

Surprised by the intrusion, Razrushitel turned his head, just in time to receive a flying elbow to the jaw, instantly knocking him unconscious.

"Nice!" An approving smile spread across Sabin's wide face,

---

[i]   Ch. 'Naked thighs of my great aunt'

making his Fu Manchu moustache quiver. "That is a sweet strike you've got there lady."

"Doris? What on Omega are you… …Karim! Wow, am I glad to see you." Dazed and confused, Tariq looked around at the rescue party. "Why did you let Doris come on a dangerous job like this? Woah, hang on a minute, you're in tac-armour Doris. What's going on?"

"Take your time Tariq, it's a long story. There'll be an opportunity later." Karim tried to soothe his old friend.

"I was beginning to wonder if anyone was coming to be honest." a weak grin touched the corners of Tariq's mouth. "Razza wasn't great company. He had a nasty habit of asking unanswerable questions and not liking my responses. He got quite cross actually."

"Oh Tariq." Doris struggled for words to express her mixed emotions. Relief, concern, mild elation, urgency all cluttered her mind and she ended up just hugging Tariq tightly.

"Drokk me Doris, let a man breathe, you'll be finishing off Razza's work for him. What are you even doing here? You are armed to the teeth, how did you… What… Where—"

"Later sweet pea," Doris put her finger on his lips again in that endearing gesture. "As Karim said, there'll be time!"

"I hate to break up the reunion, but if we don't get out of here soon, we'll have the wrath of a whole MEAT division descending on us, not to mention any backup they may have called for." Karim poked his head out of the door to check the situation and then waved them all out of the room.

Two of the team draped Tariq's arms around their shoulders to help him move.

"It's ok, I've got this." trying his best to walk, he still couldn't hide the obvious pain he was experiencing whenever anything touched his raw feet.

"Where are your socks? More to the point, where are your shoes?"

"If I knew that Karim—" the sound of aggressive shouting came down the passageway towards them saving the group from another weak attempt at a joke.

They were a well-drilled team, but caring for an injured comrade definitely made life harder for them.

"Lay down suppressive fire Sabin. I'll go round via the other corridor to flank them. Iona, with me." Doris took off with one of the group, streaking away along the passage that curved round the central hub.

"Yuito, help me with this tripod please." Sabin threw a sturdy, squat stand over to Yuito and pulled a heavy-duty laser-cannon out of his large backpack.

"You got the hardware in today Sabin! Where did you pick that ordinance up?"

"My daughter's kindergarten. Where do you think I got it from mutie? Hold that still while I attach it.

"Now hit that button."

Spikes shot out of the bottoms of the legs, driving several inches into the concrete floor and stabilising the large device.

"This thing gives a hell of a kick when it gets going and you get tired, really quickly if you try to hold it.

"Throw me those charge packs... No the big ones, this drinks juice like a thirsty shrucker."

Clipping two pairs of power cells into the side of the weapon, it powered on with a delicate beep and lights flashed across the back indicating it was ready to fire.

"Let's see what she can do.".

Fortuitously, at that moment, a pair of MEAT ran round the corner, hastily strapping on their lightweight armour.

Sabin pressed both triggers a couple of times and bright beams of light lanced across the space in front of them, scorching sizeable portions of the far wall. Recoil dug the spikes further into the concrete, creating fine cracks in the top layer. The onrushing MEAT turned-tail and scurried in the opposite direction faster than a pickpocket can lift a credit chip.

It wasn't long before they cried out in painful surprise. Doris had clearly set up position with Iona and they picked off the runners with their silenced bolt pistols.

"How long are we going to do this Karim? What's your plan?"

"To answer both questions. Firstly, for as long as it takes for us to find a way to get Tariq moving. B, we keep punching them in the mouth so they can't formulate a plan. And three, we stay unpredictable to keep them guessing."

"I didn't ask three questions."

"What does that matter, concentrate on your job and I'll let you know what to do when the time comes."

"Yes boss." Sabin opened up the laser-cannon again, this time catching a MEAT by surprise. As his legs detached just below the knees, his shock momentarily spiked before he passed out. "Ouch! That's going to sting when he wakes up."

"Don't worry Sab they'll grow him some new ones." Yuito was the eternal optimist of the group, "I'm on my fourth right hand already. It only takes a few months."

"Watch your ten Yuito." Sabin was holding off the advancing MEAT, mostly by their fear of losing body parts, but he couldn't cover the whole width of the passage.

Swinging his pair of hand-flamers up and to the left, Yuito unleashed a torrent of fire at the suddenly retreating soldiers.

"Stars, what did you bring those along for? We've got to get out of here later. Any more of that, the blast doors will slam shut and the sprinklers will come on."

Yuito grinned wickedly at Sabin and roasted the backside of another cowardly MEAT. "Afraid of getting a bit wet Sab?"

Slowly, but definitely faster than they really wanted, a heap of decommissioned enemy was beginning to grow.

"We've got to move soon guys, we're starting to block our own escape route." Sabin pulled the laser-cannon off its support and slung a wide strap across his shoulder. "Don't leave the tripod Yuito, let's press our advantage now, before we get pinned down."

"I haven't had this much fun in—" Yuito stopped mid-sentence as one of the weapons that a MEAT had been carrying exploded, sending shards of shrapnel, muscle and bone across the hallway. At the same time, half of the clothing on the pile of carcasses ignited, acrid black smoke rising with the dirty flames.

"Woah. Intense!"

"I told you Yuito."

"Never mind that Sabin, Tariq is ready to go, let's move.

"Doris, Iona, do you copy?" Karim was already pushing forwards.

"Yeah, we've got a growing collection of unwanted MEAT here, what's your status?"

"Ready to exfil. Hold your position until you see us approach that massive door we came through."

"That door that set off all the alarms when you opened it?"

"I don't need to be reminded of that right now, until those med-packs take effect, Tariq can't walk so I've strapped him to my back like I'm some kind of mutant tortoise."

"Can he shoot things?"

"Doris! I can't believe that's your first thought. Though actually, yeah, he's my rear-gunner."

"DOWN," Sabin screamed, ducking and holding his ears. "STUN GRENADE."

An earsplitting crack, accompanied by the bright strobe of a powerful light punctuated their conversation.

"Everyone ok?"

Everyone *had* managed to protect themselves from the device.

"Good. Move, move, they won't expect us to be on them straight away." Karim followed closely behind Sabin who was already up and pumping energy rays into the smoke haze in front of them.

"Pardon?"

"Keep up Yuito, we're moving out."

"Pardon?"

It was the sound of a body hitting the floor that made Karim turn.

"I said— ...Kark! ...Man down. Unrecoverable. Lets go. Yuito's not going to be able to re-grow any of that."

Looking back over his shoulder before rushing head-first into danger, Sabin saw what Karim was talking about.

Yuito lay on his back, arms splayed out, a dinner plate sized hole in his torso. His eyes were wide, mouth open with disbelief. A hollow-headed bolt had hit him in the chest, no armour would have been able to withstand the devastating impact.

Karim ran back to close the staring eyes as a mark of respect. He grabbed the hand-flamers and pulled off the tac-packs, then pounded back towards their exit, letting loose alternate volleys of bolts and white-hot vengeance as he ran.

Sabin timed his throw to coincide with their jump as he and Karim vaulted the collection of casualties, sending an electro-grenade into a squad of MEAT that scattered on reflex, just not fast enough.

Blue arcs of high-voltage current spat at the retreating fighters as the charge electrified the fine wires that had burst out and attached themselves to anything in the vicinity. An incapacitated collection of arms and legs juddered in a comical, jerking, slow-motion dance as, they sank to the floor in spasmodic stages.

"Careful Karim, I'm not a milkshake." The jolting of Karim's landing had rattled Tariq's teeth together and he almost dropped his laser pistol.

"I'm at your six." They heard the voice of Doris in their ear comms as they flattened back against the security door and sent out covering fire for her to get through.

Moments later, the heavens opened. Well, not literally. It's possible that it started raining outside, but inside the facility, the flame-retardant clothing that MEAT wore in combat had clearly been sourced on a shrinking budget. Instead of completely suppressing the flames, the fabric just let off a steady plume of dark, sooty smoke, triggering the sprinklers.

"Kark. Even though he's clearly to blame, I can't even berate Yuito over this. I knew the flamers were a bad idea the moment I saw him whip them out." Sabin looked around at the team gradually getting soaked through, "I guess at least it will clear the smoke."

"Yeah, but now we're going to be trapped in," Iona spoke up, "that rumble is the blast doors closing at every major corridor junction."

A knowing grin crept up Sabin's face, lifting the sides of his mouth and setting off fireworks in his mischievous eyes.

"Don't worry about that Iona, we can get out any time we want." He lifted the detonator switch from a pocket on his combat shorts and kissed it melodramatically, "this baby here is the freedom button."

"Hold on a moment Sabin, let's just take a second and work this out." Doris held up one hand to Sabin whilst she took down a pair of MEAT that had been attempting to sneak up on them from a side-tunnel. "They will be trying to flank and out-gun us. They may have us completely outnumbered, but they're still reeling because every time they come up with a new plan, we punch them in the mouth again."

"Yeah, I expect they want to contain us and use the blast doors like airlocks in an attempt to pin us down. Our next mouth-punch needs to be a big one. As soon as Sabin hits that button, their world will collapse in on them and if that's not a complete knockout blow, it will leave them very dazed." Karim was eager to make their next action really count.

"I think we've got a chance, we need to move quickly once we blow the walls." Doris agreed with the next stage of the fluid plan, "Stay alert everyone, we don't want any sneaky MEAT picking us off as we escape, we can't afford to lose anyone else."

The thirty centimetre thick, reinforced concrete walls of MEAT PIP were formidably built, but there is very little that can withstand the power of a large block of RDX. Developed as a more powerful alternative to TNT, its extreme instability means it requires very delicate handling. It packs such a punch that it is commonly used in the controlled demolition of buildings. Sabin's use of the compound on this occasion could not, even in the most imaginative of minds, be classed as controlled. Although, technically, he was demolishing a building.

The whole structure shook with a succession of skull-crushing explosions that got louder and more violent every few seconds. The final detonation was so enormous that they felt like their guts had temporarily left their bellies and it took Doris' team a moment to catch their breath again. Most of the sprinklers were still active, clearing the dust rapidly to reveal, through a haphazard progression of openings, the bottom of the stairwell they had come down.

"We're just going to have to make a run for it. They won't stay down for long and our way out is also their way in... ...GO."

After his rallying cry, Karim led the charge; bolter in one hand, flamer in the other. He dodged through the disarray of shattered concrete lumps and steel reinforcement rods and kept up as good a speed as he could.

Strapped to his back, Tariq scanned the side-passages for movement and sent indiscriminate ion-blasts in the direction of anything that even vaguely resembled activity. Every now and then, he pulled out stun or electro grenades to lob into open and opening doors, throwing the site personnel into the kind of confusion that he could only have dreamed of.

Owing to the 'fun' Tariq was having, passage for the rest of the team was largely unhindered, save for the rubble they had to navigate and the increasing amount of running water on the floor.

"Drokk, this stuff is slippery when wet."

Doris' rubber-soled combat shoes were designed to be super-grippy in almost any situation, but she considered this to be testing them to their limits.

Turning to check for pursuit, she slowed down as she saw a MEAT warrior looming on Sabin's position and blew the blaster out of his hand.

"What are you doing Sabin? Get out," she called through the damaged wall.

Finishing his task, Sabin hurried towards her again, emerging from the rough-edged hole with rivers of dusty water running down the parts of his euphoric face that weren't covered by his lightweight helmet.

"Wait and see Doris, you're going to love it."

"Just keep moving," she screamed into the haze.

They ran another twenty metres and he paused again, reaching up to the ceiling and fiddling for a moment, before carrying on.

"Stop it, you're putting us all in danger, what are you playing at?"

Doris tried to drag him along by his sleeve, letting off a volley of warning shots as she spotted a few heads peeping round a corner.

Sabin just smiled, shook his arm free and stopped again.

"SABIN!!!"

"Run Doris, just kriffing run."

CHAPTER 39

OMEGA 4 | WEEKS EARLIER

ariq sat across from General Hideki's secretary, frowning. Having spent a significant amount of time reading Nigel's notebooks and scanning some pages into his modified Omni to search for patterns, he had drawn a blank.

Eventually, when he and Doris had run out of ideas, he turned to the only place he could think of that wouldn't attract attention.

———

He had been directed to an unkempt building in downtown MC3 with damaged shutters and a defective neon sign. After waiting for a few minutes in the cold breeze, the intercom finally crackled to life.

"Yes?"

A scratchy voice greeted him from the scruffy-looking speaker.

"I have a meeting with the General."

"Enter."

There was a quiet click and the door opened at Tariq's push to reveal a badly-lit, dusty room with a pair of worn chairs against one wall.

At the far side of the small space sat an elderly gentleman who looked like he hadn't moved since the dawn of time.

"Wrist!"

The gravelly croak seemed to be the limit of the man's exertion. Tariq offered the inside of his forearm to the small scanner that sat on the desk which chimed quietly.

"Codes."

Tariq recited the set of codes he had memorised many years earlier.

After what seemed an interminably long wait in the uncomfortable chair, the man croaked again.

"Proceed."

Once again, the grizzled receptionist managed to convey a general weariness with existence, thinly veiled boredom, and an instruction, all in one word.

"Thanks very much." Tariq walked through the door that opened in front of him and down a short corridor. At the end, he turned into a space that contrasted dramatically with the entrance. It was like stepping into the product guide for the ideal home exhibition. Plush contemporary fabrics blended with seamless furniture. Everything was exceptionally designed, with function married perfectly to aesthetics.

It was obvious where Tariq was supposed to sit, a comfortable chair with its back to a blank corner, no possibility of being crept up on from behind. From the chair, every visible entrance could be easily assessed and no windows overlooked it.

Despite his training dictating this to be the best position to be in, the presentation of such a perfect resting place immediately put Tariq on alert. He checked the space a few times before choosing a slightly less 'perfect' chair to occupy. Then he sat there wondering whether he was overthinking things and being a little too cautious. After a moment lost in thought, he realised that part of him missed the adrenaline of being acutely vigilant.

"Aahh Tariq Colemin." The elderly general's silver hair appeared at the door, carried in an untameable mane above his bushy, white eyebrows. A pair of bright, narrow eyes pierced Tariq as they gazed at him from above a small, round set of spectacles. Keeping the glasses from tumbling into the void was a wide nose, under-lined by the kind of moustache that drove teenage boys wild with envy.

Below the facial hair and the liberal smile, General Hideki was wiry and fit, even though he was over eighty. He looked old but otherwise, he was younger than his years and in a tight spot, could surprise a more junior man with his uncommon vigour.

Tariq looked up and nodded. "Your talkative friend sent me through."

"Pleased to finally meet you. I'm already impressed. You passed my first test, that chair is rigged." The General nodded to himself in approval. "I heard good things about you when you were with the Basilisks. Oh yes, whispers rise to the very top of an organisa-tion. I was always convinced you were leadership material, but others believed you were too good at what you did lower down the ranks." He paused to beckon Tariq into his office. "You know there's always a job waiting for you if you want to come back with us. Once a Basilisk, always a Basilisk."

"Thank you General. I'm really only here as I couldn't think of anyone else I could trust."

"Now you have my attention."

"I heard things when I was inside. Things that at first seemed far-fetched, but then I remember noticing peculiar situations on some of our missions. After I landed dirt-side, I found the work a bit tedious and my brain was mulling things over so I went digging. The further I dug, the deeper the fox-hole went, the more things added up."

"You're speaking in metaphors at the moment Tariq, but please, go on."

"Well, eventually, with the help of a modified Omni and a beautiful woman, the pieces all seemed to fall into place."

"Come on son, spit it out."

"General, do you remember the mission near Caroli? The one where a major corporation paid for us to extract what they said was stolen intellectual property."

"Yes, I remember. We put a surgical strike on a NA Frigate with an infiltration and extraction team, clean and quick."

"That's right, did it seem odd to you how easy that was? I mean a Frigate, not a Super-carrier or Super-cruiser. Those things are fairly small, normally have a fully kitted-out platoon or two onboard and would generally put up a fierce fight."

"Ok, maybe we got lucky Tariq."

"Do you not think they would normally have shown more resistance protecting that important cargo?"

"You have a point, but that's just one—"

"Pardon me sir but there's lots more like that, I can think of numerous incidences over the years where we either outgunned, outran, or outsmarted the NA forces we came up against. They used to be really tough. They had almost every sector under control and kept law and order really effectively. They always had the latest weaponry and defensive equipment. Tactically they were never a walkover. It just seems like in recent years up to my capture, they had developed a real weakness."

"Now you point it out Tariq, I think you might be right. We've gone from strength to strength while it's been easier and easier to find areas of the galaxy that are barely patrolled. The NA forces that are trying to maintain equilibrium do seem like they have gone soft and, yes, they are clearly understaffed."

"Exactly. Which is why I went searching for answers."

"What did you find?"

"Have you got a secure Omni? One that's isolated from the Omniweb?"

"This sounds interesting Tariq. Here, mine is the most secure terminal in the city. Watch this." General Hideki opened a programme that ran a series of checks on his Omni and its connections to the outside world. Visual depictions of the network demonstrated incoming probes from the NA servers being deflected as if the machine wasn't there. Following that, the application performed a deep internal scan showing it was clear from any snooping software.

"That looks pretty good to me, let me plug my portable in to transfer the file." Tariq connected his interface and deposited his findings on the General's device, where he walked him through everything he had uncovered.

"Well… I… never!" The General was impressed but not particularly surprised, "we've suspected something like this for a long time but it's clearly taken substantive effort to compile this. The evidence here irrefutably reveals the extent of the decay within NA. Well done Tariq, this will be invaluable as we push forward with our missions."

"It's the least I could do to inform you General, after all the Basilisks have done for me over the years."

"Ok son, let's have a look at what else you've got for me, you mentioned you had two items of concern."

"This one is a little more 'old-school' if I'm honest General."

"Old school is how I roll son. I never really caught on to new ways of doing things."

"Well, that's fortunate then isn't it. Because we've got our work cut out to make head or tail of these." Tariq pulled the pile of notebooks out of the bag he was carrying and piled them on the desk. "I guess we start at the beginning."

"And why not son, why not? Before we dig in, I am intrigued as to how you came into possession of these."

Tariq relayed the chain of events that had led him and Doris to the notebooks and the subsequent chase through the back alleys of MC2. Wiping tears of laughter from his eyes at their encounter with Streaks and Stinks, the General removed his steamed up glasses to clean them.

"Wow, this Doris girl sounds like a live-wire. She's a keeper. I can't believe she made you dress up."

"Looking back I suppose I must have looked quite peculiar. Her background needs a little investigation though, she let on that she's got a history. I've searched Omni at length but there's nothing on her and we've not had the chance to explore it together yet."

"I'll ask someone to get onto it. A resourceful woman like that could be a real asset to the family, if, of course, you both want to stick with us, I don't want to be presumptuous. It's possible you may find out about her past in the course of things anyway, these secrets have a way of coming out in a relationship."

"I'll keep that in mind, I can definitely see a future with her so all the cards need to be on the table. Talking of tables, we really need to get upside of these."

Pulling a notebook off the pile, Tariq opened it and they both leaned over to see what delights lay within.

After several hours, the General sent for some food. Not the substandard fare that you would need a digestive system as strong as that of a prepubescent boy to stomach, but really classy take-out that was delivered promptly by a drone.

They studied the notebooks for the rest of the day, forgetting the time until the General's secretary knocked politely to inform them that he was off home.

"Any progress Tariq?"

"I was just about to ask you the same question sir."

"I'm afraid none of it makes any sense at all to me. It's all just numbers and letters. Do you think it's some kind of a code?"

"There is a theme that seems to run throughout. Each section starts with either a name or a number and if I'm not much mistaken, some of them are remarkably familiar."

"Go on." The General's interest was piqued again.

"Well there are some pretty easy ones here: several pages of columns of numbers after the title "M92", followed directly by one page titled "M93" and then half a page after, "M94"."

"Im afraid my brain isn't as quick as it used to be, you're going to have to spell it out."

"Well General, those are the staging codes of Super-cruiser class starships. I know that the M92 was a significant design, the M93 had some upgrades and modifications and the M94 just had minor changes to iron out the last little niggles. The next entry is titled "M96" which is four or five pages again. That model was an almost complete redesign, NA didn't release an M95 for some obscure reason."

"So it's some kind of secret code involving starships then?"

"I think there's more than just ships here, look at this." Tariq pushed over notebook number seven and drew the general's attention to an open page. "IZV. Surely that can only mean one thing."

"It *would* seem peculiar if there was anything else known by those initials."

"And here, a few pages later, M-PIP. Surely that must be the MEAT Prison and training Facility in MC1."

"You are right, there's definitely a pattern emerging." The General stroked his moustache and allowed himself a wry smile, "you're definitely not just grunt material are you Tariq?"

"Then there's this." Again, Tariq showed more columns of neat jottings to the general. "Notebook twelve. Magellania. Wasn't there talk of a weapons and fuel-cell stash somewhere out that way. I know it's a long time since I was on the Chimera but the Commodore was speaking about a perfect supply depot that we could raid. I know things take ages planning but have you taken action there yet?"

"We definitely have plans in that direction. In fact, we have something else to talk about now you are here.

"An operation to extract you from IZV was set in motion a while back. It was not a success and if I'm completely honest, I was rather surprised to hear from you. We wondered where you had got to at first when you weren't available for extrication. With your mission history, you were to be a vital part of the team that was being put together for the Magellanian job.

"Initially, we decided we'd have to carry on without you. I looked into your whereabouts and you seemed quite happy with your new life. I wanted you to have the option to make your own mind up about the 'second chance programme'.

"From the outside, you were making quite a go of it."

"Yes, I thought I'd really try not to mess things up, especially as I met Doris at work and she just accepted my past without judgement."

"I told you, she's a keeper.

"You have had quite the journey to secure these notebooks, now you've seen what is inside, does your heart start hammering again at the possibility of figuring out the enigma and rejoining the Basilisks? I know my pulse is raised."

"I'm not sure General. I appreciate your offer and I am intrigued. I'm just not sure if I've still got the same fight in me."

"No pressure Tariq. Either way, are you happy to hand over the notebooks should you decide to stay on Omega-4 and make a life dirt-side?"

"Of course General, I'd be more than happy. I'd like to keep hold of them for the moment to see if I can glean anything else from their pages. Now we have some traction with the information, I'd like to press on a bit."

"Not a problem Tariq, you know where I am. I'm sure I don't need to impress upon you that everything in these books is really useful and highly classified. If we digitise it and send it over to the Chimera, we risk this kind of information getting into the wrong hands. I'm afraid I'm going to have to make a difficult comm and ask them to turn around to pick these up in person.

"As soon as they are close enough for transfer, can I send you there to deliver the goods?"

"Certainly General. It will be nice to see the old team again even if I choose to stay dirt-side in the long run."

CHAPTER 40

OMEGA 4 | PRESENT DAY

Doris and Sabin sprinted the final thirty metres to the outermost wall, he grabbed her shoulder and span her round before slapping his hand down on the detonator again.

Having taken shelter round a corner, they managed to avoid the main intensity of the blast that brought the roof down in the lower level. Wild grin on his face, Sabin turned to Doris and winked.

"GO, GO, GO!" Karim was first to react and corralled them up the staircase before following, three stairs at a time. "What does it look like up there?"

"Crawling with rotten MEAT, this is not going to be easy." Crouching two floors up at the head of the stairwell, Doris took a bead on a squad that were trying to organise a defensive position and blew out a power transformer. It erupted like a box of fireworks, frying several of the closest men and flooring the others. "I wanted us to be a bit less conspicuous in all fairness. There are too many of them, we're going to have to adapt our plan. We've still got a lot of fighting to do, how are the supplies?"

Everyone replied that they had more than enough firepower to defeat a battalion.

"What's your suggestion Doris?"

"We can't split up. We might have to just go with extreme force this level and hope for the best."

"I love a detailed plan." Sabin switched the heavy cannon to his left shoulder so he could more easily launch a couple of stun grenades to clear the next leg of their journey.

"How much RDX have you got left Sabin?"

"Enough!"

"Enough for what?"

"The whole place to be honest. There was loads of it hanging around in the armoury. I thought it would be rude to leave it."

Iona hurled five smoke bombs in quick succession into the open spaces around them and down the walkways. "We ought to get a moment's cover unless the sprinklers start on this level."

"Good thinking.

"We have two options. Go round or go through. Going through takes us into the main personnel areas and is mostly one big, straight corridor.

"Going round takes longer, but avoids the highest density of MEAT. It is a bit more of a maze. What do you all think?"

"I'm for going through!" Sabin lobbed another electro-grenade towards a scurrying enemy, scoring a spectacularly entertaining direct hit. "It's how we came in and I left a few surprises for anyone chasing us out."

"Iona? Karim? Dare I ask you Tariq?"

"I'll go wherever Karim goes." Tariq smiled at her from his position, strapped to Karim's back.

"I'm easy, but we should get going soon." Unholstering a pair of plasma-pistols, Iona certainly looked ready to traumatise anything that crossed her path.

"Let's go for it. Maximum prejudice, we'll punch through any resistance and hopefully be home for breakfast." Karim made the final call and quickly checked his surroundings before standing up and wading towards the central corridor.

The rest of the team applied a stim-strip and followed after him with well-practiced smooth movements.

"So we're just going to walk right through this complex and out of the front door?"

"No Iona, some of the way you'll be allowed to run." Sabin smirked at his own joke and hit the locking mechanism that held the centre of the laser-cannon. The oversized weapon separated into two discrete units and he draped their straps cross-ways over his chest. "Though, maybe the MEAT will be doing more of the running today."

Shouts came from up ahead and they hugged the walls to provide backup to Karim who crouched in the centre of the aisle, carefully reducing the size of a couple of squads of approaching hostiles.

"Let me have a go K." Every kick of Karim's Hurricane bolt rifle jolted Tariq's head uncomfortably and he was desperate to get in on the action, "If you turn sideways, I can shoot one-handed."

"Why didn't I think of that before?" Karim adjusted his position and Tariq lifted his ion-pistol to assist in the carnage. Quickly realising he had the flexibility with the other arm, a spare hand-flamer was also brought into the fray.

Advancing steadily down the central thoroughfare, Karim gradually got the hang of an awkward crab-like gait as the body-count grew.

"It's getting hot in here," Tariq sang as he sprayed fire over another group of MEAT coming through a wide doorway.

"U-huh, U-huh," Karim joined in, pulling his trigger in time with the beat.

"So take off all your clothes," Tariq sang again as several of the enemy tried desperately to tear off their burning combat gear.

"You are so sick, that is unnecessary. These people have families you know."

"Sorry Doris, imagining I'm in a VR game helps me focus. I'm just compartmentalising."

"I get it. It's pure survival. Them or us and I'm damn sure it's going to be us today. Just maybe hold off on the macabre jokes."

They continued on for what seemed like hours at less than walking pace, battling hard at every intersection for each metre of ground they took.

"Ouch! Kark, I've been hit." One leg went from underneath Karim, sending him heavily onto the knee. A dark ring grew around the punctured trousers at a seam in his armour, "Give me a pain patch."

Doris slapped an analgesic sticker on the back of his neck while he pulled his shin-armour aside. Fishing about for a moment, he grimaced and eventually, surprised, extracted a regular .38 bullet.

"What on Omega are they using these for? I thought for a moment I'd lost my lower leg to a bolt."

"Because we snarfed their best kit when we pillaged the armoury." Iona had arrived from behind him and taken over the job of making them difficult to fire at without suffering injury.

"There's no way you're dragging that amount of ammo around with us," Karim replied in surprise as he sprayed the wound with medical-foam.

"No Karim, we filched as much as we could load into our tac-packs and tipped the rest into an atomiser."

"You are the real deal Iona."

"Yuito's idea if I'm completely honest. Stars rest his soul."

"What's our ammo situation folks?" Doris, aware of the sheer volume of stiffs they had left in their wake, checked her own belt and spare weapons, then started to root through a couple of tac-packs.

"I'm getting low now, I think we've only got a couple of small charge packs left for these babies and then a handful of energy cells for the ion-blasters." Sabin had joined them and was indiscriminately waving his pair of laser cannons left and right, scorching anything that had the misfortune to be in the way.

"We've got three tac-packs stuffed with standard bolts in clips and I found three boxes of Hellfire[i] mags in the armoury that I was saving for emergencies. I was hoping we could take those home really." Iona was running through her inventory whilst taking pot-shots at anything that looked like an adversary.

"Well there are plenty of universal power cells that fit the laser and ion-pistols in this pack, two dozen flamer canisters in the other one and wow, would you look at this. Two full double-clips of Dragonfire Bolts.[ii]" Doris waved a couple of magazines in the air at Karim.

---

[i] Hellfire Bolts' advanced bullet technology where the core and tip are replaced with a vial of mutagenic acid with thousands of needles that fire into the target upon the shattering of the vial, pumping the acid into the foe.

[ii] Dragonfire Bolts are hollow-shelled bolts that unleash superheated, volatile gas that explodes moments later.

"There is no way we are using those." Karim shook his head at Doris. "You can see the trouble we're causing with flamers. Dragonfire should only be used on muties, they are brutal."

"I have dozens of assorted grenades here," Tariq had perked up with the adrenaline surge and his pain killers had kicked in.

"No wonder it felt like I was carrying a baby Rancor."

"If someone can re-load my hand-weapons, I'd be really grateful. Actually, I think I can probably walk now, maybe even run as fast as Karim here."

"With or without you on my back? Either way, if you can make it under your own steam, it would be a relief." Needing no second invitation, Karim quickly released the straps holding Tariq.

"Throw me that pack, I'll reload myself now I'm free from Karim."

"I think we're going to have to take a detour, the density of MEAT further down here is impassable. Our rather protracted chat hasn't helped improve the situation either.

"Doris, can you plot us a different route?"

"Yeah, give me a second.

"Hmmm, if I remember correctly, we can take that door to the training room and exit at the other end. There are some other classrooms and a couple of dorms that may be occupied, though I expect not by now! I think we can weave our way to the outer wall through rooms with two entrances and minimal use of corridors."

"I'll cause a distraction." Sabin drew out his detonator again and dialled up a different frequency.

"Why didn't you mention that before?" Doris' incredulous voice was quickly drowned out by the sounds of a mobile plasma-cannon being rolled toward them.

"Because once I hit this button, there's no way we're going back out the way we came in."

The whine of the plasma weapon powering up grew in volume to the point where they couldn't hear each other any more. Just as it reached its climax, Sabin pointed at the door Doris had indicated earlier and pressed the big red button.

Iona was first through the door, closely followed by Doris, with Karim and Tariq hobbling through behind them as the sound of a thousand thunderclaps rocked the building. Concrete cracked and dust showered from the ceiling as light fittings came loose and swung away from their anchors. Everything in their vision flickered, the room illuminations guttering like they were too exhausted to shine any longer.

Their tactical helmets had protected them against the brunt of the noise but their ears still rang and their comms sounded all muffled when they talked.

"Where's Sabin?" Doris asked.

Tariq and Karim made the universal sign for "I've no idea what you said," and just shrugged.

Doris screamed again "WHERE'S SAB?"

Understanding lit up the faces of the two men, who pointed back out of the open doorway through which dust and grit still billowed in.

Always quickest to react, Doris and Iona rushed back to where the door hung drunkenly on its remaining hinge and looked out.

Sabin stood on the other side of a gaping hole in the floor.

"Too much RDX?" He mouthed at them, a sheepish look in his dark eyes.

"Jump to us, you can't stay there." Iona shouted across at him.

"You do know your helmet mic can pick up a whisper Iona don't you?" Sabin knocked the side of his head with one hand.

"Sorry Sab. Come on, jump."

Sabin hesitated, paralysed on the edge of the pit, his legs refusing to take instructions from high command.

"I... I can't!"

"What do you mean you can't?" Iona shot back at him, perplexed.

"I just can't. I can't do it."

"Sab. It's baffling me, what are you doing? Just jump. It's not like you're an elephant or a snake!" Doris urged him over the void.

"INCOMING!" Iona turned tail and ran as she saw a grenade sailing towards them down the hall.

With mantis-like reflexes, Doris raised her bolt-pistol and fired. Simultaneously, Sabin finally overcame his mental block and launched himself towards the only plausible escape route.

Standing in the doorway, Tariq watched the scene unfold as if it was in slow-motion.

Doris' bolt glanced off the grenade's bottom cap, fortunately not setting it off, but spinning it back towards the thrower. Her projectile then ricocheted off the ceiling and embedded itself in the huge energy cell that fed the plasma-cannon, which started making strange noises.

Sabin soared in a graceless arc of flailing appendages, over the gap in the floor, missed the edge and sailed down towards the lower level.

Anticipating the danger, Doris had already dropped her pistol and propelled herself at Sabin.

Noticing the imminent catastrophe developing, Iona lurched

forwards, grabbing hold of one of Doris' feet and desperately reaching out for something else to anchor on.

Somehow, as she plummeted head-first through the opening in the concrete floor, Doris managed to catch one of Sabin's thrashing arms and hold tight.

Sabin clung to Doris, his arm stretched painfully upwards as the weight of his laser cannon dragged at them both. Doris was at the mercy of Iona, who, giving up on securing any purchase with her free hand, had wrapped herself around Doris' calf and spread her legs wide, jamming her feet either side of the doorframe.

None of them saw the grenade skitter across the floor and spin idly a few times before exploding on its timer.

Tariq stood transfixed as he watched the blast cause the floor to crumble and give-way under the plasma-cannon's mass, sending the powerful munition plunging to the level below.

He held his breath for what seemed like minutes, but was probably only a couple of seconds, before the whole horror-scene in front of him erupted. A super-heated fireball engulfed the area as the energy cell detonated, taking the plasma cannon and a significant section of the structure with it.

Tariq staggered back under the oppressive heat, just as Sabin, Doris and Iona, in that order, came flying through the door and landed on top of him in a groaning heap.

Chests heaving, they dragged themselves across the floor to sit propped up against the walls.

"Never… again," Sabin coughed some of the dust from his lungs.

"Nope, not ever," Doris wheezed in agreement.

"One hundred percent," echoed Iona.

Karim, who had been checking whether their exit was clear, appeared at the far end of the training room.

"What the kark was that? Hey, this is no time to be having a rest, we've got to get out of here. There's sure to be a platoon of MEAT arriving from the barracks across town any moment."

"Shall I tell him or do you want to?" Tariq, the only one standing again, looked at the others.

"Let's just go." Doris shook her head and hauled herself upright, then pulled Iona and Sabin to their feet.

"Is there something you want to share with the class Doris?"

"Nope, all good thanks Karim... Shall we?"

Karim shook his head bewildered, replaced his helmet and led out of the far door.

The next few minutes were relatively uneventful as they limped through a succession of rooms without meeting any resistance.

Their movements became like clockwork as they checked each space before transiting through them, made sure the exit was clear, then advanced to the next area.

They were just departing one large dormitory when they started taking fire again.

The MEAT had obviously re-grouped and sent out squads searching for them.

Bullets and bolt rounds whined through the air, scorching or embedding themselves in the wall next to the rapidly exiting team. Dust puffs decorated the air whilst tiny concrete fragments scattered across the floor.

Karim and Tariq were only able to move at a fast shuffle, both of them limping badly, so Sabin took up the position of rear-gunner. He seemed relatively unscathed by his adventure with the plasma combustion, save for heavily blackened armour and one side of his previously magnificent moustache being completely scorched away.

Doris and Iona scouted ahead and gradually navigated the team back towards their original entry point.

"I'm out of power. Throw me something smaller." Sabin, jamming the laser-cannon back into his large tac-pack, caught the bolt-pistol Iona threw at him with one hand.

"Leave the heavy weapon, it'll only slow us down." Iona flung a couple of spare clips at him.

"No way. I may be exhausted, but I'm taking this thing with us. You have no idea what fun it is. And you never know when it might be useful again."

"Planning to open a sheet metal cutting business?"

"Stop being smart and give me something else to fire, I've got two hands." He grabbed the hand-flamer out of the air and hooked it onto his belt just in time to also catch an ion-blaster that she had sent in his direction. "Thanks, this will do nicely. What a combo."

Taking the next corner as fast as their weary, broken bodies could muster, they almost ran into two squads of MEAT travelling away from them.

Doris turned with her finger to her lips and a look of mild panic on her face.

They all stood statue-still, hoping they might go unnoticed. Until Tariq sneezed.

"Sorry," he murmured as twenty armed killers stopped and turned to face them.

Throwing caution to the wind, Doris was the first to pro-act. As the echo of the sneeze died away, she drove her arm into the pack on Iona's back to pull out as many grenades as her hands could grip, which in this instance amounted to four, and immediately primed them. At the same time, she swung her arms back, and with a clumsy action, hurled them at their foe.

The team rushed for cover again, all five of them diving back round the corner from which they had just emerged. Several thousand volts of electricity curved around the passage, joining most of the victims together in a kind of asynchronous departing jitterbug.

Iona peeped round the corner and sent the last few combatants to the same grisly end with some well-placed bolt rounds.

Sabin, meanwhile, had been desperately trying to hold off their pursuers by strafing them with withering flame jets and targeted ion-blasts.

"You got any RDX left Sab? There's no way we can get out through the door we came in." Doris was watching more fire teams arrive and attempt to shift their fallen comrades. She slung a couple of stun grenades their way for good measure.

"I'm going to need some help back here if you want an exit creating."

Iona ran back to his position, turned her flamer up to 'well-done' and concurrently started pinging off bolts like she was at a fairground. A grotesque and deadly fairground where nobody gets any prizes except the possibility of leaving alive.

Sabin scrambled round the corner and placed several explosive packs along and up the wall, rushing back to cover as fast as he could.

"Cover your ears guys, we're probably too close to this one."

Hands over the outsides of their helmets for extra protection, they braced for the shock.

Sabin depressed the middle of his favourite toy and they winced.

Nothing happened.

He pressed it again and again in a rapidly growing frenzy.

"Kark. The battery is gone."

"We've got more, here, have a charge pack." Karim handed him a universal battery module.

"No, this is powered by those stupid button-batteries, the ones you can never find the right size in the vast handfuls of spares you keep in the kitchen drawer and need a ridiculously small screwdriver to get out."

"One Dragonfire bolt and that lot will go up like a handful of caesium." Karim was already crawling towards the corner as he spoke, clipping in a magazine of the deadly explosive rounds.

"You haven't got the space, you're going to get yourself hurt." Doris tried in vain to dissuade him as he lined up his shot.

"You're beginning to sound like my mother." Karim pulled the trigger and instantly rolled away from the corridor junction.

They thought the previous blast was loud but it's likely that all of them suffered permanent hearing damage when this one went off.

The hole that was left in the exterior wall was big enough to drive a pair of tanks through side-by-side and a significant portion of the floor and ceiling were missing in action.

Staggering to their feet, the shockwave having deposited them all firmly on their backs, they waved away the dust and pulled chunks of wall from the prone figure of Karim.

Hoisting him up, they looked round at the scene of devastation.

The corner they had used for shelter had largely protected them from the raw power of the RDX, but it had not itself survived the encounter.

There was a mound of dust-covered corpses that had been shunted down the hall as if by a hypersonic bulldozer. Blood was collecting at the bottom of the pile of pulverised, unrecognisable ex-MEAT, and dripping onto the storey below.

"Accidence[iii] will happen." Sabin raised an eyebrow at the scene of destruction.

"I'm pretty sure the structural integrity of this facility is compromised, we'd better get out." Tariq led the team towards freedom along the pile of rubble that had collected in the passage below. There was just enough space to tiptoe along a narrow ledge that the fractured concrete rested on, so they gingerly made their way out to the sizeable gap in the wall.

At the point they were nearly all clear of the crumbling building, the familiar sound of bolt-fire broke through the ringing in their ears.

Turning back, Karim saw a somewhat foolhardy MEAT Armed-Guard limping along the corridor, pumping round after round in their direction.

"Will this ever end?" Wearily, he lifted up his own sidearm and let off a shot that destroyed the weapon and blew the man's arm clean-off.

"Ouch! Dragonfire! He's not going to be able to do the 'guard' part of his job very well now is he... ...Or the 'armed' bit." Iona pulled at Karim as they heard the squeal of wheels behind them.

Anticipating the worst, Karim rolled his eyes. "Stars. I don't think I can cope with much more of this."

A large, black SUV pulled up next to them, leaving tyre marks on the road as it stopped.

"Get in."

[iii] Accidence - Present participle of accidere ("to happen") Inflected form of accidō ("fall down, upon, at or near"). It's a play on words where 'accidents' (unfortunate chance occurrences often ending up with personal injury) sounds very similar to 'accidence' (a deliberate falling upon 'happening' [in this case violence towards another person]). The joke is probably overly complicated and ends up being a bit 'too clever' for its own good, but it amused me.

"Drokk Morton, you had me worried for a second there." Karim helped bundle the rest of them into the vehicle which took off at speed into the early morning traffic, to the tune of a large building imploding.

"I've missed out on serious fun, going by the evidence before me. You guys look like you've seen some action."

Dog-tired, they looked at each other before turning to Morton and telling him, in no uncertain terms, to "shut up".

CHAPTER 41

OMEGA 4 | PRESENT DAY

F resh off the drop-ship, minding his own business Nigel approached an Omni-map to get his bearings. As he memorised the screen, a corpulent, flame-haired sack of sweat slammed into his back with considerable force.

"Oh smeck, I'm sorry, are you ok?" Ever polite, Nigel apologised, even when not in the wrong.

"Watch where you're going you ugly little drokker. Who do you think you are?"

Always a runner or a talker, never, until recent events, a fighter, Nigel apologised profusely again.

"I'm really sorry sir, I meant no offence. I guess I didn't see you, it's late and dark. I apologise for any inconvenience."

"You want to take this outside wingnuts?"

"Wingnuts? Woah! Wait… What…? We're already outside sir." Nigel stepped back in confusion, saving him from taking a wayward haymaker to the side of his head.

"Take 'im out Rambo," the uncouth shriek came from the excessively inflated lips of a pouting princess who looked like the kind of girl that would rent out all of her orifices to the lowest bidder. It didn't help that her makeup application could have been the work of an award-winning Venetian plasterer.

"Rambo? Seriously?" Nigel's perplexed amusement did nothing to diffuse the situation as he glanced towards Rambo's companion.

"Yeah, Rambo!" His gap-toothed, red-headed aggressor rasped back at him. "And I'll pulverise your scrawny little face if you so much as look at my bird again."

"Smeck. This is not what I had in mind for this evening. Is there any way we can just agree to disagree and calmly go about our—" his sentence was cut short as 'Rambo' hoicked up a loogie and spat it at Nigel's feet. "I guess not then," he finished disappointedly.

Not including the ridiculous pushing / hand flapping that you see in primary school yards, there are essentially three types of fight.

The first is where you have two trained fighters, normally evenly matched, though maybe of different disciplines and you see a relatively level contest, both combatants having a plan and a style of attack.

Then you have the kind of scrimmage that sets a skilled fighter against someone who shows enthusiasm and often anger, but very little craft. Those rarely last long.

Lastly and probably most commonly, there are the brawls that ensue when two puffed-up, egotistical drokkwits, often infused by some kind of mind-altering substance, swing at each other until someone lands a lucky blow, friends step in, or a member of the constabulary arrives, saving face for everyone.

The confrontation Nigel found himself in was, perhaps unsurprisingly the middle of the three.

Backed-up against a wall by the continually advancing Rambo, Nigel still held out some misguided hope that they could all walk away without a scene evolving.

Then Rambo went for him again.

Nimbly evading the wild swipes of the larger man, Nigel bounced on his toes, clearly the more skilled fighter of the pair.

Not wanting to hurt the man, only warn him off, Nigel stuck the odd jab in. Some were body shots, some to the head, but he always pulled his punches to avoid doing any real damage.

Rambo was less careful and anything but accurate. Within a couple of minutes, he sported grazed knuckles from catching the plas-crete wall and had picked himself up from the ground after overbalancing, at least twice. He was also humiliated and fuming.

"Come 'ere you little kriffer, I'm going to make mincemeat out of you."

"On recent evidence, that seems unlikely sir. Look, I don't think there's any need for continued violence." Nigel swayed backwards again to evade a loose swing, "I don't want to hurt you sir."

"But I am going to hurt you, you little scrag."

"I seriously doubt your capacity to do that," Nigel muttered, feinting one way, then the next to avoid a badly aimed jab and land a couple of his own, "I'm deadly serious Rambo. I'm not one to make threats, but settling this with violence will only end badly for you. I think you have gravely underestimated your opposition tonight."

"I don't care much for your kriffing fancy words pal. I let my fists do the talking and I don't do defeat."

"Final answer?"

As a reply, Rambo aimed an uppercut at Nigel's jaw, missing by several centimetres.

Nigel allowed the contest to roll on for a short while, easily ducking or blocking every attack that came his way. Nigel's mercenary training allowed him to react as if Rambo was moving in slow motion, while he racked his brains for a way to bring it to a close without causing his opponent lasting injury.

Not considering the possibility of playing dirty, Nigel didn't see Rambo's botoxed beauty swipe at him with her handbag until it was too late. Had he ducked a fraction faster, he would have maintained enough concentration to defend on two fronts. Instead, her clutch clipped his ear, the metal catch slicing a chunk out of the lobe.

He put a hand up momentarily and Rambo lunged, draping his leaden arms over Nigel's shoulders, perspiring heavily.

The musty smell almost made Nigel retch, but he took the opportunity to target the soft, vulnerable parts of Rambo's anatomy.

He ploughed punch after punch into the belly of his new ill-fitting meat coat. Blows that would have dropped an accomplished fighter were absorbed by the layers of insulating fat and Rambo held on suffocatingly.

All the while, Rambo's companion kicked hysterically at Nigel's shins and lashed out with her little handbag, raining down indiscriminate blows on both fighters.

Nigel swung at Rambo's jaw, his nose and his guts again making solid contacts, yet still, the hothead clung to him like a limpet. Admittedly, a limpet that needed a good shower and a crash-diet, but a limpet none-the-less.

At the point where he discovered two of his fingers in Rambo's eye-socket, Nigel decided to call the fight off. He really didn't want to cause permanent disfigurement and Rambo was likely to be pissing blood for a good few days as it was.

"Ok, ok, just get off mate. I'll stop hitting you, just get off me. You've won, whatever... just, please..."

Rambo relaxed his grip and lifted up his head.

"What the kark have you done to my beau you beast?" Horror covered the face of Rambo's girlfriend, "He looks like he's been through a cheese grater."

"Your beau? Wow, lady, you could do so much bett..." Nigel paused to take in the extravagant vision that posed in front of him. Sparkly stiletto heels shimmered with pulsating rainbow colours, lighting up legs that were clearly the result of some cut-price 'enhancement' surgery. A synthetic skin-tight, reflective micro-skirt that just about covered the top five percent of her thighs left nothing to the imagination. Her marginally concealed spare tyre was squeezed into the kind of body-sock that toned athletes would shy away from and it had the effect of an over-tight corset just failing to contain a pair of struggling cuttlefish.

Above the neck, there was little improvement. It looked like her nose had accelerated through the membrane of a tom-tom drum before the lips had been blown up to keep things from slipping. The final touch was in the scraping back of her vibrantly dyed hair, away from her forehead into a painfully tight bun that sat just too high to be practical or attractive.

"...actually, I think you were made for each other. Don't let anyone tell you any different.

"Anyway, I'm really sorry ma'am, I did warn him." Nigel extricated himself from his saggy assailant and tightened the straps on his tactical back-pack. "Now if you'll excuse me, I have somewhere to go and I think I'm going to be late."

Nigel called up a ride on his handheld and briskly made his way towards the Hovertac rank at the edge of Megacity One Spaceport.

"Sir, sir, do you need help?" A voice cut into Nigel's purposeful walk. "I've called the on-site medic, you look like you've sustained a serious injury sir."

"Oh, no, it's ok ma'am. Hardly any of this blood is mine."

The shock that came over the Spaceport Concierge's face made Nigel stop momentarily.

"I got jumped, it wasn't really a fair contest, I think the medic is probably better off going to the guy with the swollen face, spitting out teeth by the pillar over there. Yeah, the one next to that girl who looks like she's crashed her face into an 'all-you-can-eat' cosmetic surgery buffet.

Sorry, I really must go, my Hovertac is just arriving."

With that, he made off into the night and hopped into the automated vehicle.

"Welcome aboard Sir. Would you like your clothes cleaned while we travel?"

"That's a thing now? Does it cost extra?"

"There's no such thing as a free lunch sir."

"Wow, a self-driving Hovertac with attitude. No thanks, I'll give it a miss this time. Just get me to the destination as fast as you can."

———

A short while later, the taxi glided to a halt outside the grimy windows of Nova Noodles. No light escaped from around the edges of the roller blinds and Nigel wondered what kind of dive he had been brought to.

He checked his messages again and followed the instructions to go round the side of the building and down the alley.

On high alert due to the already eventful evening, Nigel sensed the large frame of Karim before he saw him.

"You must be Nigel."

"No code-words or disguises here eh? You must be Karim."

"I run a tight ship. If you weren't who we were expecting, you'd either be somewhere else or moving on to the next life by now."

"Good to know where I stand, I prefer people who can call it straight."

"You look like hell." Karim spotted Nigel's blood-soaked clothes as they passed under a security light.

"Wow, damn-straight. You're no smecking Monet yourself."

"Cultured," Karim laughed approvingly, "I like you already, let's get you cleaned up."

"You mean *you're* going to stick with…" Nigel gesticulated vaguely, waving his hand to encompass the whole seven foot of Karim's solid, filthy frame, "…this?"

"You are something else Nigel." Karim let out a hearty chuckle. "Let's go inside. I can see you're going to get along just fine with the family."

They walked up a short path and in through the back door of a property which Karim subsequently closed and triple-locked. He flicked at an array of switches that lit up in sequence, priming the alarm systems and CCTV cameras.

"Tight on security, has this area got a reputation?"

"We don't always use it. We're wary of unexpected visitors after an… adventure earlier today."

"Hence the…" again, Nigel waved at Karim's dishevelled appearance.

All was quiet as they moved through the back of the property into a brightly lit room with clean, white walls and a large table covered in more military hardware than Nigel had seen outside the Chimera's vast armoury.

"Woah, that's some serious kit. I hope you don't mind me asking, but where is Tariq?"

"Sleeping. It was a rough night. I need to get some shut-eye too before I open the restaurant, so if you don't mind making yourself at home here… You can leave your bag, there's a wash room off through that door and just over the way, you can get a drink or just relax. Help yourself to anything in the fridge."

"Thanks Karim, I really appreciate it."

"Any friend of Tariq…"

Nigel didn't want to break the spell and admit that he hadn't actually met Tariq, so he thanked Karim again and put his tac-pack on the floor. He pulled out a clean shirt and trousers and made his way into the wash room.

He realised it was exactly what Karim had said it was. He undressed, put his clothes into an auto-laundry and almost instantly, the room washed him.

Warm soapy water cascaded down his shoulders, cleaning off the grime of travel and the copious quantities of Rambo's dried gore. The scent reminded him of a summer walk by the sea, of sitting in Omega-4's manicured botanic gardens and of rich people.

Shutting off the shower, the room radiated heat and caressed him with a warm breeze, drying him quickly and leaving him feeling refreshed.

Hearing a beeping sound behind him, Nigel turned and saw the auto-laundry light flashing. He pulled the drawer out at the bottom and lifted up perfectly clean trousers, which he immediately donned, and some shredded rags which he believed had once been his shirt.

"Just when I thought my luck was changing." Nigel's habit of talking to himself had not disappeared on his travels, nor, clearly had his ability to trawl a bucket-load of bad luck around with him.

He put on the shirt from his bag and went out to re-pack his belongings, draping the chewed-up fabric over the top as a reminder to go shopping for clothes.

Everything was quiet, Nigel wandered through to the small room across the way and put the kettle on. Briefly, he got excited, thinking he might be able to make a cup of tea for himself. His momentary elation was instantly crushed as all he found was fourteen different types of coffee.

He drank a glass of milk and made his way back into the large room.

Idly, he pulled out a notebook and started itemising every-thing that had been dumped on the table, laying things out in an orderly fashion and noting down models and serial numbers.

He filled several columns with neat handwriting before the sound of someone entering the room made him turn round.

"I wasn't expecting auditors." A surprised look was Nigel's reac-tion to seeing Doris' face again. She smiled and took his notebook from him.

"Doris! What the? How?"

Doris just smiled. "Nigel's famous notebooks eh. You are a dark horse Nigel Colemin."

She started to read.

"Karim's Stash:

- Bolt-Pistol - 5 - serial numbers: blah, blah
- Hand-Flamer - 3 with serial numbers
- Ion-Blaster - 4 serial numbers again
- Laser-Pistol - 2
- Laser Cannon - 1
- Personalised Bolt Rifle - 1
- Bolts - 5800
- Hellfire Bolts - 1800
- Dragonfire Bolts - 48
- Electro-Grenades - 23
- Stun-Grenades - 17

You know, this explains what slowed us down so much last night." Doris tapped on the page, looking up at Nigel.

"Sorry, I'm being rude. It's good to see you again Nigel. In fact..." she took a step back in mock surprise. "Have you been working out Nigel? You are some level of hench above how I remember. Weren't you the scrawny nerd from conduit tracing?"

"To be honest Doris, nice as it is to have a familiar face around, I'm still not sure what you're doing here or how you fit in. I thought I was supposed to be meeting a big guy called Tariq."

"Well, it's a long story that involves a new recruit, romance, sneaking about by the Hyper-loop, a run-in with some junkies, the MG, lunch with a neurotic millionaire, a Skyway trip, a visit from the MEAT, a rather explosive climax and a nosy neighbour that could bite the cherry off a cupcake from the bakery door."

"Maeve!"

"The very same."

"But how—"

"Another time Nigel, another time."

"Ok, so... Tariq?"

"He's still sleeping, I'm sure he will surface when there's a more attractive option available. Truth is, he really suffered the last few days. Ivan Razrushitel - the Commander of the MEAT and chief of Komarov's personal security detail—"

"I've heard the name and a few rumours, but dirt-side information is scarce in IZV—"

"IZV? You've been in IZV?"

"Um, yeah, it's not what it seems Doris, mistaken identity... of sorts." Nigel quickly tried to mitigate what he took to be the beginnings of a judgemental raised eyebrow. "Anyway, it sounds like things have changed over the years. I think Razrushitel was just an aggressively ambitious Captain at the time I got put away."

She walked past him into the other room and switched a coffee machine on. "Not any more, that drokker is in charge. He's a vindictive, sadistic psychopath who will stop at nothing to get what he wants."

"Made in the image of his boss then." Nigel followed her to retrieve his notebook.

"Exactly. He tortured Tariq for several days before we could get him out. He didn't talk, Tariq is strong, after all, he is retired SCUM. And he's served his time with the Basilisks. It may also have had something to do with him not knowing anything about what Razrushitel was questioning him for."

"He sounds like a real piece of work. Razrushitel I mean."

"Like you wouldn't believe." Doris picked up a bag of coffee, poured a measure of beans into a small grinder and flicked a switch on the side. The high-pitched motor lasted only moments before Doris turned it off and popped open the lid.

"No doubt the wounds will heal, we've even got medication that will prevent most of the scarring, but I'm more concerned about the mental damage. Being subjected to that kind of prolonged torment can leave deep psychological trauma. I hope he can get over it, I hope it will all be worth it." She took a deep sniff of the coffee, then waved it under Nigel's nose. "Don't you just love that smell of freshly ground coffee!"

Nigel gagged, turning away quickly.

"What's wrong Nigel?"

"I'm allergic to coffee."

"Allergic to… I had no idea that was even possible."

"Yeah, I'm a tea drinker."

"How did I not know that after all those years working together? And how on Omega did you develop such expensive tastes? You may have been a 'team lead' but we both know that still doesn't pay all that well."

"I have no vices and had very limited interests. My life before I was arrested was uncomplicated. Unlucky, but definitely not extravagant."

"Don't get me wrong Nigel, I didn't have you down as the flashy type but tea? Nobody grows it for consumption in the Draconis system and to have it shipped from off-world…"

"I got to know an importer, it never seemed to be too expensive. I don't know if it was something to do with giving him information on how the air conditioning system at MAD IT worked." Nigel shrugged.

"Oh Nigel. Can't you see it?"

"See what?"

"That guy was going to divert heat from the server centre to grow drug plants. No wonder you got cheap tea! You're a naive mine of information. You don't even know what you know."

"Really?"

"I've read your notebooks. They may not be much to you, but drokk me, it looks like there's enough in there to take down an empire. If only we could decode it."

"That's not really my style, I just thought there were some interesting patterns. On which note... ...How did you get hold of my smecking notebooks?"

"It seems like when Tariq was released, he ended up living in Mr Colemin's apartment, sitting at Mr Colemin's old desk, you know how bad MAD IT is. Beyond that, it's a long story—"

"Oh, *that* long story?" He raised his index finger to point upwards.

"*That* long story!" She nodded. "Another time, another place."

The sound of footsteps approaching was closely followed by the majestic, yet sleepy, entrance of Tariq who stifled a yawn with the back of his hand.

"Morning folks."

"Hi love. Did you sleep ok?" Doris bounced over to him and gave him a quick peck on the cheek, "This is Nigel, he arrived in the night."

"That makes you sound very mysterious! Hi Nigel, pleased to finally meet you." Tariq's hand engulfed Nigel's like an anaconda swallowing a kudu.

"You too. Doris was just telling me how you—"

"Have a nose that wakes your brain up at the first whiff of coffee." shooting a frown and an imperceptible shake of her head towards Nigel, Doris finished another of his sentences.

"If I know Karim at all, any time now, he'll be busting through that door and serving up some spectacular breakfast." Tariq smothered another yawn and poured himself a cup of black nectar.

"As if by magic." A booming voice accompanied the sound of clattering pans that drifted through the open door at the end of the long passage. Karim appeared carrying several platters of the most delicious smelling breakfast that Nigel had ever encountered.

"This will let the lazy ones out of bed. IONA, SABIN, FOOD." The shout was directed up another hallway as he returned to the restaurant kitchens.

"Don't wait for them, tuck in," he called back over his shoulder.

They needed no second invitation. The animal centres of their brains lurched forward to satiate the fierce hunger that the last 24 hours had blessed them with. Conversation took a back seat, not even lifting its head to say "hi" when the other two arrived to fill their growling stomachs.

———

Dabbing at the sides of his mouth with a napkin, Tariq stretched backwards and looked across the table.

"If I'm completely honest Nigel, I was not expecting you to look like this.

"Maybe it's just stereotyping, but for such a major geek—"

"None taken."

Tariq laughed, "I didn't think you would be quite so... well... buff."

"I spent three months on a tiny shuttle being starved and worked like a donkey by a mad woman called Remi—"

"Remi? Wow, what crime did you commit to deserve that?"

"I think it was supposed to be a punishment for her. And then, for the last two months, Remi and Sam have beasted me in the gym and combat training deck. Again, supposedly retribution for Remi's IZV mistake."

"I heard about that." Tariq was laughing. "I can't believe they couldn't recognise that you weren't me. If only I could have seen the looks on their faces when they realised."

"It wasn't pretty actually, they smecking-well tried to blame me at first. Then in what they called 'training', they showed less mercy than Genghis Khan and then had the cheek to frame it as *saving* me from a walk outside."

Nigel went on to relay the full tale of his 'rescue' and subsequent time aboard the Chimera and by the time he had finished, the rest of the table were rocking with laughter.

"What the drokk happened to your ear?" Iona leaned over to take a look at Nigel's injury.

"Oh, that, it happened at the spaceport, I stumbled on a prick."

"I've stumbled on many pricks, sometimes multiple times, but I never sliced my ear half off!" Iona giggled, "You are the unluckiest guy I have ever met."

The room instantly silenced.

"Ah… yeah, you make a good point Iona. About your luck Nigel… You and me are going to go into the bunker downstairs. The rest of my crew are going to tidy our weapons into the armoury in super-quick time and disappear back to their anonymous lives until we contact them again. Doris, please can you call Morton and ask him to—"

"Don't worry, that SUV is already being melted down for construction materials. He's a complete pro."

With a nod from each, Tariq and Nigel picked up their belongings and walked through a concealed door, down to Karim's secret bunker, leaving a whirlwind of activity behind them.

"Nigel, this is the kind of information people would and probably have killed for. Fortunately for you, we found it first and also, fortunately for you, it doesn't make any sense to anyone without you interpreting it."

"That doesn't sound very fortunate for me really."

"Well it does mean nobody is going to kill you for these notebooks."

"Well surely *somebody* would. To stop the information getting out I mean. And *you* might after I've interpreted them."

"I see your point. Well for context, you're a fully-inducted Basilisk. You are now part of the wider family and you have the full weight of the whole organisation backing you up. Nobody who is part of that family stands by and watches another member come to harm without trying to do something. That's why you got sprung from IZV."

"No it's not, I got sprung from IZV because they thought I was you."

"True, but the family support is what I was driving at. You're family. All Basilisks back each other up, nobody gets left behind, so—"

"They only tried to spring *you* because *you* were suddenly useful. If they cared that much, they would have come to get you before. Admit it, *you* got left behind."

"Are you always like this Nigel?"

"Like what?"

"How did you survive on the Chimera? Just tell me how many times the Commodore tried to kill you."

"Oh she was quite nice actually, very kind and accommodating."

"She must have really valued the information you're carrying in that enigmatic head of yours."

"I must say, she was quite prompt at granting me ship-leave."

"Probably glad to wash her hands of you and your rotten luck for a while."

"When you put it like that—"

"We're getting distracted. Tell me what's in these notebooks." Tariq laid the nineteen black books out on the table.

"You know these are private property, how did you get hold of them?" Nigel tried to sound authoritative but ended up just coming over as a petulant teenager.

"Long story that involves a new recruit, romance, sneaking about by the Hyper-loop—"

"—a run-in with some junkies, the MG, lunch with a neurotic millionaire..." Nigel cut in on someone else's sentence for once. "And that lady with the teeth that would make a camel look like a hot date... she is annoying, but completely harmless."

Tariq's eyes widened momentarily.

"Yeah, Doris gave me the crazy outline and said to leave it to be told another time. I still can't believe MAD IT is so bad that you ended up with my old job, in my old apartment just because we share the same smecking surname."

"Never mind that Nigel, what I want to know is why you went to all that trouble to hide your diaries. The air vent, the spidrion silk, the deposit box... if you have no idea the value of this information, why go to such lengths to protect it?"

"Two things really. One, because we all love a bit of mystery and pretending we are secret agents don't we? And two, because I'm not so simple that I don't understand how a lot of it relates to confidential data. I doubted anyone could decipher it without me to help them, but better safe than trying to explain a huge leak of state construction secrets."

"So what's in them?"

"Everything. Well everything I thought was interesting, which is pipes, cabling, conduits and their specifications."

"Specifications?"

"Yeah, dimensions, volume, materials, strength, how different bits are used. You know, that sort of interesting stuff."

"You need to get out more Nigel."

"I don't know, the last months have led me to think maybe I don't."

"Are you always like this Nigel? Oh, I've asked that before. Are you seriously that literal about anything anyone says?"

"Not always, but I figure most people just say what they mean."

Tariq pinched the bridge of his nose momentarily to gather his thoughts. The conversation was proving to be harder than he had expected and he needed to keep Nigel on track.

"Do you know what information the Basilisks need?"

"I know it's something to do with Komarov's Magellanic Villa and a vast collection of resources that the Basilisk family feels entitled to. I also know that he is corrupt and there is no honour among thieves, so basically, whatever he has is fair game and guiltlessly obtained."

"Notebook twelve," they said in unison.

"You can be dazzlingly succinct when you want to can't you Nigel."

Nigel pulled the relevant book forward and opened it, flicking through to find the page he wanted. "Here it is, Magellanian Villa, pages sixty to ninety-three."

"Let's have a look." Tariq leaned over to see what the pages contained as Nigel slid it across the table.

"It's just numbers in columns."

"Yeah, but they are interesting numbers. Numbers that dance and excite, numbers that have patterns and intricacies."

"I'm glad they mean something to someone. I can't see how this is useful."

"Nor can I really, but let me talk you through what I've put down here."

For the next couple of hours, Nigel helped Tariq build a mental image of the extensive service systems of Komarov's luxury holiday home.

By the end, he found he could fill in the rest of the structure comparatively effortlessly.

"It's amazing how, when you know what goes where, the function of each space becomes clear. How many different structures have you logged?"

"Most of the main big ones are documented like this. They are interesting, I can recall pretty much anything about any of the others but I only wrote down things that got my heart rate up."

"You *really* need to get out more." Tariq held up his hand to stop Nigel responding immediately, "Are there any particular gems in the rest of these notebooks?"

"Well I really like the design for the MEAT PIP facility, that has some really elegant solutions to some tricky problems—"

"Had."

"What do you mean?"

"That campus is not quite what is used to be. I'd rather not think or talk about it ever again to be honest.

"What else do you have?"

"Every military outpost, they are pretty sexy, a few of the more obscure developments in far-flung locations had complex barriers to overcome. Oh and I've got everything there is to know about IZV, what a beauty! I collected most of the NA galactic defence fleet too, a few officially commissioned leisure-crafts. To be honest, a lot of them have very similar layouts beneath their fancy aesthetic wrapping. For example, the interesting thing about the M96 Super-cruiser class is that they only deviated from the M94 in materials - technology moves on - and the size of the living quarters for Commissioned officers. They pinched space from the non-commissioned officer's mess hall and galley. Some of that was made easier as they had dispensed with the chefs and replaced everything with food printers and pre-prepared vending stations. Oh, and changing the layout around so the galley was closer to the recycling vats helped. Also there was less accommodation needed for support staff, what with all the cooks being sacked, so they expanded the top brass' rooms into that space. The unions played merry hell because of the redundancies until Komarov crushed them when—"

"Nigel, Nigel, stop.

"I'm sure it's fascinating. *To you*.

"I think we've got what we want from this. We can get this all logged in the Basilisk system. It's going to make their assault so much easier that they aren't going in partially blind."

"They?" Nigel questioned.

"Yeah, they. I haven't quite decided whether I'm going to join up with the crew again!"

"Great. What's next then?"

There was a soft knock at the door and Doris slipped in.

"I've just been thinking about those jump-gate energy spikes."

"Oh yeah?" Tariq looked up with raised eyebrows whilst Nigel maintained a non-plussed, vacant expression.

"Well, if Komarov is somehow pinging containers through jump gates at peak times and obscure angles, all-the-while managing to avoid collisions, that's going to take some serious calculating power."

"U-huh."

"Who do we know that has some of the most powerful machines in the solar system, able to compute quadrillions of bytes of complex calculations on an almost constant basis?"

"Oh, you mean—"

"Yeah, the very same. And I did some digging. Who ordered upgrades for their hardware within roughly the same time-frame as we started seeing the anomaly in the jump-gate network?"

"Really? GWHQ? Wow… As if they are involved! It's an absolute genius move. Evil genius, but genius all the same. Time to pay them a visit I guess."

"Good cop, pretty cop?"

"You'd be welcome to tag along."

"Nigel. we've got a meeting scheduled with General Hideki in five days. You'll love the guy. Why don't you lie low, relax, enjoy Karim's cuisine and get some proper rest for a while. We'll be back before you know it and we can visit the General. Lets's see what his advice is and where that takes us."

CHAPTER 42

OMEGA 4 | PRESENT DAY

Fuming to the point of dangerously high blood pressure, First Minister Komarov had dispensed with his usual taciturn conduct to berate his personal assistant. A vein in his temple pulsed like an artery and his eyes bulged. Froth collected at the corners of his mouth giving him the appearance of an unhinged lama.

His 'office' office, rather than his home office or his holiday office looked out over the sprawling bungle of MC1. The megatropolis looked weary today, her eighty-seven-million hover-car a week habit was beginning to show, despite the NA clean air directive.

Komarov strode to the window, looked down at the wreckage in the middle-distance that had once been MEAT PIP, inhaled the essence of recent destruction that lingered over the place and discharged the full venom of his fury.

"Mark my words Chupa, mark my words. May the Galactic Spirit herself strike me down with a meteor if I do not find and punish the perpetrators of this atrocity towards my person."

"Meteorite."

"Don't interrupt... What?"

"Meteorite… Sir?"

"What? No… Shut up, I'm beyond formalities with you Chupa. What did you say?"

"I said Meteorite. Sir."

"How in the name of all things holy is that relevant?"

"You said strike you down with a meteor sir."

"What's your point Chupa?" Though put off-course from his original rant, Komarov was still simmering.

"Meteors are what you see in the atmosphere. We call them shooting stars. Meteorites are the pieces of rock that hit the ground. Or indeed, the things you were hoping the Galactic Spirit would strike you down with."

"I was not hoping She would strike… Don't divert me Chupa."

"Sir."

"This is a disgrace. I want the heads of those who allowed this violation to happen, but first I want them to give me an explanation."

"I hate to—"

"You're interrupting again Chupa. I will not tolerate interruption.

"I want explanations and I want them fast, and I want you to convene an emergency sitting of the Megacity Elect Security Synod to sort this situation out.

"Well, what are you waiting for?"

"For you to finish Sir. I was trying to say, far be it for me to disappoint you sir, but those that were directly responsible for the facility are currently under several million tonnes of rubble. I expect an explanation may be outside their capability right now."

"And the Security Synod?"

"Ah, well… How shall I put it sir?.."

"Spit it out Chupa, you know I hate it when you prevaricate."

"If I might draw your memory back to the last convocation of the Synod… …You decided heads should roll after the debacle at IZV and took it upon yourself to oversee all security matters. The Synod was dissolved as you were unanimously elected Supreme Chief Of Care-Keeping."

"Are you blaming me Chupa?" The tattoo that Komarov's carotid vessels beat on the inside of his skin was approaching fever-pitch, causing his assistant to chose their next sentence extremely carefully.

"We do not apportion blame Sir. We step up to responsibility. I should have been more bold in my opposition to your suggestion."

It wouldn't have mattered what Chupa had said at that instant. Komarov would have boiled over in an ice-bath. He picked up the heavy cut-glass ash-tray that lay on his desk and hurled it at Chupa with all his strength.

As the sharp corner of the redundant ornament (Komarov was no smoker) struck Chupa between the eyes, he blinked slowly. The ash-tray disintegrated into a billion crystal shards that sprayed the wall behind and showered the floor underneath the statuesque assistant.

"I'm sorry sir." Chupa apologised and stepped to the side to allow the robot vacuum cleaner to suck the area clean again.

"You're lucky you are a synth Chupa, or I'd… I don't know what I'd do, but you wouldn't like it."

"I didn't like that if I'm entirely honest sir."

"Well, do something, call Razrushitel, get him to set up a special investigatory unit to fix this. Tell him I am very disappointed that he allowed someone to escape our most secure facility."

"Sir, Razrushitel is currently convalescing. He was in the building, interrogating Colemin when it all happened. He managed to climb into a metal cabinet and communicate his location to the recovery teams. It'll be two days before the medications restore full health. He was pretty beaten up."

"Yuàn tiān kōng luò zài wǒ chǔ nǚ zǔ mǔ de tóu shàng[i] Chupa, what did they have? Thirty? Fifty insurgents? Military vehicles? A hover-tank?"

"Survivor accounts said, there were five that came in and five that got out including the Colemin fellow."

"Five? So a battalion and a half of MEAT lost over 500 soldiers and only managed to cause one enemy casualty."

"That is correct Sir.

"And one more thing sir."

"Go on Chupa, more bad news I suppose."

"I'm afraid so sir. They emptied the armoury."

"Emptied? There must have been tonnes of stock in there. How in the name of all things holy did they manage to carry all that out?"

I think they carried the most valuable items and extrapolating back in time, judging by the power-spike we saw in the system, they atomised quite a lot."

Komarov paused for a moment for the news to sink in and to control his rage.

"It's not like there is an armoury to re-stock at the moment. How long to clear the site and rebuild?"

---

[i]   Ch. 'May the sky fall on my virgin grandmother's head'

"By my estimation—"

"I don't want estimations, I want hard facts." Komarov's temper was worsening with each new bombshell and was in no mood for vagueness.

"It will be three days to clear the site, the construction machines are already in place. Once the old material has been returned to its atomic constituents, the building printers will take two weeks to replicate the old structure. More time will be needed if we modify anything, which I suggest we do for the sake of security."

"Better! We can look at the plans with an architect this afternoon and make decisions on improving our defences... Now, run me a bath and prepare my cocktail of relaxants, I don't want to feel like my brain will explode at the slightest noise for one moment longer."

CHAPTER 43

DRACONIS SYSTEM | PRESENT DAY

t was beginning to look like Rob had life back under control. The regular exercise, cutting down his cannabis habit and restoring a jettison cycle that had margin for the unexpected arrival of what he referred to as his 'secret slingshots', was relieving his stress.

The new station had arrived and been placed into orbit to synchronise with the original installation. With no more than a few minor tweaks, it had fitted in almost seamlessly.

GWHQ was running like a well-stocked food printer, though not as deliciously aromatic, in fact it would have hummed like a skunk drowning in sewage if smells could travel in space.

Rob stood up from receiving the doc-bot's daily health check and vitamin-mineral infusion and stretched. He felt pretty gruntled about life in general as he made his way effortlessly through the small station, floating up past the main concourse on his way to the control room.

Something felt wrong. He looked around. Something looked wrong but he couldn't put his finger on it.

"Ella, Kimi, what's up?"

"Hi Rob, sir, please clarify your request." Kimi - the newest SAI that Rob had employed on the station was, unlike Ella, still polite to him.

"Somethin' jus' seems off ladies. Any sensors makin' any noise?"

"Nothing at all Rob. Are you sure your paranoia isn't playing up again?"

"I got that unner control Ella, it's mah spidey senses goin' haywire."

"Everything has been reading normal, apart from a minuscule flicker of the airlock door contact on the docking gantry, but those wobbles happen on one system or another on a daily basis. It's often when another motor draws power or the solar arrays are shifting position. I can't see any anomalies."

Rob frowned, pushed off, and floated up the stairs to his control deck, where two black-clad figures stood silently waiting, arms folded, sphinx-like faces.

"Um… You weren't goin' to tell me 'bout the extra heat signatures in m'room?"

"The extra… How on Omega did they get there without us knowing?"

"I'm askin' the same question Ella…. Well, I guess they ain't too host'l, 'f they'd want'd me dead, I'd 'a been bleedin' out, or walkin' wit the waste b'now."

He turned his attention to the ominous visitors. "So mah friends, what can Rob do f'r'all y'all t'day?" Broad smile, Rob opened his arms in a magnanimous greeting.

"We've never met Mr…?"

"Jus' call me Rob. Surnames mean nothin' when you're the only darn human in charge of all the sh—"

"So Rob, we've got a problem."

"Well I'm the one everyone comes to f'r cleanin' up their problems. I'm a bit like The Wolf." He tried to smile again but the pain was back.

"It's not *that* kind of a problem Rob. But we aren't the only ones that have a problem are we?"

"Look, I'm not quite sure what y'all drivin' at." He winced again as his discomfort intensified, "But we're doin' fine, we got space in our roster f'new work since our station upgrades and addin' our sister unit over there. 'Fact, I'd say we in better shape than we been in f'years."

"Allow me to introduce myself. Lieutenant Tariq Colemin of the Basilisks, I'm sure you've heard of them."

Rob gulped, nodded and grimaced in suffering again.

Tariq went on, "Retired Captain Tariq Colemin of the Space Commando Ultimate Marines, and now possibly one of the top five most-wanted men in the galaxy, having recently escaped from the Megacity Elite Armed Tacticians Prisoner Interrogation and Processing facility in Megacity One."

Looking uncomfortable but not fazed, Rob put out a hand for Tariq to shake. "Well there's a hist'ry ain't it. I'd rather be on your team than meet you in the cold, dark vacuum o' deep space." A feeble attempt at a grin touched Rob's lips, his mouth was drying up and his pain throbbing again.

"And I'm Doris, ex Megacity Elite Armed Tactician Security Liaison Intelligence Collecting Executive, Section Commander for MC2. No need for second names when you're pretty much the only woman in a man's world."

"Charmed t'meet y'r acquaintance ma-am. You got quite the title there. I'm mighty impressed."

"Time is not our friend Rob, I'm going to cut to the chase... We know."

"Y'know what sir?" The bemused face would not have won him any Oscars.

"Everything Rob. We know the contents of the dark shipments you're getting from NA, we also know the destination and how much you've been paid."

Sweat started to collect at the base of Rob's spine, his heart was racing and he was struggling to think of a way out of this new difficulty. Whenever he was under pressure it always made the pain worse so it was harder to think.

"We also know about your pain Rob." As Doris started to play 'pretty cop', Rob was unable to hide the genuine surprise in his face. "Yeah, you live alone, with only SAIs for company. Nothing wrong with that Rob, but it means you haven't had any practice at hiding things from people."

"I ain't trying t'hide that. I don' 'spec' anyone out there's least bit innerest'd."

"Knowledge is power Rob, just like there's money in muck, there's leverage in learning." Tariq wandered around Rob's improved control room and made impressed noises at all the big-ticket equipment. "My word Rob, you've got a serious operation going on here, this kit must have cost millions. You have any security on these stations?"

"Oh I git it, you're in th'extortion racket. Well I ain't too bothered, what's the worst you can do? Torture me? Kill me? I'm being permanently tormented by this pain, so that ain't gonna make a lot of difference. An' if y' kill me, won't be too long afore every planet 'n' station in this galaxy ends up knee-high in its own filth. Ain't no-one got time for that."

"No Rob, we've got better bargaining chips than that. We know you know what you're doing is wrong. We know you're not comfortable with it. We know if there was another way, you'd take it." Doris was warming to her role.

"You sure knows a lot."

"And we know a thing or two about pain.

"What we're here for, is to offer you a way out."

Rob suddenly perked up. "I'm a lis'nin'."

"A way out of being tangled up to your neck in the desperate corruption at the heart of the NA. A way to make amends, a way to get a clean conscience and a pain free life back." With this last sentence, Doris flashed her biggest, friendliest smile and held her palms out, facing upwards to demonstrate her openness.

"If you ain't messin' then I'm all in. You're right, I'm tired o' all this cloak 'n' dagger stuff and it ain't like I need the cash, I jus' di'n' want anyone closin' us up. I got multiple AIs and SAIs employed here, fair wages 'n' all, I grown t'like 'em, wouldn't wanna let 'em down or see the sector go to sh—"

"We're not messing Rob. We just need you to do one thing for us and we can blow this thing out of the water once and for all."

"Whatever it is, I'll do it. I'm in. Where do I sign?"

"Well, actually nowhere. We were never here, you've never met us. Let me talk you through what's going to happen. We can sort your pain on the Chimera - one of the Basilisk's Super-carriers. The ship is in system and the doctor there has some incredible technology. I guarantee she'll fix your issue, she's awesome and it's all been cleared by senior command. Then we need you to screw up one of your clandestine projectile 'shipments'. A small course change at the right time could cause just the right amount of mayhem."

This really got Rob's attention. "Hey I can't do that, I've a reputation to uphold and there could be lives at stake."

"It's all about timing Rob, when we send the signal, you get your computers to set a slingshot up that looks normal but hides a trajectory tweak. We have a target in mind that avoids loss of life but can disrupt the system enough to get on the news."

"But then I'm a gonna get in a whole heap a trouble with my intimidatin' messenger lady."

"Don't worry about that Rob, we can protect you if necessary, but a public apology from you is really all that will be required. The powers that be at NA won't want coverage but we'll leverage the event to our ends and you can uphold a veneer of plausible deniability. You alway get some teething problems with new systems, the spotlight will turn away from you in no time at all. Once it's discovered what is in those containers, everything will start to unravel for Komarov and his cronies."

"Well if you're sure I'll be safe, I definitely would sleep me better if I can get cleared of this darn contract…"

"We needed to know we could trust you and I think we've got our assurances." Tariq grinned at Rob, with a weary and beaten face, secure in the knowledge they had gained an ally in the battle that was about to begin.

CHAPTER 44

OMEGA 4 | PRESENT DAY

eneral Hideki shifted in his armchair and pushed his glasses back up his nose, a gesture borne of habit rather than function. Immediately, they slipped forward to the tip again, perching precariously as if ready to dive over the precipice into his magnificent moustache.

"Gentlemen, gentlemen, please pull up a chair... Ah, of course, they don't actually move, um, it's an old turn of phrase. Make yourselves comfortable, no need for formalities, relax. Whiskey? Rum? Brandy? Heaven forbid Vodka!?" He stiffened involuntarily at the word. "Maybe not, maybe not, you're too young of course. It's lovely to see you again Tariq, how have you been? Thinking hard I imagine."

Nigel shot Tariq a questioning look which was dismissed with a slight "not now" shake of the head. Without actually replying, the pair sat down and smiled politely.

"I'll get water, or would you like some fizzy pop? Can't abide the stuff myself but you young folk these days," he chuckled to himself as if sharing a private joke, "you must be wondering why I've asked you to see me. You both have some pondering to do and fairly quickly, you need to choose whether you are going with the fleet or staying on Omega-4. I don't want to influence you either way. I can see the attraction of both options. I understand the pull of adventure and the draw of peace and comfort. I just thought you might benefit from some time for reflection and a word of advice."

Nigel glanced sideways again at Tariq who caught his gaze. Both of them realised the General was just warming up.

"My good fellows. Good judgment comes from experience and experience comes from poor judgment." He looked from Nigel to Tariq and back again, adjusted his glasses - which immediately returned to their perilous state - and continued. "You both have a vast wealth of experience." The corners of his mouth curled slightly at his own quip, "What you learn from that experience will inform your choices and lead you down a path. You have only one path ahead of you. Decisions cannot be un-made. You can no more un-do your actions than you can un-say your words or un-see the effects of them. The repercussions of your next steps may be hidden but I assure you, they will be far and wider-reaching than you are capable of calculating."

Pausing for breath again, the General settled into his chair and, seemingly, his rhythm.

"As Al Franken once said - 'Mistakes are a part of being human. Appreciate your mistakes for what they are: precious life lessons that can only be learned the hard way. Unless it's a fatal mistake, which, at least, others can learn from.' He was, of course, quite a wit. Gentlemen, don't be afraid of the choices you both need to make. Don't be fearful that you might make a mistake, for - anyone who has never made a mistake has never tried anything new. - That was Albert Einstein my good men. Not that I am suggesting you should try to do something 'new' just for the sake of it."

Nigel was wondering where the General was going with this pep talk.

Tariq was wondering if the ageing leader had taken leave of his faculties since their last meeting.

As if to answer their silent thoughts, the General changed tack.

"I know the temptation will be to see a piteous, shrivelled man who can only talk laboriously, and discount him as an old fool to be spoken to loudly and slowly... Old people might not have the same vision or reflexes as you young bucks, but remember, we were young once and felt the same way as you do."

He paused momentarily to sip from a glass of water, his gnarled hand wavering slightly as he placed the tumbler back on the ancient oak table-top.

"We might seem old and slow and stupid sometimes, but I counsel you not to patronise or be condescending. To think first and act later has been what has kept me alive more times than I care to remember... The S3 is leaving port after resupply in a little under five hours. The shuttle will rendezvous with the Chimera on the dark side of Gamma-3 only four hours later. If you stay and have a sudden, last minute change of heart, there is an individual with a racing yacht that we can charter quietly to reunite you with us but once the S3 has docked, we are only 45 minutes from departure to the inner star-gate and, then, our destination system. Once the Chimera has reached the jump-gate, there will be no catching up with her.... If you have any questions gentlemen, please feel free to ask, I have already gone on too long."

Caught slightly on the hop at the abrupt ending, the two Colemins sat mutely for a moment.

"Just how old do you think we are?" piped up Nigel. Mildly nonplussed at the inanity of his question and surprised his mouth had voiced the inner monologue. He unsuccessfully grasped at some way to sound less like an idiot. "I mean, Tariq's got arms covered in tattoos and over the last month, I've even grown a beard."

Admiral Hideki looked bemused, clearly unable to fathom where this left-field question had come from.

"Never mind Nigel sir," interjected Tariq, "I think he is still nervous about the prospect of having a free choice after all this time."

Nigel nodded vigorously, relieved to have someone else taking command of the awkward situation.

"I'd like to know what the odds are for a successful mission, now that we are running almost four months behind schedule on this Magellanian job."

"Ah Tariq. I always had you down as one for the details. I was told you were more brawn than brain, but I never believed it." The old General smiled generously, "I'm not one for all the nitty-gritty myself to be honest. I'm more… let us say… strategic. You know, the bigger picture, 40,000 foot birds-eye-view stuff. The Fleet-Admiral and I set the overall agenda, you'd have to talk to Commodore Andrade really."

Tariq nodded and sat back again.

———

Five hours later, the little cargo shuttle S3 - Nigel's first action-filled transport - silently drifted from the backwater bays of MC1 Spaceport. Within minutes, she was accelerating north over Omega-4's great ocean heading for Gamma-3, finally breaking atmo in a transient flash of white vapour.

———

Another four hours passed and from the shadows, one pair of eyes watched the drop-ship noiselessly jetting across the lunar horizon towards the dark side, matter and antimatter painting a sparkling drive-trail in their annihilation dance.

ACKNOWLEDGMENTS

Huge thanks are due to Kate - my patient and long-suffering wife who allowed me time to indulge my creativity.

Thank you Jacob for being so stubborn about not reading it on a screen that it finally went to print. And for the helpful feedback to smooth the reader's journey.

Thank you Lily who suffered my random reading of paragraphs during the creative process and who shamelessly spread the fact I was writing a book to everyone who would listen.

Thank you Harry who not only endured the reading of this as it evolved, but actively encouraged me every time I had run out of chapters to read to him at bedtime.

Thank you all four of the above for being so hyper-critical that it made the whole story much better than it could have been.

Thanks to my sister Abi for her candid and very valuable feedback throughout.

Huge thanks to Jenny Green (no relative) who selflessly gave her time and tips and very detailed feedback despite having a heavy publishing schedule of her own.

Thanks to Amy for editing and providing the kind of grammar and punctuation fascism that was sorely needed.

Thank you Rob, for asking to be in the book, your character has turned into one of my favourites.

Thank you Ben for the initial idea that gave this whole adventure a springboard.

Big thanks to the incredible Crowther tribe who inspired the resolution to the only serious case of writer's block I had.

And thanks to anyone else along the way that was kind enough to read early / late drafts and point me in the right direction. You know who you are, I am forever grateful.

If I've missed you and you think you deserve thanks, then I'm sorry and I thank you. Submit your complaint in writing and I'll credit you in book two or three.

EMBERS OF THE NEW ALLIANCE

Streaking through the sky like a white-hot meteor, Ash wrestled with the controls of the only Mensa ship that couldn't fit in the bay of the Chimera.

"Stars, flying this heap of spare parts is like trying to wrestle an alligator. She's got the turning capability of a sledgehammer and none of the sensors are reporting honestly."

Sweat was dripping off her forehead and making her hands slip on the manual flight-yoke.

"NO, I don't need your help Nige. Why the drokk the Commodore put you on this boat in the first place is beyond me if I'm being completely frank."

"So, completely Frank, where can I go if I can't help or even touch anything?"

"Just… somewhere else right now. I've got a lot on my plate and you breathing down my neck, making weak jokes is only going to make me homicidal.

"Drokk, cloaking is down."

"That will be due to the speed Captain, it's not stable once we get above—"

"I don't need the details Tariq, but drokk me, how do you know that?

"Actually, don't answer me now, I'm preoccupied in my attempts to not completely write-off this trug of rusty scrap.

"Oh stars, now we're getting hailed."

"You knew it would happen Ash." Sam was standing at the comm console and patched the incoming call across to the main bridge PA.

"Unspecified frigate with the disguised drive signature, this is Alpha Control, you are coming in hot with no security clearance and no destination jump codes. Turn your transponder back on and alter your trajectory to avoid the jump-gate before we are forced to fire on you."

"That's the last drokking thing we need right now." The usually ice-cool Ash was beginning to show ragged edges, "Sam, give me an open channel."

"You're on Captain."

"No can do control, this boat is unresponsive and coming right through. Please clear the shipping lanes and give us a bit of space."

"Unspecified Captain of unspecified frigate, that will not be possible, we have a three hour holding queue and the next security clearance packet will put you at the back of that line. Please alter your course, to avoid damaging other vessels in the area."

"Sorry control, what's your name and position?"

Caught momentarily off-guard by her question, the jump-gate operator blurted out his name before he could stop himself. **"Andrew, junior jump engineer, but I fail to see—"**

"Look Andrew, can I call you Andy? You sound like a reasonable guy and I don't want to make threats or come across all heavy, but we are the least of your worries right now."

"You're right Captain, I have a hundred and sixteen separate starships to transition through this gate before my shift ends and I will not let your recklessness derail my timetable."

"Ok Andy, maybe I misjudged you. You are clearly an unreasonable, self-important jerk who, if he isn't careful, will find his jobsworth attitude is going to cause a serious incident. I hope your public liability insurance is good enough to cover the significant damage to your precious starship queue because, security codes or not, we are going through that jump-gate and we are not slowing down." Ash could barely get the words out fast enough, what with her struggle to keep the ship flying straight. "And before you make idle threats, any attempt to engage the jump-gate defences, will be utterly pointless. I only know one person with the necessary reflexes to target-lock us at this velocity without cutting several expensive shipping freighters to pieces, and they are sitting at the drokking controls of this particular flying skip."

There was a short pause before Ash continued.

"I suggest you shift the rest of your little holding stack to a wider orbit because hot on our tail is something that will make you fill your underwear. And I don't mean in a good way. DONG-luh-MAH?"

Sam cut the communication and looked across at Ash who maintained her laser focus on the centre of the jump-gate.

"Can you get the coordinates spliced into the gate system to match our intercept time Sam?"

"That's what we've got Norm here for. I'll get a tight-beam locked for the hack." With time slipping away fast, Sam managed to fix a network access portal in the main jump-gate computer system and handed the channel over to Norm.

"We've not got long Norm."

"Long enough Ma'am, I'll be able to inject the codes for the Chimera at the same time."

"Good man. You see that Nige? Helpful, efficient, and no drokking breakages."

Nigel chose not to reply but just rolled his eyes at Tariq who shrugged back."

"Unspecified frigate with the ill-tempered, rude Captain, this is your last warning, alter course immediately or you will be fired upon."

"This lad is clearly trying to make a name for himself. Junior engineer. I ask you," Ash complained as she continued in her battle to maintain stable flight, "he won't be so cocky when the Chimera's cloak drops."

"You have ignored your final warning unspecified frigate, Jump-Gate Alpha will open fire in WOAH DROKK ME!"

The control operative had clearly just seen the limitations of stealth technology unveil an accelerating M94 Super-cruiser, bearing down on the carefully choreographed space transit queueing system.

No-one on the bridge was able to suppress their mirth as the all-channel announcement blasted out from Jump-Gate Alpha control.

"All ships, clear the vicinity immediately at full burn, your position in the queue will be maintained. Jump-Gate Alpha will not be held accountable for any vessels that fail to comply."

The level of panic in the voice that came over the broadcast was palpable.

"Basilisk Super-cruiser Chimera, this is Alpha Control issuing a formal notice to urgently change your bearing to avoid a notifi-

able incident. Your transponder code and drive signature have been logged and should you ignore our directive, access to the whole jump-gate network will be restricted or officially revoked."

"I guess he's forgotten all about us then." Ash smirked, "Increasing burn in five, four… prepare for the jump."

Rapidly losing control of the situation, the young jump-gate operative was completely misplacing his frass, allowing total pandemonium to develop in local space.

"Evacuate all gate structures, all craft take emergency evasive action. DO NOT, I repeat, DO NOT attempt to use the jump gate.

Super-cruise Chimera, you have been reported for flying without due care and attention in a restricted velocity zone, alter course immediately."

In the middle of the disarray, Ash gripped firmly on the fusion drive boost lever and slammed it forward.

"Kiss my ass…teroid dust mutie" she muttered as they hit the centre of the jump-gate and blinked out of the system.

―――――

Read Book Two - Embers Of The New Alliance

Find out what happens when, having burned hard for the main Jump Gate, dragging Nigel's particular brand of calamity with them, the Basilisks rush to strike on Komarov's secret residence before it's too late and their nemesis completes his private army to take control of the whole galaxy in his toxic iron grip.

With Nigel on board, nothing is ever straightforward so they have to wildly improvise their plans in the rapidly changing landscape. They meet resistance, incompetence and plain old misfortune, a predictable inevitability when the unluckiest man in the galaxy teams up with the most reluctant bad-ass in the solar system.

Taking down the corrupt administration from the top is not going to be easy, Komarov is a slippery operator who, despite the team's determination, seems to have the ability to evade them at almost every turn.

To complicate matters further, like a looming shadow over their whole operation, nobody is entirely sure how the 'Colemin effect' is going to influence the final outcome.

ONE MORE THING

I love books. Given the choice, I'd curl up with a good book and while away days at a time.

Sometimes, though, I'm either unable to take a proper book with me or am so engrossed in a story that I have to keep going with an electronic book, or listen to an audiobook.

One thing that annoys me is being forced to buy books (or films for that matter) in multiple formats so I wanted to redress the balance a little where I can.

If you are holding this physical copy of Fires of The New Alliance and have actually bought it, then just take an original photo of yourself reading it and share it on instagram, remembering to follow and tag @NewAllianceSeries.

When I see that post, I will DM you with a link to download the book in electronic format COMPLETELY FREE.

NOTES

CHAPTER 13

1. gǒushǐ yùn - dog shit luck. A phrase that has its roots in ancient rural China, when crops were fertilised with animal manure and human waste. Dog excrement was a good source of nutrients for crops, so early in the morning, enterprising villagers would collect it to sell to farmers. Finding and even accidentally treading on dog shit was therefore seen as a good thing as it meant making extra money. It eventually became slang for any bad situation that ended up being good for you. But it is often used ironically.